SHADOW IN
THE GLASS

Also available by M. E. Hilliard
The Greer Hogan Mysteries

The Unkindness of Ravens
Shadow in the Glass

SHADOW IN THE GLASS

A Greer Hogan
Mystery

M. E. HILLIARD

CROOKED
LANE

NEW YORK

Published in the United States by Crooked Lane Books, an imprint of The Quick Brown Fox & Company LLC.

Crooked Lane Books and its logo are trademarks of The Quick Brown Fox & Company LLC.

Library of Congress Catalog-in-Publication data available upon request.

ISBN (trade paperback): 978-1-63910-337-9
ISBN (hardcover): 978-1-64385-894-4
ISBN (ebook): 978-1-64385-895-1

Cover design by Alan Ayers

Printed in the United States.

www.crookedlanebooks.com

Crooked Lane Books
34 West 27th St., 10th Floor
New York, NY 10001

Trade Paperback Edition: January 2023
First Edition: April 2022

10 9 8 7 6 5 4 3 2 1

For Jeanne and Helene

Chapter One

It is a truth, universally unacknowledged, that a single woman in possession of a good fortune has no practical need of a husband. However firmly stated the feelings or views of such a woman may be, this truth is so fixedly unaccepted in the minds of those who meet her that remedying her woeful marital state is considered a righteous project for any number of meddlesome, though well-meaning, friends, relatives, and distant acquaintances. And so it was that I found myself driving northward one beautiful autumn afternoon, to attend the third wedding of my friend Sarah Whitaker, who was brilliant, beautiful, and stinking rich.

I was happy to support Sarah in her latest, and hopefully last, trip down the aisle. I was planning on staying a few extra days in Lake Placid and turning it into a mini-vacation. After the events of the previous spring and a busy summer at the Raven Hill Library, I needed a break. Late September was the perfect time of year for a week in the Adirondacks, and Sarah's wedding gave me the perfect cover for my ulterior motive—investigating a murder.

Any wedding is always fraught with emotion. I confess my own feelings were mixed. While genuinely happy for my friend, I had attended her second wedding with my late husband, Danny. The two of us had later visited the newlyweds at the

Whitakers' summer cottage on Mirror Lake. Though I had seen Sarah a few times since, this was my first trip north after that last getaway with Danny. And here I was, on my way to several days of nuptial festivities, with my own agenda: to determine if any of the guests, including my own first love, had any knowledge of my husband's murder.

I had lived for some time with the suspicion that I had let an innocent man go to jail in order to keep a secret. From the moment I walked into our apartment and found Danny's body on the floor, there were things that didn't add up. But in the welter of grief and guilt and rage, I had ignored them. The part of my brain that was still functioning logically noted them and filed them away, but the day I buried Danny I decided to bury every memory related to the night he died. Any facts that didn't fit the case the police came up with were simply added to that mental box, and there they stayed for years, until the nightmares started. Even then, I tried to ignore them. But life happens. Circumstances change. I changed my profession. I changed where I lived. But my new and supposedly peaceful life had brought me within seconds of being a multiple murderer's latest victim. It's the kind of thing that focuses your attention like very little else can. I emerged from the experience a different woman than the one who had arrived in Raven Hill determined to forget. I wanted answers. And I would get them. The fog had lifted.

I left the village of Raven Hill Wednesday afternoon. I'd gotten up early, for me, and gone for a brisk-walk–slow-jog combo through the winding streets of the village. After my adventures of the previous spring, I had decided it was time to get in better shape. The everyday exercise I'd taken for granted as a city girl had disappeared into the suburban car culture of the Albany area. I wanted to make sure that the next time I had to outrun a murderer, I could do it. I was aided in my quest by local police officer Jennie Webber.

The two of us had become unlikely friends after working together to find a killer. The former soldier was younger and in better shape, but with her encouragement I was getting back to fighting form. That didn't stop me from packing a full complement of Lycra shapewear to ensure I looked great for the wedding weekend, though. At forty, I was taking no chances. The underpinnings taken care of, I'd pulled out several outfits I couldn't decide between. In the end, I packed them all. I decided this was one of those times when more was more—for whatever parts I needed to play, I wanted the confidence that came with the perfect costume.

It wasn't a long drive up to Lake Placid—most of it was on the Northway, and the weather was good. But once you got off the highway, you spent a lot of time on winding country roads. I twisted through the woods and the small towns that were scattered across the Adirondacks, windows rolled down and music turned up, enjoying the mountain air and the scenery. The foliage in late September was a blazing spectacle, but leaves had already started to fall. They twirled and danced, sometimes leaping into the road in front of me before spinning away as I passed. When not passing through the shadowed woods, the narrow roads were carved into the mountains. Two lanes, with a steep wall of jagged rock on one side and cold, rushing water on the other. Not a trip for the faint of heart. I found it exhilarating. Over the river and through the woods, a-hunting I would go.

By the time I reached Lake Placid, I had a renewed appreciation for the beauty of the Adirondacks and the effort it took to get there. The trip to the 1932 Winter Olympics must have been an event in and of itself. It probably wasn't much better in 1980. The ski jump loomed over me as I drove into town. The trip down Main Street required a more sedate pace, giving me a few minutes to relax and enjoy the scenery. Much of the village of Lake Placid was on the shore of Mirror Lake, with the lake that gave the place its name located a little to the north and west of downtown. It was a charming blend of old and new, with something to do in every season.

The wedding was a multiday affair. Sarah said she wanted to spend time with her friends and family, so she and her fiancé Jack had arrived the previous weekend and wouldn't leave for their honeymoon until a few days after the ceremony. There was a ladies' tea Thursday afternoon ("Lets me do my face time with the elderly aunties and my mother's friends," Sarah had told me), and I'd volunteered to attend and provide moral support. The rehearsal on Friday night would be followed by a "small party" with a band, buffet, and open bar, all on the Whitaker waterfront. The actual ceremony would be midday on Saturday, followed by lunch at a local venue. There would be a breakfast on Sunday for those guests still in town who wanted to carb up before heading home or off to other vacation pursuits. Various activities had been arranged between wedding events. The whole thing reminded me of something out of a Regency romance. I was sure Sarah's mother would have had croquet as well if their lawn didn't slope down to the lake at such an angle. And knowing the Whitakers, the food would be excellent and the alcohol free-flowing. My plan was to drink a lot of water between parties and tell my liver to brace for impact.

I'd been invited to spend the weekend at the Whitaker cottage. The term was an emphatic understatement, even by the standards of the wealthy. Situated on a waterfront lot on Mirror Lake, the "cottage" consisted of a main house, a guesthouse, and a boathouse. All were original, dating back a century or more. Back then, the place was less crowded, extended families spent the summer or ski season in large houses, and waterfront property was expensive, but not obscenely so. Sarah's family had always been comfortable enough to hang on to the place. Each building had since been renovated to include all the modern conveniences but still retained the look and feel of an earlier era. Even the boathouse had a sizable apartment on the second floor. The whole place was tied together by gravel paths and a rambling garden. The only thing it lacked was parking, but Desmond Whitaker had remedied that by buying a rundown house on a small lot across the street, tearing it down, and building a garage. The rich are different from you and me—they are so rarely inconvenienced.

I figured I'd be stashed on the third floor, in what used to be the servants' quarters. The few spare rooms on the second floor would be reserved for older relatives who might have trouble with all the stairs. This was no hardship as far as I was concerned. The views from the top floor were gorgeous. The Whitakers had knocked out walls and updated the plumbing to make a couple of guest rooms. Sarah's dad had taken one side for a home office, complete with a door to a covered stairway leading to the garden. He often worked late and liked to go for a stroll along the lake before bed. I'd wondered about that private entrance, but the one time I'd mentioned it to Danny, he had laughed and told me I had a suspicious mind. Like Miss Marple, I thought the worst of people because it so often turned out to be true.

Wherever I'd be sleeping, it was kind of the Whitakers to invite me. Sarah's mother had always been fond of me. She seemed to think I was a good influence, probably because she didn't know me well, and Sarah wasn't talking. I'd offered to help with last-minute wedding things but was told that was in no way necessary. As far as I was concerned, it was. There were at least half a dozen people attending who had some connection to Danny and the company he was working for when he died. Since I had only a passing acquaintance with most of them, guest lists, seating arrangements, and contact information would be very handy to have.

I had tackled Sarah first.

"You know your mother will be making you crazy," I said. "This way, you and I get more time to catch up, and I can run interference between the two of you. Besides, it's awkward being the widow at the wedding. The guests I know also knew Danny, and I haven't seen most of them since his funeral. This will give me something to do, and something to talk about if things get uncomfortable. And I really would love to help."

I'd like to say I was above playing the widow-of-a-murder-victim card, but I'd be lying.

Sarah sighed.

"I hadn't thought about that. Well, if you're sure. It would be fun to have you helping me out and keeping my mother off my back. I thought not having a wedding party would make things simpler. I guess I didn't realize how much grunt work my brides-maids did last time."

"Now you know why I went on that European business trip with Dan and didn't come back until the day before the service."

She laughed and said, "I totally get it. And I appreciate the offer to help. I just don't want you to feel like one of Mother's minions."

"I can manage your mother. And she's such an organizational wonder I doubt there will be much to do beyond keeping you from strangling her. So—settled?"

And it was. Sarah had talked to her mother, and I had made a follow-up call to Jane Whitaker repeating my offer and suggesting a gin and champagne cocktail perfect for the tea. Jane liked her gin as much as she liked me—she'd never been a pastel party punch kind of girl. So the deal was done. Greer Hogan, wedding guest, would double as Greer Hogan, undercover Girl Detective, without anyone being the wiser. I was pleased with myself as I pulled up to the Whitaker house. I needed a vacation, and Lake Placid was beautiful this time of year. All I had to do was show up, keep the bride and her mother from killing each other, give a reading at the service, and begin an investigation into a murder that was technically already solved, without tipping anyone off that I was nosing around. Easy-peasy.

Had I but known . . .

Chapter Two

~

"I'm *so* sorry!" Sarah was agitated, alternately wringing her hands and waving them around. This was out of character for my usually poised friend. She'd met me in the driveway, bounding out the door before I'd even gotten out of the car. After hugs and hellos, we were standing at the edge of the lawn. While I stretched after the long drive, Sarah told me there was a change of plan. Apparently, more out-of-town relatives had decided, at the last minute, to attend the wedding, and all the rooms at the Whitaker house were needed.

"So everyone is being rearranged. I can't believe it—Mother always has a plan B and C, but this time she seems to have been caught unprepared. We both feel terrible. But don't worry—we're going to put you up at a hotel. The Mirror Lake Inn. Right up the street. Hadn't you planned to do a spa day there? On us. Mother decided, after all you've been through, that you deserve a treat. Whatever you want. Let me get my bag, and we'll go get you checked in."

Sarah was hopping with impatience. She turned toward the house.

"Oh, that's so kind. Shouldn't I say hello to your mother first and thank her?" I said.

"She can wait. I think she's busy anyway, triple-checking something with the caterer or micromanaging the housekeeper. I'm not even sure where she is. We can go get you settled, and maybe grab a bite to eat? You can thank her later. Though we should be thanking you for your understanding."

Not hardly. The Mirror Lake Inn was way out of my current price range. Danny and I had spent an anniversary weekend there once as a special treat, but my librarian's salary wouldn't cover it. I'd wanted to be in the thick of things, and I was willing to bet some of the people I wanted to talk to would be staying at the inn. And I'd be spending a lot of time at the Whitaker place anyway.

"You know me—always willing to take one for the team. Especially if it involves a luxury hotel stay! I was going to come early for the tea anyway, remember? I'll talk to your mom then."

"You're the best!" Sarah said. "Be right back." She bounded toward the house.

I went around to the passenger side of the car, to move the stuff for the trip I'd piled there on to the back seat. That done, I turned in a slow circle, taking in the scenery. The sun was going down, casting long shadows. The rays of light that came through the trees created blinding reflections off the windows of the Whitaker house and those of its nearest neighbor. I'd always wondered about that house. The two homes looked as though they had been built around the same time. There was never anyone there when I visited, but it was always kept up nicely, from what I'd seen of the exterior. Right now, though, very little of that was visible. A row of evergreens ran along the side of the driveway, hiding all but the top floor. The trees swayed gently in the breeze, revealing several windows. The waning daylight flickered across them. For a second, I thought I saw someone, a moving figure, there and then gone. I watched, but it didn't reappear.

"All houses in which men have lived and suffered and died are haunted houses." I quoted Mary Roberts Rinehart, one of my favorites among the old school American mystery writers. I felt chilled—the sun set fast in the mountains. Deciding that what I'd seen must have been a trick of the light, I walked back to the driver's side of my car and got in. But while I waited for Sarah, I continued to watch the windows next door. I saw no movement. Seconds ticked past, and then a faint red glow appeared. It held steady for a moment, then floated across the pane and vanished. I stared, waiting for it to reappear. The sound of a voice made me jump.

"Let's go," Sarah said, settling into the passenger seat. She smiled as she pulled on the car door, which closed with a solid Germanic *thunk*. "You kept Dan's BMW. How old is this thing now?"

"Old enough to be cool, instead of just plain old," I said. "I couldn't bear to part with it, Dan loved it so much. And now that I have to drive everywhere, it's nice to have. Solid and safe."

I started the car, giving the house next door one last, long look. Nothing. *Trick of the light, of the setting sun*, I repeated, *or maybe someone's there this time.* But it left me with an odd feeling. I backed out and turned the car toward the inn.

We chatted about my new home, the village of Raven Hill, on the short drive to the hotel. Once parked, we headed to the front desk, where I picked up my room key while Sarah ordered some wine and a fruit and cheese plate to be sent up. A bellman was dispatched for my luggage.

"You must be hungry. I could use a little something, too. I haven't really had a chance to eat today. So many last-minute things. I'll help you unpack and we can catch up," Sarah said as we waited for the elevator. My room was lovely, with polished wood furniture and thick carpets. The sitting area in front of the window looked out on Main Street and Mirror Lake. Once my luggage and the food had arrived, we settled in with a glass of wine. Sarah still seemed edgy. Bridal jitters? I decided to do a little gentle probing.

"So, ready for the big day?" I asked. "And the two days before? And the day after?"

Sarah laughed. "It seems over the top, doesn't it? But for once I can't pin it all on my mother. I wanted something informal, something fun, and a chance to visit with everyone. I guess I pictured myself in some boho dress, barefoot in the garden, with a French country picnic lunch after. Then the planning seemed to take on a life of its own. It probably seems silly, since it's my third wedding. Still, I thought it would be nice to have one more big get-together before everything changes. And it's not like I'll ever do it again."

"Third time's the charm?" I teased. "And what's going to change, other than you and Jack settling into wedded bliss?'

"I can't believe I'm doing this for the third time. You know something, Greer? This is the only one that feels real. Like this is it, until death do us part. The first one was because I was young and stupid and wanted to piss off my parents. The second one was because everyone was pairing off and it seemed like it was time. With Jack, it feels right. Like I've met my soul mate."

"That's wonderful, Sarah. I'm really happy for you." And I was. I had actually introduced Sarah to her current fiancé back in the day, but at the time she had been dating the dull and appropriate young man who had become husband number two. He was likable enough, so blandly handsome I couldn't remember his face, and met with full approval from her parents. I guess he was qualified for the job he got in the family business, though he hadn't set the world on fire while he was there. And though she did get married in the same two-year period as everyone else we knew, I always thought she was trying to atone for that brief, disastrous marriage to an avowed Communist with whom she'd eloped during a rebellious phase her sophomore year at Columbia. Jack Peterson, the current groom, had shared an apartment with Danny while both were in graduate school. Jack was now a successful architect, unfazed by Sarah's wealth and ambition. He was also a genuinely nice guy. They were a good match.

"Thank you, Greer. It means a lot that you can be here, especially since you introduced us. I'm only sorry that, well—" She trailed off.

"It's okay, Sarah. I'm glad I'm here."

"So am I." She hesitated for a second, and then asked, "Would you ever get married again? After what happened to Danny?"

She caught me by surprise. *Would I?*

"I don't know. I hadn't really thought about it." I truly didn't, and hadn't. Though we were not in a good place when he died, my husband and I had, for the most part, been happy. I shrugged. "Why do you ask? Planning on fixing me up with someone? Your brother is still single, right?"

"Very funny. Of course he is. Jeremy keeps saying he's not the marrying kind. I'm sure he does it just to annoy my mother. All her friends have grandchildren, and she's finally given up on me. I've sensed a spark between him and Isabelle—Jack's sister, you've met her, right?—but they're keeping a low profile. Neither is the type to shout it from the rooftops. You'll have to tell me what you think."

She fiddled with her engagement ring.

"I told you Ian Cameron is coming, right?" she said.

"You did. He does some consulting for your dad, right? And he's Jack's poker buddy whenever he's in town. Danny used to play with them, too."

"Yes. Didn't you two used to date?"

"We went out a few times my senior year in college." That was an understatement. We had a crazy hot fling that ended badly. Ian was a friend of Danny's from business school. The whole thing went down years before I got married. Dan and I didn't even start dating for quite a while after. Sarah didn't know the whole story, nor did Jack. Few people did.

"Oh," she said. "I thought it was more of a connection than that, I don't know why."

Probably because she was both perceptive and intelligent, and I'd had a few drinks when I told her the story. But I kept my mouth shut now.

"Well, I mentioned to my mother that Ian had asked Jack if you'd be here, and that you two had something of a history, bad timing, that sort of thing. I wanted to seat you together whenever we could, and for Jack and me to casually include you both in some things, and just, generally—"

"Play matchmaker?" I said.

"Well, okay, yes. I hope you don't mind. But listen—when I mentioned you and Ian, my mother got this funny look on her face and said that wasn't an option. When I asked why, she got kind of defensive, but she finally told me that it was because Ian was about to be engaged to Brittany Miles. But it's not common knowledge so not to say anything."

"Oh," I said. My stomach gave a little lurch, followed by a sense of relief that surprised me. I'd think about that later. First things first.

"So, who is this Brittany?" Ugh. That was my mother speaking through my body.

"Brittany's the new VP of Strategic Initiatives, or something like that. I think my father just made up that title to keep her with the company."

Whitaker Inc. was one of the last small advertising agencies left after decades of mergers. It had been family-owned for generations. Their creative team was behind quite a few well-known commercials, so they had some very loyal, very big accounts. Jeremy had worked in creative before leaving to follow his own star. Sarah had rotated between all the departments, but her strength was in sales. Her father, Desmond, was CEO, and Sarah was expected to follow in his footsteps.

"What kind of initiatives is she working on?" I asked.

"We've struggled with the digital side, so she's been focused on that. It's why we brought Ian in—we need better analytics. And she's been looking into our global partnerships."

"What's she like? Personally, I mean."

"I don't have much to do with her, so I don't know her well. She seems very bright. Ambitious. She's around thirty. Awfully young for the job she's got."

"We were bright, ambitious, and awfully young once, too. Not that forty is old," I hastened to add.

"Of course it isn't. I'm only now starting to feel like a grown-up," Sarah said. "But this thing with Brittany and Ian, it just doesn't feel right."

"Well, it doesn't bother me. I think he's been married a few times since we dated. I'll be happy to see him and have a chance to talk to him."

"Hmph. Still."

Time to change the subject. I wanted to process the Ian news on my own time.

"If you're hell-bent on matchmaking, doesn't Jack have a few single friends?"

She brightened up. All happy lovers want everyone to be in love.

"You know, he does have one or two that you might like, and they'll be at the wedding. I'm not sure when they're arriving, but—"

"Sarah! I was kidding!"

"Okay, okay. I'll leave it alone. For now." She smiled and blew me an air kiss. "So you said you were bringing a bunch of outfits because you couldn't decide what to wear. Let's see what you've got." Sarah reached for my garment bag. "You know my motto—better hot than not. Especially when there's an ex-boyfriend in the room."

I couldn't agree more.

After Sarah and I had sorted out my wardrobe for the weekend's major events (pretty and classic for the tea, sophisticated and sexy for the rehearsal dinner, elegant and understated sexy for the service and lunch), she left. I finished my unpacking and decided to get the lay of the land at the inn. I was feeling edgy and wanted to sort out my thoughts. I also wanted a real meal. Fruit and cheese were nice as long as I could follow it up with something like a burger and a beer.

I went downstairs and confirmed my spa appointments. Mani-pedi before the events, relaxation and pampering after. I'd had my roots touched up the previous weekend. Even a hint of gray in my dark hair washed me out when combined with my pale skin. I then strolled around the main floor, peeked into the dining room, and then headed for the bistro. I found a seat at the far end of the bar. It gave me a good view of the lobby and the people coming and going from the restaurant. I sat down, ordered dinner and a drink, and started making friends with the bartender.

I'd been raised in and out of my family's pub, so I knew from experience that bartenders were good observers and better listeners. I waited for a lull in business and chatted him up. This was no hardship. Mike was good-looking and funny, and clearly a pro. I complimented his skill with a shaker and presented my family business bona fides. This led to a conversation about the chemistry and creativity required in putting together a good craft cocktail. We established a nice rapport when he wasn't helping other customers. When he was, I took the opportunity to look around. Would I even recognize some of the people I was looking for? At one point I could have sworn I saw Desmond Whitaker in the lobby. It was quick—I only saw him in profile. He was walking past the bar entrance with someone I couldn't quite see. He checked his watch, then stopped. There was a break in the crowd, and I saw a thirty-something brunette beside him. He leaned close, apparently whispering something to her, and then turned toward the stairs to the exit. At that point I lost them both in a group coming in.

Things were picking up in the bar, so I gave Mike a big smile and asked for a shot of Bailey's and my check. I signed it and left a generous tip. Mike was busy at the taps, so I gave him a wave as I went by and received a wink in return. He might never have information I needed, but I was glad to have cultivated the source anyway. I took my drink to a comfy chair by a fireplace off the lobby and curled up to review what I'd learned so far.

I was glad Sarah had told me about Ian. After everything that had gone down around the time Danny was murdered, I wasn't sure how I felt about our relationship, historical or otherwise. We hadn't been in touch since the funeral. I hadn't been in touch with anyone from that crowd, really. I'd kept to myself, ignoring all unpleasant memories, for about three years. I'd been reaching out to people over the past few months though, so it was strange that I hadn't heard anything through the grapevine. Ian likely had information relating to my husband's death, whether he knew it or not. I needed that information. I had to start somewhere. And it's not like I hadn't dated anyone since Danny died. My last year of graduate school in Philadelphia had been made all the more pleasant by a much younger law student from Penn. His mother had been on his case to find a nice Jewish girl and settle down ("You're nearly thirty!") and David had not been so inclined. Neither had he been inclined toward being single or celibate. As the older, Catholic widow of a murder victim, I was so unsuitable I was perfect. We both liked hockey and nice restaurants, and he was always willing to do the Sunday morning bagel run while I lounged and drank coffee. We didn't need to be in each other's pockets all the time, which worked for our study schedules. We had parted friends and kept in touch. It was good to have a hockey buddy in your contact list. Especially if his father was a partner in a big criminal law firm in Manhattan. You never knew.

Whatever the situation with the pending fiancé, I'd have to get Ian alone and ask him some questions. This Brittany had me curious. Sarah didn't like her. That much was obvious. It seemed as though she sensed some threat. Professional rivalry was unlikely, since Sarah was set to inherit both her father's job and the majority of the company. But Sarah was competitive. We'd started taking a yoga class together once, and she'd quit after two sessions because she couldn't figure out how to win. Still, the tension seemed more personal. Sarah hadn't referred to her father as "Daddy" once. Jane Whitaker was always "Mother," but Desmond Whitaker was either Dad or Daddy. One of the things that had cemented my friendship with Sarah early on was our mutual and perpetual annoyance with our mothers. We were both daddy's girls, but while I had no interest in inheriting my father's pub, Sarah was all in on taking over the family firm. The company we both worked for right out of college was part of Sarah's plan to get a variety of experience before going to work for her father. She had always been clear on her goals and confident that she would reach them, so why had this woman gotten under her skin? And what was up with the "before everything changes" comment? That sounded like something more than the wedding. She'd skated past it. I planned to ask her again later.

And what was Daddy doing in the hotel lobby, having what looked like an intimate conversation with some woman I didn't recognize? I hadn't seen Desmond in a few years—but I was sure that was him.

Speaking of—the woman I'd seen with Desmond now rounded the corner, accompanied by a man in his thirties. They paused just inside the room, the woman with her back to me. Her companion was dressed for a cool night in the mountains, but somehow still looked wrong. His trousers were too sharply creased, his shirt too neatly pressed, and his hiking boots were pristine. He had the erect posture of a man of medium height who wanted to appear taller. His hair was precisely cut and neatly styled, and his glasses had the kind of low-key trendy frames beloved of bankers and other suits trying to look cool. He was droning on about something—the woman couldn't get a word in edgewise. The tension in her shoulders suggested mansplaining, as did the self-satisfied expression on his face. He finally wound up with "I'm sure you'll see I'm right," and without waiting for a response, he patted her shoulder and left. Delightful.

The woman let out a sigh audible from where I was sitting, briefly studied the glassy-eyed stag head mounted over the fireplace, and then she left as well. What was going on here? The Whitaker family mysteries seemed to be mounting. Sarah's cryptic comments about one last big get-together and about Jeremy's evasiveness, and then Desmond's encounter in the lobby.

Then there was the always unflappable Jane, thrown into a tailspin by some last-minute changes in the guest list. What relatives could upset her that much? And why hadn't she just packed the late additions off to the inn? Not that I was complaining. The place was busy, warm, and blessedly normal. The image of the shadowed figure and mysterious red light in the house next to Sarah's flashed before my mind's eye. After more than a year of working at Raven

Hill Manor, every unexplained event took on a fantastical feel. But there was a simple explanation for what I'd seen, I was sure. Not my problem, even if the place was haunted. No, the Whitaker family issues would have to wait. I had bigger fish to fry. I just had to catch them first.

Chapter Three

After sleeping in and enjoying a light breakfast in the hotel dining room, I decided to do a little shopping. I was meeting Sarah and Jack for an early lunch but had the morning to myself. I roamed around, stopping in various shops. The nighttime temps were a little colder than I'd expected, so I bought myself a sweatshirt with a moose on it and a knit scarf with a fun polka dot print. The scarf would see a lot of action on chilly days at the Manor, and the sweatshirt would come in handy now that I was working out more. Winter was coming. Feeling virtuous about all the exercise I'd be getting once my vacation was over, I bought a box of candy to bring back to the library and tucked in a few buttercreams for myself just in case.

My only other purchases came from the library book sale display. The Lake Placid Public Library was on Main Street. From the front, it looked like a cheerful little cottage, hardly big enough to hold a bookshelf, let alone a whole library. In actuality, the slope from the street to the lake gave it another floor and an annex that stretched behind the building next to it. Since I was on vacation, I resisted the urge to go in, but I did pick up a few things from the sale shelves in front. With some time to spare before lunch, I went down the stone steps next to the building, settled into one of the Adirondack chairs at the edge of the lake, and pulled out my finds.

I'd scored a couple of Golden Age mysteries and a short story anthology from the same period. I didn't think I'd ever read Christie's novel *The Hollow*, one of those in which Poirot braves the countryside. I find nothing more relaxing than a country house murder. I was not particular about method. Poison was always good—there were so many options among common household products, not to mention the items found in the garden shed. Knives were a bit tricky unless you really knew your stuff; hit an artery and you have a lot of bloodstains to explain. Awkward. There were always old service revolvers tucked into desk drawers for those less concerned with noise. As far as blunt instruments went, I was a fan of the croquet mallet. There was a nice solid head, the shaft was long enough to give you a little insurance against the aforementioned bloodstains, and fingerprints could be explained away as long as one had the foresight to arrange a game on the day of the planned head-bashing, and remember your color when choosing the mallet of death. Really, the possibilities were endless. There was even a Christmas story in the anthology—"The Mistletoe Murder" by P. D. James. I loved a good holiday homicide. I slipped a receipt into the anthology to mark the story for bedtime reading and tucked everything back in my shopping bag.

I stretched out and admired the scenery. The sky was bright blue, and I watched a hawk circle and glide above me. Some crows landed at the edge of the grass. One had coloring that made it look like it was wearing a hood. That one studied me for a moment before losing interest and looking for food elsewhere. Mirror Lake was living up to its name, reflecting the autumn foliage on the surrounding mountains. The village of Lake Placid wound along it. What was once a hard-to-reach vacation spot frequented by a hardy few had become a slightly less hard-to-reach vacation spot frequented by people from all over the world, but it still had a wild beauty to it. Winding along the shore were homes of varying size and age. The

Whitaker house was at the far end, tucked into its own little cove. I wondered what was going on with Sarah's family. I didn't expect the weekend to play out like a Christie novel, but there was tension in the air and there were secrets being kept. It was none of my business, though, and I had my own mystery to solve. Still, I was curious. I wanted the weekend to go well for everyone's sake. I would try to get Sarah alone after lunch and find out what was worrying her.

I met Jack and Sarah at the combo crepes and sandwich place. Jack's younger sister Isabelle was with them. Half sister, I recalled. I had a vague memory of meeting her once before at some event. She was eight to ten years younger, so not quite thirty. Jack's mother had died when he was quite young, and his father had remarried. Isabelle gave me a shy smile when we said hello but was otherwise quiet. We ordered our lunch and found a table and made small talk until the food was ready. Jack and Sarah went to get it. I turned to Isabelle and found her studying me.

"I remember now where I know you from," she said. "You're Dan Sullivan's wife. I met you at the Christmas party. I was working for him that winter . . . well, right up until he died, actually. I was so sorry. I felt bad, he was under so much pressure those last few months, but he was always kind and patient with me. He was nice, everybody liked him. That's why I was so surprised when somebody murdered him."

Sarah and Jack returned with our lunch in time to hear that last bit. Both looked dumbfounded. Isabelle didn't notice. She was looking at me, her head tilted like an inquisitive bird.

"You look different. Did you change your hair?"

"I have. I've changed many things. More laid-back job, more laid-back look." I smiled at her and turned to Jack and Sarah. "Isabelle and I just figured out where we met."

"Yes, I—" Isabelle began.

Jack shot her a look. She closed her mouth. Sarah jumped in.

"Speaking of all those changes—tell me about them. Are you missing city life?"

"Only all the takeout options and the free exercise I got just going from place to place."

We talked for a while about village life in Raven Hill, the library, and the people I'd met. Sarah quizzed me thoroughly about how I felt about leaving the busy city, high-powered job, and friends who traveled in the same circles I had.

She finally wound up with, "You know, you're the only person I know who's ever done anything like this. Decided to change her life, quit the job, left town. And you don't regret it, do you?"

There was a little bit of a plea in her question. Even Jack looked apprehensive.

"I don't," I said. "I was ready for a change, for a lot of reasons. But I flailed around for a while, you know, after Dan died. It took me time to figure out what I wanted to do. But we've talked about this. What's this really about, Sarah?"

"Well," she said, reaching for Jack's hand, "I've decided to make a change, too."

"I thought so," I said. "Spill."

She took a deep breath. "Jack has an opportunity to work on a project, a big project, in Europe. He's going to take the job, and I'm going with him."

"Wow. That is big news. What did your dad say?"

"I haven't told him yet. We're going to tell everyone after the wedding."

"This project was only just finalized," Jack added.

"Where will you be based? Time difference makes it tough to telecommute, but you can do it," I said.

"The project is outside of Paris, but we're not sure where we'll live yet. Or exactly when we're leaving. Or—anything. Lots of details to work out."

Sarah bit her lip. Jack looked around the room. Isabelle frowned.

There was more to this.

"Your dad will be sorry not to have you around," I said.

"I don't know about that," she answered. "We've been butting heads a lot lately. I don't understand some of his decisions. And he's been distracted. I'm not sure what's going on, but I think this will be for the best. It's time for a change."

We talked a little more about their plans, but there was nothing too concrete yet. It was a recent development. I still had the sense that I wasn't getting the whole story, but it was their business. They probably wanted to share it with their families first. We moved on to talk of the wedding festivities. The rest of lunch was uneventful.

When we were clearing our table, Jack leaned over and said, "I'm sorry if Isabelle upset you. She's brilliant with numbers, a genius—literally—but not so great with people. She just doesn't think."

"No worries," I said, "she didn't upset me. She meant well, and I find her honesty refreshing."

"You're very kind," he said.

The happy couple was off to visit some members of Jack's family who had just arrived. Isabelle and I were headed in the same direction, so we walked together.

"So you're staying near the Whitakers?" I asked.

"Yes, next door. Jack and I are there now, and our parents when they arrive."

"Is that the big house with all the tall trees? Just the other side of the driveway?"

"Yes."

"Hmm. I thought that was empty. I've never known anyone to be there when I've visited. I guess the Whitakers know the owners."

"The Whitakers are the owners. At least, Jane Whitaker is. It was her family's house, the Granvilles, but no one's lived in it in years."

"That's odd. I'm surprised they haven't sold it."

"There's some story there, I'm not sure what. Jack says it has 'good bones.' He may be an architect, but his first love is restoration. Sarah says they've always done any repairs, but that it needs updating." She put updating in air quotes and added, "I guess most people want something fancier, but I think it's okay. It reminds me a little of my parents' house. Except it doesn't have the same feeling. This house feels sad. I guess that sounds strange."

"No, I know what you mean. Some places get like that, when no one has lived in them. I wonder why they're working on it now."

"They're going to rent it out. There's already new appliances and some new furniture. The plumbing is all good, but they're not quite done with the electrical changes. Something about a generator for the party. But Sarah said everything should work fine. It's only my family, and only for a few days."

"So the Petersons are going to be the test renters?"

"I guess so. It's okay. It was Jack's idea. I don't mind, and my parents won't care. They never notice things like that. It has a nice library, too, so they'll like it."

"So would I. I've always loved old libraries. You should see the one I work in." I gave her a brief description of Raven Hill Manor.

"This isn't quite as interesting, but if you want to see it, come visit. I'd like the company. My parents don't arrive until tomorrow, and Jack's busy with all the wedding things. We were supposed to come earlier, but he got tied up, so we just got here last night."

"That would be nice, thanks. I guess it must have been you, or maybe Jack, that I saw in the window upstairs while I was waiting for Sarah. Since I'd never known anyone to be in the house, I decided it was a trick of the light. Sunset."

"No, we didn't get here until late. After dinner, nearly nine. So it couldn't have been us. Maybe one of the contractors stayed late?"

"Maybe, though I didn't see any trucks. That might explain the red light though. Headlamp of some sort? Are they still working on the third floor?"

Isabelle shook her head. "They're not working there at all. Jane wanted it left alone until after the wedding for some reason. It's not even emptied out yet."

"Then I guess it must have been the light. With the sun setting and the breeze—well, it was probably a combination of reflection and shadows."

We walked in silence for a few minutes. Then Isabelle cleared her throat.

"You know," she said, not making eye contact, "I heard something up there, on the third floor. Last night. And then later, the piano. In the library."

"It wasn't Jack?"

"He'd gone to see Sarah. I was reading, so I would have heard him come in."

"What did you hear?"

"I'm not sure. It wasn't exactly footsteps, but it seemed like the floorboards were creaking in a sequence, if that makes any sense. And then a noise like a squeaky hinge, but that was farther away. I could barely hear it. Then nothing." She shrugged. "I listened for a bit, then decided it was just old house noises. Old wood, you know? And the trees in the wind. So I finished my chapter and turned off the light."

"What about the piano?" I asked. I could see the logical explanation so far. Old houses settled, wood swelled and shrank according to the weather. But piano wire?

"That was later, but not much later," Isabelle said. "I wasn't asleep. I was listening, because of the other noises, but the wind had come up, so it was harder to hear. The tree boughs were scraping and tapping against the house. Then the wind died down, just for a minute, and I heard it. The piano. A few notes, repeated. Nothing for a few seconds, then the wind again. But I think I'd have heard the piano over it. Maybe."

"What did you do?"

"I turned the light on, got up, and put a chair in front of my door. Then I waited for Jack to come home. I called him when he came up the stairs. He said the house was locked—he'd used his key to get in, and shut it up behind him. He looked around upstairs with a flashlight but didn't see anything. Or anyone. He chalked it up to the house settling."

"The piano?"

"Music coming over the water. Or me dreaming. He said he'd check the locks and look around again in the morning."

"Hmm. It probably is the age of the house and the temperature swings this time of year. Well, we can poke around, see if we find an explanation. It might even be fun. Will you be all right tonight?"

"I'll be okay. I'll be out for a while, and I'll make sure to find out when Jack will be back. I'm not usually—well, I don't want you to think I'm silly."

"I don't," I said. "I've scared myself a few times at the manor, especially when I first started working there."

She looked relieved. After a minute she said, "I'm sorry if I was tactless, what I said about Dan. I probably shouldn't have mentioned it."

I repeated what I'd told Jack and added, "Besides, being the widow of a murder victim leads to some awkward conversations."

"Awkward is the only kind of conversation I seem to have," Isabelle said. "But if you don't mind my asking, what did happen to Dan?"

"The police said he interrupted a burglary."

"But you don't believe that?"

"I—why do ask?"

She shrugged. "The way you said it. And I always thought it had something to do with work."

"Why?"

"I don't know. I just presumed, but when I didn't hear anything else, I didn't think about it. I went to work for Jack right after, and he never mentioned it."

"Do you remember why you thought what you did? Was there anything in particular?"

"I don't think so. If it were one concrete thing I would remember. It must have been a lot of small things that didn't make sense. People hardly ever say what they really mean, you know? And I always hear things the wrong way."

"It sounds to me like you hear them the right way, Isabelle, just not the way they're intended to be heard."

"Oh, well, maybe." She didn't look convinced. "But anyway, I remember a lot of that kind of thing that spring. At first I thought it was because I was new. I didn't know much about the business—the whole cannabis product industry. I'm sure Dan hired me as a favor to Jack—I had just left my PhD program and was at loose ends. But I don't think it was just me."

"Was there anything in particular?" I asked.

She shook her head. "I don't know. I'll think about it. There was one thing—Dan said he wanted me to look at some data and tell him what I thought. He said something about 'something wrong with the pattern' or something like that. But he never showed me."

"And that was right before he died?"

"Yes. Maybe a week?" She gave me a sidelong look. "He mentioned you, too." Apparently deciding I wasn't going to dissolve into hysterics, she continued. "He said that he was going to check some things with you, that you were good at making crazy connections that turned out to make sense. If you could do it with the people, and I could do it with the numbers, he'd have an answer. I didn't understand. People don't make sense, but numbers do. If you start getting crazy answers, there's a flaw in the logic. You just have to find it. It's really very simple."

Maybe for Isabelle. I was proficient with basic financial statements, and could do some useful analyzing and forecasting, but I was about as good at complex, theoretical mathematics as Isabelle was with more nuanced social interactions.

"He did mention something like that to me, but he never explained. If anything else comes back to you, will you let me know?"

She nodded.

"And Isabelle? Please don't mention this to anyone. If we're both right and Dan's death had something to do with work, it could be dangerous if the wrong person hears we're curious."

"I understand. I'll keep this to myself and let you know if I remember anything else."

"Thank you. Now let's figure out when I can see that library."

We compared calendars and exchanged cell numbers. After making tentative plans, Isabelle went on her way, and I climbed the hill to the inn.

Chapter Four

꩜

I arrived at Sarah's house that afternoon at the appointed time for the tea and was greeted by her mother, Jane, a petite blond whirlwind who was always impeccably attired. After a Chanel-scented hug, she held me at arm's length and looked me over. It could've felt like an inspection, but Jane's face was etched with concern. After a moment she stepped back and smiled.

"Greer, you're looking wonderful. Have you lost weight? No? Then you've changed your hair. Beautiful! And I love your dress—such a flattering color. I've been so concerned. First Dan, and then that dreadful business last spring. It sounded most unpleasant. We're all thrilled you could be here. I feel terrible about the last-minute change of plans. I told Des—well, never mind. It's not important. As long as your room is comfortable? Yes? Excellent. Well, there's not a thing to do before the guests arrive. You'll want to freshen up and change your shoes after your walk here. I know it's not far, but those sidewalks are treacherous, aren't they? Just run up to Sarah's room—you know the way. And make sure she's down here in fifteen minutes, will you? So happy to see you, Greer."

And with a kiss on my cheek and a gentle squeeze of my arm, she was off. As instructed, I climbed the stairs to the second floor and knocked on Sarah's door. It was flung open by the bride-to-be. Her hair and makeup were perfection, in spite of what appeared to be a small explosion involving the closet and several suitcases.

"Thank God it's you," she said, gesturing me in.

"Your mother says you have fifteen minutes. How can I help?"

"Oh, for heaven's sake! This one or the blue?"

After getting Sarah's dress and accessories sorted out, I sat down to change my shoes while she rooted through her jewelry box.

"Your mother looks great," I said. "And she's a bundle of energy. I got a little breathless listening to her."

Sarah turned to me, a tiny frown line appearing on her forehead.

"She seems more wound up than usual. Does she seem a little, I don't know, manic? It's just that I'm worried about her drinking."

"I wouldn't say manic," I replied. "Your mother's always been tightly wound. And given the circumstances, I didn't notice anything unusual. But I haven't seen her in a while. Do *you* think she's drinking too much?"

"I don't know. It's more that she always seems to have a glass in her hand. She's never sloppy, but she seems edgy."

"Hmm. Well, there's a lot going on, so that could be it. But if I notice anything I'll let you know."

"Thanks," she said. "I really want everyone to have a good time, my parents especially. Jack keeps telling me I'm worrying too much. It'll be a beautiful weekend, and in a few days it'll be just the two of us. That will be so nice."

But the little frown was back. Was this about more than the move? I was about to ask when she jumped up.

"Look at the time! We'd better go down."

And with one last twirl in front of the mirror, we were off.

* * *

I've always thought that one of England's greatest contributions to civilization is the late afternoon meal known as "tea," the higher the better. From dainty finger sandwiches with exotic fillings to flaky scones generously topped with clotted cream and jam, every possible flavor and texture were covered. The cocktails, while not traditional, were a very nice addition. I'd put away my first a bit too quickly, after an unexpected fit of nerves hit me when I started to greet people I hadn't seen in years. Halfway through the second I felt light-headed and decided a plate of cucumber sandwiches, with some smoked salmon thrown in for variety, would fix me right up. Veggie platters were for amateurs. I'd loaded a plate and spotted a quiet place to sit and observe the crowd when I heard a familiar voice, one that carried above the noise of the crowd.

"Lovely party, Janie. Where's the bar?"

I turned and saw Jane Whitaker in the entrance to the dining room. At her side was a statuesque woman of about seventy, her dark, silver-streaked hair and colorful outfit windblown, her bright blue eyes scanning the room. She was leaning on an elaborately ornamented cane, smiling as she looked at the guests. In contrast, our hostess wore a look of quiet desperation. She spotted me and waved me over, beginning introductions before I was within five feet of them.

"Carolyn, this is Sarah's friend Greer Hogan. I'm not sure if you've met? Greer, this is Desmond's cousin Carolyn Quinn."

"Yes, we have met, but it's been a few years. So nice to see you again," I said.

"Carolyn's had a very trying trip. Perhaps you could find her a seat and get her something to eat while I make sure her room is ready. You must be exhausted, Carolyn." Jane gave me a pointed look. "I'll be as quick as I can."

I got the message. Keep Carolyn quiet and tucked away until Jane had time to deal with her. I didn't mind. Caro, as she liked to be called, was one of Sarah's more colorful relatives. She was the family rebel—skipped college to model, traveled the world, never married, was rumored to have had affairs with famous men, and was plainspoken in the extreme. She was the anti-Jane. Several years older than Sarah's father, "Great-Aunt Caro" had always been a favorite of the Whitaker children, and of Desmond himself, so Jane tolerated her eccentric in-law. I'd met her only once, but I liked her.

I settled Caro in the spot I'd picked out for myself, a corner of the living room partly screened by a potted tree, with a good view of the party and a nice breeze from the nearby French doors. She plucked a sandwich off my plate. "Mm, these are good. Get another plateful, won't you, darling? I'm famished. And find me a drink. It's been a helluva day. Don't worry," she added, waving the finger sandwich, pinkie extended, "I'll behave."

I sent a waiter with a tray full of cocktails in Caro's direction and loaded up a few plates. It was the kind of event where my waitressing skills came in handy. Sarah gave me an odd look as I wove through the crowd. I mouthed "Great-Aunt Caro" as I went by, and she smiled. When I arrived with the food, Caro was studying her half-empty glass.

"I never trust a pink drink," she said. "Too precious. But this isn't bad."

"It's gin and champagne, and usually clear with a lemon twist. They must have used pink champagne. Maybe the caterer wanted it to look a little more 'ladies' lunchy.'"

"Well, Janie's always liked her gin," Caro said, draining her own glass. She waved the waiter over and plucked a few more glasses off the tray, sliding one over to me. I'd barely touched the one I had, but that didn't seem to bother Caro.

We'd been eating in companionable silence for a few minutes when a couple of women who looked like mother and daughter walked into the room. The younger one looked familiar, though I couldn't place her. She glanced my way and did a double-take. Then she pasted a smile on and gave me a little finger wave. I responded in kind. She bent toward her companion and started to whisper something, and the two veered off. I sighed.

Caro gave me a look.

"Know them?" she asked.

"I think the younger one probably knew my husband. My late husband, I mean."

"He's the one who was killed during a burglary?"

"Yes," I said, "or so the police tell me."

Caro studied me for a moment, then pushed my drink a little closer.

"I'm sorry," she said. "That's a terrible thing to have happen, and there's nothing I can say to make it better."

I appreciated her bluntness. I'd gotten tired of euphemisms and platitudes years ago. Dan was not lost, he had not passed. He'd been murdered. He was dead. Caro's straightforward statement mitigated the spurt of rage I always felt when someone mentioned it.

"I hope you're not feeling too much like the specter at the feast. Do you know many of the guests?" Caro asked.

"A handful. If I haven't seen them since, well, it can be a little awkward. But most have been fine. And the Whitakers have been wonderful."

Carolyn nodded. "Janie was always a good girl, and I suppose Desmond is no more a fool than any man. He has a good heart, always did."

"So you've known Jane since she and Desmond married?"

"Before. I was at school with her older sister, Barbara. Now there was a wild child. Made me feel positively timid."

Wow.

"I've never met her," I said. "Will she be coming to the wedding, do you think?"

"She doesn't get out much. Not sure that would be a good idea. Though she seemed better the last time we spoke." Caro frowned. Then she glanced over at me and went on.

"Jane was quite a bit younger, of course. My parents always treated Des as part of the family, so I guess you could say he was the baby brother I never had. Our fathers were brothers, and Des and I were both only children. There were a lot of families that spent summers in the Adirondacks, not just the ski season. We had a little place over near Saranac. So I've known Jane since she was a child. I didn't see much of either her or Desmond for a while. I was traveling. Then I came home from a trip one day and they were fresh out of college and engaged. At first I was surprised—they were so young—but Jane was so much the opposite of his mother. Eleanor Whitaker drank like a fish. The household was always in chaos. And there was Jane, with never so much as an eyelash out of place. I could see the appeal. And after what happened to Barbara— ah, speaking of brides—"

Sarah had found us. She greeted Caro with a hug and a kiss. I gave her my place on the loveseat and pulled over a chair. The two spent a few minutes catching up—Caro's trip, the schedule of wedding events, who was here, and who had yet to arrive.

"Did you know Auntie Barbara was here?" Sarah asked Caro. "I'm sure she'll be happy to see you. She's resting in her room now, but the two of you can visit later."

Caro looked surprised. "I'm glad she's feeling up to it," she said. "Isn't this an awful lot of—activity for her?"

"She's only coming to the wedding, and then lunch afterward. Jeremy said she's been doing very well, and this way she can visit with the family. It was a last-minute decision, but her doctor cleared it. Said it would be good for her."

"Oh, well, that'll be nice then. I do visit her at home, but it's been a few months. The older one gets, the faster time passes." Caro smiled, but I thought she still looked uneasy.

"Oh, look—wait, don't look—okay, now look," Sarah said, gesturing with her glass. "It's the one and only Brittany. Surprised she made it in time. *Very* important meeting this morning, she told me."

I turned my head slightly in the direction indicated. I saw a thin brunette with shoulder-length hair. She was wearing a sleeveless sheath dress and a bright raspberry wrap that had slid down to her elbows, revealing bony shoulders. The wrap looked like cashmere, and the handbag was designer. No hosiery, unless she was channeling Kate Middleton and wearing those nude tights that clung like a second skin. She was attractive rather than pretty, or would have been if she hadn't looked so bored. I disliked her instantly.

"So what do you think?" Sarah said.

"She reminds me of that line in *Bridget Jones*—something about an American stick insect."

Sarah snickered. "Tell me about it," she said. "She goes sleeveless year-round. That's what the wrap is all about. The style and color change seasonally. She's in good shape and has decent arms, but honestly."

"She's no Michelle Obama," added Caro. "This one's a little too thin. It'll start showing in her face in a couple of years." Caro popped another sandwich into her mouth and continued her assessment of Brittany. "So what's her story?"

"She's my father's new favorite employee, and the rumored future wife of Greer's ex-boyfriend."

"And this is why we dislike her?"

"I've never actually met her," I said. "I'm leaping to conclusions."

"Trust your instincts," Sarah said. She made a face. "To be honest, I didn't dislike her on sight—it's more that I didn't trust her from the moment I met her."

"Trust *your* instincts," Caro told her. "Get her to come over. I want to size her up."

We all sipped our drinks and studied our target while Sarah waited for her moment. Upon closer inspection, Brittany was not as tall as I had originally thought. She was wearing very high heels. Barefoot, she'd be closer to my own five and half feet, rather than eye to eye with Sarah or Caro, who were closer to five ten.

Her jewelry was vintage, and her makeup was tasteful. Still, she looked a little more corporate cocktail party than afternoon tea. Beyond the brightly colored wrap, it was a fairly standard outfit. She handed her empty glass to a passing waiter and pushed her hair back. The gesture and the profile seemed familiar, like I'd seen exactly that before. It took me a minute, but I realized that Brittany was the woman I'd seen with Desmond Whitaker at the inn. Odd, if she was supposed to have arrived today.

Brittany's companion made one last remark and turned away. Brittany stood where she was, looking around. I thought she was looking for someone she knew but then realized she was studying the house rather than the crowd. She reached out and ran her hand along the wood of the banister. She turned toward us, and Sarah waved her over.

"Brittany! So glad you could make it! Are you enjoying yourself? Lovely. Let me introduce you."

She started with Caro. I hid a smile. I knew Sarah's "fake nice" voice from way back.

"And this is my friend Greer Hogan. I don't think you've ever met, though Greer and I go way back. She introduced me to Jack. Greer, this is Brittany Miles. She's worked for Whitaker Inc. for—what is it?—nearly a year now."

"Eighteen months, actually. And no, I've never met Greer."

It took effort to keep my jaw from dropping. She sounded like a little girl. I couldn't imagine sitting through a meeting listening to that high pitch. How could anyone take her seriously? I couldn't believe Sarah hadn't warned me.

We exchanged greetings and made small talk. Caro asked her a few questions about herself. She was polite, though not very forthcoming. The conversation was petering out when another Whitaker relative came over to say hello to Sarah and Caro. With the two of them distracted, I decided to indulge my curiosity.

"Are you enjoying your stay at the inn?" I asked.

"What?" She looked startled, but only for a second. "I'm sorry, I don't know what you mean."

"Oh, I thought I saw you last night. At the Mirror Lake Inn, in the lobby. Several of the wedding guests are staying there."

"No, I just got here. And I'm staying in the guesthouse."

"My mistake. Must have been someone who looks like you."

"Yes, I guess so." She turned to include Sarah and Caro. "Well, if you'll excuse me, there's someone I need to speak to."

Caro gave her a wave and said, "So nice to have met you, Brita," and went back to her conversation. Sarah smiled and mouthed "Bye."

"See you," I said. "Enjoy your visit."

"Thanks," Brittany said, and went back to the hallway. She paused, looking first left, then right, and once again pushed her hair back. It must be a nervous gesture, I thought, her hair didn't seem to be in her face. She decided on a direction and disappeared from view. But that last look convinced me that it was indeed her in the lobby last night. So why lie?

I was starting to feel warm from all the alcohol, so I told Sarah and Caro I needed some fresh air. I slipped out the French doors and stood on the fieldstone patio, enjoying the cool breeze and the view. The Whitakers had done some landscaping since the last time I visited. The steeply sloping lawn had become a terraced garden. They'd always had nice old trees and some flowers, but a bit of judicious pruning and grading and the addition of new plants gave it a more finished look. They'd kept the hedge that ran along the old gravel driveway on one side and added what I thought were flowering trees on the other. It enclosed the back of the property without seeming fussy. A winding path started at the patio and disappeared behind shrubs, reappearing farther down, only to disappear again. Always a sucker for a mystery, I decided to follow it. My guess was it ended at the boathouse.

I went down the steps into the garden, keeping to the stone pathway. This would be an invitation to a broken neck in icy weather, but right now it kept my kitten heels from sinking into the grass. A few steps brought me to the first turn and into a small clearing with a bench. Another small path entered the clearing on the opposite side from where I stood. There were a couple of steps up, and then it disappeared around a corner. Based on the location, I thought it led back to the driveway. The shrubbery behind the bench grew fairly high. I could hear voices from the living room, but I couldn't see anything, not even the patio. It afforded privacy, if not always quiet. If you had a suspicious nature, it would also be a great place to eavesdrop. I continued my explorations. The sounds of the party faded quickly as the path wound on. For the most part it was just a garden path, creating a gently sloping means of getting to the lake. But at irregular intervals it would open up, and you'd turn a corner or enter a small glade to find a statue, a birdbath or a feature plant. The effect was surprisingly playful. There was even a reflecting pool, with another little bench nearby. It had a stone border, designed to look random, with loose stones here and there. The same stones were scattered around the clearing, grouped with different plants. I went to the edge and peeked in. I saw a rippling version of my face, with the trees and the top floor of the Whitaker house looming over me. The water was deeper than I expected, sloping up to a shallower depth in the center. A soft hum revealed some machinery hidden behind a trellis—probably a pump and heater. That would keep the birds happy all winter—they'd have water when most things smaller than the lake were frozen. There was a pile of folded green tarps behind there as well and some tools. Looked like the work wasn't quite done.

I walked on. The clever layout gave the impression of a much larger space. Though many of the plants were not in bloom, the garden had obviously been designed with an eye to year-round color. I couldn't identify much of what I was looking at but knew enough to tell that where it was lovely now, it would be spectacular in the spring and summer.

I rounded the final corner and stepped onto a small area of lawn facing the lake, with the boathouse and dock off to my left. A pair of lounge chairs, one of them occupied, centered the scene. As I headed toward them, the lanky lounger pushed up his sunglasses and then raised his drink in salute.

"Greer Hogan! You're a sight for sore eyes! Join me, won't you?"

"Hello, Jeremy," I said, settling into the other chair. "It's nice to see you again."

Jeremy Whitaker, Sarah's younger brother, had always been something of a disappointment to the family. Though not exactly the black sheep, he was usually described as "not living up to his potential." Classic underachiever. I liked him, but I had to admit he'd never seemed to have much purpose. Good-looking and with no shortage of charm, Jeremy seemed to skate through life, leading most people to write him off as superficial. Though he often adopted a mocking, cynical tone, I knew him to be thoughtful. After Danny died, Jeremy had made a point of taking me to lunch whenever he was in the city and sending funny emails for my birthday. I suspected he was more sensitive than he let on.

"And you. Get tired of the Mad Hatter's Tea Party?"

"It's a lovely party. I just needed some fresh air. Your Great-Aunt Carolyn arrived, did you know?"

"I picked her up from the airport. She still flies her own small plane but refuses to deal with rental cars. It's her twenty-year-old Range Rover or nothing. She likes my convertible though. Made me leave the top down the whole way."

I had visions of a septuagenarian Phryne Fisher, winging her way north and then ordering her chauffeur to floor it through the mountains. No wonder Caro looked windblown.

"So is that your job this weekend? Ferrying people around?"

"Some of that, and making sure the band and bar are set up for the party after the rehearsal dinner."

"Your mother's not handling every detail?"

"Amazing, but no. I spent most of last winter here and stayed through the summer. I'm a little more connected locally than she is, and Sarah wanted something fun and informal, so I'm a better bet."

"Sounds like it. Did you do a lot skiing?"

"Some. I did this and that. I helped with the garden redesign."

"Really? It's great. I thought it was different from your mother's style. It's almost mischievous."

"Whereas she represents all that is deeply regimented and orderly."

"Well—"

"You don't have to say anything. We all know. I'm not sure she likes the design, but she's thrilled with my initiative."

"I'm sure. I understand you're all working on the house next door, too. I never knew the family owned it."

"It technically belongs to my mother and her sister, Barbara, though my mother's the trustee. The Granvilles built at the same time the Whitakers did, and it's still got the original floor plan. Jack's overseeing the project. Nice to have an architect in the family—he'll make sure we don't decide to take out any load-bearing walls. It's past time it was made habitable again. It can't stay there like some kind of macabre time capsule forever."

There was distinct edge to his tone. I decided to change the subject and asked about the band for the party. We chatted for a few minutes more, and then I said I needed to get back to the tea.

"I volunteered to pitch in with any last-minute tasks, so I need to check in with your mother and sister. Sarah really wants to make sure everyone has a lovely weekend."

"Can't blame her. One last hurrah."

"She said something like that, too. What's going on, Jeremy?"

"All will be revealed, Greer, but not yet. Let's just say the family is in for a big surprise, and for once, it's not my fault."

With that, he stood, gave me a peck on the cheek, said he'd see me later, and left.

So I wasn't imagining things. Something was up with the Whitakers. But what? I sighed as I turned back to toward the house. I was in Sarah's camp—I just wanted everyone to have a nice time. I had my own issues to deal with. I'd had a pleasant afternoon and made contact with a few old acquaintances, but I'd have to get serious. I couldn't let subtlety turn into outright avoidance. I'd gone down that path before and sometimes still wavered. I'd known it would be a long process. Time to get methodical.

I walked back through the garden. I had it to myself until I reached the reflecting pool. I heard Brittany—there was no mistaking that little girl voice—talking on the phone. The one-sided conversation carried down the path that led toward the driveway—she had to be there, just out of sight. She sounded agitated. No thanks. I scooted onto the path that led to the house before she came into view.

Once inside, I looked for Jane. I found Sarah and told her I planned to meet with her mother and then go back to the inn but wanted to say goodbye to her and Caro first.

"I saw my mother a few minutes ago—she said she was going to her study to print some things out for you. You know where it is? And Caro's around here somewhere. She said something about needing some fresh air. I'm sure you'll bump into her. Thanks again for pitching in. See you tomorrow?"

We said goodbye, and I went in the direction of Jane's office. I found her in the hallway just outside it. She looked startled when I rounded the corner.

"Hi. Wedding assistant, reporting for duty. I know you've had a lot of last-minute changes. Sarah said there were some calls to make. If you'd like to give me the guest list and seating charts, I can do that and adjust the seating. I'm planning a quiet night."

"Thank you, Greer. That would be wonderful. I just have to take care of a few things. Fifteen minutes? Then I'll meet you in my study."

I told her I'd get my things and meet her there. I went up the back stairs and retrieved my things from Sarah's bedroom, came back the same way, and slipped into Jane's study. It was an oasis of calm after the noise and color of the party. She'd done some redecorating since my last visit. Though the room was small and trimmed in the same dark wood as the rest of the house, it had large windows and pale yellow walls. There were French doors that opened onto a tiny patio with steps leading down to one of the garden paths. One door was slightly ajar, letting in a soft breeze. These doors and windows, combined with several strategically placed mirrors, gave the illusion of space. "All my walls are mirrors," I murmured. How did the rest of that verse go? I shook my head. It would come to me.

I set my things down next to an overstuffed chair and ottoman. Beside the chair a large basket held Jane's knitting. Sharp silver needles in a variety of sizes skewered skeins of yarn in as many colors. She must have several projects going at once. To my left was an end table piled with books, mostly on gardening and knitting. There were also a couple of paperback mysteries— *Resurrection Row* by Anne Perry and Carolyn Hart's *The Christie Caper*. I'd read and enjoyed both. Against the window was a desk. When seated there, Jane would overlook the old gravel drive leading to the boathouse, with a partial view of the lake and garden. A chair and ottoman faced some bookshelves with a small television. A love seat was near the door, and a thick carpet with a watercolor pattern tied all the colors together. The overall effect was feminine and warm.

The room showed Jane's usual sense of order, with the exception of the desk. There were piles of papers and folders strewn across the top, with pens scattered over them. The vase of flowers in the corner seemed to have been shoved sideways, leaving a trail of fallen petals and splashes of water. Those would leave a mark. No matter how long it had been since I left home, my mother's training had stuck. I plucked a tissue from the box on the desk and tried to mop up the spill. Still wet—I really needed a towel. I picked up the stray petals and put the whole mess in the trash. I couldn't put the vase back without moving the folders. I didn't want Jane to think I'd been going through her desk. That being said, I eyed the files, wondering what had inspired this small eruption of disorder. They were all labeled and all seemed to have to do with the wedding—caterer, florist, entertainment, seating charts, guests. The first three files were closed, their contents only slipping out a bit. The last two were open. These were the pages scattered on the desktop. They were also the ones I wanted copies of.

I studied the printouts. Everything had been done using one computer program or another, but apparently Jane liked to make notes by hand. Couldn't blame her, so did I. There were scribbled comments, arrows, and things crossed out, sometimes with new information written in. All pretty run of the mill, except for one corner of the seating chart. There was a huge red X through one table. A single line was drawn across all the names but one. That one was scratched out so hard there was a hole in the paper. Next to it was a sketch, in red ink, of a knife dripping blood.

That wasn't annoyance at a last-minute change. That was rage. Who had inspired that kind of response?

I started reading some of Jane's comments. They covered everything from dietary issues to how the guest knew the bride, with a few notes on which guests were recently divorced and had to be seated far from their former spouses. It was a gold mine of information, but I wasn't going to be able to tell whose name was obliterated without taking time to compare it to the guest list. It was unlikely Jane was going to give me a copy with all these notes and comments.

I nipped over to the door and eased it open. No one in the hall, though I could hear Jane's voice around the corner. It sounded like she was giving instructions to someone. I shut the door and pulled my phone out of my handbag. After adjusting the magnification on the camera a few times, I got some clear pictures of the chart. I tried to work across it methodically, with a couple close-ups of the table with the red X through it. I was sliding everything back to where I'd found it when I heard the doorknob squeak. I dove for the ottoman, threw my phone into my bag, and grabbed my spare shoes. By the time Jane walked in, I was bent over, slipping on the ballet flats I'd walked over in.

"I'm so sorry to keep you waiting. Couple of issues with the caterer." She looked at her desk and frowned.

"Oh, no, I was glad to have a minute to sit. My feet are killing me." I bent over to massage my instep. Out of the corner of my eye I saw her glance in my direction and move some of the papers with one hand. In the other she held a small towel. She glanced at the open door and back at me. She shut it.

"There we go." I gave her a bright smile as I slipped my shoes into my bag. "Oh, did you knock that vase over? Here, let me help."

"No," Jane said. "No, I'll do it. More of it ended up on me." She gave me a tight smile. "This is what I get for rushing." She dabbed at the remaining damp spots on the desk and then sat down, once again moving papers around and adjusting the vase.

"The tea went well, don't you think? Everyone seemed to be having a good time. And the food was delicious," I said.

Jane smiled. Her shoulders relaxed a little. "Thank you. I thought it went well, too. Now we just have to get through the rest of the weekend." Her jaw tightened as she looked down at her desk.

"Sarah's idea of simple and informal? It'll be fun, but I know it's a lot of work. Though Jeremy is helping with the rehearsal dinner and dance, isn't he? I saw him a little while ago at the bottom of the garden. Which looks wonderful, by the way. I understand he helped with that, too."

She glanced out the window. "Jeremy did a lot of the design work. It's not what I'd have chosen, but it does look nice, doesn't it? He's always had a good eye. Perhaps he's finding his way at last." She sighed. "And Sarah, Jack, and Jeremy between them are managing everything—well, almost everything—tomorrow night. I'm not sure about that band on the lawn. I've invited all the near neighbors, and it shouldn't go too late. But sound does carry over water—"

"I'm sure it will be fine. There's always a lot of action at night along the lake. It's never really quiet. This way you can devote yourself to all the details of the more formal event. And maybe even enjoy yourself a little. Now, what can I do to help?"

Jane sat at her desk and rattled off a short list while booting up her computer. After making a few changes, she printed out clean copies of the guest list and seating chart. She looked them over, penciled in a couple of things, and handed them to me. She thanked me again for volunteering to help.

"It's no problem," I said, "I don't mind at all. The last thing I want is for you and Sarah to exhaust yourselves trying to do everything." Especially when I wanted to nose around.

"You've always been such a lovely girl, Greer. I'm so glad you and Sarah maintained your friendship. And I am a little tired."

"Well, then, take some time to put up your feet and get some rest. I'll take care of these few things tonight." I blew her a kiss and got up. She smiled and turned back to her desk. I looked over my shoulder when I got to the door. Jane was looking out the window, lost in thought. She did look tired, and sad. I left quietly, closing the door behind me.

I'd reached the street in front of the Whitakers' when I realized I didn't have my sunglasses. I must've taken them off in the garden or while I was talking to Jeremy, probably the latter. The quickest way back was down the old gravel driveway at the side of the house. I could start on the lawn and work my way back through the garden if need be. I looked up at the house next door but saw nothing in the windows today. The only sound came from the whispering evergreens and the cawing of a crow somewhere in their boughs. I was rounding the corner by the hedge when I heard a familiar voice. I stopped.

Ian Cameron. He was standing with his back to me, talking on the phone while he pulled a suitcase out of a rental SUV. He was wearing his usual uniform of jeans, loafers, and button-down oxford. Ian was a few years older than I, but from what I could see, he had so far avoided the paunch and thinning hair that often arrived with middle age. He looked the same as he had when I'd seen him a little over three years ago. His call finished, he shoved his phone in his pocket, then reached up to close the hatch of the car. I took a few steps forward. I didn't want him to think I'd been eavesdropping. The gravel crunched under my feet, and he turned. I walked a few more feet and paused.

"Hi," I said. It was lame, but it was a start.

"Hi yourself," he said, taking a few steps toward me.

We stood there, about three feet apart, looking each other over while trying to look like we weren't doing exactly that. After a few seconds he looked up at the house, then back at me. He smiled.

"You look very pretty. Ladies' tea party this afternoon, right?"

"Yep. All the older relatives, Jane's friends, and some of Sarah's that arrived early. Afternoon dresses and china teacups. You missed quite a spread. If you're quick, you may be able to snag some left-over finger sandwiches and scones."

"I wouldn't dare attempt it without my hat and gloves," he said, his grin widening. "Jane might have me tossed out."

I grinned back. "Maybe not. She seems to be mellowing. She actually let Jeremy take charge of the rehearsal dinner. With Sarah's input, of course."

"Then it should be a good time."

"Yes, sounds like it."

An awkward silence followed. I could find no way to segue from our brief easy banter to the questions I needed to ask: "Do you have any idea who killed my husband or why? Was there something shady going on?" So I defaulted to my usual response to conversations I didn't want to have—recalling an urgent task elsewhere.

"Well, I'd better go—"

"No, wait—um," Ian said, looking around, "were you on your way to say hello to Jeremy? Because he left me a message to let myself into the boathouse—I guess he's been shifted down here due to some last-minute guests. But it didn't sound like he planned on being here until later."

"I think he's doing another run to the airport or the train station. He mentioned it when I saw him earlier, and his car's gone. No, I'm looking for my sunglasses. I think I left them in the garden."

"I'll help you look."

"Oh, no, that's okay, you've had a long trip. I'll find them, and I'll see you later."

"Please, Greer." He touched my arm. "Listen. I wanted to say how sorry I am. About—"

He stopped. Opened his mouth. Shut it again. Repeat.

"About Danny?" I asked.

"Yes. And about everything that happened. Not getting in touch for all this time. Since the funeral. I should have. That night, the night Dan died, I said and did some things I shouldn't have. I'm sorry. It's never an excuse, but I'd had a lot to drink." He blew out a long breath, and said again, "I'm sorry."

"Thank you, Ian. I appreciate it. But really, it was only a kiss and some conversation. Nothing to worry about." I tried to make my tone light. Ian shot me a look.

"Okay," I said. "So it wasn't nothing, but we'd both had too much to drink." I took a deep breath and decided to forge ahead before I chickened out. "And there are some things I want to talk about, but not that. I need to know some things about the night he died, and about the weeks before. I know he was in touch with you. There are some things I don't understand. I'm hoping you can help. Something strange was going on, I'm sure of it."

"Hmph." Ian took a step back. He frowned, his eyes moving as though he were reading something there in the hedge that only he could see. I knew that look. It meant his wheels were turning. After a minute, he nodded.

"I think you're right, Greer. There was something going on, but I'm not sure what. He wanted to discuss something, but we never connected. He was supposed to be there that night. I thought we'd talk then."

"Yes. But something held him up. He kept texting. Do you remember anything?"

"Not really. I can do some checking, and give you some background. But not now. Why don't we meet for dinner? Do you have plans?"

"I have to take care of a couple wedding-related things for Sarah and Jane, but that won't take long. I was planning an early night."

"We'll do something casual, right here in town."

I hesitated, not sure how I felt about having dinner with Ian. Not sure how I felt about Ian in general—it varied by the minute. But it might be my only chance to talk to him alone for any length of time, and I wanted some idea of what I was heading into before I started asking questions.

"All right."

We set a time and place to meet and said our goodbyes. Ian went into the boathouse, and I resumed my search for my sunglasses. They were on the ground near the lounge chair, just as I'd thought. I dusted them off and put them on. I looked up at the house and garden, admiring how they looked in the end-of-day light. A movement caught my eye. Great-Aunt Caro, making her way to the bench by the reflecting pool. I watched her go. She was in good shape for her age, but she'd had a few drinks and didn't seem to be making good use of her cane. I decided to go up the driveway, and detour into the garden to say goodbye, as I hadn't found her earlier.

I had almost reached the break in the hedge when I saw Isabelle coming out the side door. I called out to her. She turned and waved and headed toward me. She looked like she was limping.

"What's up?" I said as she got closer. "Blister?"

"I think so," she said, "and my feet are killing me. I hardly ever wear these shoes. At least I don't have far to go."

We chatted for a minute about the party, and she continued on her way. I went through the hedge and down the steps into the garden. I came into the clearing and found Caro bent over the pool. It looked like she was searching for something.

"Caro! I was about to leave—do you need anything before I go? Did you drop something?"

She gave a start and lost her balance for a second. I darted toward her, but she righted herself and leaned on her cane.

"I'm so sorry!" I stopped next to her at the edge of the pool.

"Oh, that's all right. I was just trying to remember—I think they used to have koi in this pond, but no sign of them now."

"I think you're right," I said. "There's a heater over there—they would have needed it in the winter." I gestured toward the trellis and once again noted the pile of tarps. Odd, they didn't seem as tidy as before.

"Of course," she said, taking my arm and turning me back toward the path. "I remember now."

"I like the reflecting pool," I said, "though it's a little less like a mirror when it's breezy."

I glanced into the water as we walked. A bright flash of color caught my eye. I stopped, but it disappeared in the rippling water. Caro gave my arm a tug, and we started walking again.

"If you'd help me to the bench, Greer, I'd appreciate it. I'm afraid I can't party like I used to."

"Would you like me to go get you something?" I asked once she was seated.

"No, no, I'm fine, darling. Just a little tired. I want to enjoy having the garden to myself for a bit. Very peaceful."

"Well, all right. If you're sure . . ."

She waved me off.

"Go along, don't worry about me. And you'll want to stick to the driveway. It's getting dark, and the paths aren't lit. I'll see you tomorrow."

"Okay, bye then." I waved back and started toward the driveway. She sat and turned her face up to the last rays of the setting sun. Once I reached the tall hedge I couldn't see her. She was right, darkness was falling fast. I paused to fish a pebble out of my shoe. Without the noise of the gravel crunching, it was very quiet, the only sound the wind in the trees. I must be among the last to leave. Or maybe not. I caught the sound of voices, briefly, coming from behind me. I turned but saw no one. Maybe Caro didn't have the garden to herself after all. I looked up at the house next door—the Granville house—but there were no mysterious figures in the window, no strange lights, no sound of piano music. That made for a nice change.

I made my way back to the road and set a leisurely pace to the inn. I had a lot to think about, chief among them, what to wear to dinner?

"It's not like it's a date," I told myself as I walked back to my hotel. I needed to put on my detective persona. This was an interview. That's it. So I'd be businesslike. A casual but pulled-together look. I might even take notes. Greer Hogan, Girl Detective, on the job. Mindful of what had happened the last time Ian and I were together, I vowed to stick to sparkling water. Besides, I was already getting a headache from the champagne cocktails. How many had I had? I'd lost count. So absolutely no alcohol at dinner.

My resolve firm, I pushed the elevator button and went to get changed.

Chapter Five

~

"This wine is delicious," I said, swirling it in my glass. *It's not like I'm drinking martinis*, I told myself.

"I'm glad you like it. This place always has a nice selection."

We'd met at a small wine bar and bistro on Main Street. I'd opted for black pants and a black rib-knit turtleneck, pointy black flats, and a washed denim jacket to add a casual element. My hair and makeup were equally casual for the simple reason that it had taken me more time to make the calls I was handling for Jane than I thought it would. Most were to answer simple questions about directions and the weather. It was like an average reference shift, where I was often tempted to reply, "No problem. Let me google that for you." There were a couple of last-minute requests, dietary and seating. One of these was from April Benson, who was in the midst of an ugly divorce. Both she and her soon-to-be ex were attorneys, and he had worked for the same company as Danny. She was in a chatty mood. I'd met her a couple of times, so I let her rattle on and then made plans to get together with her at the rehearsal dinner. She seemed inclined to gossip, which was all to the good. When we hung up, I spent a couple of minutes comparing the seating chart Jane had given me with the pictures of her originals I'd taken with my phone.

The name she'd scratched out was Brittany Miles. No love lost there—she must suspect, or know about, an affair. After that, I'd had just enough time to clean up, change, and meet Ian.

We ate bread and perused the menu. My dinner decision made, I looked out the window while Ian discussed the specials with the waitress. We'd opted for indoor dining but had a nice view from our table at the back of the restaurant. The sun had long since set, but the water glittered with shards of silvery moonlight that cut a path across the cool darkness of the lake. Floating above the darkness, Ian and I were reflected, our images blurred in the window. A memory swam to the surface from two decades past. Another small restaurant, this one in Greenwich Village. I'd looked out at the dark street, shadowy figures hurrying past in the late winter twilight, the warm light within projecting a colorful picture on the glass. Ian and Greer, newly acquainted, not really on a date, just grabbing a bite. And here we were, in a different restaurant in a different village. Greer and Ian, getting reacquainted, not on a date, just having dinner. The same and not the same.

A little wave of melancholy swept over me. I sighed and turned away from the reflection. I stared into my wineglass, which had somehow emptied itself while I was lost in thought. I eyed the bottle. Maybe just half a glass. Before I could make a move, the waitress beat me to it and gave us both a generous pour. I reached for another piece of bread.

When I looked up, Ian was studying me. I raised an eyebrow.

"You've let your wild Irish hair down," he said, raising his glass.

"Does that surprise you?"

"I don't know, I figured with the new job it might be frowned upon."

"Oh, picturing me with a bun and glasses and a baggy cardigan?"

"Something like that."

"You clearly don't know many librarians."

Although, truth be told, my hair often ended up in a messy bun on a busy day at work, and the temperamental heating in Raven Hill Manor had resulted in an old sweater living on the back of my desk chair. No glasses, but I'd had to squint at the menu, so who knew how long that would last. No matter how many classic wardrobe pieces I'd salvaged from my previous life, my fashionista days were behind me. Having a high-paying job with a global cosmetics company in Manhattan required a much different wardrobe, and wardrobe budget, than being a small-town librarian. On the upside, I'd become a champion consignment shopper.

"You're the one and only," Ian said.

My stomach gave a little flip at his phrasing, but I just smiled and took a sip of my wine.

"What was it you wanted to talk about?" he asked. "That is, if you still want to talk?"

"I do."

Where to begin? I was sure Ian had nothing to do with Danny's murder, but he might know something about who did, whether he knew it or not. Did he have any reason to keep quiet about it? It occurred to me that, in spite of our history and his friendship with Danny, I didn't know that much about his life for the past twenty years. But he was my best source at the moment.

"I don't feel like I really have closure around Danny's death." True. "I'm trying to understand what was going on with him when he died, what he was worried about." Also true. "I feel bad because I wasn't really there for him when he needed me." Very, very true. "And I think the wrong man is in jail, and whoever murdered Danny is still out there." True, and frightening. But there it was. Ian was only the second person I'd told. He'd probably think I was crazy.

Silence. Seconds ticked by.

"Wow," Ian finally said. "Are you sure about this?"

"Pretty sure." I took a slug of my wine. Maybe another bottle was in order. Where was the waitress?

"Hunh," Ian said. He also took a hefty swallow of his wine. When he spoke, he seemed to be choosing his words carefully. "If you think something was off, I believe you. You've always had good instincts. But—murder? As in premeditated? I thought the police determined it was manslaughter. Dan interrupted some petty crook robbing the place. What makes you think they were wrong?"

"Well, for one thing, the guy said he didn't do it."

Ian raised an eyebrow.

"I know, but here's where it gets interesting. He admits that he broke in, and that he knocked Danny out. But he said he was paid to break in and told what to take, but he was also told that nobody would be home and he should make it look like a regular robbery."

"What was he supposed to steal?"

"Anything computer-related. Laptops, tablets, smartphones, flash drives. Those he was supposed to turn over to the guy who hired him. He'd get paid for that, and anything else he took he could keep."

"And is that what he took?"

"Mostly. He'd done a pretty thorough search for the electron-ics, but he'd left a couple of things. He missed some cash and jewelry, probably because Dan came home. There were a few other things that were strange, but that's the gist of it."

"But couldn't he sell the electronics?" Ian asked.

I shook my head. "Maybe, but you know how there are always a few retired cops hanging around my dad's pub? They said the big three for thieves are cash, jewelry, and guns."

"But there's a lot of information stored on devices," Ian said. "Banking, personal info, things like that."

"Different kind of crime, different kind of criminal. It's more sophisticated."

"And more traceable, that kind of activity."

Ian was catching on.

"Yes, and this guy was not that kind of crook. But the police never found the electronics. They did find some of my jewelry, but that was the only thing they could trace back to the break-in."

"What about the payoff? Any sign of that? Or any info on who hired him?"

"That's where his story broke down. He said all the contacts were anonymous, and that he never got the money when he dropped the bag of devices. But he swears that he knocked Danny out and then left. Dan died of blunt force trauma, and this guy was an amateur boxer. Maybe he hit him harder than he thought, I don't know. Look, there are a lot more details, but the bottom line is I believe him. I listened to him in court. He's just not smart enough to make up a story like that. But whoever hired him was after something, knew we weren't supposed to be home, and arranged to have us robbed. It had to be someone we knew. Whoever that is hasn't been caught, or even identified. But I think this person worked with Danny. Something was going on at New Leaf."

Ian leaned back in his chair. The waitress appeared with our appetizer and asked if we wanted another bottle of wine.

"Bottle of Pellegrino," I said. The wine had been good, but my nervousness about this meeting was gone. The game was afoot. I wanted a clear head. I waited until she was out of earshot.

"So, will you help me?"

Ian rested his elbows on the table and laced his hands together. Then he nodded.

"I have to admit that the staged robbery and murder theory is a little far-fetched. But Dan was worried about something. And in any IPO, there's a lot at stake. Money, reputation. And some unusual personalities." An understatement, as far as I was concerned. "So it's possible. But how are you going to investigate a murder, Greer?"

"I don't need to investigate a murder," I said. I'd done it before, successfully, but now was not the time to go into that. "I only need to get enough evidence to get the police to reopen the case. I need information. That's where you come in. Do you have any idea what was going on? Did he give you any hint?"

"Dan was very circumspect in his emails, and he always wrote from his personal account. I answered one or two questions, and gave him my opinion on a couple of things, but without context it was tough. I don't remember much. It was a few years ago, and I had a lot going on."

A divorce, as I recalled. His second, not that I was counting. I kept my mouth shut and waited for him to continue.

"There was something funny, though. He sent me something in the mail. Spreadsheet, but no labels, just numbers. Didn't look like his usual stuff. I couldn't figure it out."

"Did you keep it?"

"I'm sure I did, but I don't know where it is. I've moved since and haven't unpacked everything. And I don't think I deleted the emails."

I couldn't fault him. I had lots of boxes in my parents' basement. I'd packed them up before selling the apartment Danny and I had owned, and I hadn't touched them since, despite my mother's nagging.

Ian promised to find what he could. I pulled out the guest list and asked for any background he could give me on anyone he knew. I was stumbling around in the dark with all of this, hoping I'd run into something useful, but I had to start somewhere. He ran through the list, making a few notes next to names, telling me anything he knew. It wasn't much, but it helped me narrow the field.

"Thanks," I said. "I'm trying to keep this very quiet. I'm not sure what, or who, I'm after. I don't want to tip my hand."

"I understand," he said.

The waitress arrived with our meals, and we decided on a second bottle of wine after all. The conversation turned to more mundane things. My new home and job, his current projects and travels, people and places we knew. There was caution on both sides when talking of personal things, but an easy familiarity on other topics. I decided it was time for the two questions that most interested me.

"Something's up with the Whitakers," I said. "Something seems off."

He shrugged. "I just arrived. I've seen Desmond and Jeremy briefly, but that's it. Everyone's probably just wound up about the wedding."

"Speaking of weddings, I understand congratulations are in order."

He looked surprised. Well, I knew it was supposed to be hush-hush, but I wanted to know, and I wanted to see his face when I asked.

"Britta, or something like that?" My turn to shrug. "Heard it through the grapevine. Anyway, congratulations."

"You must mean Brittany." He smiled and shook his head but didn't say anything else. The check arrived then, so we settled up and left.

The town was still hopping, though the temperature had dropped. I was glad I'd dressed warmly, and put on my new scarf. Ian had his thinking look on. I remembered it from days gone by. It meant I'd get cursory responses while he focused on something

I was not privy to, a habit I'd always found irritating. We walked back to the inn, but other than a few general comments on the weather and the activity on Main Street, we were quiet. He saw me into the lobby, looked around, then told me he'd see me tomorrow and left. Not even a peck on the cheek. He was technically almost engaged, but still.

Chapter Six

My phone rang at a ridiculously early hour the next morning. When I saw the time, I was presented with more evidence that I was turning into my mother—I presumed someone had died. Then I saw the caller. Ian.

"Mmph," I said when I picked up.

"Good morning, gorgeous," he said, sounding cheerful and alert. He had always been an early riser. Good God, what had I ever seen in him?

"What?" I rolled over and sat up. My mouth felt like cotton. Had I had that much to drink yesterday? Must have been the champagne. And the wine. I should stick with martinis. Where was my water? I found it and took a swig.

"We have plans."

"I know. Tonight. Big party."

"That, too. But we're also having breakfast. A picnic on the lake."

"That's barbaric. Who eats outside in the middle of the night?"

"Where's your sense of romance? The sun's coming up. It's a beautiful day. Your first quart of coffee should be there any minute. So get yourself caffeinated and meet me at the boathouse in an hour. I have some things to tell you, and I don't want to be overheard."

And with that, he hung up.

"Bossy," I said to the blank screen of my cell phone. "And since when are we romantic? You're getting engaged."

My soliloquy was interrupted by a knock at the door. Room service. I hauled myself out of bed and grabbed my robe. A helpful bellman deposited a tray on the table and aided me in my struggle to open the curtains. The daylight, what there was of it, was painful. Once he'd gone, I fumbled around until I found my sunglasses. I put them on, collapsed on the love seat with a cup of steaming coffee, and parsed my conversation with Ian. Picnic breakfast. Would serve him right if I didn't show. But then the caffeine kicked in, and I started wondering. *"I have some things to tell you, and I don't want to be overheard."* What could that mean? Something about Danny? The Whitakers? The pashmina-wearing stick insect? And who would overhear us at this time of day?

I looked out the window. The sun was, indeed, rising. Mist rose from the lake, where the water temperatures had stayed higher than the air overnight. It blurred outlines and highlighted the autumn foliage, leaving everything washed in shades of scarlet and amber. What would that look like from the middle of the lake? I checked the weather. Temps cool but going up. It would be a lovely day. And I could always squeeze in a nap. Curiosity had won.

I tossed back the rest of my coffee and reviewed my wardrobe options while brushing my teeth. If Ian Cameron was expecting anything particularly fetching he could think again. I opted for a clean and presentable "just threw this together because I'm on vacation" look. I topped it all off with the moose sweatshirt. There was no mistaking that for romantic.

Ian was waiting on the dock, a picnic basket at his feet. He grinned when he saw me and checked his watch.

"Only five minutes late. I'm impressed. The coffee will still be hot. Hop in."

The canoe was tied to the end of the Whitaker dock. I saw that the Granville house also had a dock, running parallel to this one, but it was shorter, and looked older and less sturdy. There was a sawhorse placed where it met the Granville land, probably to discourage anyone from walking onto it. There were a few overgrown shrubs nearby, and one of the wheelbarrows that seemed to be everywhere.

Ian helped me into the canoe. It was more comfortable than I expected, thanks to the addition of some cushions that looked like they'd been scrounged from old lounge chairs. I rearranged a few of them and leaned on the side—gunwale?—of the canoe while Ian untied us and settled in with the oars. The water was calm in the little cove, and we drifted gently toward the Granville dock. Ian took a deep breath and looked around.

"Isn't this great?" he said. "What a beautiful way to start the day."

"Right," I said. "Very scenic. Also very early. Please understand that I'm wearing a T-shirt that says 'Always been indoorsy.'"

"It must be hidden by the moose," he said. "Nice rack, by the way."

I stifled a snicker and said, "You're very fresh," in my best prissy librarian voice. I reached over the side to flick some water at him. As I pulled it up my hand brushed something, something with a silky, slimy feel. Ick. It took my morning brain a second to realize there was no seaweed in a lake. Some kind of water plant growing around the unused dock, maybe. I twisted around and looked over the side. The water was cloudy—we'd kicked up sediment. The cove was shaded, but there were still tendrils of mist snaking across the surface. Ian gave a deep pull on the oars, and as the water moved I saw it. A face, pale and feminine, dark hair undulating around it. I gasped and leaned farther out, but the image twisted, the face turned away. Something glinted blue, and then sank out of sight into the dark water. Another strong stroke and we were out of the cove and into the sunshine. For a second I saw my own white face in the water. It vanished as the mist closed around us. I could see nothing but reflected light.

I turned back around. Ian was watching me.

"I just saw . . ." What, exactly?

"Your reflection?" Ian asked. "They do call it Mirror Lake, you know."

"Yeah, I know. I guess so. But . . ."

"Have some more coffee. You'll be fine. Yours is in the pink mug. And I made sure the bagels were the real thing—no doughnut-shaped bread for you. I know what a snob you are."

He was probably right. I was hungover and bleary-eyed. Another trick of the light? Perhaps, likely even. But like the face in the window, it was eerie. It felt wrong, like something that shouldn't be there.

I peeked into the basket as Ian rowed. There were a few items wrapped in deli paper, a couple of thermal mugs, bottled water, and some linen napkins. I took the pink mug and sipped. My head was clearing, the faint throb of the headache disappearing. The mist on the lake was burning off as the sun rose. It was like being inside a mirror. Or a prism, I thought, looking at all the colors, created or reflected. It was hard to tell what was real. There were a few other early birds in sight, but it felt like we had the whole place to ourselves. No chance of being overheard.

"I think we're safe from eavesdroppers," I said. "Why don't you tell me what's going on? Otherwise I'm holding your coffee hostage."

"You're a hard woman, Greer Hogan. Give me a minute."

Ian looked around and did whatever you do to secure your oars. I handed over his mug and one of the bagels.

"Here you go," I said. "I can see the poppy seeds. Yours." I tossed one of the napkins at him and unwrapped my own breakfast.

"First things first—there's nothing going on between me and Brittany Miles. Never has been."

"You don't owe me any explanations about your love life, Ian."

He gave me a long look. I took another bite of my bagel.

"Maybe not, but I'd like you to understand," he said. "Brittany and I have attended a few professional events together. Her idea. She was my primary contact while I was doing the consulting work for Desmond. We got along fine, so why not? The strange thing was, I never got the sense she was that interested."

"So you were—what—her standard plus one? Or at least in the rotation?"

"As unflattering as that is—yes. I did ask her to something once, and she came with me, but—it was strange. We had a nice time, but no spark."

"Sounds like she's just not that into you, but then why keep inviting you to things?"

"My thoughts exactly. I finally realized it was only work-related events, and always with roughly the same people attending. I suspect she was using me as a cover. I think she's dating a married man. Possibly—likely—someone in the business."

I considered that. It made sense. "Could be. Or a woman. Married or otherwise not out. In the company, or a competitor."

He looked surprised. "I never thought of that," he said. "But maybe."

"Maybe or maybe not." I flashed back to that scene in the hotel lobby. "What about Desmond Whitaker?" I asked.

He gave that some thought, then shook his head. "I can't see it. He's got to be thirty years older. And I thought he and Jane were solid."

"I don't know." I told him what I'd seen at the hotel, and about my conversation with Brittany at the tea. "And Sarah smells a rat about something. She thought it was professional, but maybe she senses something going on with her father. And Jeremy says there's a big, ugly surprise on the horizon, but that could be something else."

"He hasn't said anything to me, but that's not surprising. We're friendly, but we don't know each other that well. Sarah may be onto something though," Ian said. He proceeded to tell me about a potential deal to merge Whitaker with another company. Brittany had been instrumental in putting it together. But suddenly all talk of it had ceased. It had been very hush-hush but seemed like a real possibility. Then silence.

"So do you think it's totally off the table? I can't believe Sarah wouldn't know."

He shrugged. "I don't understand the dynamics there myself. That's one of the reasons I wanted to make sure we weren't overheard. I got the feeling Desmond was keeping the rest of the family out of the loop. All I know is that I was analyzing some things for them, and then I wasn't. Brittany told me they were going in another direction. She still wanted me to work on recommendations for some systems and analytics, but to keep it quiet. The official story was that I was there to help with some system upgrades, but it was kept vague. I overheard her flat-out lie to Jane about it at a cocktail party. But some of those people involved in the original merger plans are here this weekend, for the wedding. Old friends of the family."

"I may have seen one of them last night," I said. I told him about the conversation I'd witnessed after dinner and described the man with Brittany as best I could.

"That descriptions fits a couple of people," Ian said. "Hard to say for sure."

We debated possibilities while we finished our breakfast. We were left with more questions than answers. I wasn't even sure it mattered, but I enjoyed the easy point and counterpoint of the debate. It had always been like this—I'd never once felt talked down to with Ian. He was brilliant at what he did but acknowledged that there were some things I was better at. Our strengths complemented each other. It was easy to slip back into some elements of our old relationship, but there were still tensions. How it ended, what had happened to Danny, who we both were nearly twenty years later. But right now, on this beautiful morning, neither one of us wanted to go there. He did circle back to the topic of Brittany.

"Anyway," he said, "regardless of what's going on with the Whitaker family business or her personal life, I'm making it clear to Brittany that I'm out of that loop. I tried to talk to her last night, but it kept going to voice mail. I know she was around—I saw her leaving near midnight. I'll find her today and straighten things out."

"You don't have to do that on my account, but thank you for telling me all this."

"I should have done it a while ago. I was hoping you and I would be able to spend some time together this weekend. So—do I get a place on your dance card for tonight?"

I laughed. "Sure, as long as you don't value your toes. Remember I have two left feet."

"You do not," he said. "I'll take my chances."

We talked a little more about the party and the band Jeremy had hired. Then he dropped me at the public dock near the inn.

"Shorter walk for you," he said. "And more exercise for me. I'll see you tonight. Want a lift to the rehearsal?"

We made plans, and he rowed off. It was a short walk to the inn, so I had time to shower and change before my visit to Isabelle. Ex-boyfriends, mysterious mergers, murdered husbands, and a wedding weekend worthy of the Bridgertons made exploring a potentially haunted house look positively relaxing.

Chapter Seven

The Granville house was a beehive of activity when I arrived, at least on the outside. A team of landscapers in matching caps and several carpenters were there, all of whom seemed to be wielding some tool that made noise. Isabelle had told me to come around to the back. I made my way through tidy stacks of lumber, piles of gardening tools, and wheelbarrows full of yard waste. All of this must have been disguised by the green tarps I saw lying nearby, because I hadn't seen any of it the night I arrived or yesterday during the party. I also passed two big generators, one with heavy-duty wires running into a basement window. Isabelle had said the wiring needed work. She was waiting for me on the back porch.

"Jack was up and out early," she said, "and the work started soon after. The walls of this place are pretty thick, so the noises from the work are muffled and a little strange. I decided to just wait out here. It's such a nice day. Can I get you anything?"

"No thanks, I'm fine. Did you have a more restful night last night?"

"It was very quiet. I had dinner with Jeremy, and we sat outside and talked afterward. There's a little chiminea on the lawn by the boathouse. He walked me back when we heard Jack's car. I told him I didn't like being there alone, but I didn't tell him about the noises. He was very nice about it."

"Jeremy is very nice. He's thoughtful." And it looked like Sarah's suspicions about his love life were on target.

"Yes, he is. And very easy to talk to. I never feel awkward. He's an artist. He asked me to pose for him. I was surprised, but he said I had good bones. Which is funny, because that's what Jack says about this house."

"That sounds nice, Isabelle."

She frowned. "I guess so. It's just that I'm not sure what to wear."

"I'm sure he won't care. Wear whatever you want. You always look nice."

A faint pink crept up her cheeks. "Oh, thank you, but that's not really me."

"What do you mean? Of course it is."

"Oh, no, I mean it's *me* in the clothes, but I don't pick them out. I have a lady at Nordstrom. I met her when I was in college, looking for a dress for graduation. I'm really hopeless at that kind of thing. I always have been. It's not the kind of thing you learn at math camp, you know? Anyway, she found something for me right away—it was very nice—and gave me her card and said I could call anytime I needed something. So a couple times a year I tell her what kind of places I need to go, and she knows how I should look, so she sends things. She even tells me how to make different outfits. It's so much easier, and quicker, but it's kind of embarrassing to admit I can't figure it out on my own."

"Lots of people have personal shoppers, Isabelle. Fashion sense is not a given. And you're right—it takes time. That's why some people just wear the same outfit every day. It's called uniform dressing. Lots of people do it." Most of them men, but I'd known a few women to find their look and stick to it.

"Yes, that's what Ilsa said. It's what I do for everyday stuff. Jeans or black pants, and the same shirt or sweater in different colors." She seemed less embarrassed now. "But I still don't know what to wear this afternoon."

"You can wear what you've got on, or if you want, I'll help you pick out something. I love clothes as much as old libraries. And we have time. Let's go."

Isabelle gave me a tour as we walked through the downstairs. The kitchen was recently renovated—all fresh cabinetry and pristine granite. The new appliances gleamed. I was sure that if I could cook I'd think it was grand. The main floor was similar to the Whitaker house in layout and style, though with more and smaller rooms. Whereas the rooms next door had been opened up and connected, here that was true only of the library and what looked like a small den repurposed as a music room. It held a baby grand and a couple of chairs and some music stands shoved into a corner. There were librettos and sheet music scattered around, with some still upright on the piano's music shelf.

Double doors opened into the library, which was everything a library should be. Floor-to-ceiling shelves, complete with rolling ladder, map stand, comfortable overstuffed chairs, even an old-fashioned library table with a green-shaded lamp. The woodwork was gorgeous. The shelves were separated by carved wooden beams. Closer inspection showed that some were solid, but others held built-in cabinets. They opened with mechanisms disguised in the carving. In the center of each were designs in wood inlay. I found the same delicate work on a game table. The only flaw I could find was the selection of books. It was a collection frozen in time. There were actual encyclopedias, beautiful to look at, but dated in the late 1960s. Encyclopedias, like most print reference sources, were now nearly all online, so that updates could be made in real time. The nonfiction was outdated, though I spotted some biographies that had stood the test of time.

I roamed the room and discovered several low shelves of children's books, battered and well loved. Nancy Drew began with the original blue cover for the earlier titles and moved on to the more familiar bright yellow as the series progressed. I hadn't liked Nancy much until I read the originals, when she was a bold, independent young woman ignoring convention, rather than the ladylike bit of perfection-in-pearls-and-pumps that she became. Next to these was one of the cleverly disguised cabinets. I pulled it open using a knothole just large enough for my finger and smiled when I saw a folded blanket and a flashlight. Someone used to hide and read here.

I stood and examined the adult fiction. There were a lot of classics, nicely bound hardcovers, and popular fiction from Golden Age mysteries and early adventure stories onward. The contemporary fiction thinned out between *Valley of the Dolls* and *Princess Daisy*. Other than some tired-looking paperbacks from the early eighties, it ended there.

From a professional perspective, the collection was well organized but needed a good weeding and the addition of more modern titles. From the perspective of someone getting the place ready to rent or live in, it was pretty much the same, though I might keep the old encyclopedias and nicely bound series for the sake of nostalgia and visual appeal. The place had been kept clean and dusted, so getting rid of the more dated-looking items and filling in with best sellers and some light reading would do the trick. I wondered about the time capsule quality of the place—a lot of this could have been done as part of general upkeep.

"How long has it been since someone lived here? Do you know?" I asked Isabelle, who was flipping through an old atlas on the map stand.

"I'm not sure. I think Jane's parents lived here until they died. I don't know when that was. Jeremy told me that his mother just shut the place up after his grandmother died. She owns it with her sister."

"Hmm. I wonder why she wanted to keep all this," I said.

"I don't know, but you should see what's upstairs. Some of it's kind of cool. Jeremy's been emptying out rooms, with some help from Jack and Sarah. They're not allowed to throw anything out without Jane looking at it first. She keeps saying she'll do it, but she never does. Maybe after the wedding."

I thought of all the boxes in my parents' basement, all that remained of my married life. I kept saying I'd deal with them, too. But still they sat. Pretty soon I'd have to go through them—they might hold some clue to what had gone on in those weeks before Dan died. I couldn't tell you what was in them. Some friends had helped me pack. I'd made decisions on autopilot. Who knew what I'd find? Probably nothing, but it had to be done. Emotional avoidance no longer served my purpose. I wondered if something about this place made Jane sad, so she avoided the task. In my case it was just over three years. In hers it was well over thirty.

Isabelle and I went up to the second floor. More work had been done here at various times. I was sure the master bath had once been a small bedroom adjacent to the larger one. Isabelle told me her parents would be staying in it when they arrived. She and Jack occupied the remaining bedrooms and shared a large bathroom at the end of the hall. The furnishings were a mix of new and antique. Everything was updated, from the bath fixtures to the bed linens. Isabelle's room had a lovely view of the lake. I looked out and saw both docks, though shrubbery hid part of the one on the Granville property. I could also see the guesthouse, and a bit of the boathouse behind some trees. The lake shimmered in the distance, with the mountains behind it.

Isabelle was picking through a small pile of clothes on the bed. She sighed and said, "Why don't we look around upstairs before we do this? That's where I found some of the cool stuff, but the lights don't work so I didn't have much time to look around. We'll take flashlights. Jack and I each have one in our rooms—the wiring is unreliable, and he said they get sudden storms sometimes."

She collected the flashlights and handed me one. We started up the stairs. I expected some creaking, but they were surprisingly solid. We reached the upstairs hall. There was light coming in the windows at either end, but all the doors were closed. I wondered why and asked Isabelle.

"They swing shut if you leave them open. That's what Sarah told me. It probably has to do with drafts and the placement of the windows." She opened the nearest, and light flooded into the hall.

"Is this where you heard the footsteps?" I asked.

"I think so. They seemed to come down the hall. But they weren't like step-step-step, more like step-step, then nothing, then farther along a step, then nothing, then step-step. Then something like a creaky gate."

I walked down the middle of the hallway. No discernible noise, not from where we were standing. I tried the side of the hall, and then the other. Still nothing.

"It was probably just the house settling," Isabelle said, but she didn't seem convinced.

"Probably, and you were hearing it from below, so hard to tell for sure. And the temperature dropping at night would affect it."

"That's true. Well, look what I found in here."

I stepped through the door she'd opened. Inside was some standard bedroom furniture, a pile of cardboard boxes, an old trunk, and stacks of records. She was holding up two—the Rolling Stones and Janis Joplin.

"Wow! Quite a find," I said. The records, old LPs and some of the small ones—45s?—were stacked all over the bureau and nightstand. There was even an old-fashioned record player in the corner.

"My dad would love these," Isabelle said. "He's got quite a collection already, but there's a few here I've never seen. I keep telling him he can download whatever he wants, but he says it's not the same."

"I've heard a lot of people say that. Well, if he's looking for that scratchy-needle-on-vinyl sound, he can always try that." I gestured to the old machine.

"I wonder if it works," she said, and went to investigate.

I turned and looked down the hall. What was it about a door that someone else has closed that made you want to open it and look? Some of us are natural snoops, according to my coworker Dory. I liked to think of it as healthy curiosity, or a love of mysteries. I pushed open the door across the hall. The room was small and dim and empty of furniture. Some drab curtains, half open, hung at the window. I walked over and pulled them aside to look out. Just a view of the street and the neighbors. I let the drapes fall, then took a closer look. In the creases, where the light hadn't touched it, the fabric was such a virulent shade of green that the best thing that had ever happened to it was being left to fade. I shook my head. The seventies, man. The music, the drugs, the social unrest—all this I could understand and appreciate. The design aesthetic? Never.

I went back into the hallway and tried to orient myself. Where was the room whose windows I had seen from the Whitaker driveway? To my right, if the street was behind me and the lake in front. I passed the stairway and found two doors. I turned the handle of the first, and though the door stuck a little, it opened with a creak of the hinges. This room was still furnished—another bedroom. It was what I'd call early Adirondack. There were no drapes or bed linens. Nothing on or in the dresser. It was a corner room, with windows on two walls. One overlooked the Whitaker driveway, though it was hard to get a clear view through the trees. They moved a little in the breeze, and for a second I was looking straight down at where I'd parked the night I'd arrived. This must be where I thought I'd seen someone watching me. The light shifted as the trees moved, and there was a brief flash behind me.

I turned. The light flashed again. There was a full-length mirror in the corner, the kind that you could tilt at different angles. All the furnishings in this room were antiques, but this was the star of the show. The wood was dark, and the frame was carved with all manner of woodland objects—acorns, oak leaves, flowers, and animals. Mixed in, so cleverly that you had to look closely to see them, were magical beings. There were faces in the tree trunks, pixies peering through the leaves, small, winged creatures that looked at first like butterflies but were actually fairies. All looking back at me as I looked at the mirror. It was extraordinary. It had the same feel as the woodwork in the library, but it was more detailed and more imaginative. Who had made it? I hunted around for some kind of signature or label. Maybe on the back.

The mirror was heavy, but I shifted it away from the walls enough that I was able to wedge into the corner behind it. It was dark, but I could see some kind of writing on the back. I pulled my flashlight out of my pocket and turned it on. I sucked in my breath and backed into the wall as the lettering came into sight. The words were big, and red: "I AM HALF SICK OF SHADOWS." There was something aggressive about them. The size, the depth of color. I reached out and ran my fingertips over the words. Some of the pigment flaked, leaving spots of red on my hands. I rubbed at them with my thumb. As they warmed, they felt less powdery. Almost oily. Not a crayon, but some sort of pastel? An old lipstick? Whatever it was, it had been here a long time, and whoever wrote it meant it to stay.

"I am half sick of shadows." That was familiar. Where had I heard it? It came to me. The title of a Flavia de Luce mystery. She was one of my favorite young detectives, but the title phrase came from something else. Tennyson maybe. I felt like I should know, but I'd have to look it up. I slid out from the corner and took a deep breath. The simmering anger I felt in the scrawl on the back was at odds with the whimsy of the front. Although . . . I eyed the carved faces peering out at me. As any Irish girl knows, the good folk were not benign. Any gifts bestowed came with a hidden price. The relationship was always transactional.

Regardless, the mirror was a work of art. Someone had taken a lot of time over it. It was fantastic—I couldn't look away. There had to be a signature hidden somewhere. If it were me, I'd hide it in the carving, disguise it, and put it somewhere near the bottom. Or around the rim, out of sight. I reached up and ran my hands along the outside of the frame. Smooth. Then I knelt and did the same on the bottom. Nothing. Worked into the design then. I started at the left, tracing the outlines with my fingertip, from the bottom rim to the glass. I heard a sound in the hallway. Maybe Isabelle could help.

"Isabelle, come here. You've got to see this," I yelled, not taking my eyes off the mirror.

"Just a sec," came the muffled response.

I studied the actual mirror while I waited. The glass itself was old and wavy. My image seemed to shift, though I was holding still. The silvering at the edges was beginning to fade, leaving a black rim. It reminded me of the reflecting pool. But in spite of its age, or maybe because of it, it seemed to pull in all the light in the room, reflecting it back in a way that made the walls recede.

"All my walls are lost in mirrors," I recited, thinking of Jane's office. "All my walls are lost in mirrors, whereupon I trace . . ." How did it go? "Left hand, right hand . . ." Something like that. I moved my hand along the glass as I spoke. The mirror tilted on its stand. I adjusted it, and when I looked into it again a woman I'd never seen before looked back.

I froze.

She lifted her hand, moving it the way I had moved mine.

"Self to left hand, self to right hand," she paused and tilted her head.

"Self . . . selfsame . . . self . . . self . . ." She shook her head and dropped her hand. She studied my face in the mirror. "Who are you?" she asked. She didn't sound threatening, or aggressive, just curious.

"I'm Greer. Greer Hogan. Sarah's friend."

"Ah," she said. "Sarah's friend. Yes. Sarah's getting married." She smiled.

"She is. I'm here for the wedding."

"So am I." She held my gaze a moment longer, then her expression went blank, her eyes vacant. She frowned and turned her head. I stayed where I was. There was a sound in the doorway. I looked over my shoulder. A tall, striking Black woman stood there.

"Barbara?" she said, stepping into the room.

The woman stood still for a moment, then looked at me in the mirror again. Her focus was back, her gaze sharp.

"Where are my manners?" she said. "I'm Barbara Granville. Sarah's aunt. Jane is my sister. And this is Margaret. Margaret looks after me. Margaret, this is—Greer. Sarah's friend. She's here for the wedding, too. The wedding will be lovely. Janie makes everything lovely."

Barbara looked down at me. I could see her register that I was still kneeling on the floor. She stepped forward and reached out. I grasped her hand, and with the other on the mirror pivot I stood. I needn't have worried about pulling her over—she was strong enough to give me a good tug upward. Her hands were small, but her grip was firm. She was petite, like Jane, and I could still see some blond in her silvery pixie cut hair. Once I was up, she stood beside me, so that we were both facing the mirror.

"Do you like my mirror?" she asked, speaking to my reflection.

"It's gorgeous," I said. "I was wondering how old it was and who made it."

Barbara frowned and shook her head again. "I don't know. It's always been here. The mirror has always been here. It's always here, looking back at you." She reached out and touched the carved frame.

"And the writing on the back?" I asked.

"What writing?"

"It says, 'I am half sick of shadows,'" I said. "Tennyson, I think."

She gripped the frame. "Yes," she said. She stepped toward the mirror. At that moment, Isabelle bounced into the room, her arms full of something colorful.

"Look what I found—oh, hi," she said. She stopped right inside the door and looked from face to face.

"Isabelle, this is Barbara Granville. Jane's sister. And this is Margaret . . ."

"Jackson," Margaret said.

"Margaret Jackson," I said. "This is Isabelle Peterson, the groom's sister."

"Hello," Isabelle said. She stood in the doorway, looking awkward.

"Isabelle," Barbara said, "Jeremy has told me all about you. So nice to meet you. And look, you've found my shawl." She smiled and walked over to Isabelle, who had blushed at the mention of Jeremy's name. Definitely something going on there.

"Oh, I'm sorry. I didn't know. Sarah said—"

"It's fine. Let me see." Barbara took the shawl from Isabelle and held it up in front of her.

"How beautiful," she said. "It's yours. You should wear it when you model for Jeremy. He told me at breakfast he'd asked. He told me all about you."

"Erm, uh, how nice. That's nice. It's—nice of you to give it to me. I'm just not sure—what to wear it with." Isabelle bit her lip.

"Why, nothing at all," Barbara said. "You're lovely. And the colors suit you. Look."

She guided Isabelle over to the mirror. I moved aside. Barbara was right. The colors suited Isabelle. Blondes looked good in black, and the paisley and floral embroidery brought out her blue eyes and peachy complexion.

"Oh, it does look nice," said Isabelle. She held the shawl in front of her with one hand. She was still holding something in the other.

"Here, let me take that," I said.

Isabelle handed me something red and silver and shaped like an hourglass and continued studying her reflection. I took what she'd handed me over to the window to get a better look. It was a red lamp—a red lava lamp. Vintage. It had a brown electrical cord wound around the base. I wondered if it still worked. It seemed to be in good enough shape. I was about to plug it in when I remembered there was no power up here.

"I thought that might be what you saw, Greer," Isabelle said. She and Barbara had turned from the mirror. "It's some kind of light, isn't it?"

"It's a lava lamp," said Barbara. "I'd forgotten all about that. We used it with the Ouija board. The red light is more conducive to spirits." Barbara gave a little laugh. "Come, Isabelle, and show me what other treasures you've found. That's all right, isn't it, Margaret? We have time?"

"Sure, we have a little time. It's fine." Margaret said.

Barbara walked toward the door. She stopped and looked back.

"Rossetti," she said. She waved her hand at the mirror. "The poem. The one about being lost in mirrors. It's Rossetti. Christina, not the brother. She wrote about more than goblins, you know. Though Janie always liked the goblins, when she was small. I can't remember the title." She made a tsk of annoyance and turned to Isabelle.

"Show me," Barbara repeated. "I thought everything would still be in my room, but I guess not. It's been such a long time."

"Everything is still here, it's just been moved," Isabelle said as they went into the hall. I heard her mention the wiring as they moved away.

I looked at the lamp in my hand and then out the window. Not possible. When I looked up, Margaret was watching me.

"What did Isabelle mean, 'It might have been what you saw'?" she asked.

"Oh, it was probably just a reflection from the setting sun. The night I arrived, I was waiting for Sarah and I thought I saw something up here. First a person, then a light. Hard to tell, with the trees moving."

"What night was this?"

"Wednesday, around dinnertime."

"We got here yesterday. There's been people all around this house—are you sure it wasn't one of them?"

"Could be. There's been lots of activity because of the wedding," I said. I didn't want her to think I was delusional. She looked so pragmatic. And competent. She also looked like the new 007, if Nomi were in her early fifties and shopped at Talbot's.

"I'm glad Barbara was able to come. I've known Sarah since right after college, and this is the first time I've met her aunt. I understand she hasn't been well," I said.

"She has good days and bad," Margaret said. "More good lately. Her doctor thought it would do her good to come."

"I thought maybe you *were* her doctor. You don't look like a home health aide to me."

Margaret laughed. "I get that a lot," she said. "I'm a nurse. I worked in the ICU until I had a kid—then the shift work was hard to manage. My husband is a teacher. I've been working for the Whitakers for years now. There are usually two of us. I don't do nights. I leave that to the youngsters." She looked at her watch. "We'll have to get going soon. We're having lunch with Mrs. Whitaker."

"It sounds like they're having fun," I said. I could hear conversation and laughter from down the hall. "Let's see what else they've found."

I started to put the lava lamp on the dresser, then hesitated. I didn't want to leave it in this room, where I thought I'd seen its light. Besides, everything was being cleaned out. "I'd better bring this along and put it back where Isabelle found it," I said. Margaret nodded, but I saw her glance at the window and frown.

We went down the hall and found Isabelle and Barbara sitting on the bed, looking at the old records. The trunk in the corner was open. I could see a jumble of things in it. Maybe that's where the lava lamp had come from. I walked over and set it down on the nightstand and looked into the trunk. It wasn't as old as I first thought, but it wasn't new. There was a matching suitcase next to it, both by the same maker and of excellent quality.

Barbara stopped what she was doing and watched me. "Those were mine, too," she said. "High school graduation gift. I was going to take them with me to Vassar. I never went, of course." She stopped, and the blank look came over her face again, just for a second. Then she shook her head and turned her attention to the luggage. Her expression was puzzled, and then sad. Looking at her in profile, I could see Jane. She looked much older, but then she was older. And Jane had certainly had a few things tweaked. Margaret watched for a second, then spoke softly.

"Barbara? It's time for us to go. We don't want to keep your sister waiting."

"Of course," Barbara said and stood. "She's so busy. Janie takes care of everything, doesn't she?"

"I'll see you tomorrow," said Isabelle. "Thank you again."

"Yes, I'll see you both at the wedding. I'm looking forward to it."

We finished our goodbyes, and the two women went down the stairs. We could hear Barbara telling Margaret about the things they passed and what had been changed. Their voices faded. I looked at Isabelle and said, "Looks like you've got your outfit for this afternoon." I wiggled my eyebrows at her.

"Oh, I couldn't. Could I?"

"Why not? I'm sure the artist won't be fazed. Delighted, more like."

"I don't know about that," Isabelle said, then stopped. She held up her hand. "Listen," she whispered.

I heard it. The piano. Five notes. Silence. Then the same sequence again. We waited, but there was no other sound.

"It must be Barbara or Margaret, at the piano. I guess they're still downstairs," I said.

"It's what I heard the other night. I'm sure of it," Isabelle said.

"Why don't we go see if they're still here," I said. "Besides, your parents will be arriving soon, won't they? We can go through more of this another time."

Isabelle nodded and picked up the shawl and a similarly embroidered headband. We left everything as it was and went down to the second floor. She put her new treasures in her room. We were on the stairway when I heard the first door close. Not from downstairs, where I expected it, but from the third floor. Isabelle glanced at me. I shrugged. Another door shut. Then we heard the squeak of an angry hinge, followed by a slam. Barbara's room. In unspoken agreement, we kept going, without looking back.

There was no one on the main floor. Barbara and Margaret must have gone straight out. We went to the music room. Everything was as it was when we had left the room earlier. I walked over to the piano and looked at the music on the shelf. "The Unanswered Question" by Charles Ives. I wasn't musical—that was my sister, Frances—but enough had rubbed off that I knew this sheet music was for more than one instrument. Maybe that explained the clump of music stands. I moved the yellowed pages around. There seemed to be one sequence that repeated.

"Do you read music?" I asked Isabelle. She shook her head.

"My mother does," she said. "Why?"

"I'm just wondering if any of this is what we heard," I said. "It doesn't look like my sister's piano music, but I don't know enough to tell."

The piano, like everything else, was dusted and polished. I played a few random notes. It seemed to be tuned, too. That was work and expense for an instrument in an empty house. I wondered if Jane played. I didn't remember seeing a piano in the Whitaker home, and I knew Sarah didn't play, and Jeremey's art of choice was drawing. Why keep this in tune if no one played it?

"So do you know anything about Aunt Barbara?" Isabelle asked. She'd perched in a window seat where she could see down the driveway.

I shook my head and sat in one of the overstuffed chairs. "No. This is the first time I've met her. Sarah rarely mentioned her—she talked more about Caro when she was telling family stories. Margaret is a nurse, though. She told me that. She said someone else does nights. I get the impression Barbara has round-the-clock care in her home."

"I wonder why," Isabelle said. "Although, you can tell that she's not all there all the time. I don't mean that in a bad way," she hastened to add.

"I know, and I think you're right. She seems to zone out periodically. But she's clearly intelligent."

"Yes," Isabelle said, "though her speech pattern is a little odd sometimes. Sort of singsong, odd repetitions. In a poem, that would be significant."

I raised my eyebrows. I hadn't thought of it like that. Isabelle interpreted my surprise differently.

"My mother is a poet," she said. "She's had quite a lot published. She's always drilling into me how much word choice matters, even in everyday life."

"I think Sarah mentioned it. And your father is a physicist? Something like that?"

"Yes. They're both college professors."

"So I guess you take after your dad, then. The math and science gene."

"I don't know. Music and poetry are both very mathematical, I think. Though I am a lot like my dad. He's not too great socially either."

"I think you're doing fine. And that's an interesting point you made about Barbara's speech. I don't know that it's conscious."

"Maybe a head injury?" Isabelle suggested.

"Maybe. I remember Sarah once said something about Barbara being in a car accident when she was young, but I got the feeling there was more to it."

Our speculations were cut off by the arrival of Isabelle's parents. We went out to greet them. Dr. John Peterson was tall and silver-haired, with thick glasses and a rumpled outfit I called "academic casual." Raven Hill was surrounded by colleges and universities, so I'd learned to spot the standard professorial looks. There were only two, so it wasn't hard. The second involved the addition of a sport coat and tie to the rumpled khakis and shirt for dressier events. Isabelle's mother, Nancy Clyde Peterson, was also tall, with the high cheekbones and strong nose that her daughter had inherited. She was dressed a little more colorfully.

We had finished introductions and were about to take the luggage in when Desmond Whitaker came from the direction of the guesthouse. He'd met the Petersons, but I was surprised that he wasted no time on formalities.

"Have any of you seen Brittany Miles?" he asked.

"Not since the party yesterday," I said.

Isabelle said the same but added, "I think I did see someone walking around the guesthouse late last night, or it might have been very early this morning, but it was dark. Something woke me up and I looked out, but I couldn't see very well."

"Is something wrong?" I asked.

Desmond blew out a long breath. "She's missed a meeting. No one has seen her since late last night."

"Maybe something came up that she had to deal with. Family, or something. I'm sure you'll hear from her soon," I said.

"She doesn't—she's never mentioned her family," he said. "It's unlike her to miss a meeting with me. She's very conscientious."

"Well, you could contact the police," Isabelle's mother said, "though I think they wait twenty-four hours. But you are her employer, so I'm sure they'd try to be helpful."

And the Whitakers had lived in town for generations, and had a lot of money, so the police would at least humor him.

"I'll keep that in mind. She'll probably turn up. Don't let me keep you."

He turned and walked toward his own home. I was surprised at how abrupt he was. In all the time I'd known Sarah, I'd never seen her father behave that way. The Petersons either weren't offended or didn't notice. They had started to talk about their plans for the afternoon. I had my own plans. I wanted to look up those poems Barbara had mentioned. But first—lunch. Once I'd helped with the suitcases, I said my goodbyes and went on my way.

Chapter Eight

❧

I've always wanted to be one of those women whose appetite faded to nothing in the face of any kind of stress or emotional upheaval. Alas, I was doomed to disappointment. The meeting with Barbara had unsettled me. Though Isabelle and I had a nice visit, and I had enjoyed meeting her parents, I was a little out of sorts. The business with Brittany was odd, too. Hadn't Ian said he'd seen her drive away last night? Maybe he'd reached her since. Desmond would probably talk to him. Not my business—he could speak for himself. I flashed back to the moment when I thought I'd seen a woman's face in the water but quickly dismissed it. If someone had drowned, I would have seen a whole body. Probably. I shook it off. It was a reflection. That brought me back to Barbara, and the mirror, and the writing on the back of it.

I stopped on the way back to the inn, got myself a solidly built roast beef sandwich and bottle of water for lunch, and retreated to my room. I wanted to process the morning's events and look up the Rossetti poem. Poems, actually. Barbara had mentioned something about goblins. That rang a bell, too. And find the source of the quotation on the back of the mirror.

Fortified by half a sandwich, I did a search for the poem fragment. Once I included the author it was easy to find. "A Royal

Princess" was not a happy story, though at least, in the end, she chose for herself. The stanza I had half remembered was haunting:

All my walls are lost in mirrors, whereupon I trace
Self to right hand, self to left hand, self in every place,
Self-same solitary figure, self-same seeking face.

I shivered as I recalled Barbara appearing in the mirror, reciting the lines she knew. The repetition of the word "self." Her words were vague, but her gaze was sharp, at least at first. I reread the stanza a few times, committing it to memory. Then I scanned Rossetti's title list for anything to do with goblins. There it was. "Goblin Market." The Poetry Foundation site really was a gem. I remembered reading this one in college. If I recalled correctly, it was her best-known work. Apparently, the morality of the tale was considered instructive for children. That raised my eyebrows, given a lot of the imagery. But it was imaginative. Barbara said Jane had liked it when she was young. Maybe because it was about two blond sisters? I skimmed it again. Not my kind of thing. I preferred the stories where the daring sister got away with it, whatever it was.

Now on to the red-lettered phrase on the back of the mirror. Of all the things I'd seen that day, that creeped me out the most. I typed it in. Tennyson, as both Barbara and I had guessed. It was from *The Lady of Shalott*. The poem was often quoted and depicted in art. I had never liked it—I thought the woman got a raw deal. When I first read it, I just didn't like her. As I got older, I decided her choices were limited and all of them bad. That phrase though— *"I am half sick of shadows."* I could feel that one, understand it in a different way. I was sick of shadows, too. A shadow had hung over me since my husband died. A shadow walked between me and Ian. Shadows hung over the Whitaker family, and the Granville house, the latter for a long, long time. At least forty or fifty years based on what I'd seen inside. How long that writing had been on the back of the mirror I couldn't tell. At least that long. My mentioning it had upset Barbara, whether because she knew about or was surprised by it was hard to judge. My guess was she knew something. But the mirror was old. It had always been there, looking back at you, she had said. The workmanship was that of a much earlier era. The fantastic creatures didn't have a hint of Disney about them. I was fascinated by it, but I had to leave it for now. I had my own shadows to banish. Besides, those who trafficked in magic mirrors never came to a good end.

Back to the mystery I came to solve. I put down my phone and picked up the guest list, studying the notes Ian and I had made at dinner. Did any of these people know anything related to Danny's death? But my mind kept drifting. I went back to my sandwich. Nothing like a blast of horseradish mayo to clear the head. No good. I kept spinning through the same questions. Was it the lava lamp I saw the night I arrived? Must have been, though we found it in another part of the house. But who had held it? Wait—that wouldn't fly. The wiring. Isabelle had said the power to the third floor was off because something needed to be rewired, and that wouldn't happen until after the wedding. And why had Margaret seemed so interested in what I had seen and when? Had Isabelle really heard footsteps? And the piano? I should look up that music—"The Unanswered Question." I had quite a few of those of my own. And though it was none of my business, the one that bothered me the most was—what had happened to Barbara all those years ago? What kind of accident? And why did Jane leave the house as—what had Jeremy called it—some kind of macabre time capsule?

My phone chimed. Almost time for my salon appointment. I cleaned up my lunch, slipped into yoga pants and a loose shirt, found my flip-flops, and headed downstairs. I'd have to ask Sarah about that, and about Barbara. Or maybe Isabelle would find out something during her modeling session with Jeremy that afternoon.

I pondered that pairing. Not one that I would have put together, but it could work. Jeremy wouldn't be threatened by Isabelle's brilliance, and he had enough social acumen for both of them. Isabelle wouldn't care if Jeremy wanted to study art, or design gardens, or paint artisanal flowerpots, as long as he was happy. He made her feel comfortable in her skin, and that's what mattered. They'd been keeping things under the radar. Not surprising—Isabelle was a little shy, and Jeremy wouldn't want Jane trying to manage things. They'd let people know in their own time. *Not my business.* It was time for this Cinderella to get ready for the ball.

Chapter Nine

Ian had volunteered to drive me to the rehearsal and then to the party. Ten minutes before the appointed time, I was doing a final, 360-degree check of how I looked. I was wearing a fitted dress in a deep, autumnal green that brought out my eyes. It hugged my curves, thanks to the clever addition of Lycra to the fabric and my liberal use of shapewear underneath. Those parts of me not nipped in, smoothed, and flattened were either boosted, rounded, or both. I tried a few experimental dance moves. I could move and breathe comfortably, and all parts of my ensemble stayed put. Success. Now for the makeup check. I moved to the brighter light in the bathroom.

I'd gone with a more dramatic look than usual. My everyday cosmetic routine was considerably pared back now that I no longer lived and worked in the city, but tonight was a special event. It was fun to glam up again. I leaned in toward the mirror. My mascara had not flaked, my eyeliner was still where I'd applied it, and there was no lipstick on my teeth. Perhaps I needed a dab of gloss just to bring out the color? There. Perfect. I wiped my fingers on a tissue as I studied my reflection. What was going on with my jawline? I placed two fingers on either side of my face, above and below my ear, and pulled gently upward. That was better. Hmm. Well, nothing to be done about it now. I stood up, lifted my chin, and pulled my shoulders back. Good enough. I picked up my coordinating wrap and handbag, made sure I had my phone and key, tucked in the lip gloss, and off I went.

Ian pulled up right on time. He whistled when he hopped out of the car to help me in. He was looking good himself. On the way to the rehearsal, I quizzed Ian about Brittany's alleged disappearance.

"Did Desmond talk to you?" I asked, after telling him what happened when the Petersons arrived.

"He did," Ian said. "I told him I'd seen her drive off late last night, and that I'd been trying to reach her but that she hadn't returned my calls. I've tried her a couple of times today," he added, "but no response."

"Don't you think that's strange?" I asked. "Desmond said she'd missed a meeting, and that was unlike her."

"I guess so. She was always on top of things when I worked with her. Maybe something personal came up, some sort of emergency."

"That's what I suggested, but Desmond said she didn't ever mention her family. I thought he started to say she didn't have one, but then he changed course."

"She was raised by a single mother. Her mom died young—she was around forty, I think. It happened right after Brittany graduated from college. I never got the sense there were any other close relatives. She didn't talk about it much. In fact, she didn't share a lot of personal information at all. You know how people will share anecdotes over lunch or drinks? She never really did that, and if she was asked directly, she seemed . . ." Ian frowned.

"Secretive?" I suggested.

"Not really. It's more that she thought about it before she said anything. Like she wasn't in the habit of sharing."

Or was trying to get her story straight, I thought, though I had no reason to suspect her of anything. Possibly I read too much crime fiction.

"Maybe it has something to do with this secret relationship you think she's having," I said. "Although that would let Desmond out of the picture, since he's the one looking for her. Or maybe this mysteriously aborted business deal."

"Maybe," he said as he parked the car. "But it's not my problem. Let's just have fun tonight, Greer. Show off your stellar dance moves. Forget about everything else."

I laughed. "Okay," I said. "And we may be observing a budding romance." I told him about Jeremy and Isabelle as we walked in. But one part of my mind was still turning over the Brittany issue. She seemed to be a woman with secrets. And I didn't want anything to spoil Sarah's wedding.

The rehearsal went smoothly. Sarah and Jack were happy and excited. The Petersons were cheerful and relaxed. Isabelle and Jeremy seemed to be getting along just fine, exchanging whispered comments throughout the rehearsal. Sarah's parents were another story. Desmond Whitaker seemed anxious, and Jane looked like she hadn't slept in days. She was beautifully dressed and made up as always, but I could see the circles under her eyes. She kept a close eye on Desmond, who was too distracted to notice. I went over to Jane before we left and put my arm around her.

"You look beautiful," I said. "Do you have your dancing shoes on for the party?"

"Thank you, Greer, you look lovely, too," she said. "I don't think I'll be doing any dancing. The kids have everything in hand. I may just go to bed early. I'm quite tired. So much excitement."

"I'm sure. It's been wonderful so far, and I'm sure tomorrow will be, too."

"I hope so. I do so want Sarah to be happy."

"She will be."

I saw Ian talking to Desmond. He looked up, and I raised an eyebrow. He said something to Desmond, and the two walked toward us.

"It seems we have a missing wedding guest," Jane said. She tried to make her tone light, but I could hear the tension.

"I'm sure she'll turn up," I said. "Are you sure you won't join us tonight?"

"No, you all have fun. I'll see you tomorrow." She took Desmond's arm, and the two went out. We followed at a distance. We walked to the car in silence.

"Desmond has talked to the police about Brittany," Ian said, once we were in the car. "They seem to be taking him seriously, but it's been less than twenty-four hours. It's not like they can do much."

"Can she swim?" I asked, the face in the water rising out of my memory. It could have been her.

"I saw her leave in her car, remember?"

"Right. But we don't know what happened after that. I guess she could be anywhere."

"She's an adult," Ian said, but I could tell he was starting to worry.

When we got back to the Whitakers', the place had been transformed. By putting down temporary flooring on the end of the driveway and along the dock and using parts of both Whitaker and Granville lawns, there was enough space for everything. Tables and chairs ringed the dance floor, with others set farther away for those who wanted a little less noise. Brighter lights shone on the center of activity, and strands of twinkle lights hung from the trees and bushes. The whole effect was festive and romantic.

The event wasn't due to start for another half hour—they'd left time in case the rehearsal ran long—so there was still last-minute setup going on. Ian and I snagged a table at the edge of the lawn, close to the action but far from the speakers. It also gave a good view of the proceedings. Party or not, there were a few people I needed to speak to, and I didn't want to miss them. I wandered over to say hello to Jeremy, who was talking to one of the band members, while Ian went to see if the bar was ready to serve.

"The place looks great," I said to Jeremy. "I can't believe everything you've managed to fit in here."

"Thanks," he said. "Sarah and I have been working on it for a while. Of course, everyone we hired is experienced with outdoor events. The only wild card is the power. We've done a lot with batteries and generators, and all the path lighting is solar, but if we blow a fuse in either the boathouse or the Granville house, we'll be dancing in the dark."

"I'm sure it will be fine. Did your mother get to see it all? She said she was tired and probably wouldn't make it to the party. She can see everything from the house, though, can't she?"

"She did a walk-through before the rehearsal. She said it was wonderful. She seemed really pleased, in an exhausted kind of way." He shook his head. "I don't know, this is taking a lot more out of her than I would have thought."

"She did seem exhausted," I said. "Sarah said she was worried about her drinking. Do you think that has something to do with it?"

"I know what Sarah means, but I haven't seen her with a drink in her hand in a couple of days. I know she's been having trouble sleeping. I actually found her in the upstairs hall one night, and I'd swear she was sleepwalking, but she said no." He shook his head. "Maybe the house renovation on top of the wedding was just too much. But I didn't see how we could hold off until next spring."

"Why—" I started to ask, but the lead guitar player called to Jeremy with a question.

"Sorry," he said, "gotta deal with this."

I walked back to the bistro table Ian and I had chosen. He was already there, cocktails on the table, checking his messages.

"Good work," I said. "I wasn't sure they'd be ready to serve."

"The bartender recognized you from the inn. Apparently, you have a fan." Ian said, putting his phone away.

"Professional rapport," I said. "We have a mutual appreciation of a good craft cocktail."

"That must be it," Ian said. "Cheers."

Within minutes we were joined by Isabelle, Sarah, and Jack. We talked for a few minutes about how well the rehearsal had gone and how nice everyone looked. No mention of the missing Brittany. I wanted to hear how Isabelle's modeling session had gone but figured it would be better to wait until I got her alone. Jack and Ian decided to make another bar run before it got crowded—guests were starting to drift in. Sarah looked around and let out a happy sigh.

"Everything looks great, doesn't it?" she said. "I'm going to enjoy a drink and the company, and then I'm going to have to get busy. I can't leave it all to Jeremy."

"Everything seems to be well in hand," I said, "and as the bride, you'll need to mingle. You wanted to spend time with your guests, remember? You know I'm willing to lend a hand."

"Me, too," said Isabelle. "But really, I think it's going to be fine."

"I guess you're right," Sarah said. "It's just that I'm so used to my mother managing every social event, I'm convinced something will go wrong since she's not here. It's strange not to see her zipping around."

"You've all done a wonderful job. And she looks like she could use a rest before tomorrow," I said.

"True," Sarah replied. "It's somehow all become too much for her. I'm surprised—she normally thrives on this kind of thing. She had suggested some minor additions to the decorations and the layout, and when we came out this afternoon to check on them, I thought she was going to pass out."

"When was this?" I asked. "What happened?"

"After lunch," Sarah said. "I asked if she'd eaten, and she said yes, but I'm not sure. We were looking at the lighting along the driveway, and we turned and started to walk down here. She looked up, then sort of gasped and swayed. I put my arm around her to keep her steady, but she got so pale I thought she was going to keel over. Then she took a deep breath and told me she was fine, just a little dizzy."

"That sounds like low blood sugar," said Isabelle. "It happens to me once in a while, if I'm working on something and forget to eat."

I couldn't comment, since I'd never in my life forgotten to eat, especially if I was under any kind of stress. But it sounded reasonable. Sarah still looked concerned.

"She'll get some sleep, and if you make sure she has breakfast tomorrow, she'll be fine," Isabelle went on.

"You're probably right," Sarah said. "Ah, perfect!" she added as Jack appeared with a glass of champagne. I wasn't so sure. From everything Sarah and Jeremy had said, Jane seemed to be doing a slow unravel. I glanced at the Granville house. Jeremy thought it might have something to do with the renovation. It was possible Barbara's presence, complete with nursing staff, had thrown her. My guess was that they were the last-minute guests who had precipitated my move to the inn. Or maybe there was something between Desmond and Brittany, and Jane was on to it. Any or all of it on top of the wedding extravaganza would be enough to put anyone over the edge.

I spotted April Benson and excused myself to go talk to her. She greeted me like an old friend. Air kisses and compliments were exchanged. The latter were sincere on my part—April looked great. Her outfit showed her fabulous legs to advantage, and though she was five years older than I, her face was smooth and flawless. I'd have to talk to her about her skincare routine. *Or find out where she'd had her work done*, I thought, thinking of my jawline. But first things first. I was hoping she'd be as chatty as she had been on the phone, and I wasn't disappointed. No sooner had we gotten in line for the bar than she began. After once again expressing condolences about Danny's death, she turned to company gossip.

"I'm not surprised you're wondering about what went on there. I always thought there was something shady. Couldn't put my finger on it. Our firm did some work for them, and as they got larger, Frank went to work for them. Hoping for a big payoff when they went public—those CBD products are all the rage, and I think it made him feel younger, and trendy. He never brought in business the way I did, and he's competitive. I got a big bonus and gave him a vintage Mustang that he'd had his eye on, thinking that would make him happy. But no—he was mad that he couldn't do it himself. Never even let me drive it. Of course I'd take it out when he was out of town, just on principle. Anyway, the next thing I know he's off to the corporate counsel job."

She paused as we got to the front of the line. Mike gave me a big grin and asked if I wanted my usual. I nodded and said, "Moonlighting?"

"Helping out a friend," he said. "Their bartender called in sick." He handed me my drink and started on April's.

"Nice-looking guy," April murmured, as she angled for a better look at Mike turning and bending over to pick up a new crate of glasses.

"Um-hmm," I said, sipping my martini.

April smiled and thanked Mike and, after a lingering glance at him, got back to the topic at hand. Frank, she said, was at first very tight with the CEO, Clarice Philips, and the chief technology officer, someone named William Warren. Then she got the sense that he was being left out of the loop on certain things. This was ringing a bell. I remembered Danny saying something like that after we'd met the Bensons at a company party. He couldn't figure out why they'd hired Frank. He had a solid reputation and stellar credentials, but Danny said April would have been a better fit in terms of age and acumen. The Bensons had formed a boutique law firm with a specialized clientele. They'd done well enough to add a couple of associates. According to Dan, Frank was intelligent and detail oriented; April was just as smart and had both charm and vision. Maybe Clarice had realized her mistake and settled for a workmanlike job? There was something else, too, but the thought flitted away as April continued to speak.

"So he stayed for a while, but after they'd been public for a year he came back to our firm. I think he'd started to figure out he wasn't in with the cool kids, though to her credit, Clarice seemed genuinely sorry to lose him. I admit I was surprised. I think that's when his midlife crisis really hit, and he started chasing around after other women. With the kids in college, we were both a little bit at loose ends. Now he's engaged to some cocktail waitress thirty years younger. Ah," she said, "speak of the bimbo."

April gestured with her glass. I looked over and saw a man I recognized as Frank Benson greeting Sarah. At his side was a much younger woman built more like a Barbie doll than anyone I'd ever seen. I'd always wondered if Barbie could actually stand on her own if she were a real woman, and now I knew. The answer was yes, and in four-inch heels to boot. She was wearing a short, sparkly dress, carrying a tiny, sparkly handbag, and flaunting an enormous, sparkly diamond on her left hand. Her hair was platinum and her skin was tanned. I was sure both were fake, but at least it wasn't obvious.

April was eyeing her up and down. "That's what my grandmother would have called 'putting all the goods in the shop window,'" she said.

"And then sprinkling on some sequins," I added. "What's her name?"

"Shelby. Shelby Travis," April said.

"Soon to be Benson, I take it?" I asked.

"Not soon enough for her, I'm sure," April said. "Two lawyers divorcing each other is never a fast process, especially when there's a profitable business involved."

I studied Frank Benson. He'd always been a genial-looking man, and he still was. He'd put on some weight since the last time I saw him, and his hair was more salt than pepper. Other than being awfully red in the face for a cool night, he seemed to be in good shape for a man in his early fifties. I'd talk to him tonight but wait until he'd had a drink or two and I hadn't just been standing next to his estranged wife.

Someone came over to greet April, so I drifted off. There were a lot of people I knew from various places, or who knew people I knew. It never ceased to amaze me that once you reached a certain level of education and professional achievement, you kept running into the same people, even in a big city or one of its satellite vacation spots. On one hand, it could get a little dull. On the other, you were never more than one person away from anyone you wanted to meet. Or needed to talk to about your husband's murder.

I moved from group to group, getting reacquainted and being introduced. Gentle steering of the conversation elicited the kind of information I needed—who'd been doing what and working where, who was in touch with whom, and who seemed either too hesitant or too eager to discuss New Leaf. I exchanged contact information with a few and made some mental notes on where to find the rest. Ian would appear once in a while, introducing me to someone he thought might be helpful or whispering a comment. He was doing great at the sidekick gig.

After I talked to everyone I thought might be useful, I went back to the bar. I'd switched to sparkling water and finger foods while I mingled and detected, so I decided it was time to relax and enjoy myself. I ended up next to Shelby Travis. She apparently hadn't noticed me talking to April, because she gave me a polite smile and said hello. I responded, and as she moved, I got a better look at her sparkly little handbag.

"Is that a Judith Leiber?" I asked.

"Yes, it is," she said with a genuine smile. "My fiancé gave it to me." She held it up so I could see it better. It was a crystal-covered metal cat, one of the minaudières Leiber was famous for.

"It's gorgeous," I said. "I remember seeing a display of those, all animals, when I was a little girl and my mother brought me into the city to shop."

"It's twenty or thirty years old," Shelby said. "I've always liked vintage clothes and accessories. Things that were really nice and made to last."

"Me, too," I said.

I introduced myself, and we chatted about fashion. Once we got our drinks, I told her I'd find her later, since I'd love to say hello to Frank. She seemed happy to have found a friendly face and said she'd tell him to look for me.

I went back to our table. Sarah was off visiting with guests, but Isabelle and Caro had joined Ian, and Jeremy had decided to take a break and came over as well. The band, Penny Dreadful and the Novelettes, was swinging into action. They were all women, with a lead singer who looked and sounded a lot like Adele. I asked Jeremy how he'd found them.

"They play a lot of local bars and festivals," he said. "Mostly in the Hudson River Valley between here and Albany. They do a lot of oldies, from the sixties to the aughts."

"So I guess that makes us oldies, too?" I asked.

"Pretty much," he said. "But they're perfect for the age range in this crowd."

I looked around. He was right. Most of the guests would have grown up listening to the musical holy trinity of my childhood— Billy, Bruce, and Bono, all middle-aged when I was young. This was a band that would go over well in the Concert on the Green series the library sponsored every summer. I'd have to get their contact information. Jeremy said he'd introduce me later. We finished our drinks and Ian asked me to dance, and for the next hour or so all thoughts of murder and family tension were left behind. We drank and danced and had fun. The bride and groom both seemed to have a spin around the dance floor with everyone. I saw April with one of Jack's friends, and even Caro joined in for a few songs. A good time was being had by all, but I was glad to sit down and catch my breath when the band took a break.

I fanned myself as I looked around. It was a cool night, but the dancing and drinking had kept me warm. Sarah would be pleased. Everyone was having a good time. Well, almost everyone. Desmond Whitaker was standing at the edge of the seating area, scanning the crowd, a frown on his face. He turned and walked away, heading toward the guest cottage, sticking to the semidarkness at the perimeter of the party. He disappeared behind some shrubbery near the dock. There was a light on in the cottage, but I didn't see anyone moving around. If Brittany had returned, she wasn't at the party. Either she was back and Desmond was annoyed she hadn't shown, or she was still missing. I'd have liked to see his face on his return trip, but Jeremy told me he could introduce me to the band, so off I went.

The lead guitarist, Penelope, was the de facto leader of the group. We chatted briefly and she gave me her card, saying she'd be happy to discuss the concert series. The band members all lived closer to Albany and could tailor the show to our needs. The next set was based on requests from one of Jeremy's older relatives, she said, so I could see more of their range. Had to be Caro, I thought, so this should be good. I had some time before the band started playing again and decided to take a walk around. Sarah would want to discuss all the details of the party, and I wanted to make sure I'd taken everything in.

I skirted the seating area bordering the lawn where I'd found Jeremy the day of the tea party. There were a few tables at the edge of the lighted area. They were mostly unoccupied, probably due to the dim lighting and the distance from the food and drinks. When I reached the grass, I slipped off my shoes and carried them. My feet were hot and sore, and it felt good to free them for a few minutes. I walked up the slope to the edge of the garden and turned to look at the party. All the different kinds of lights, the low flames under the food, and the reflections off the lake combined to create an otherworldly effect. People moved in and out of view, from light to shadow, with flashes of color and the sparkle of jewelry marking their passage. The murmur of conversation and the soft strum of a guitar floated on the breeze. It was like a party in fairyland. I hoped Jane had seen it. I looked up at the Whitaker house. There were lights in a few windows. I saw a shadow move briefly, as though someone had just stepped back. I glanced at the Granville house next door. Mostly dark, only a few lights from the first floor. Isabelle's parents were here somewhere, enjoying the festivities.

I walked back to our table along the bottom edge of the garden. The path leading into it from the lawn was blocked with a wheelbarrow. That seemed rather inelegant. The Granville dock had been marked off-limits with a couple of potted trees and a neatly lettered sign on a sawhorse. Perhaps closing this off had been a last-minute decision. The path lighting was dim. Solar, Jeremy had said. I'd thought he said they weren't working at all. Maybe they'd been replaced. Navigating the twisting trail in near darkness would be treacherous. However clunky, the wheelbarrow appeared to be effective—I saw nothing in the garden but shifting shadows accompanied by a whispering breeze. Still, the whole thing was odd.

Moving past the dance floor and the bar, I wound my way through some tables at the end of the driveway. There I found Shelby and Frank Benson, who invited me to join them. After a little small talk, I went into my well-rehearsed spiel about finding closure. Danny had been so concerned about something at work, had I missed something important? I felt terrible for rushing out that morning, and when I got home it was too late. I was sure it was nothing, but it bothered me. It was more than I usually tossed out as gossip bait, but I phrased it as though I was just looking for reassurance. Frank had been a key player, until he wasn't, so he might have an ax to grind. And Shelby found me sympathetic, which could only help.

Frank heard me out but didn't offer much. It was frustrating, but I couldn't push. We moved on to other subjects. Shelby wanted to open her own business—vintage clothing and reproductions. I was surprised at her grasp of what was involved. I shouldn't have written her off as all boobs and hair. Other than a few comments, Frank was silent. After a short time, I made my excuses and rose from my chair. Frank stood and offered his card, inviting me to get in touch if I had any other concerns. Then he added, as though it were an afterthought, "Dan didn't leave anything work-related with you, did he? Something he brought home to study?"

"Work-related? I don't think so. What sort of thing are you talking about?"

"Oh, I don't know. It's just that there were some reports and files we couldn't find."

That didn't make any sense, unless he'd smuggled home something incriminating. And everything would be backed up somewhere. I shook my head.

"Remember, we were robbed that night. Afterward, I stayed with friends and threw away or packed up anything that was left. It would have been on a drive or his laptop, right? All of those kinds of things were taken. Most of what was stolen was never recovered."

"Well, it's not important now. Just trying to solve a little mystery. Take care," Frank said.

I mulled that over as I walked away. What could he mean? This was the computer age. There was never just one copy of anything. Frank must have been fishing to see if Danny had gotten his hands on something he shouldn't have. It wasn't too clever of him to ask, but he'd had a few drinks. And why ask now? As far as I knew, he'd done a workmanlike job and gone back to his practice. *Trying to solve a little mystery? Join the club, Frank. I'll add yours to my list.* But not right now, I decided as the band swung into action. It was time to revisit the Age of Aquarius.

Chapter Ten

Caro had Ian out on the dance floor when I got back to our table. The Petersons were breaking out some moves they'd probably perfected during their courtship. The bride and groom were trying to mimic them without a lot of success. One of Jack's friends whom I'd met earlier appeared, and we hit the dance floor together. Within a few minutes, April, Isabelle, Jeremy, and the rest of Jack's poker buddies had joined us. What we lacked in coordination we made up for in enthusiasm. We were a few songs in when I spotted her. Just beyond the tables, in between the party and the dark lawn, was Barbara. She was smiling and swaying to the beat, occasionally doing a little shimmy. A couple feet away stood a young woman I didn't recognize. Probably the night nurse. I tapped Jeremy's arm and gestured. He nodded and walked over to the two. After a brief conversation, he and Barbara joined us on the dance floor, and the young woman, who Barbara said was called Melissa, sat down at one of the tables. Caro reached out toward Barbara, who took her hand and did a twirl under her arm. I watched them dancing and laughing, and in the dim light could see the teenagers they'd been when these songs were on vinyl. Hard to believe Caro used a cane and Barbara didn't get out much. I hoped I was in that kind of shape in my seventies.

By the time I sat down again, I'd done something called the Frug, the Shimmy, and the Swim and, for a few minutes, done all of them at once. I gulped water while Barbara and Caro sang along about marching to the beat of a different drum. Once the lead singer started belting out "Respect," all the ladies hit the dance floor again. When the song ended, Sarah put an arm around each of her aunts, actual and honorary. All of them were flushed and happy. I took a picture with my phone. This was the kind of thing that Sarah had wanted from this weekend. We were all ready to take a seat when we heard a scream.

It was a woman. The band was between sets or we wouldn't have heard her. She screamed again, and then started yelling for help. It came from the other side of the dance floor. I heard a man yell, "Someone's in the water!" Barbara's nurse took off running. We all followed. Jeremy pushed his way through the crowd, Ian right behind. By the time I got close enough to see what was going on, the two men were hauling someone onto the bank at the end of the dock. It was Frank Benson. Melissa knelt by him, did a quick check, and yelled, "Call 911!" over her shoulder. Several people pulled out their phones, but Isabelle had the sense to move closer to Melissa and ask her questions as she spoke to the operator. Shelby was standing by, shifting from foot to foot, uncertain what to do or where to go. I went to her and guided her to the nearest table.

People continued to mill around until Penelope turned on her mic and said, "Hey, everybody. Looks like someone needs medical attention. Please take a seat and give them some room. Our great catering staff will be making the rounds with drinks, hot and cold, and some dessert. Relax and give the medical people some space. Thank you." She sounded so calm and matter-of-fact that everyone did as she'd requested and moved away.

Caro and Barbara came over to where I was sitting with Shelby and sat just behind us. I wanted to distract Shelby, who was staring at Melissa and Frank. He didn't seem like someone who was getting up anytime soon. I touched Shelby's arm to get her attention. Once she turned to me, I started talking.

"What happened?" I asked her. "How did he fall in?"

"He went out onto the dock to make a phone call. He thought it would be quieter. I was listening to the music. When I looked up, he was bent over, staring into the lake like he was looking at something. I got up to go see. He stood up, saw me coming along the dock, and pointed into the water. Then when he bent down again, he leaned forward and fell. I screamed for help. No one heard me at first, but then the music stopped and I yelled some more and everyone came running. I knew I couldn't get him out myself. I don't think he can swim."

Shelby stopped. She seemed dazed. Shock. I looked over her shoulder and saw Melissa performing CPR. Crap. I felt movement behind me and two steaming cups were placed on the table. I took Shelby's hand and wrapped it around the hot mug.

"Drink some," I said. "It'll help."

"What?" she said. Then she looked down. "Oh, thank you." She took a few sips.

I heard sirens in the distance. Only a few minutes until help came. I looked up and saw that Ian had replaced Melissa on the chest compressions. I had no idea if Shelby was the type to get hysterical, so I wanted to hold her attention until the paramedics got to Frank.

"Does he have any health issues? Any problems with his balance?"

Shelby shook her head. "He takes medicine for high blood pressure, and some vitamins I think, but he's in pretty good shape for a guy his age."

The blood pressure would explain the red face. The CPR suggested a heart attack. Not good.

"Do you have any idea what he saw?" I asked.

"No," she said. "He just looked surprised, sort of confused. He was trying to tell me. He was shouting, but the music was loud. That's why I went over. Then he bent, and swayed a little, and fell."

"Was he still on the phone?"

She frowned. "No, he must have put it in his pocket. The only thing in his hand was his drink."

So it wasn't the phone call that had triggered whatever had happened. It sounded like he really had seen something. Reflection? That's what I'd decided in the canoe. But I was starting to get a bad feeling about what was going on at the end of the dock. I'd like to take a look. No one was down there now, but I didn't want to leave Shelby alone. I'd decided it would have to wait when Shelby stirred.

"My bag," she said. "I dropped my handbag!" She started to get up.

"Wait," I said. "I'll look for it. You'll need to go with Frank when the ambulance comes." I could hear sirens. It would be here any minute. I turned in my chair. Caro was still behind me, but Barbara wasn't in sight.

"Bathroom," said Caro. "I'll stay with her while you look. If you're not back, I'll see that she gets on the ambulance or arrange a ride to the hospital. Go."

Caro took my seat when I stood. I went toward the dock. Other than the group around Frank, the area was deserted. Most of the guests were seated around the dance floor, drinking coffee while the Novelettes played an instrumental, acoustic set. Sarah and Jack were mingling.

The ambulance arrived with a shriek of sirens. While everyone's attention was fixed on that, I moved out onto the dock. I stayed to one side, ostensibly studying what was in front of me, but actually looking over the edge into the cove. I saw nothing but rippling water. I was so focused that I stumbled over something. I regained my balance and looked down. There was something dark and soft at my feet. I reached down and touched it. A sweater of some sort. I lifted it and saw the Leiber cat. It had come open, the chain tangled with the sweater. A lipstick had rolled out. I knelt down and put it back in the open bag, then set that on top of what I could now see was a small cashmere shrug. I looked toward the base of the driveway. The ambulance was pulling away. No sign of Shelby. All righty then. I poked through the contents of the minaudière. Driver's license—not a bad picture. She was a little older than I'd thought. Combination credit-debit card. Some actual paper money. That was getting less common, but I always carried cash just in case. Call me old-fashioned. Apparently Shelby was, too, because in addition to the money she had a dainty, embroidered handkerchief. Well, she was into vintage clothing. I put everything back in and snapped the bag shut.

I started to stand but realized there was no cell phone in Shelby's bag. It would only hold a small one, so maybe she had it with her. Still, if I was going to snoop through her handbag, I should do the right thing and make sure I'd found everything she'd dropped. I started feeling around. Anything small might have slipped through the wooden slats. The dock was in good repair, but some of the spacing was uneven, leaving crevices. I was about to give up when I felt something smooth between the edges of two warped pieces of wood. I couldn't see what it was, since there was only a slight difference from the color of the wood around it, and a dull gleam where the light hit it. I tried to get my fingers in, but no go. I could feel it move, so it wasn't wedged in tightly, but I couldn't grasp it.

I sighed and sat back on my heels. I could give up and come back tomorrow with help and some kind of tool. Really big tweezers? I hated to leave it, whatever it was. Probably a phone, given the shape and feel of it. And if it was, and it was Shelby's, she'd need it. Maybe I could find a stick. I brushed my hair back as I leaned over for another look. Wait a minute—I did have something. I couldn't pick a lock with a hairpin, but I had some heavy-duty clips in my updo that might do the trick here. I tugged one loose. It slipped into the crack easily. The metal tips slid around the object. I gave a gentle tug. The clip slid along the smooth surface and popped out, but not before pulling one side up. It was indeed a phone. I gripped it again and pulled. One side stuck. No amount of wiggling would move it, and I couldn't get a good grip on it with my hand. I also didn't want to give it such a hard pull that I sent it flying into the water.

I studied the situation. If I sacrificed another hair clip, I could hold onto one end and work at loosening the other. I'd known I'd be dancing tonight, so I had enough metal in my hair to set off airport alarms. I pulled out another clip, wiped my sweaty hands on my dress, and went to work. It took some doing, but I finally felt it start to give. One last tug and it popped free. I made a quick grab for it. One hair clip sailed over the edge of the dock and into the water with a tiny plop, and I landed on my butt, but I had the phone.

I looked it over. It was the smallest version of a high-end brand. No fancy case, just a gunmetal cover. It was sleek and minimalist, not what I would have expected from Shelby, but she'd surprised me before. I was going to see if it had a screen lock when I heard footsteps. I looked up. Ian, his trousers damp and his sleeves rolled up, looked down at me.

"Whatcha doing?" he said.

I must have made quite a picture—legs at odd angles, dress hiking up, hair coming down, and sweaty in spite of the cool night. I thought of all the time I'd spent primping and sighed.

"Shelby dropped her things when Frank fell in," I said. I tucked the phone into the handbag. It barely fit but I was able to close it. "They went everywhere. I was making sure I found what I could."

"I see," he said, looking me over and raising an eyebrow.

I sighed again. I bundled Shelby's bag into her shrug and made sure I had a good grip on both. I sat for a second, feeling more of my hair slip down. I stuck the remaining clip in a random spot, then looked up at Ian.

"Well," I said, "are you going to help me up?"

He reached down. I grabbed his hand with my free one and scrambled up. It was an inelegant maneuver, but at least I was upright.

"So what's the status?" I said.

Ian shrugged. "Frank's on his way to the hospital. Looked like a heart attack. If he makes it, it'll be because Melissa moved so fast. Lucky for him, she was a paramedic before she started nursing school—she said she's dealt with a lot of cardiac arrest. Jack and Sarah are saying goodbye to their guests. Jeremy is supervising the cleanup, with help from Isabelle. Most people don't realize how bad the situation with Frank was."

"Jane must be having a cow," I said.

"No sign of Jane. Desmond showed up and is pretty rattled. He said Jane took a sedative and hasn't stirred. She's been having trouble sleeping and wanted to be fresh for tomorrow."

"Well, that's a blessing," I said. "With any luck he'll be stable by tomorrow morning, and everyone can relax and enjoy the wedding. And I don't think we'll need to change the seating," I added as an afterthought.

Ian gave me an odd look.

"I'm helping with the seating—oh, never mind. Let's just hope there's no disruption tomorrow."

"I've always loved your pragmatism, Greer."

"Don't be a smartass, Ian. I'd like you to drive me home, but because I'm so pragmatic I think you should change out of those wet clothes first."

"I appreciate that. I hadn't expected to go wading tonight," Ian said. "It's getting chilly."

It was. The temperature was dropping, and the breeze had picked up. I'd worked up a sweat a few times and now felt cold and clammy. My sweater was back at our table. Ian's lips were looking blue. I was sure the water was freezing. I turned to take a look. The moonlight shimmered over the surface. It might be cold, but it was beautiful. That's when I saw it. Something white, more solid than the moonlight, moving slowly in the water.

"Ian," I said. I watched as more of the narrow white object came into view, bobbing in the water just off the Granville dock. Then it stopped with a jerk and started to sink.

"Ian!" I yelled it this time. He was back at my side in a second. "Look!" I said, pointing at the water.

He stared and shook his head.

"I don't see anything, Greer."

"There's something there," I insisted. I kept my eyes fixed on the spot where the pale, white thing had sunk. I could swear I still saw it, just under the water.

"You're tired," Ian said.

"No. Shelby said Frank saw something. He was pointing into the water. He was yelling to her, but she couldn't hear him, so she doesn't know what it was."

"He'd had a few drinks," Ian said.

"Yes, I know, it's just that I thought I saw something, too. When we were out in the canoe. I told you. It could have been a woman's face, but it was distorted. And Brittany's missing. Wait—there!"

It was back, just visible, something long and white. The breeze moved over the water, creating small waves that lapped against the dock. They skimmed over something coming to the surface, something attached to what I'd seen. An arm. A bare arm and shoulder, and now a face. Dark hair wrapped around it, but a face.

"Oh my God," I whispered. "Brittany."

Ian reached into his pocket and swore. "I left my phone in my jacket. Took it off on my way into the water."

"Petersons," I said. "Granville house. It'll be faster." Not that speed mattered now. It was too late for Brittany. I stared at the body, barely blinking, unable to look away.

"Wait here," Ian said. "Don't let her—I mean—"

"I know," I said. "Go."

Ian took off at a run.

I watched Brittany's body sway in the water. It never seemed to move far. It—she—must have been caught on something. If she weren't, she would have floated away by now, wouldn't she? It's not as though the lake water was still. And she must have drowned last night, or early this morning, so it was likely that I had seen her and not my own reflection from the canoe. But what was she doing under the Granville dock?

Once again, I heard sirens in the distance. Good. I was ready to be relieved of this grim task. Ian returned and put his sport coat around my shoulders.

"The police will be here any minute," he said.

I nodded.

Jeremy arrived a moment later, Isabelle right behind him. She held two steaming mugs.

"Here," she said, "I thought you might need something hot, and the caterers are cleaning up."

"Thank you," I said. I shifted Shelby's things to one arm and took a mug. The warmth was welcome, as was the jolt of caffeine. Ian was gulping his.

"Why don't you two go inside, wait in the boathouse?" Jeremy said.

"The police will want to talk to us," I said.

"I'll deal with them. Go get warm and dry."

We walked up the dock. As we turned toward the lawn, a police car pulled into the driveway

"I have to get my things," I said. "They're still at our table."

We detoured around the dance floor. The area was mostly deserted. Only the catering staff was left, collecting glasses and cups with practiced efficiency. I gave Ian his jacket and pulled on my sweater. I picked up my evening bag, and we wound our way through the tables toward the boathouse. As we passed the stage, Penny called to me. She let me know she'd be in the area for a couple of days if I wanted a band CD or to see another show, since this one was interrupted. The girls were almost done packing up. They'd probably have to talk to the police before they left. The stage wasn't high, but it gave them a good view of the crowd, and for all the cops knew, Brittany had gone into the lake more recently. Ian didn't say anything until we were inside. Then he turned to me.

"The thing is, if Brittany fell in the lake and drowned, wouldn't her—I mean, don't bodies either sink, or if not, wouldn't she— it—drift out into the lake?"

"I don't know," I said. "I read mysteries, but I'm not into forensics. I think it has something to do with gases, and maybe water temperature, but I'm not sure." It wasn't something I wanted to go around asking at this point either. "Look, go get changed," I said to Ian. "The police will have questions. You might as well be dry."

"You're right," he said. "Make yourself at home. I won't be long."

I drifted around the room. Jeremy obviously used this as his studio. It was the part of the boathouse that jutted out over the water. One wall was mostly windows. They gave a view up the lake. The light would be good for painting. An easel, a pile of sketch pads, and a corkboard with pictures and sketches was pinned up in one corner. There was a galley kitchen near the door. I peeked down the small hallway opposite the wall of windows. There was a bathroom straight ahead. An open door showed a small bedroom, with books and more sketch pads scattered around. Opposite was another door, partially closed. I could hear Ian moving around. The place was cozy. A little tight for two, but from what Sarah had told me when I arrived, it was just supposed to be Ian here. Jeremy got booted from the main house at the last minute, just like I had.

I went back to the window and settled into an overstuffed chair. I kicked off my shoes, tucked my cold feet under me, and picked up the top sketch pad on the table next to me. I flipped through it. All the drawings featured the same woman—lean, strong, with angular features. I was no critic, but these seemed to be pretty good. Figure studies, if I recalled correctly. I found Isabelle toward the back. She had taken Barbara's advice and worn only the shawl. She had draped it carefully—you could see the length of one leg and a little bit of hip, but otherwise the pose was quite modest. Sexier because of it. Isabelle was no dummy. I put the sketchbook down and leaned back in the chair. A wave of fatigue washed over me. I closed my eyes. The only thing keeping me upright was all the shapewear I had on.

"Greer?"

"Hmm? Oh, I was starting to doze."

"Are you okay?" he said. "All this has been—a lot. On top of—everything else."

"Yes," I said. "I'm okay. Just tired. It was a busy night. And I was up awfully early."

"Right. My fault. But I had a great time. I had a lot of fun tonight. Well, up to a point."

"Me, too," I said. "It was really nice."

"Great," he said. He leaned forward, elbows on knees. He looked sideways for a minute, then back at me. "Listen," he said, "I have an idea. I was wondering if—"

Oh my God. It sounded like he wanted to have a Serious Conversation. We'd have to do it eventually, but I wasn't ready to do it now. I was exhausted, distracted, and didn't know what I wanted. The only thing I was sure of was that it wasn't the same thing I'd wanted the first time around.

The door rattled. Saved. Jeremy walked in and collapsed into a chair.

"So what's going on out there?" I asked.

"I told the police what I could. They'll have some questions for you, but right now they're getting her out of the water. I left my dad in charge. I want to get some dry clothes on." But he didn't move. He looked exhausted.

"Coffee, pal?" Ian said.

"That would be great," Jeremy said. Ian went to the kitchen counter and got to work with the one-cup coffee maker.

"How's your dad doing? And Sarah?"

"My father is shocked, but functional. He's dealing with the police. Sarah's doing okay. I think she and Jack are trying to figure out what to do about the wedding."

"Do you think they'll cancel it?" I asked.

"I don't see why they should. Most of the guests were gone by the time we found Brittany. Few people knew her. I think the best plan is to keep it quiet and go ahead with things. It sounds harsh, I know, but I don't know what good it does to cancel it."

He was right. It was sad, but true, that Brittany's absence wouldn't be noticed. With most of the guests having traveled some distance to attend Sarah's wedding, making any changes would create more disruption and disappointment than just going ahead with it.

Ian came back with Jeremy's coffee. We all sat quietly for a few minutes, too tired to talk. When Jeremy had finished his coffee and there was still no sign of a policeman at the door, I roused myself.

"I've been enjoying looking at your work. I never knew you were an artist."

"Well, it was on the back burner for a long time, but I decided it was now or never. I'm glad you like it. Did you see my version of Caro as the hero of a graphic novel?"

Jeremy pulled a couple things off the corkboard and handed them to me. One was a black and white photograph of a very young Caro wearing go-go boots, hot pants, and a maxi vest. The other was a sketch with the exaggerated features and stylized background of characters in graphic novels. It wasn't as good as his other work, but it was cool and discernibly Caro. I complimented him and asked where the picture had come from.

"It's from her modeling days. I told her I was going to make her a supermodel crime fighter, but she said no go unless she could also be a jewel thief or something fun like that."

"Sounds about right," I said. "I'm surprised she never tried acting. She's not afraid of the spotlight, that's for sure."

"I asked her that once. She said she'd always rather play herself. She is a superb mimic though. When Sarah and I were little, she used to crack us up imitating everyone from the dog to the neighbor's nanny."

We chatted for a couple of minutes about the party, the guests, and Frank's apparent heart attack. Finally, there was a knock on the door. Jeremy let in a uniformed officer, who told us that due to the lateness of the hour he wanted to get preliminary information and someone would follow up the next day. He asked a lot of questions all the same. We asked a few ourselves, which were met with "It's really too soon to tell." With one final "We'll be in touch," he packed up his notebook and left.

I let out a jaw-cracking yawn, and we decided to call it a night. Jeremy headed for a hot shower. The walk to the inn wasn't long, but Ian and I were both cold and tired. His SUV was parked alongside the Whitaker garage across the street, so we went there. Since the passenger door was up against some bushes, I waited in front while he pulled out. There were no windows in the garage doors, but there was one in the service door. I peeked in. A dim light burned near the entrance. I could see the garage was full, mostly with family vehicles I recognized. A few cars in the back were covered with what I thought of as automotive dust sheets.

Ian pulled up, and I hopped in. He had the heat blasting, for which I was grateful.

"See anything interesting in there?" he asked while I buckled up.

"Not really," I said. "What did Brittany drive?"

"A Prius," Ian said.

"Really? I would have thought she'd have something that made more of a statement."

Ian shrugged. "She told me once she hated to spend money on gas. She was surprisingly budget conscious for someone so successful. Why?"

"I've been wondering what happened to her car," I said. "Unless it's under a cover, it's not in the garage."

"Desmond has a couple of classic cars, and Jane has a convertible she uses around town in warm weather. He showed me last time I was here."

"That's right. I've seen them, and I remember Jane's car. No Prius there. So where is it?"

"I saw her leave in it, remember? I guess it's wherever she went."

But she had gone into the lake, and if she'd done it in her car, we wouldn't have found her where we did. But I was too tired to argue.

"Okay," I said. "What time should we leave tomorrow?"

We made plans, and he pulled away. I looked up at the full parking lot. Maybe Brittany had left in her car, but that didn't mean she hadn't come back in it and then ended up under the dock. But that still left the question—if she was in the lake, where was her car?

Chapter Eleven

I overslept the next morning. It had been a restless night, punctuated by disturbing dreams. I remembered very little of them when I woke, but the emotions they evoked remained. The feelings faded to a vague unease as I rushed to gulp down some coffee and pull myself together. Still, I was ready when Ian picked me up, and off we went to the wedding and brunch. They were being held at another venue in the area, with stunning views and autumn ambience to spare.

Everything went smoothly. Sarah came down the aisle solo, looking not so much radiant as happy and comfortable in her own skin. She and Jack smiled at each other through the entire service. I hadn't been a weepy bride either. Danny and I had smiled and laughed at some inside jokes throughout our wedding. It had been a happy day, and a mostly happy marriage. But as I watched Sarah, a thought drifted to the surface of my mind: *I will never do this again.* Something inside me, unsettled since Sarah had asked me if I'd ever marry again, shifted into a calm certainty. No, I wouldn't. That part of my life was done, but I couldn't close the door on it yet. I had unfinished business.

The service concluded, pictures were taken, toasts were made, and lunch was eaten. A good time was had by all. Jane looked more relaxed than I'd seen her in days. Even Desmond's mood had improved. Sarah and Jack drove off to the honeymoon location they'd picked out in town, where they'd stay for a few days before departing for two weeks alone in wedded bliss. There was a little bit of a scramble as everyone left, and Ian and I ended up giving Caro a lift back to the Whitakers'. Barbara had gotten quite tired, and Margaret had taken her home right after lunch.

"Just as well," Caro said, settling into the back of the SUV. "That little Mini Margaret drives doesn't have much of a back seat. It's a go-cart, is what it is. Fun when I was young and limber in London, but that was before either of you were born."

We were laughing and chatting about Caro's misspent youth when we pulled up to the Whitaker house and saw the police car. We all went silent. The excellent meal I'd had rolled in my stomach. I heard Caro sigh. After a couple of seconds, she said, "I guess we'd better go and see what this is about." As though we didn't all know. We were getting out when Jeremy and Isabelle pulled up, followed by Desmond and Jane. I presumed Barbara and Margaret had gotten home and gone in before the cops showed up.

Desmond went immediately to the police officer. Jeremy joined him. Caro went to Jane, who had stayed by the car. Isabelle walked over to us. We stood quietly. I saw Caro whisper something to Jane, who nodded. There was a brief conversation between the policeman and the Whitakers. The officer took something out of his pocket and showed it to Desmond and Jeremy. Both shook their heads. The officer gestured toward Jane and Caro. Desmond shook his head, then turned and walked to his wife and cousin. Jeremy came over to us while the officer took out his phone and made a call.

"They need a formal identification of the body," he said. My father will go. There's some question about her injuries. I'm not clear on the issue. They've also got some jewelry. The police want us to take a look."

The officer finished his call and walked over. He introduced himself and showed us a small plastic bag holding a bracelet and earring. Did we remember seeing Brittany wearing it, and if so, was it a complete set? Earrings, necklace, bracelet?

"I'm sorry, I don't really notice things like that," Isabelle said.

"Neither do I," said Ian. "Unless she wore it often, I wouldn't recognize it. It doesn't look familiar."

The officer moved the bag closer to me so I could see it. There was a brief flash of blue. That seemed familiar somehow, as did the jewelry itself. I frowned. What was it the flash reminded me of?

"Ma'am?" The officer was waiting for an answer.

I shook my head. "It looks familiar, but I only met Brittany briefly. I remember thinking that she looked nice, and that her jewelry was vintage, but I couldn't tell you exactly what it looked like, or what pieces she was wearing. I'm sorry. Is there some missing? Do you think she was robbed?" Unlikely he would say anything, but nothing ventured, nothing gained. As expected, the officer was noncommittal on my robbery gambit.

A few minutes later, Desmond left with the police officer. Caro went in with Jane. The rest of us stood there debating what to do. It was finally decided that Jeremy would get in touch with Sarah and Jack and let them know what was going on. He thought they'd want to come back. Ian would drop me at the inn. We'd all reconvene later at the house and plan what to do when we knew more.

Back in my room, I stripped off my wedding finery and wrapped up in the provided robe. Hair and makeup next—I brushed out my updo and rinsed off my friend-of-the-bride face. After a brief study of the result, I patted on some moisturizer, soaked a facecloth in cool water for my puffy eyes, and got a bottle of water out of the fridge. When in doubt, rehydrate. Then I settled in with my feet up to consider the situation.

The body was Brittany, and Desmond would confirm it. There was no other explanation. Brittany had drowned. Whether she'd fallen in or been pushed would need to be determined.

The car was another question mark. It was possible that she'd gone off somewhere, but unless it was some incredible emergency, why hadn't she told someone? I wondered if anyone had checked to see if her luggage or clothing were missing. That would tell us a lot. Even if I dashed off in a hurry, I'd take my handbag. And I'd do that only for a family emergency. With Brittany's mother dead, and no father around, what other family did she have? Ian might not know; Desmond probably would. Their HR department would have an emergency contact on file.

I circled back to what I'd seen from the canoe. Was it a woman's face and not a reflection? It had been distorted by the water and the sun reflecting off the fog and the surface. If it was Brittany's body, it should have floated off. Unless she'd just gone under. I thought of Ian waiting on the dock. "I have to take care of something," he'd said. No. A crime of passion I could see—I could believe that of anyone. But to get rid of an ex-girlfriend, or even a business rival? Not his style. He wasn't that kind of killer. I moved on.

Had Frank really seen something, and if so, was it the same thing I had? More important, to me at least, was what had prompted that private call? It wasn't right after our conversation, but it was soon enough. Shelby might know. I didn't think I'd get anything from Frank, even if I decided to go visit him in the hospital. I didn't know him well enough to justify a trip to his bedside, but I did have Shelby's things tucked away in a drawer. She would want them. I'd have to find out if she'd called the Whitakers—she didn't have a way to get in touch with me. I might be able to finagle dropping them off at the hospital. That would have to be tomorrow. I wanted to get back to the Whitaker house and see what was going on.

Decision made, I put on jeans and a sweater and applied a little makeup. With the right lipstick, a girl can face anything. A brisk walk through the cool evening air would provide a healthy glow. Off I went, hoping for the best and expecting the worst.

The newlyweds had returned. Sarah had taken charge. Jane was not doing well, and Margaret was looking after both her and Barbara. The two were resting upstairs. Sarah's father wasn't back. He'd called; there'd been some delay.

"The guys are all watching baseball in the den," Sarah said. "There's really nothing for anyone to do but wait. I need to figure out food. Would you mind checking on Caro? She's in the living room. She keeps saying she's fine, but I think this has taken a lot out of her."

"Sure," I said. I found Caro in a wing chair drawn up to the fire, which had been lit against the chill of the evening. I perched on the hearth and asked her how everyone was doing.

"Jane's completely undone. I think she's in shock. With Barbara it's hard to tell. The medication blunts things, I think. Margaret has taken charge, so they're in good hands. Though she's apparently a firm believer in tea liberally laced with sugar in cases like this, based on the tray that just went up."

I was a firm believer in tea liberally laced with whisky for shock, or whatever else ailed you. Caro believed in skipping the tea and going straight for the whisky if the glass she was holding was any indication. She took a sip and sighed.

"It was such a lovely day, and the party last night was such fun. I was really hoping that wretched girl would turn up elsewhere in a few days. Though obviously not like this," she added.

"I'm sure we all were, to the degree we thought about it at all," I said.

The only people who'd seemed upset were Desmond and Jane. Though Jane had appeared more on edge than worried. I'd disliked Brittany on principle. Now I felt a little sorry for her. She'd gone from a person to an inconvenience.

"Greer, darling, may I ask a favor?"

"Of course," I said. "Can I get you something?"

"My cane," she said. "I dropped my usual one last night during all the excitement. Adrenaline, you know, so I didn't even miss it until I was getting ready to go to the wedding. This one is my spare, and I don't feel quite as steady on it. I know it's getting dark, but would you be a dear and take a look? It's not just my favorite, it was a gift."

"Yes, certainly, I understand." I stood.

"Thank you. I'd feel so much better if I had it back. An MI5 agent I once dated gave it to me. He said if he wasn't around to look after me, at least I'd have that. I never saw him again."

"What happened to him?" I said.

"Nobody knows. Or if they did, they didn't tell me. Close-mouthed bunch. But that cane has come in handy more than once."

I probably didn't want to know. Deciding that if I was going to once again spend time hunting for something on a chilly night in the dark, I'd at least take a flashlight, I found Sarah and told her about Caro's request.

"She's very attached to that cane," Sarah said. "I appreciate you going to look. There's always a flashlight in the mudroom. Come on."

I followed her to the mudroom. She found the flashlight and grabbed the jacket on the peg beneath it. "Here, wear this. It's getting cooler. It's Caro's, but she won't mind."

I shrugged into it, tested the flashlight battery—still good— and went out and down the driveway. *At least tonight I'm wearing comfortable shoes*, I thought, as I crunched through the gravel. I hunted in all the likely places, starting with where we'd been sitting the night before. I couldn't remember when I'd last seen Caro with her cane. Other than the odd bit of disturbed grass, there was little sign a party had taken place. The stage, tables, and chairs had disappeared. The landscapers would probably put the rest to rights on Monday. If Caro had left her cane here, someone would have found it.

I moved toward the dock and hunted there. When I got close to the guest cottage I stopped. There was a light burning inside, visible through the sheers that covered the windows. There had been last night, too. I clicked off the flashlight and looked around. There was no one in sight. This was my chance to satisfy my curiosity about what Brittany had taken with her, if she had left in her car for reasons unknown. I had no reason to go in, but I could always say I needed the bathroom and didn't want to interrupt my search by going back up to the house. It wasn't like it was a crime scene. More likely the scene of a tragic accident. That would be my story anyway. With one last look around, I moved into the shadows around the cottage.

I went as far as the door and stopped to listen. I heard nothing but water slapping against the wooden dock. I pulled the sleeve of my sweater over my hand and tried the handle. Locked. I didn't bother trying a window. No one would go to those lengths for the bathroom. Besides, I wasn't that athletic. Unwilling to give up, I thought for a minute. Danny and I had visited here a few times, and we'd stayed in the cottage once. Sarah had been delayed and her parents were at their home in Westchester, so there was no one to let us in. She had told us where to find the spare key. I thought it was quaint that they left one. That was years ago, though. I looked at the door lock. It didn't look as though it had been replaced any time recently. Maybe I'd get lucky.

I tried to remember where the key had been the last time. I moved a flowerpot. Nothing. I didn't think it would be that obvious, but I checked another pot just the same. I bent down and turned on the flashlight. There were some small plants and scattered rocks near the door. I felt around. All the stones felt real and were solidly planted, except for one, which rocked a little when I pushed it. I got hold of it and lifted. Bingo. There was a key in a depression underneath. I picked it up and put the rock back. After brushing the dirt off the key, I tried it in the door and heard a satisfying click. I was in. I dropped the key in the jacket pocket and stepped inside.

The little house had an empty feel, as though no one had been there for days. Even the Granville place had felt more lived in. I closed the door behind me and looked around. It was as I remembered—small living room, bedroom and bathroom off a short hall to my right, kitchen straight ahead. It was tiny, but fine for one person or a couple for a weekend. Whether for reasons personal or professional, Desmond had apparently wanted Brittany close by. The only lights on were a lamp in the living room and a light over the sink in the kitchen. I looked more closely at the lamp, following the cord down behind the end table. It was plugged into a timer. No need to smart-home the cottage. It was used occasionally for guests, and only in warmer weather.

I went into the kitchen. The light over the sink was more of a nightlight, but it was enough to work with. I didn't want to draw attention by flicking lights on and off. I stepped on the pedal on the trash can. Nothing but a couple of wrappers and some used individual coffee pods. There was a mug in the sink. Next to the coffee maker was a bottle of red wine and a box of crackers. Also a pile of mints with the inn logo. That was more than one turndown service.

I pulled my sleeve down again to open the fridge. Nothing but green tea and soy milk. It figured. Still no sign of a handbag or car keys. Not that surprising. Some people dropped their stuff as soon as they walked in, but I never left mine near the door. On to the bedroom.

This time I used the flashlight. Nothing seemed out of order. Clothes were unpacked and hung up in the closet. There was a nice suitcase open on the luggage stand. It looked to me like at least a day's dirty laundry had been tossed in, maybe two. A pair of pants and a top had been tossed on the bed, probably what she had on before she changed for the tea party. The small desk by the window held a lamp and a sleek laptop plugged into a charger. I debated taking a look at the computer before deciding that it probably had a screen lock. There was a tablet on the bedside table, next to another small lamp. No phone that I could see, and no handbag. Under the bed? I got down on hands and knees and swept the light back and forth beneath the bed skirt. If you're going to snoop, be a good snoop. But there was nothing there.

I was backing up when I heard a click. The light went on. I froze. I was running through a brief list of reasonable lies to explain my presence on the floor of the dark bedroom with a flashlight when I heard another click. I peeked around the corner of the bed. The living room had gone dark. I held my breath and waited. No other sounds, no footsteps, no one breathing. The timer had turned the light off. I scooted back and looked at the desk lamp. It, too, was plugged into a timer. I let out my breath.

I'd started to stand when I realized that I'd be in full view through the window. The drapes were open, and the sheers wouldn't give much cover. If anyone was looking, they'd see me moving. Unlikely, but I didn't want to risk it. Using the bathroom didn't require being in the bedroom. I dropped back to the floor and rolled sideways until I was nearer the door. I tucked the flashlight into the waistband of my jeans and then crawled out the door. Once in front of the bathroom, I stood and dusted myself off. This was all getting a little too Agatha Raisin for me. One more thing to check, and I was out of here.

Since the bathroom was the reason for my visit, I turned the vanity light on. There was an open cosmetic case on the counter containing all the usual suspects. No meds. If she took any, she had them with her. A tissue with a lipstick blot was on the counter, along with an unplugged hair dryer. All the haircare products were still in the case. Thinking of the mints, I checked the shower in case she'd taken the little bottles of shampoo and conditioner from the inn. Nothing. So she hadn't showered or washed her hair while she was here. The trash can held an empty bottle. Hand lotion, and I could see the inn logo. Deciding there was nothing else to be learned, I flushed the toilet for the sake of verisimilitude, turned off the light, and left.

I was on the stoop reaching for the key in my pocket when I heard footsteps. I held still, hoping whoever it was would turn to the dock or the boathouse. No such luck. The steps came closer. I stepped off the walk and eased along the wall, careful to avoid the flowerpots. I had just crouched behind a juniper bush when Desmond Whitaker rounded the corner. He stopped, looked around, and went to the cottage door. He had pulled a set of keys out of his pocket and inserted one in the lock when a door slammed. The Granville house, I thought, though it was hard to be sure from my position behind the shrub. There was the sound of voices, indistinct conversation, and the crunch of gravel. Desmond paused, waiting until the sounds faded. Then he turned the key and tried the handle. It was locked, because I hadn't had time to lock it, so he'd done it himself. I bit my lip. Desmond swore, pulled the key out, studied the key ring, then tried again. It worked, and he disappeared into the cottage.

I watched the windows as I debated my next move. The light in the living room stayed off. I wanted to know what Desmond was doing, but I couldn't stay where I was for long. My calf muscles were starting to cramp. I didn't want to try to wait him out and then tumble in a heap at his feet as he was coming out the door. I had the excuse of the hunt for the cane, but still. He might put me together with the unlocked door. I shifted position and decided to give it another couple of minutes. I didn't have to wait long before Desmond emerged. When he turned to lock the door, he set something down. I couldn't get a clear view through the juniper branches. Frustrating—he hadn't gone in with anything, so I wanted to know what he was leaving with. I finally got a glimpse when he passed through the light coming out of the bedroom window. It looked like a briefcase, or maybe a laptop case.

As Desmond got farther away, I eased out from the behind the bush. I moved along the wall of the cottage, stopping before I hit the lighted window. Desmond continued up the driveway, keeping close to the hedge. When he reached the house, he went to a side door. I was certain that was the one that led up the stairs to his office. I was right—a minute later he appeared in a lit window on the third floor and closed the drapes.

I sidled closer to the bedroom window of the cottage and peeked in. I could see the desk, now empty. Brittany's laptop was gone. I leaned forward, trying to get a look at the bedside table. From what I could tell, the tablet was gone, too. I stepped back. There was undoubtedly a very good explanation as to why Desmond Whitaker had just made off with a guest's computer equipment. Perhaps they belonged to the company? Brittany was an employee. But she was also dead, under unexplained circumstances, and there had been something furtive about Desmond's visit to the cottage. I smelled a rat.

Whatever he was up to, I still had a mission to complete. I moved away from the cottage—Caro had been nowhere near it as far as I knew—and went back to my search. I was ready to give up when I spotted the cane under some shrubbery near the Granville dock. It must have rolled down there when Caro was helping Shelby get to the ambulance. I picked it up and dusted it off. It was heavy. I could see why Caro would feel more secure using this than her spare. The wood was old, a varnished hardwood, and the handle was a roaring silver lion. There was more silver detail on the shaft. It really did look like a sword cane I'd seen in a museum. I held it as though I were going to use it, and pressed on the fittings, separately and in combination. I felt something shift. I lifted the head of the cane and a silver blade slid into view. Impressive. I pushed the cane back together until I felt another click. It was plenty useful as a blunt instrument as it was. I tucked it under my arm and went back to the house and straight to Caro, who was still by the fire.

"Desmond's back," she said when I walked in. "The body was Brittany. No doubt about it."

"I can't say I'm surprised," I said. "It would have been too much of a coincidence otherwise."

Caro was giving me an odd look. I looked down and realized there were bits of juniper stuck to the jacket and some dirt on my knees. Note to self—after lurking in shrubbery, clean up before you see anyone.

"Sarah said you wouldn't mind if I borrowed your jacket. I had to crawl under some bushes to get the cane. It must have rolled down there while you were helping Shelby."

"Yes, of course. I remember now. I didn't think to look for it once the ambulance left. Thank you, Greer."

"You're welcome. Do you need anything before I go?" I asked. "I thought I'd see if Sarah needs help with anything."

"I'm fine. I'm sure she'll be glad to have an extra pair of hands."

I had put the flashlight back and hung up the jacket when I remembered the cottage key. I'd forgotten to put it back after

Desmond left. I reached into the pocket and came up with a key fob. Caro's car keys, probably. I felt around some more and found a cough drop, and then deep in the corner, the cottage key. I slipped it into my back pocket. I'd return it tomorrow sometime.

I found Sarah in the hall. She looked grim. I told her I'd found Caro's cane and heard about the positive ID.

"It gets worse," she said. "Shelby Travis just called. Frank Benson died an hour ago."

Chapter Twelve

Brittany turning up dead hadn't surprised me, but the news about Frank was a shock. According to Sarah, he'd been in the ICU but had been holding his own. Everything had seemed stable. Shelby had left his room to get something to eat, and when she got back, a crash cart and a bunch of nurses and doctors were in his room. A few minutes later, he was gone.

"And that's really all I know," Sarah said. "Shelby wasn't in good shape, I couldn't get much sense out of her. She said she called because you had her cat, of all things."

"I do. It's her handbag. A Leiber cat." I told Sarah about collecting Shelby's things after Frank was fished out of the water.

"Oh, I see. She left a number. Mrs. Henderson took the message. I'll get it for you."

Mrs. Henderson was the housekeeper. I was surprised she was still on her feet, but there she was in the dining room, arranging platters of sandwiches. She gave me the phone number, told Sarah that Caro had gone to bed, and that the buffet would be ready shortly. Her tone implied we were in the way, so we went to the living room. Everyone else, including the Petersons, had gathered in the den.

"I'll let them know when the food's ready," Sarah said. "Right now I just want some quiet."

We settled in front of the fire and discussed the situation. I told her I'd help any way I could.

"I appreciate that. Right now I don't know what's going to happen. The police will be back tomorrow. We're going ahead with the breakfast—it's small and casual, so Jack and I will go. There's some guests we didn't get to visit with. My mother's not up to it. She's normally all about keeping calm and carrying on, but all this has just knocked her flat. I'm sure Brittany's death was an accident, but I don't know how long the police will be here."

Until they're satisfied that it was an accident, I thought, *and if they find something that suggests otherwise, they're going to be around for a while.*

"I'm sure they'll be able to tell tomorrow. Did they give your dad any idea of how they'll proceed?"

"He just said they'd be here tomorrow. Then he said he had to take care of some things in his office, and he's been there ever since."

He hadn't, but I didn't want to tell Sarah what I'd seen. There might be a perfectly good explanation. Or not. Either way, my friend had gotten enough bad news on her wedding day. I decided to change the subject, and for a few minutes we talked about how the wedding had gone and what everyone had worn. By the time Mrs. Henderson appeared to let us know the food was ready, Sarah was looking more relaxed.

It was a subdued group that gathered in the living room. The Petersons kept the conversation moving, catching up with those they knew and asking questions of those they didn't. They really were very nice people. After we'd all finished our light supper, they excused themselves, with Jack's father offering an upbeat, "I'm sure this will all be cleared up in the morning." Isabelle opened her mouth and shut it again. Ian was staring out the window, frowning. The rest of the room murmured agreement and then gave a collective sigh as the door closed.

Over coffee, the six of us discussed plans for the next day. Everyone spoke as though Brittany's death was a tragic accident. I think Sarah and Jack even believed it. Ian was non-committal, Isabelle looked thoughtful and said little, and Jeremy looked worried. As for me, I presumed the worst, which came from reading too much detective fiction and stumbling upon the occasional body.

It was decided that we'd reassemble around noon, unless the police wanted us earlier. My guess was that the police would step carefully around the Whitakers—a wealthy family who had lived in the area seasonally for generations. I opted to walk back to the inn and took my leave.

Once in my room, I pulled out Shelby's things. The shrug I folded up and put into one of the shopping bags I had. The minaudière kept falling open. If I took the phone out, it closed easily and stayed shut. Either there was some trick to it I couldn't figure out, or Shelby kept her phone elsewhere. From what I remembered of her dress, it wasn't likely to have pockets, but you never knew. It was also possible this wasn't Shelby's phone. Maybe Frank's? Shelby had said he had his phone in his hand when he fell into the water, but she could have been wrong. I wanted to know who that last call had been to. Maybe I was grasping at straws to think it had something to do with our conversation or Danny's death, but after the odd question Frank had asked, I wanted to be sure.

I hit the power button. There was still battery left—the phone came on. Time and date on a black background. No picture. I pushed the power button again. Screen lock. I stared at it for a minute, then set the phone down and found the list of guest contact info Jane had given me. There was a number for Frank. I got my own cell phone and dialed. It rang a few times on my end, but nothing happened with the phone in front of me. I checked the volume button on it. Not muted, and also set to vibrate. So this was not Frank's phone.

I got Shelby's number out and called. She answered right away. I was surprised—I'd expected the phone in front of me to ring. She sounded weepy, but coherent, and glad to hear from me.

"Thank you for calling, and for getting my things. That cat was the last gift Frank gave me. For my birthday." This was followed by a sniff.

"I'm so sorry. Frank was such a nice man. I'm glad I could help. The bag fell open, but I think I found everything. I have your sweater. I found a phone, too."

"Phone? I have my phone. That's the number you called. It didn't fit in the bag. I had it tucked in my bra." Another sniff.

"Oh. Maybe it's Frank's?"

"I don't think so. That's why he got up—he said he had to make an important call. Business. I'm sure he had it when he fell in the water. At least, I thought I saw it. It was dark. Maybe I'm confused." This was followed by a yawn.

"Well, it might belong to one of the other guests. I'll let you take a look just in case."

"Sure," Shelby said and yawned again. "I'm sorry," she added, "I took a sleeping pill. It's all just been so awful."

"I understand. I'd do the same in your shoes. Why don't we meet tomorrow morning, not too early, and I'll give you your things and you can look at the phone. Will that work?"

Shelby said it would, and we agreed on a time and place to meet at her hotel. I hung up and put the pretty jeweled cat and the sweater into the bag. Then I put the phone on the table. I looked up Brittany's number on the guest list. I got my cell and dialed. The phone on the table neither rang nor moved. So much for that theory. I got ready for bed and picked up one of the paperbacks I'd bought at the library. Maybe I'd have better luck with Agatha Christie's county house murder.

A few hours later, I woke from a sound sleep. My phone was ringing. I picked it up. No call. The ringing continued. I got out of bed and grabbed the phone on the table. I swiped the screen, then fumbled it. By the time I had it to my ear, a man was talking.

"Are you there? For God's sake, stop playing games!"

He hung up before I could say a word. No way to tell who it was or who he was trying to reach. I brought the phone over to the bedside table and put it next to mine. Probably an irritated wedding guest. If he called back, I'd let him know what had happened.

* * *

Shelby was having breakfast when I arrived at her hotel the next morning. I joined her for coffee. Her eyes and nose were red. She was wearing very little makeup and had her hair in a ponytail. She was pretty in spite of her disheveled appearance, but today she looked the age on her driver's license. She shook her head when I showed her the phone.

"No, I've never seen that," she said. I handed over the bag and asked how she was doing.

"I'm okay, I guess. I'm still just so shocked, you know? It seemed like he was getting better. They were going to move him out of intensive care soon. I went to get something to eat—I hadn't had anything all day, and I figured if he was resting it was a good time. I wasn't gone for very long. Then when I got back . . ."

Shelby's eyes filled up.

"I'm sure there's nothing you could have done," I said. "He was hooked up to all kinds of monitors, right? The doctors couldn't have gotten to him any faster even if you were there and noticed something was wrong."

I really had no idea how a cardiac care unit worked, having only seen fictional ones on TV, but Shelby seemed comforted.

"I suppose not," she said. "I told the nurse at the station that I'd be downstairs for a little while, and she said everything looked fine, go ahead. Later, after, she asked me if I wanted her to page my friend. I told her I didn't know anyone here. She said that right after I left, a woman came wanting to visit Frank. Since he wasn't allowed visitors, the nurse told her where to find me. But no one came to the coffee shop."

"Maybe it was April," I said.

"No," Shelby shook her head. "She arrived later. She's his next of kin. They're still legally married. He never changed anything." She bit her lip.

"Those things don't occur to people," I said. "Neither my husband nor I ever thought anything would happen to one of us. There are things we should have done but didn't. I wouldn't take it personally. And as for the woman the nurse saw, it must have been someone else here for the wedding that Frank knew. Or a friend of April's."

"Maybe. She's been very nice to me, actually. April. She's going to help with the arrangements and everything. I'm supposed to call her this morning."

"That's good. It was very hard after Dan died, but I had friends and family around. Here, take this." I pulled one of my library business cards out of my wallet and wrote my cell number on the back. I gave it to her. "If you ever want to talk."

"Thank you," she said.

I had plenty of time to get to the Whitakers after I left Shelby, so I decided to take the long way around Mirror Lake and call it exercise. I thought about our conversation. Everything I had told Shelby was true. I wasn't just being nice. Many people never thought of dying, especially if they were reasonably healthy and nowhere near retirement. Frank had been in his fifties, and in the throes of a midlife crisis, with a much younger girlfriend. He wasn't going to contemplate his own mortality. Danny had been not quite forty and in good health. Other than the forms we filled out for our employers and banks, ones that asked for a beneficiary, we never gave dying a thought. No one expects to suddenly drop dead, let alone be murdered.

It was also likely that the woman who had come to see Frank was someone he knew who had attended the wedding. Perhaps she hadn't known Shelby, or was a friend of April's and had no use for Shelby. Still. I talk to Frank Benson about my husband's last days at the company where they both worked. He asks if Dan brought any work home, since something was "missing," which makes no sense. Frank then makes a phone call to a person unknown. Then he has a heart attack. The next day he's on the mend when he has a mysterious visitor and suddenly dies.

All of it could be coincidental. The heart attack certainly was. And there was no sign of any foul play at the hospital, mysterious visitor or not. But if there was something sketchy going on at Frank's and Dan's old company, that coincidence might have been awfully convenient for someone. In the words of a retired cop I knew, "If a coincidence is really convenient for someone, it's probably not a coincidence." But I had no evidence. There were moments even I thought I was reaching. It was worth talking to April again, though. If she was helping with the formalities, she'd be in town a few more days. I'd give her a call and ask her to meet for a drink.

When I got to the Whitaker house, there was a cruiser in the driveway. Behind it was a sedan so nondescript it shrieked "unmarked police car." Sarah had told me to let myself in, so I went to the side of the house with the door into the mudroom. I looked down the driveway to the dock. There were two men, one in uniform, heads together, standing at the end. I was much too far away to eavesdrop, so I went into the house before they noticed me watching them.

The Whitaker family, including their newest in-law, were gathered in the sunroom overlooking the garden. There wasn't a clear view of the lake, but you'd be able to see anyone coming and going from the dock through some breaks in the hedge along the driveway. Intentional or not, they'd picked the best spot to keep an eye on the police. Isabelle and Ian arrived shortly after I did. Caro, Barbara, and Margaret had gone for a walk. Desultory conversation was made. The degree of tension in the air surprised me, given that this was still officially an accident. *Though perhaps not so surprising*, I thought. It might not have anything to do with Brittany's death. It might be all about secrets these people wanted to keep. I had some experience with that. Whether those secrets would matter to the police depended on what they were.

Desmond was definitely hiding something, based on the times I'd seen him where he wasn't supposed to be. That might or might not have to do with Brittany. My guess was that it did. Sarah had yet to break the news about moving to Europe with Jack. She certainly wasn't going to drop that bombshell right now. Jeremy had said the family was in for a big surprise, but that had yet to be revealed. I didn't think that had to do with Sarah, or else she didn't know he knew. Jack was distressed on Sarah's behalf but seemed reasonably calm. Jane had been tense for days, but that could be because her beautifully planned weekend had spun out of control, a worst-case scenario for a type A personality. And she was dealing with the unexpected presence of her older sister, in company with her husband's most eccentric relative. Barbara and Caro had been wild cards in everyone's life for more than fifty years. That would put Jane on edge.

And then there was Ian. He didn't seem so much tense as distracted. Of course, it had been a long time since we'd spent significant time together, but I knew that look. His wheels were turning. He was problem solving. My guess was the problem had something to do with Brittany and whatever she'd been up to before she died. He was convinced she'd been up to something and that it was business related. I didn't think it was a bruised ego. He'd always focused on work first, real life second. I could see it more clearly now in hindsight.

As time ticked on, eyes turned more often to the window. Desmond stopped pretending to pay attention to anything else. Finally, Jane stirred and looked around.

"I'm so sorry, I'd forgotten Mrs. Henderson is off today. Can I get anyone anything? Coffee? Tea?"

"I'll do it," said Sarah. "I'll bring in some drinks, and we can serve ourselves." She seemed relieved to have something to do. I couldn't blame her.

"Would you like some help?" I asked.

"That would be great," she said.

We went to the kitchen. While we pulled together hot and cold beverages and some cookies, Sarah vented.

"Honestly, everyone seems to have lost their minds. That ridiculous woman fell in the lake and drowned, and people are carrying on as though there's an ax murderer lurking in our midst. I'll be glad when the police clear this up. I don't know what's taking so long."

"Autopsy," I said. "Unattended death, or something like that."

"Really? Oh, I forgot, you read all those mysteries. And—oh my God! Danny! And last spring—I'm so sorry, Greer! I'm being insensitive. I wasn't thinking."

In her distress, Sarah bobbled a cup. She made a grab for it, but it hit the floor with a crash. Her shoulders slumped.

"I'm so sorry," she said again.

"It's all right, Sarah. All of the most useful things I know I learned from reading crime fiction. And I've been dealing with the other deaths pretty well. Now, where do I find a broom?"

"I'll get it," Sarah said. "I should probably leave you in charge of the crockery." She rummaged in a closet for a minute and came back with a broom and dustpan. She swept, and sighed, as I arranged cups and saucers. I waited. She had something to get off her chest.

"If you're sure you don't mind talking about this kind of thing . . ." she said, and stopped.

"I don't," I answered. Truth. While I would undoubtedly benefit from some sort of therapy regarding the murders I'd been involved in, I found investigating and plotting revenge therapeutic enough. I didn't want to be talked out of it. I did want to help my friend. Also, I was nosy. Trifecta.

"It's not so much what happened to Brittany that bothers me. I know that sounds terrible," Sarah said.

"Well, you never liked her, and she's put a damper on your wedding weekend," I said. "But I know what you mean. I didn't know her, but I feel like I should feel worse about her death, just because."

"Yes. Exactly. But I resent her for being dead. From the moment she started working for us, she was a problem. Not because she did anything wrong, but because she—I don't know—she threw off the dynamic? But at the same time, it was freeing, in a way. Jeremy left. He was never happy there anyway. My father's focus shifted. I decided it was okay to make a change. But I never trusted her. And now that she's dead, it feels like none of us trust one another. There's some undercurrent. Like everyone's keeping secrets."

"Well, you are," I pointed out.

She flushed. "I know. But the rest of the family's acting so strangely."

"Maybe they're keeping secrets, too, but they have nothing to do with Brittany drowning." Although I'd put money on the fact that some of them did. "I think you should wait and hear what the police have to say and go from there."

"I guess you're right. I'm only sorry if this is bringing up a lot of bad memories."

"I'm all right. Let's bring this in before the tea gets cold."

The group was much as we had left them, though Caro had returned. Barbara and Margaret had gone upstairs. Everyone took something to drink, mostly to have something to do. Finally, Desmond had had enough.

"I'm going down there. I want to know what's going on," he said.

He set down his cup, but his exit was preempted by a knock on the door. The police. The younger, uniformed officer was the one we'd met yesterday. He was accompanied by a casually dressed older man he introduced as the assistant chief, Bill Kent. Kent apologized for keeping us waiting and for the intrusion. He went on to explain what happened in the case of an unexplained death, reassuring everyone that it was all very routine. His associate would check our contact information; he understood it was very late when the body was found. Meanwhile, he had just a couple of questions.

"When was the last time any of you saw Ms. Miles?" he asked.

This was met by silence, some thoughtful frowns, and little bit of nervous shifting. Hard to tell where that was coming from. I decided to play helpful witness.

"I met her for the first time Thursday afternoon, at the tea party," I said. "Sarah introduced us. We talked for a few minutes, then she excused herself. I went outside for some fresh air. I thought I heard her on the phone a little later—I was in the garden, and I think she was on the path that led out to the driveway, but I didn't actually see her. I left a little later. I'm staying at a hotel."

"I think that's the last time I saw her, too, though I was busy with the guests. I may have seen her but not to speak to," Sarah said.

"I saw her after the party," Caro said. "She was walking down the driveway." She turned to me. "It was right before I saw you. I sat in the garden for a while, enjoying the sunshine."

"Thank you, ma'am. Did anyone see else see her?" Kent asked.

"I saw her leave in her car late Thursday night. I'm staying in the boathouse. You can see the driveway and part of the guest cottage," Ian said. "I didn't see her come back."

"She must have come back late," Jeremy added. "I was up sketching, and I saw her walk into the garden. Later I saw lights on in the cottage. Then the lights went off."

Isabelle stirred. "I didn't see Brittany, but I did see you." She looked at Desmond. "It was around midnight."

All eyes turned to Desmond.

"I was out there. I often take a walk around the lake late in the evening. I noticed there were lights on in the cottage, but Brittany's car wasn't there. I thought it was odd but decided she might have gone to meet someone for a drink or something," Desmond said.

"There's something else," Isabelle said. "I didn't see anyone, but I heard something. A splash, and then someone walking up the driveway. I looked outside, but I didn't see anything."

"What time was this?" The younger officer was taking notes.

"I'm sorry, I don't know. Very late, or early morning even. I should have checked. But that house makes a lot of strange noises."

"She's staying next door," Jack clarified. "The house is old and being renovated. It makes all the usual old house noises."

"And you may well have been dreaming," Caro added, "so I wouldn't worry, Isabelle, about not checking the time."

"I see," Kent said. "So the last anyone saw Ms. Miles was late Thursday night or the early hours of Friday?"

There were general sounds of agreement.

"Thank you," Kent said. "Was anyone else here who might have something to add?"

"My wife's sister and her caretaker," Desmond said. "But my sister-in-law is not in good health. I would rather she weren't disturbed."

"I understand. What's her name?"

"Barbara Granville," Jane said. It was the first time she'd spoken since giving her own name. "I can certainly check with her physician and see if it's possible for you to speak with her, if it's absolutely necessary."

Jane's delivery was polite, but there was old money in her tone. Whoever wanted to speak to Barbara would have to go through Jane and a number of professionals on the Whitaker payroll. The police might have their way in the end, but it wouldn't be easy.

Kent nodded. "I appreciate that, ma'am. I'm hoping it won't be necessary. I'll know more once the medical examiner is done."

"Well, how long will that be?" Desmond said. "I should think you'd know something by now." His tone was belligerent. Concern for his family? Or a more personal concern for Brittany?

"We know that Ms. Miles appears to have hit her head and drowned. We don't know where or when or how. That's what we're trying to find out. I'll be in touch. Thank you all for your help."

And with that, they left.

There was a brief silence. Then Desmond began sputtering. Jane shushed him and said, "I'm sure this was an unfortunate accident and everything will be cleared up. Now, tell me about the breakfast, Sarah."

Sarah gave me a look and moved over to sit with her mother, who seemed more herself than she had in days. Jack joined them.

Desmond muttered something about his office and disappeared upstairs. Ian came over to me.

"How about an early dinner?" he said. "I've got a couple work-related things to do this afternoon. I think, after this, we could both use a chance to unwind. Say around five?"

"Sure," I said. "I have a couple of things to take care of myself. I'll meet you at the boathouse."

Dinner arranged, Ian left. I joined Isabelle, who was cleaning up coffee cups. Sarah mouthed a "thank you" from across the room. Isabelle invited me over for another visit. I accepted but told her I needed about half an hour. The key to the cottage felt heavy in my pocket. I wanted to put it back without worrying that the police would show up asking awkward questions. Once we were done tidying up, I waved goodbye to Sarah and left through the side door. I wanted to get to the cottage without attracting any notice and decided the best way to do that was through the garden.

I went along the house until I reached the beginning of the hedge. There was a narrow path that led past Jane's office and ended at stone steps that led down through some shrubbery. I followed the path, went down the steps, turned a corner, and found myself at the edge of the clearing with the reflecting pool. Not exactly where I thought I'd end up, but close enough.

I walked toward the pool. The day had turned overcast, but there was no breeze. The surface of the water was smooth and dark. It seemed more reflective than usual in the odd half light. I could see the house and trees behind me clearly on the surface, their outlines sharp. I walked around to the other side. Something was niggling at my memory, something I'd noticed in the pool the day of the tea. I leaned forward, my face appearing in the water below. Not as clear as an actual mirror, but not as distorted as what I'd seen in the lake. I was convinced now that had been Brittany, dead and caught below the surface of the cove, her body disturbed by the action of the oars.

That wasn't what was pinging in my subconscious though. I leaned back, studying the pool, hoping something would jog my memory. With the toe of my shoe, I pushed at some of the beach stones that rimmed the water, filling in a couple of gaps. But no matter how much I stared and fidgeted, nothing came to me. Nothing was visible beneath the still surface, nothing rose up out of my memory. *Probably not important,* I thought. *Just some oddity.* I stepped back and looked up at the house one more time.

There was movement in one of the windows. I took another step back. A curtain was pulled aside. Caro's face appeared, then Barbara's right next to her. I smiled and waved. They waved back. I turned and ambled down the path, around a corner and out of sight. Nothing to see here, folks, just Greer taking a walk. I'd have to be more alert if I was going to sneak around replacing keys I shouldn't have to places I shouldn't have been.

I made it through the rest of the garden without running into anyone. The lawn was empty. I fought the urge to sprint and walked at a leisurely pace. I looked around before crossing the driveway, saw no one, and headed in the direction of the Granville house. Once off the driveway, I veered toward the door of the cottage. I pretended to study it, in case anyone was watching, then walked toward the stoop. I fought the urge to look around to see if anyone could see me. If I was just engaging in idle nosiness, I wouldn't care who saw me. If I was up to no good, I would. I bent down, found the correct rock, and lifted it. I pulled my sleeve down over my hand, wiped the key clean on my jeans, and dropped it into its hidey hole. I'd replaced the rock and stood, pleased with my work, when the front door of the cottage opened.

Ian.

It took a second for him to notice me, which gave me enough time to decide how to play it.

"Whatcha doing?" I said.

"Looking for something," he said. "What are you doing?"

Nice recovery. The best defense is a good offense.

"Just looking around. Wondering if the place had crime scene tape up or anything."

He grimaced at the mention of crime scene tape. Maybe that hadn't occurred to him.

"Apparently not," he said.

"Hmm," I said. "Surprised it was unlocked though. Maybe we should tell someone."

Ian looked skyward and made another face. Then he looked back at me. I stood my ground, doing my best to look both innocent and helpful. A few seconds passed in silence. Finally, he spoke.

"I have keys," he said.

"How convenient."

"They're Jeremy's."

"Nice of him to lend them to you. Did you tell him what you were looking for?"

More silence.

"Oh, I see," I said. "He doesn't actually know you borrowed them, does he?"

"Not exactly."

If Ian Cameron thought he was going to stonewall me, he was nuts. I wanted to know what he was up to. I was also enjoying myself.

"So you'd better get them back as quick as you can. Why don't you tell me what you're looking for and I can help." I smiled. I really wanted to help. I'm nice like that.

Ian rolled his eyes, then smiled back at me. "Okay, Greer," he said. "I'm looking for her computer. She always traveled with her laptop."

"Ah, I see," I said. "So no screen lock? Trusting."

"I don't know," he said. "But I figured it was worth a try."

"Well, I'm guessing you didn't find anything. I saw Desmond leave here with a laptop case last night. I was looking for Caro's cane." I wasn't going to tell him I was snooping around in the cottage until he told me why he wanted to snoop around in the laptop.

Ian glanced up toward the Whitaker house.

"Pretty sure he's in his office. Along with what you're looking for," I said.

"Probably so, since there's no sign of any electronics in here," Ian said.

"I think we should put our heads together later. You can tell me what you're looking for, and I can tell you what I've found out." Which was not much, but he didn't need to know that. "Meanwhile, you better get those keys back. Unless you need to break into somewhere else?"

"Not this afternoon. You're right, we should figure some things out over dinner. I don't like the looks of some of this. I need to make some calls, though."

"Deal," I said. "See you later."

We went in opposite directions. Dinner would be interesting. It sounded like Ian was finally thinking of Brittany's death as more than an accident.

Chapter Thirteen

I had a pleasant and uneventful visit with the Petersons. There were only two items of note in our conversation. The first was an offhand comment from Mrs. Peterson while we were rehashing the visit from the police.

"I'm not surprised something woke you, Isabelle. This house does make some odd sounds. I could have sworn I heard footsteps last night," Isabelle's mother said.

"Probably the wood contracting. It got chilly. Or the plumbing. In our house, it's always the plumbing. More knocks and raps than a Victorian séance," Mr. Peterson replied, and then returned to the volume of Conan Doyle he had found in the library.

"Perhaps," Mrs. Peterson replied, sounding unconvinced.

The other interesting tidbit came about when we were discussing Jack and Sarah's post-honeymoon plans. The Petersons were aware of the opportunity in Europe, but not that it was decided. Isabelle gave me a look, suggesting she knew as well, but we both kept it to ourselves. Regardless, Isabelle's parents thought it time that she move on, too.

"Now I know you enjoy Boston, and your brother values your help, but it's time you finished your doctorate. Have you gotten back in touch with that woman in Albany? Dr. Arsenault, isn't it?" Mr. Peterson said.

Isabelle sighed. "I don't think I'm suited to academia, Dad. Or at least, not to the politics."

"I know it's tedious, muffin, but if you can master calculus at ten you can learn to navigate departmental infighting. You just need a mentor."

"And you know people in the area now. You'd have friends nearby," Mrs. Peterson added. She smiled at me, but I saw her glance in the direction of the boathouse. Isabelle's budding relationship with Jeremy had not gone unnoticed.

"I'll get in touch. Maybe I can drive down and see her before I come home."

The conversation moved on to other things. Isabelle and I decided to forgo more exploration on the third floor. The cloudy day made it too dark in rooms with no electricity. Isabelle's mother joined us in rooting around in the library. She commented on the dearth of poetry in the collection but eventually found a couple of shelves in a corner, one of which held a first edition Sylvia Plath. I was about to say good-bye and go meet Ian when my phone rang.

"Greer darling, it's Caro. I got your number from Sarah, I hope you don't mind. Listen, I've just got to get out of here for a while. Let's have dinner. Soonish. We can go right over to that place on the water, the one near the inn."

"Oh, well, I'd planned to have dinner with Ian—"

"Perfect! Nothing like having a handsome man to squire you around, is there? I'd love to treat you both. What time?"

I told her fifteen minutes. I buzzed Ian and explained. Within half an hour we were seated and studying our menus, drinks on the way. Caro sat back in her chair, dinner decision made.

"I'm so glad you two were willing to indulge an old lady. I couldn't stay in that house another minute," she said.

"Tense?" I asked.

"Oh yes," Caro said. "It's all the uncertainty. At least the whole wedding rigamarole is over. Don't get me wrong—I'm happy for Sarah and Jack, and I'm sure they'll be happy together. I'm all for a party, even one that goes on for several days, but there's no need to get married to have one."

She paused while our drinks were served. We ordered, and once our waiter was gone, she started again.

"Jane is exhausted. Everything according to plan, you know how she is, and this is all too much. Desmond is distracted and upset—I don't know what this Brittany did in the company, but I'm sure her death will cause problems. The kids are doing all right, both of them stepping up. Sarah's quite calm, all things considered, and Jeremy is handling quite a few things. He's wonderful with Barbara."

"Yes, I've seen that," I said, as Caro buttered a roll. "And I've spoken to Barbara a few times. But Caro, if you don't mind my asking . . ."

"What's wrong with her?" Caro said.

"Well, yes. I mean, sometimes she seems fine, and other times, it's as though . . ." I hesitated, trying to find the right phrase.

"She's not all there?" Caro asked. "You don't need to be delicate with me, Greer."

"I know, it's just that I wouldn't put it that way. It's not that she's not *all* there, it's more that she's not *always* there. She seems to fade in and out, if you know what I mean. I heard there was some sort of accident—Sarah mentioned it once. But I don't ever remember her, or Jeremy, talking much about Barbara at all. Of course, it's none of my business."

Caro waved this off. "No, no, it's all right," she said. "You and Sarah have been friends for a long time. You're both close to the family at this point," she added, giving a nod to Ian. "With everything that's going on, you should know the story. Or as much of it as I know at least. You have to remember, I was away quite a bit." She sighed. "I don't think I could have done anything even if I had been here. We were all so young." She paused. "I think this calls for another round."

She got the waiter's attention and ordered. That taken care of, she turned back to us.

"Where to begin?" she asked. "What do the two of you know about the late sixties, early seventies?"

"Sex, drugs, and rock 'n' roll," Ian said.

"In a nutshell, yes." Caro took a sip of her drink. "But there was so much going on. So much change. It felt like a revolution, and in a way, it was. A necessary one, in my opinion. We grew up thinking our lives were going to be a certain way, and then all that changed. It was as if from one day to the next, we didn't know who we were anymore. No, that's not right. We didn't know who we were supposed to be, and who we were supposed to be changed depending on who we were with. Depending on our age, really, or their background. And there we were, trying to figure it out."

"I take it some of you found it easier than others?" I said.

"Some were happy with the status quo. Some wanted to upend it, especially with the war going on. Some of us wanted adventure, and freedom. We'd just graduated high school and were ready to take on the world. Barbara was always a rule breaker. She liked to push the envelope. We all tested, and broke, boundaries. Barbara blasted right through them. She was very bright, smarter than I was, but her judgment sometimes . . ."

Caro shook her head.

"I think initially everyone thought it was drug use. Everyone over the age of thirty thought we were all high all the time. But we were just at that age, and there was so much energy in the air."

Ian and I exchanged a glance. Caro saw us and smiled.

"All right, there may have been some mind-altering substances involved. But our crowd wasn't that wild. There were a few, of course. Barbara was far from the worst. We all smoked weed—hookahs were popular with a few of the boys. Pretentious twits to this day, I'm sure. Anyway, acid was available, and we all tried it. Barbara liked it more than I did, but she was far from a heavy user. Of anything. No, in retrospect I think it was a mental health issue, and all the risk-taking stemmed from that."

"What kind of mental health issue?" I asked.

"Today they'd probably diagnose bipolar disorder, though there could have been more going on. Barbara would swing from quiet and withdrawn to wild. She was always happiest with her books and her music, but sometimes she'd disappear into herself. Other days, it was party time. She was always a night owl—still is, but back then she wouldn't sleep for days, it seemed. The only person who could reach her when she swung to an extreme was Jane. She was always very protective of Jane. But Jane was still a child, not quite twelve that summer."

Our food arrived, and we were quiet as plates were handed around. Once the waiter had gone, Caro continued the story.

"It was near the end of the summer. August. Everyone was excited about going away to school. Or in my case, just going away. I'd already started modeling, and I was off to the big city."

"I've seen your picture. Jeremy has one," I said. "Loved the hot pants." Ian nodded in agreement.

"Yes, well, I was quite something, wasn't I?" Caro said, laughing.

"You still are," Ian said, raising his glass to her.

"Aren't you delightful!" Caro said. "Those really were the days. For me at least. Not so much for Barbara."

"She was supposed to go to Vassar, wasn't she? That's what she told us," I said.

"That's right. She was going to study literature. Poetry was her thing. She was always scribbling in a journal. I asked her once if it was a diary. She said no, it was more. She showed me a few pages— her thoughts, some poems she had written, or was working on, quotations, a few sketches. Though some of the drawings were Jane's. She would tell Jane what a poem was about, and Jane would draw a picture. Sometimes there were slips of paper stuck in, random things Jane had drawn and given to her. It was charming. I said when she was a famous poet, some eager graduate student would be using her journals to write a thesis. She said she'd probably be famous only if she died young."

"Sylvia Plath," I said. "There were a few of her books in the library at the Granville house."

"Yes, Barbara was a fan. I always found her work a bit morbid, but Barbara thought she was a genius. Just don't get her started on the husband."

Caro stopped again. She stared out the window, down the lake in the direction of the Granville and Whitaker homes. I sensed we were getting to the hard part of the story. I waited a minute, then prompted her.

"So it was August, and everyone was excited," I said.

"Middle of August, a couple weeks before Labor Day. It had been a quiet stretch—hot, lazy days, people on vacation, picnics. Then the weather turned, like someone flipped a switch. Cooler nights, not so muggy. You could feel the shift in the atmosphere, everyone knew the end was coming, the idyllic days over. Time for back-to-school shopping, getting back to business, closing up the house."

Another pause. I looked over at Ian, who had been silent. He was watching Caro, who was fiddling with her glass. I shifted in my seat and, when he looked over, gave a little nod. He leaned toward her.

"There was a party?" he said.

"The Granvilles were away overnight," she said. "I don't remember where. Desmond's father had gone back to the city. Some meeting. And of course his mother was always three sheets to the wind. I was staying with the Whitakers. We didn't live far, but I didn't have a car, so Barbara came and got me that morning. We were happy, talking about our plans. Barbara was very chatty. We spent the day hanging out, swimming. Janie and Des were around in the morning, then disappeared off to a friend's house. There was a boy, a young man really, Phillip. He was interested in Barbara, had been for a while, but he was a few years older. Anyway, he came by in the afternoon and stayed. She liked him well enough, but she had her own plans. Being a doctor's wife in White Plains wasn't one of them, and Phillip was all set for med school. A real golden boy, that one, literally and figuratively, although I think he had a wild streak. Kept it well under wraps, but he was far from being the straight arrow people—adults—thought he was. I always suspected that some of the harder drugs came from him, but Barbara never said.

"People started to drift in after supper. The younger kids went to bed, and Eleanor was passed out in the Whitaker house. We were all at Barbara's, on the porch and in the music room. It was all the usual stuff—music, snacks, joints, a couple of bottles being passed around. Bunch of prep school kids playing at being hippies, really. God, how I've always hated the smell of patchouli! Someone was playing the guitar on the porch. Inside, a few kids messing around with a Ouija board. Barbara and Phillip were in there. Barbara had this lava lamp, a red lava lamp. That was the only light they had on. She said she'd read that a red lamp was more inviting to spirits. I was in the kitchen, talking to some people, drinking rum and coke. Things were pretty mellow. By this point, some of the kids were passed out. Others had gone down to the lake. It was just Barbara and Phillip and one other girl around the Ouija board. The girl's boyfriend was out cold on the couch. Barbara went up to check on Jane, and that's when all hell broke loose."

Caro took a hefty swallow of her drink. Ian and I stayed quiet. She was painting a vivid picture. It helped that I'd been in the Granville house. The parts that weren't renovated yet had to be much the same as they were that summer. The lava lamp I'd seen for myself as well. And I couldn't fault Caro on the patchouli.

"It was the girl who screamed," Caro continued. "I'm not sure what happened, but we ran into the music room and Phillip had her by the throat. Someone knocked him down, and he started raving about the spirits in the lamp trying to kill him. They were taking over people's bodies, he said, so he had to stop them. Barbara came running downstairs. She told most of us to get out, and then she just talked to him. She told him she controlled the lamp and would make them go away. She turned it off, and he did seem to calm down, but then he started saying his heart was going to fly out of his chest. None of us had seen a bad trip before. That's what it was, of course. We thought Phillip might have a heart attack. Someone suggested an ambulance, but that was shot down. Cops. People started to bolt. A few stayed. Barbara seemed calm. Unnaturally calm. She was like that—always good in a crisis. She said she would take him to the hospital. I offered to go, and so did one of the other boys, but she had a two-seater. She said no, she could handle him. She asked me to look after Jane. We got Phillip into the car—he was off in another world, still talking about spirits, but manageable. They left, and the rest of us started getting rid of the evidence. Those of us that were conscious, that is.

"I forgot about Janie at first. Once things were cleaned up and under control, I went to check on her. She wasn't in her bed or anywhere in her room. I was panicking, standing there in the hall-way. Then I heard crying. I followed the sound into Barbara's room. I couldn't see anyone at first, but then I found her."

"Hiding behind the mirror," I said, picturing the room and the small space in the corner.

Caro and Ian both looked surprised.

"I've seen it. It's the perfect hiding spot for a little girl. Jane's always been petite, hasn't she?"

"She has. She looked much younger than her age, and she was so tiny," Caro said. "Barbara was the same—she always made me feel like a giraffe. But strong. Both of them. The Granvilles have always been swimmers. The grandmother set some sort of record. Anyway, I found Janie and made her wash her face and take a couple of aspirin, then I put her back to bed. I went downstairs. The only people left were the boy I'd been talking to in the kitchen and the other couple that had been in the music room. The girl had bruises on her neck where Phil had grabbed her but seemed all right otherwise. We'd all sobered up by then. They were going to wait with me for Barbara to come back. We thought everything was okay. Then the police showed up."

"The accident," I said.

"How far gone was she when they left?" Ian asked. "Didn't anyone realize that she was too drunk, or stoned, to drive?"

"For God's sake, it was fifty years ago. No one who could stand up was too drunk to drive. None of us gave it a thought. But honestly, she seemed fine. I'm not convinced she'd had that much to drink, or used anything, for that matter. Though later she did say she'd dropped a little acid. I got the impression that summer that she used LSD in small doses pretty often. She said it helped her find her muse, or something like that."

"Microdosing," Ian said. "I've known people who swear by it. Enhances creativity and focus."

"You're kidding me," I said to him. "This is a thing with techie types? What, it improves their gaming scores?"

Ian looked annoyed. "There are many creative people in tech. And I didn't get half a dozen patents sitting around playing video games. Do you think all those froufrou fashion types you worked with are just dreaming things up sober? Not from what I see."

"Drugs are old news in fashion," I said. "And seriously— 'froufrou'?"

Ian was about to respond when Caro interrupted.

"Well, whatever you call it, Barbara was doing it at seventeen. It's not a recent invention. And I think she'd been doing it that day, or all week. All summer. I don't know."

"What happened when the police came?" I asked. "What did they say?"

"There was a terrific crash. The car was totaled. Off the road and into woods. Phillip was thrown from the car and killed. Went straight into some rocks. Barbara was hurt, but she crawled out and headed up to the road. She managed to flag someone down. I'm not clear on the details. They went to the nearest house and called an ambulance, but it was too late of course. Phil must have been dead on impact. Barbara had a head wound and a lot of bruises and cuts. They took her to the hospital. The police came to the house to find her parents. Instead, they found us and the remains of a party."

Ian let out a low whistle. "What a mess," he said.

I agreed.

"It gets worse," Caro said, her tone grim.

"Did they arrest anyone?" Ian asked.

"No, no. The four of us were all old enough to drink, and we'd gotten rid of anything else. Barbara was seventeen—her birthday was a few weeks later. They asked us some questions, and we told them very little. One officer was very interested in the bruises on that girl's neck—what was her name? Juliet? We told them it was Phillip, that we didn't know what had come over him, but that he'd had an awful lot to drink, and that once he'd calmed down, Barbara decided to take him to the emergency room. They bought it to a point, though they had to know there was more than rum involved. I called my parents, who tracked down the Granvilles, and I stayed with Jane."

"And Barbara?" I asked.

"She came home the next day. It was the last time I saw her before I left. She was still dazed. She kept saying, 'I was only trying to help,' over and over again. Jane wouldn't leave her side. Barbara tuned in enough to thank me for staying with Jane. I told her I was happy to, that I'd always look after Jane. Then Janie piped up with 'And Desmond, too.' It was very sweet. I promised. I sat with them a little longer, and then I went home. Two days later, I left for the city. I didn't know what had happened until the next week, when I got a frantic call from Des."

"Desmond? How old was he?" I asked.

"Fourteen that fall," Caro said. "That kid didn't have much of a childhood. I think he only had fun when he was with us. My parents behaved like adults, so he didn't have to. He could always call them, and if I wasn't going to be around, I gave him the number where I'd be. It made him feel better. Took him a while to reach me that day. Puts my love-hate relationship with cell phones into perspective."

That brought the stray cell phone in my bag to mind. I'd have to show Ian and Caro. Maybe they'd recognize it. But right now I wanted to hear the rest of the story. Caro continued.

"He didn't make much sense at first. He told me that Barbara was back in the hospital and that no one could find Janie. He said people were looking everywhere. They'd asked him about all the places they went and checked with other kids. No one had seen her since that morning. He'd overheard someone say they were going to call the police and look in the lake."

"Oh my God, he thought she'd drowned?" I said.

Caro shook her head. "I don't think he believed that. He thought she'd run away, or gotten hurt. But he was frightened and getting desperate. It was dark. His parents wouldn't let him leave the house. He said he tried to call my mom and dad, but they weren't home. He thought if he looked, and she was hiding, she'd come out. He had a point. I told him to stay by the phone, and I'd see what I could do. I called all my parents' friends until I found them. They had no idea what was going on, but they left for the Whitakers right away. I didn't remember finding Jane in Barbara's room until I was back on the phone with Desmond. I told him to tell my mother as soon as she got there. But he didn't want to wait. He sneaked out somehow, and when my parents arrived, both kids were gone."

"Panic time," Ian said.

"Yes, but my mother kept her head. She called me, and I told her what I'd told Desmond. She went right over and found the two of them, sitting on the floor of Barbara's room. Jane didn't understand what had happened to Barbara. Apparently she'd never come all the way back from the night of the accident. So her mother told her that Barbara was sick and had done something bad. That someone had died and Barbara had been hurt and couldn't get well unless she went away for a while. That Jane was a good girl, and healthy, and that if she always behaved, nothing bad would ever happen to her."

"Are you serious?" I asked. "She told her that? That's—"

"A load of shit, I know," Caro said. "Elise Granville was never great with kids. Very distant and appearance conscious. My mother was there but didn't feel she could say anything."

"But what actually happened?" Ian asked.

"The boy's parents blamed Barbara for everything. Their darling boy could do no wrong. Bright future lost. You get the picture. They were going to press charges. There were doctors and lawyers involved. I think the police report about Juliet's bruised neck came into it in Barbara's favor. So they made an agreement."

"They institutionalized her," I said.

"Yes, they did. They wanted to keep her out of jail and avoid scandal. Truly, I think she needed some kind of psychiatric help, but I don't think she needed to be locked up. Even if it was a very discreet, very upscale kind of mental hospital. I didn't learn about all of that until sometime later. I was back at my parents' at Christmas. At the time, I thought it had to do with the head injury. I really didn't know. I felt terrible. Still do."

"I doubt there's anything you could have done," Ian said.

I agreed, then asked, "So she never got better?"

"She did, and then she'd get worse. She was in and out of the place for a while. I don't know if it was the drugs she used when she could get her hands on them or the drugs they gave her in the hospital. Probably both. There was just no telling what you'd get with her from one day to the next. Once Jane was grown and her parents died, she took charge and things got better. Barbara lives in her own home with twenty-four-hour care now. She has a very good doctor. She'd made such progress, and now this."

"She seems to be holding up fairly well," I said.

"Oh, yes, I guess you're right. Well, let's hope it lasts. Now, tell me, what do you think happened to that poor girl? Did she just stumble and fall in?" Caro asked.

We discussed it for a while. I pointed out that Brittany had been wearing very high heels.

"Maybe she caught one in the dock and hit her head as she tumbled in?"

"Yes, those shoes were a bit much, especially for an afternoon event," Caro said. "The only time I ever tried to walk in something that high they were platforms, and I still nearly broke my neck. Couldn't believe Elton John could do it and I couldn't."

"She was self-conscious about her height," Ian said. "She liked to project a certain image and thought she looked more authoritative in higher heels. I asked her once. I was teasing her, but she took that kind of thing very seriously. Appearance was important to her, though I never got the feeling she was vain. It's hard to explain."

We discussed the drowning for a little longer. Neither Ian nor I mentioned Desmond or the missing laptop. Ian did bring up the business deal that had apparently fallen through. Caro hadn't heard anything about it.

"I can't see Jane going for any kind of merger, never mind a sale," Caro said.

"Why would she care?" Ian asked. "She's never been involved in the company, has she?"

"Not in the day-to-day, but she owns a considerable portion of it."

"I thought it was Desmond's family business. Didn't his father or grandfather found it?"

"Mmhmm," Caro said as she sipped her coffee. "But Jane provided the capital to expand it. The Granville family has had money since the year one. Jane is pretty shrewd financially and always able to spot a trend. Takes after her father. She put a lot into the business and takes pride in what they've built."

"Maybe that's what happened," Ian said. "Desmond talked to Jane about a merger, and Jane didn't go for it."

"Maybe," Caro said, and then yawned. "Well, my darlings, I'm afraid you've worn me out. It's time for me to go home and to bed. I appreciate you inviting me along."

"Our pleasure," said Ian.

"And thank you for sharing Barbara's story," I said. "A lot of things make sense now."

"It was good to talk about it. I don't think any of us ever really have. I wanted you to understand. I just hope Sarah and Jeremy do. It's time to make sure they know what happened as well."

We were back in the car before I remembered the phone. I was in the back seat and leaned forward to show them when we got to the inn. Neither one had seen it before.

"All right. It must belong to a guest."

"Or even one of the workmen," Caro said. "They've been all over the place."

"I'll let Sarah know tomorrow. Spa time in the morning. I'll see you both in the afternoon," I said.

Barbara's story was a sad one, I thought as I got ready for bed. She'd had a softer landing than many, cushioned by wealth and a protective family. She'd never lived the independent life she wanted. Though with the mental health issues, that might never have come to pass either. Brittany's life was over. She was thirty, tops. She had carefully constructed her life, and I wasn't convinced the end of it was an accident.

I crawled under the covers and turned to "The Mistletoe Murder" by P. D. James. After a tense and depressing day, I needed a little Christmas. A nice holiday homicide was just the ticket.

Chapter Fourteen

My spa day was mostly uneventful, which at this point qualified as relaxing. My massage therapist informed me I stored all my
stress in my shoulders. This was not news to me, but she did show
me some stretches she said would help. Then she sent me off to my
facial. Here, my puffy eyes were discussed, with the advice that I
abstain from alcohol and salty foods for a while. This didn't stop
me from having a glass of wine with my spa lunch, but I vowed to
do better once home. After some reflexology, a soak in the hot tub,
and a shower, I felt like a new woman.

Any hope that my muscles would remain unknotted was
dashed when I turned on my cell phone. There were a few missed
calls and a series of text messages. They'd all come in close to the
same time, but one was a little earlier. Isabelle had said, "Please call
when you're done at the spa. Something strange happened."

The next was from Sarah. "More bad news. Please come right
over."

And Ian, short and to the point—"Call me"—followed by
another, "Please." Nice.

Whatever was going on, I wanted to hear it in person, not get
it via text message or multiple phone calls. I got my bag and headed
over to Sarah's, where I found quite a crowd. There was a police

cruiser and the unmarked car in front of the house. I went to the side door, figuring I could let myself in the usual way. I was reaching for the handle when I heard voices in the garden. I walked along the hedge until I got to the break. Not sure where the sound was coming from, I stayed on the driveway side, where I was sure I couldn't be seen. I could hear men talking, but no voices I recognized. I couldn't make out much of what they were saying either, which was irritating. I did catch the words "get into the lake" and "unconscious." Those were a little louder and sounded like questions. That was about it, so I gave up and went inside.

The whole family, plus Isabelle and Ian, were gathered once again. No sign of the Petersons. Barbara, Margaret, and Caro were sitting in the living room, while everyone else was in the sunroom. It was late afternoon, but everyone had a drink in hand. Mindful of my puffy eyes and wanting a clear head, I decided to hold off until I knew what was going on. Sarah started talking as soon as I walked in.

"Greer, you'll never believe this. The police are back—they've finished the autopsy and they're saying that Brittany drowned, but not in the lake. The think the reflecting pool, based on water quality or something. They're taking samples."

"I think this whole damn thing is ridiculous," Desmond said. "They don't know what they're talking about. There's a mistake somewhere."

"Of course there is, Daddy. Here, let me get you another drink," Sarah said. "Do you want anything, Greer?"

She gave me a pointed look.

"I'll come with you," I said, and followed her to the bar in the next room.

"If she drowned in the pool, what was she doing in the lake?" I whispered to Sarah as she plopped some ice cubes into her father's glass.

"Well, that's the question, isn't it?" she said. She finished making a very watered-down drink. "I mean, how did she get there? Did someone find her and tote her body down to the lake?"

"Sarah," I said, "I think you have to consider that someone killed her and then decided to get rid of the body."

Sarah made a face. "But who would do such a thing?" she asked. "And who could have been roaming around here in the middle of the night?"

Any one of your family members or guests, I thought, *but most likely your father*. My face must have given me away.

"What aren't you telling me?" she asked.

At that point there was a knock on the door. I grabbed a bottle of sparkling water and a glass, and Sarah and I went back to the sunroom. The same two officers we'd met previously were back. I knew there had to have been more out in the garden, so I drifted over to the window to see what I could see. It put me a little behind and to the side of everyone else. Caro, Barbara, and Margaret all came in and stood in the opening between the two rooms. The police stood facing the rest of us. They were not invited to sit. Desmond went on the offensive.

"I'd like to know what all of this is about," he said. "Because I'm not hearing anything that makes any kind of sense. My daughter's wedding has been disrupted, our family home overrun, and now you're saying that a guest who was found in the lake actually drowned somewhere else."

There was a bit of the lord of the manor about his delivery. In fact, the whole scene was very *Masterpiece Theatre*, in an updated, outdoorsy kind of way. I didn't detect any fear in his voice, just genuine anger and confusion. Interesting.

The assistant chief, Bill Kent, I recalled, gave us an update. Based on evidence from the postmortem, Brittany had struck her head and drowned. Though she was found in the lake, there was water in her lungs that came from another source. The reflecting pool was being tested.

"But this is absurd," Jane said. "No one would move her. No, she must have hit her head and taken in some water, and then gotten up and gone back to the cottage. There's some kind of brain injury where people do that. Remember that skier? You knew him." She turned to Jeremy. "He ran into a tree, picked himself up, finished the run, and dropped dead hours later in the bar. No," she said, "it was an accident. An accident."

"Of course it was, Janie," Barbara said. She came and perched on the arm of Jane's chair. "We all understand it was an accident." Barbara patted her sister's shoulder. Jane looked surprised, but then reached up and took her sister's hand. Caro had said Barbara was always protective of Jane. Even after years of Jane being in charge, it looked like she still was.

"I'm afraid that's not possible, given the amount of water in her lungs, Mrs. Whitaker. She definitely drowned but was put in the lake after she died," Kent said. "We're going to have to take a closer look at the guest cottage and grounds. We'll also want to talk to you individually to review the information you've given us. We'll try not to be too disruptive."

"I don't see what we can tell you that you don't already know," Sarah said. "Brittany had been here less than a day. I'm sure this has nothing to do with us."

"Actually, Ms. Whitaker, she had been in the area for a few days. We believe she was staying at the Mirror Lake Inn. It would be helpful if any of you could tell us what she doing, or who she might have been seeing, while she was here."

I was looking at Desmond Whitaker from behind and saw his shoulders tense. Sarah became more indignant.

"What makes you think that?" she said. "I find it hard to believe. Wasn't she meeting with a client in the city?" She directed this to her father. He shrugged.

"There were some mints and a bottle of hand lotion in the guest cottage with the inn's logo, ma'am," the other officer said. "It looked like she might have been there a few days."

Sarah made a noise of disgust. "Why would she take them? It's not like she couldn't buy her own. We certainly paid her enough."

I rolled my eyes and sighed before I could stop myself. Good thing no one could see me. Sarah was one of the most thoughtful, supportive friends I'd ever had, but the fact that she'd never met a problem she couldn't solve by throwing money at it sometimes made her oblivious. The price of hand cream or really nice chocolates never registered with her. Or the price of gas, I thought, remembering Ian's comment. Which told me something about Brittany and her background. That could be important.

I looked up to find Kent watching me. He quirked an eyebrow and then turned his attention back to the group. The officer asked for keys to the guest cottage. Desmond went to get them. He also wanted to know if any us planned to leave the area. The police couldn't keep any of us at this point, but I didn't want to look like I was bolting. I also didn't want to leave in the midst of all of this but wasn't sure what my options were. There was something niggling at me about that reflecting pool. I wanted to take a look and see if it came back to me. I hadn't seen anyone coming or going while at the window—the garden was well designed for privacy. Which was irritating while I was spying on the police but would be helpful while I was snooping.

I waited until Kent and his officer had left. While everyone else was breaking into groups and putting their heads together, I slipped out onto the terrace and down the steps. I walked slowly along the path, listening for voices, but heard nothing. The clearing was empty when I entered it. There was some flattened grass, and a few twigs had broken off the surrounding shrubbery, but other than that it was as serene as always.

I sat on the bench for a moment, then stood and walked closer to the edge. The pool reflected the trees behind me and the top floor of the Whitaker house. The air was still, and so was the surface. Today it truly was a *miroir d'eau*, a water mirror. It showed me nothing I couldn't see with my own eyes, though backwards, I thought as I glanced up at the house. I walked around to the other side. I had done this same thing on Thursday. What was it that was bothering me? I looked up again. From this side, you could see the windows of the third floor above the trees. Different angle. I looked down at the water again, studying the surface and the rim of the pool. Everything looked the same, but I still felt something was off.

"Ms. Hogan, isn't it?"

I gasped and stepped back, blinking as I looked up. Bill Kent was standing at the edge of the path.

"I'm sorry," he said. "I didn't mean to startle you. It is Ms. Hogan?"

"Yes," I said. I waited. I had learned years ago that babbling to police officers at murder scenes was unwise. I held his gaze and threw in an inquisitive head tilt. He looked back for a minute, then smiled. He scratched the bridge of his nose with his ballpoint pen.

Cork O'Connor, I thought, *the Adirondack model*. O'Connor was another of my favorite fictional detectives, a red-headed mid-western version.

"Lost in thought, were you?" he asked.

He stood there, looking pleasant and unthreatening. Also solid and unmoving. He wasn't going to go away and leave me with my thoughts. Well, maybe I could get some information.

"I was wondering where her car was," I said. "She drove off in it. Someone saw her. And there's a pool at the inn, at all the hotels, I'd think. Could she have drowned in one of those? You should be able to tell, right? I confess I'm more into Agatha Christie than those forensics shows."

"Good questions. We're looking into all of that. Now, do you have a few minutes?" Kent asked.

"Sure," I said.

He flipped through his notebook.

"How long have you known the Whitakers?" he asked, still turning pages. The tone was casual, but I had the feeling the absent-minded search through his notes was for show.

"I shared an office with Sarah for a couple of years at our first job, right after college. I met her family around that time. So, nearly twenty years."

"And Ms. Miles?"

"I met her Thursday, briefly."

"First time? Never seen her at another event with the Whitaker family?"

"No. I don't go to any of their business functions. I don't live in the city anymore. And I hadn't seen Sarah's parents in a couple of years until this weekend." Except for that brief glance of Desmond Wednesday night, but I wasn't going to share that. I could throw Kent a bone though.

"Although . . ." I started, then paused. "On Wednesday night, I saw someone who looked like Brittany in the lobby at the inn. She was with a man, no one I knew. I thought I recognized her when I met her Thursday, but when I mentioned it she said she'd only just arrived that morning. So I decided I was mistaken. But based on what you said, maybe not."

"Can you describe this man?" he asked.

I gave him the description and couldn't resist adding, "and a general air of being insufferable," which made him smile.

"Duly noted," Kent said. He asked me a few more questions, when I had arrived, where I was staying, and wound up with "Is there anything else you think I should know?"

I smiled at him. I'd no idea if he had looked into anyone's background, but I was about to find out.

"My late husband was also friendly with several of the guests. He was murdered over three years ago. A friend of mine in Raven Hill, where I live now, was murdered last spring. I didn't kill either one of them, but you'll probably want to check up on me anyway. Would you like the names of the detectives involved?"

His eyebrows went up. Either he hadn't known, or he was surprised by my helpful and forthcoming attitude.

"Yes, please," he said. He flipped open the notebook again and wrote down the names I rattled off.

"Thank you," he said.

"Anytime," I responded. "If there's nothing else?"

"Not at the moment," he said. "If I need you, I'll find you." He waved me off.

I went up the path. Right before the bend, I looked back. Kent was standing at the edge of the reflecting pool, staring in. I turned and kept going.

Chapter Fifteen

When I got back to the house, Sarah, Jack, and Isabelle were huddled in the sunroom, deep in conversation.

"Oh, good, you're back," Sarah said when she saw me.

"Just needed some fresh air," I said. "Where is everyone?"

"Barbara and Caro are upstairs. Margaret's in the kitchen with Mrs. Henderson, making a pot of tea. Jeremy and Ian went off with another police officer who arrived. My father got the keys for the one that was here, then went to his office. My mother followed him up. Pretty sure they're having a fight, from the look on her face. Don't know where the assistant chief went."

"He's in the garden," I said. "I ran into him there."

"He said he wanted to talk to my parents," Jack said, "but then he disappeared."

"I'm sure he'll find them," I said. "How long are they staying?"

"Until tomorrow. That's when everyone had planned to go home," Sarah said. "And I know you planned to leave then, too, Greer. But we were wondering . . ." she glanced at Jack and Isabelle, "if you wouldn't mind staying an extra day or two. Until all this is cleared up. Will that be a problem at work?"

"I'd be happy to stay. I took the whole week off," I said, "so that's not an issue." There was the issue of where I'd be staying. The luxury inn was a treat, but I'd rather be on the spot. I wasn't sure how to broach it, but Sarah beat me to it.

"That's great," she said. "And we have one more favor. Isabelle's parents are leaving tomorrow morning. Jack and I are going to come back here and stay in my room. Caro and Barbara are staying. Would you mind moving in next door with Isabelle? If you'd rather stay at the inn, that's no problem—Jack and I can stay there."

"I'd be happy to stay with Isabelle. It'll be nice to be here with everyone," I said. And easier for me to keep an eye on things. I'd had a bad feeling about all of this from the time Brittany had gone missing, and that feeling was getting worse by the minute. And then there was the matter of Danny's death. I felt guilty that I'd back-burnered that, but being on the spot would give me some time to work on that problem as well. I knew Ian was staying a few more days—he'd planned to work with Desmond on a project. Jack and Dan had been in touch, and though I didn't think he had direct knowledge, he might have some insight. Add in Sarah, Jeremy, and Isabelle, and I'd have some fine minds at my disposal.

"Thank you!" Sarah jumped up and hugged me. "I appreciate it. I'm worried about my mother—about everything, really—and I'll feel better being right here. Now, let me see what I can do about food. I have a feeling the police will be here for a while. We'll need something informal. If Mrs. Henderson doesn't quit before all this is over, it'll be a miracle."

As Sarah disappeared down the hall, Jack sighed.

"Not exactly the honeymoon you'd planned, is it?" I asked him.

He smiled. "No," he said. "We knew we'd be dealing with family issues, but these are not the ones we were expecting."

"I take it Sarah hasn't broken the news that you're leaving the country?" I said.

"Nope," he said. "We were going to do that this week, after all the guests had left. I think we're going to have to wait until this situation is resolved. And if you've got to move in with your in-laws after the wedding, we could do worse. I can always escape next door and work on the renovation if I need some quiet. Excuse me," he said, as Sarah called from the kitchen.

"And how are you holding up? I got your message a few hours after you sent it and decided to just come over," I said to Isabelle.

"Oh, I'd forgotten that with everything that's been going on," she said. "It didn't have anything to do with Brittany. It's something that happened last night." She glanced around, and then came and sat next to me on the sofa. "I don't want Sarah to hear this—I don't think she can handle anything else."

"What happened?" I said.

"Well, remember how I'd been hearing footsteps and doors closing? And sometimes the piano?"

"Yes," I said. "On the third floor. I heard the doors closing the day I was there."

"Right, they slammed shut," Isabelle said.

I nodded.

"This is different. And my mom heard it, too. But now the footsteps are downstairs, like someone walking in the hall. The doors shut, but quietly, and there's a click, like a lock turning. You wouldn't hear it if you weren't already awake. My mother was up reading, so she heard it. My father sleeps through everything. She's heard it twice. Last night, she got me. I was in bed, but not asleep."

"What happened?" I asked.

"She had heard a door close. She went into the hall and thought she heard someone moving around downstairs. She came to my room, to make sure it wasn't me. While I was getting the flashlight, my door swung shut. Not exactly a slam, but it closed hard, you know? We both jumped, but that door has done that before, so once I had the flashlight, we opened it—it creaks a lot—and went to the top of the stairs. As we got there, we heard another door close. We waited, but there was nothing else. We put on all the lights, all the ones that are working, anyway, and we went downstairs."

"That was brave," I said. "Did you find anything? Or—anyone?"

"No, but someone had been there, I'm sure of it. We checked the kitchen door, and the front door, and they were still locked. But the side door wasn't. No one uses that door; it goes right into some overgrown shrubs. And there was something else strange—my mother swore she smelled perfume. She said it was familiar, maybe Chanel, but she wasn't sure. It was very faint."

"That is strange. So a woman, then. Jane wears Chanel. But would she use the side door?"

"The family always uses the back door. And why would she be sneaking around at night?"

"Sleepwalking? It's a stretch, but possible. Something about this place upsets her, I think. That's why she doesn't want to deal with it."

"Maybe," Isabelle said. "But wouldn't someone have noticed?"

"I think Jeremy did." I told her what he'd mentioned about finding his mother in the hallway. "But you're right—to come over here and sneak in and out—we may be reaching. What about all the contractors that have been in and out?"

Isabelle hesitated. "They don't typically use that door. But I know once or twice they've opened it, to run wires or bring in something heavy. It's closest to the driveway and the basement. But I checked all the locks before I went to bed. I know it wasn't open."

"Hunh," I said. "Do you think this is the first time? Or were some of those other times you heard noises also someone getting in?"

"I don't know. Some of the other noises could just be old house noises. But the footsteps—I think that had to be someone moving around. But it would have to be someone who knew the house, don't you think?"

"I would think so, yes," I said. "Which would mean the family, unless some of the workmen have been in and out so much that they know the floor plan."

"I don't think we can rule it out," Isabelle said. "Jack hired a local firm, and he likes to have the same crew as much as possible. He wouldn't use someone who had a lot of turnover. But what could they be after?"

"I don't know," I said. "It seems more likely that it's someone in the family, but that leaves the same question: what are they doing? Of course, there are keys floating around. That expands the circle to anyone who's spent any time here recently. It seems unlikely though."

I told Isabelle about the key to the guest cottage under the rock. She nodded.

"A lot of people leave spare keys hidden," she said. "My parents do. I leave one with a neighbor at my place in Boston."

"I live above my landlord, so I can always call him. The whole smart home thing is very hit or miss where I live. I'm sure the Whitakers have all that security in Westchester, but I don't think they've ever bothered up here. They probably have someone checking on the place when they're not here, but that's not 24-7. Jeremy should know—he's been here full-time for nearly a year."

"I'll ask him," Isabelle said. "And I'll see what Jack knows about keys. I just don't want him worrying, or mentioning it to Sarah. She's got enough to deal with." She paused, and then added,

"You know, I don't feel like I'm in danger. I'd just like to know what's going on."

"I would still be careful. It probably doesn't have anything to do with Brittany's death, but you never know," I said.

"I know," she said. "It's clear that somebody killed her and then tried to get rid of the body, but I just can't imagine anyone doing that. I can see hitting someone over the head, but figuring out how to move the body without being seen—that takes a cool head."

All true. It also took a knowledge of the grounds, since toting a corpse around in the middle of the night with no light wouldn't be easy even if you did know your way around. Which pointed back to the family.

"And what about the car?" I said. That was another point that bothered me. Isabelle was about to respond when Sarah returned and said we'd be going the buffet dinner route again.

"I think we're going to be doing a lot of this," she said. "With people coming and going, it's not like regular meals will work."

"Hopefully it won't be for too much longer." Even as I said the words, I knew I was being optimistic. I'd always heard that murders not solved in the first twenty-four hours were likely to remain unsolved. The trail went cold fast. And Brittany had died either late Thursday or early Friday and spent a day in the water. Physical evidence would be scarce. Brittany's killer might never be discovered. And that meant a cloud over the family, over anyone who could be suspected, forever.

"I hope you're right," Sarah said. She looked doubtful.

I wondered what she really thought, but it wasn't an easy ask. "Do you think one of your relatives killed your least favorite employee, and if so, which one?" was not the kind of thing you could drop into conversation over dinner. I'd have to come at it sideways. This was not the murder I had come here to investigate, but it was the one I might be able to help solve. I still wanted the truth about Danny, for myself and for the man who went to jail, but I'd always known that would take time. We were running out of time on Brittany's murder. I wanted the truth for Sarah and her family, and for the rest of us who were here and suspected. Even if one was found guilty, the rest would be free.

The three of us chatted for a while, but the conversation was forced. Jack came back and told us his parents were packing up. They were meeting some friends in the area for dinner and would say goodbye to everyone tomorrow. Since they hadn't arrived until after Brittany had died, the police didn't have any further need of them. Eventually, Ian and Jeremy drifted in. They'd both answered a lot of questions and figured there were more to come. We ate and drank and tried to avoid talking about the thing we were all thinking about. Finally, Sarah couldn't take it anymore.

"I just can't understand any of this!" she said. "It had to be someone she knew from somewhere else. I know it wasn't any of us, but it doesn't look to me as though the police are looking anywhere else. We may never know."

"I'm sure they'll find out who did this," Jack said, though he didn't sound like he meant it.

"I'm not," Ian said. "As far as I can tell, they think it was me."

"Or me, or my father," Jeremy said.

"That's ridiculous," Sarah said.

I saw Isabelle raise her eyebrows. She didn't think it was ridiculous. I didn't think Ian and Jeremy were likely suspects, though Desmond was high on my list. But here was my opening.

"You know, maybe if we all put our heads together, we could come up with something," I said.

"You think we can do better than the police?" Jack asked.

"I know it's a stretch, but we were all here, at least some of the time. We may have noticed something. Or we each noticed things,

things that separately don't mean anything to us, but put together they do."

"That makes sense," Isabelle said. "Fewer unknowns. But we have to be prepared. We may succeed and not like the result."

"Isabelle—" Jack began.

"She's right," Jeremy said. "We have to admit—it's likely to be someone we know."

Sarah bit her lip. "All right," she said. "I think we have to do this. And if we're not sure, well, it doesn't need to go beyond us. Agreed?"

There were cautious nods all around. It was reasonable. Sarah turned to me. She was very businesslike, now that there was a plan.

"Greer, you've done this before. How should we proceed?" she said.

Good question. I'd always been better at working alone. Also, I had no actual plan. Just a desire for information. I got a reprieve when there was a brief flurry of activity in the hall. Desmond getting a plate to take upstairs and letting Mrs. Henderson know the other ladies would be down shortly.

"Well, now is obviously not a good time," I said. "Tomorrow? When can we all get together?"

There was a brief debate. It was finally decided that we'd all meet for dinner.

"I'll arrange everything," said Sarah. "I know just the place. Is there anything else we should do?"

"I think if we all write down what happened, what we saw and when, that's a good start," I said. "And if you talk to the police, take note of what they ask. It could tell us something."

This was a long shot, and though I sensed some skepticism from Jack and Ian, they went along. Everyone wanted to feel in control, and this was what we had. The group broke up then. I claimed the need to pack and a desire to go to bed early. I really wanted some time alone to think and make some calls. Ian walked me out.

"I think I have an idea what was going on with Brittany and the deal that fell through," he said in a low voice. "But it would help if I could get a look at her files. I'm pretty sure I can get into her computer. I just need to get my hands on it."

"Well, unless Desmond handed it over, or disposed of it, I'm guessing it's still in his office somewhere," I said. "But most of the time, he is, too. I don't know, but I'll call you tomorrow when I'm settled next door. I'm a librarian, you know, not a burglar."

"I have faith in your creative problem-solving abilities," he said. "Want me to walk you back?"

"No, I'm fine. Enjoy your poker game," I said.

"From what Jack says, Isabelle is going to clean us out, but it will be a nice distraction." He gave me a kiss on the cheek and went back inside.

When I got back to the inn, I went directly to the bar. I lucked out and found Mike on a dinner break.

"Mind if I join you?" I asked. What was he going to say? But his smile seemed genuine as he gestured to the seat next to him.

"I never say no to a pretty lady," he said. "I've only got a few minutes left on my break, but once I'm back on the bar I'll make your martini. I've got a new brand of gin for you to try."

"You've got a deal," I said. "I could use a drink. What a day. You've heard about that body they found in the lake?"

"Lots of people talking about it. She wasn't from around here though, was she?"

"No, she was a guest at the wedding. She worked for the Whitakers."

"Was she at the party the other night?" he asked.

"No, apparently she died the night before. She was in the water for a while."

Mike grimaced. "That's awful," he said. "What happened to her? I've heard all kinds of stories."

"The police aren't sure. At first they thought she'd fallen in—now it's possible someone killed her. You know, they think she might have been staying here for a few days. If I can find you a picture, do you think you'd recognize her?"

"Maybe," he said. "Depends on whether she came in the bar. You get the picture, I'll get your drink."

He got up and went around the bar. I pulled out my phone and started searching. My best bet was the Whitaker website, but any pictures there would be formal and edited. It would be good to have a candid shot as well. I was scrolling through some results when I heard Mike greet someone. I looked up and found April Benson standing next to me.

"Hi there," I said. "How are you? Join me for a drink?"

"That sounds great," she said as she sat down.

Mike came over and slid my martini across the bar. He greeted April with a big smile and took her order.

"What are you doing there?" she asked as he walked away.

"Looking for some pictures," I said. I'd found two that should work—one the formal headshot from the company website, another a full-length shot from a professional function. "Do you recognize her?" I asked April. She'd been staying at the inn, so she might have seen Brittany.

April took the phone and studied the pictures. She shook her head. "No," she said, "should I?"

"Not necessarily," I said. "That's the woman whose body was found in the lake. Brittany Miles. The police think she was staying here for a few days last week."

Mike came back with April's drink, and I showed him the photos.

"Yeah, she was here. Came in last Monday night. Mondays are slow. White wine spritzer."

"Was she with anyone?" I asked.

"Not at first, but then some guy came in and sat with her. Tonic and lime. They were here for a while."

"What did he look like?" I asked. It could be Desmond, or the other man I'd glimpsed her with.

"Average height, thin, pointy chin, glasses. I don't know—he was wearing casual clothes, but he still looked kind of out of place. Still formal, in a way."

"Like he was wearing a suit even when he wasn't wearing a suit?" I said. "And kind of smug and self-satisfied?"

Mike laughed and said, "Well, I can't really comment on the guests, though honestly, I don't think he was staying here. He paid cash, and I didn't see him around. Let's just say he looked like the kind of guy who'd go to a bar in the mountains and order a salad and a tonic and lime."

April and I both laughed. Mike winked, said he'd be back, and went to take care of another customer. April watched him go, and then turned to me and said, "Any interest there?"

"No, too many other things going on," I said.

"Ah, the tall redhead?" she asked.

I rolled my eyes. "That's a long story," I said.

"Let me guess—'it's complicated,'" she said, making little air quotes.

"Yep."

"Men," she said.

We both sighed and took a swallow of our drinks. After a suitable pause and another sip, I asked her how she was doing.

"Okay, I guess. Frank and I hadn't lived together in a couple of years and hadn't had much of a marriage for a while before that, but it's still a shock. And I had to tell the kids." She went on to tell me about making the arrangements with Shelby. "She's smarter than I gave her credit for, and her grief seems genuine. It's awkward—he changed some of the financial things, so she'll get his life insurance, but I'm still next of kin. So there's a lot to sort out."

"I know," I said. We commiserated briefly on the formalities of widowhood. That reminded me of the phone call Frank had made right before his heart attack. April was holding up pretty well, all in all, so I decided to ask her about it.

"I haven't gotten his things back. They will come to me, I'm not sure when. Though I'm sure the phone is dead—even in his pocket it would've gotten soaked. I'll see if I can find out who he called," she said. "We weren't on the same account anymore, but I'll come up with something to get the records. I've always smelled a rat where New Leaf was concerned."

"One more thing, if you don't mind," I said, pulling out the cell phone I'd found. April didn't recognize it. It had been a long shot. I'd have to remember to give it back to Sarah in case one of the guests called looking for it.

Mike came back and asked if we needed anything else.

"Sure," I said, taking a stab at another question that had been bothering me. "Where would you stash a silver Prius if you didn't want it to be found?"

"Well, in the movies, it's always at the airport lot. But I'd leave it at the biggest used Toyota lot I could find. Was that the kind of car the dead lady had?"

I nodded.

"Then I can tell you it's not here. The police were all over the lot when I showed up for my shift. No tow trucks leaving since.

They'd have found it. Funny though. I'd have thought a woman that dressed like that would have a sports car. Something sleek and new."

"You like fast cars?" April asked.

"I'm more of a vintage car guy," Mike said. "I'm old school."

"Are you really?" April said, leaning forward.

I thought of the cherry-red Mustang, now undoubtedly April's. I settled up and left her to it.

Chapter Sixteen

After I left the bar, I called my landlord, Henri, and let him know I'd be staying for a few more days. He told me he was glad I was having a good time, and to let him know what day I'd be back, and he would make a nice dinner. Henri was a wonderful cook. He was also convinced that I was one missed meal away from becoming too thin. I adored him.

My next call was to Officer Jennie Webber, one of Raven Hill's finest. We'd become reluctant allies during a murder investigation the previous spring and unlikely friends after the killer was found. She had heard about Brittany, but hadn't thought much of it. She wasn't pleased to hear that I was involved.

"I thought you were going to a *wedding*," she said. "With fancy dresses and tea parties. Rich people stuff. Not to mention the ex-boyfriend. How did you manage to get involved in another suspicious death?"

"It's not like I went looking for it. I wasn't even there. It just so happened that she was killed at my friend's house. Probably."

I gave her the whole story, including the odd things that had happened at the Granville house. She listened attentively, asking the occasional question. She'd be telling me to mind my own business before we hung up, but she was interested. Jennie had been a soldier, and I suspected that being part of a small police force was a little too quiet for her.

"So do you think your friend or someone in her family killed this woman?" she asked.

"Sarah, no. The rest of her family, probably not, though her father's a dark horse. Any of the other guests, also probably not, though there's the possibility of something business related that went south. I can't see an obvious motive for any of them."

"Motives are overrated," she said. "Who could actually have done it—who had the opportunity, who was strong enough—that's the question." We debated this for a while longer, my emphasis on the why, her belief that the how mattered more. Then she asked me about Ian. She ended as expected, with the admonition to keep my nose out of the investigation.

"I'll tell Sam someone might be calling to check up on you," she said. "I can just picture his expression. Be careful, Greer. And call if you need backup."

I was touched. It was reassuring to know Jennie would have my back. Her boss, Lieutenant Sam O'Donnell, would be relieved that I wasn't getting involved in another murder on his turf. He'd found me helpful last spring, but I didn't think he was ready to deputize me anytime soon.

"Thanks," I said. "With any luck, I'll be home safe and sound in a few days."

After I hung up, I thought about her question as I packed. "Who could actually have done it?" From what I could see, any number of people, known and unknown. Maybe I'd have a better idea after dinner tomorrow. Someone must have noticed something unusual. I tucked in with my Christie novel, hoping for inspiration, but remained clueless.

I'd checked out and was watching a bellman load my car by midmorning. *I could get used to this kind of service*, I thought. I looked around the parking lot while he worked, thinking about Mike's comment. I admired his ingenuity where the used car lot was concerned—the man clearly had hidden talents—but I thought the Prius must have been ditched closer to the lake. That's where the body had been found. There were no used car lots, or airports for that matter, within walking distance, so unless the killer had an accomplice, the car was somewhere nearby. But why move it at all? It didn't make sense, unless the killer thought Brittany was already dead when she hit the water and wanted to make it look like she'd gone into the lake somewhere else.

I tipped the bellman and made the short drive to the Granville house. The unmarked police car was out front, but no cops in view. I parked in the turnaround, leaving room for the Petersons to get out. Isabelle appeared to help with my suitcase, and before long I was settled in the bedroom recently vacated by her brother. It had been freshly made up, with flowers on the nightstand next to a heavy-duty flashlight. Everything was pristine. I sensed the capable hand of Mrs. Henderson. A housekeeper was another thing I could get used to, though my tiny apartment hardly warranted it. I managed to keep it neat enough, if you didn't count the piles of books scattered around, but I hated to dust. Sarah had once complained about having staff around all the time. She loved being alone in her New York apartment, though she had been quick to hire a cleaning lady, one who had her own key, and appeared only when Sarah was at work herself. I'd have to ask her who else the family employed here, other than Mrs. Henderson. They might have keys and would certainly know their way around.

"Any activity last night?" I asked Isabelle as we went downstairs.

"No, it was very quiet. I didn't get in until late—my parents were already asleep. But I checked all the locks, and I didn't hear anything. My mother didn't either. But she did find something interesting in the library. We wanted to show you."

Mrs. Peterson was in the kitchen, filling a thermos with coffee.

"Mom, where did you put that notebook you found?" Isabelle asked.

"Back where I discovered it, or as close as I could get to it," she said, wiping her hands and walking to the library. She went to the back corner of the room and bent down to reach one of the lower shelves.

"Here it is," she said. "Let's look at it in the light."

The three of us gathered around the library table in the center of the room and put on the lamp. She set down a notebook of medium size, with a heavy paper cover, stitched rather than spiral-bound. Without opening it, you could tell it was well used, with smudges and fraying at the edge of the cover. There was some yellowing on one side. It was old but had held up well. Mrs. Peterson gently opened it and started turning pages. They were full of short paragraphs, verses, doodles and drawings. Interspersed were some longer entries, whole pages on which the writing was less neat, with underlining and exclamation points. In some cases the writer had pressed so hard into the page that the reverse side couldn't be used. Pencil, ink, marker—it looked like the author wrote with whatever was at hand. The entries ended abruptly three-quarters of the way through.

"Barbara always kept a journal," I said. "Caro told me that. I think you've found one."

"She was a poet," Mrs. Peterson said. "Lots of good work here. How old would she have been, do you know?"

"A teenager. Maybe seventeen, almost eighteen?" If the sudden end to the entries meant what I thought it did, this would the last journal Barbara kept before being shipped off to a mental hospital.

"That seems about right. It reminds me of what some of my freshman turn in. The ones with potential. Some of the drawings, though, seem a bit immature. More like the work of two different people."

"Some would be Jane's," I said. "She would've been closer to twelve at the time."

"Kind of Barbara to share this with her sister. Journals full of works in progress are personal things. They must have been close, in spite of the age difference."

"You never let me look at your notebooks, Mom," Isabelle said.

"You were always more interested in equations than iambic pentameter, Isabelle. Besides, there's a lot in those notebooks that should never see the light of day. Don't know why I keep them. I want you to burn them when I die."

Isabelle rolled her eyes. "Okay, Mom."

I had to laugh. My mother, though in good health, had already left written instructions for my sister and me on how to clean her Waterford and her silver. Apparently, academic families had different priorities.

Mrs. Peterson closed the notebook. "We should put this back," she said. "I don't think it was ever meant to be seen, the way it was wedged into the bookcase." She went back to the corner and tucked the notebook away. She looked around as she came back and added, "I'm surprised there aren't more. Strange that there would be just that one tucked behind the music books. If it weren't for the ravens, I wouldn't have found it."

"What?" I said.

"The ravens," she repeated. "The light slanting in the window at the end of the day showed them quite clearly. There, in the carving." She pointed.

"Oh," I said. "I see. There are ravens, live ravens, all around the library I work in. A full unkindness."

"Or a conspiracy," Mrs. Peterson said. "Another word for a group of ravens, though lesser known."

"A conspiracy," I said. "That would describe them better some days, especially when they want some of my lunch."

Mrs. Peterson smiled. "Try giving them peanuts in the shell. They like those." Then she frowned. "I wonder, though, where the rest of them are. She had to have more than one journal."

"They would probably be upstairs, don't you think? If they were something she didn't want anyone to see, she would have kept them in her room," Isabelle suggested. "Of course, everything's in boxes now, because of the renovations."

"That would make sense. Still odd that this one ended up here," She looked around at the library. "I'm so glad your brother isn't falling prey to the obsession with open floor plans. Getting rid of this woodwork would be a crime," Mrs. Peterson said. "This will be a lovely home when he's finished. It just needs cheering up."

"Jack never goes for trends for the sake of trends, you know that," Isabelle said. "But I agree—it is a bit gloomy and sad."

"Trim those trees!" Dr. Peterson had appeared in the doorway. "Let in some light. Car's all packed. If you've got some coffee for the road, we're ready to go."

With a minimum of fuss and one final "Let me know how it goes in Albany, muffin!" from Dr. Peterson, Isabelle's parents were off. Isabelle and I went back inside. We rummaged around and put together a lunch of leftovers and took it out on the porch. We were in time to see Bill Kent leaving the boathouse and walking up the driveway. He nodded, we waved. We sat in silence until a few minutes had passed, and then we both jumped up and peeked around the corner of the house. We heard the sound of an engine and saw the car go past the driveway. We went back to our seats.

"So, Jeremy or Ian?" I said.

"Jeremy is out this morning. He had some errands. He'll be back soon though. I'm supposed to model again this afternoon."

"Right, I didn't see his car when I pulled in. I'll keep Ian out of the way for a few hours."

On cue, my phone rang.

"'Tis himself," I murmured, and picked it up.

"Know a good lawyer?" Ian said, without preamble.

"As a matter of fact, I do," I said. "In the city, but I'm sure he could recommend someone local. Come on over. Isabelle and I are having lunch on the Granville porch. You can tell us all about it."

"Be right there," he said, and hung up.

Isabelle raised her eyebrows.

"Ian thinks he needs a good lawyer," I said. "You better keep your clothes handy in case the cops come back for him this afternoon."

"Seriously," Isabelle said. "And we don't know if Jeremy's off the hook either. Or us, for that matter."

"I think they'd be asking us more questions if they thought we killed her, but you're right. We had as much chance as anyone. You were on the spot, and I was a short walk away."

"But why would we?" she asked. "Why would any of us?"

"That's what we need to find out," I said, watching Ian come striding across the lawn. He was agitated, I could tell. He bounded up onto the porch, threw himself into a chair, ran his hands through his hair, and then jumped up and began to pace.

Finally, he came to a halt, leaned against the porch railing, and said, "Do I look like a murderer to you?"

His red hair was standing on end, his hands were fisted, and his blue eyes were blazing with righteous anger. Even his usually crisp oxford and jeans were in disarray. To be honest, he looked sketchy. I saw Isabelle look him over, tilt her head, and raise an eyebrow, but she decided discretion was the better part of valor and kept her mouth shut.

"Of course not," I said. "What happened?"

"Deputy Barney Rubble has got hold of the fact that Brittany and I used to date, and that you and I used to date, and has put that together into some kind of crime of passion."

"So, what, you killed her off to be with me?" I said.

"Something like that," he said. "Someone told him about the rumored engagement."

A line from Lerner and Loewe's "The Simple Joys of Maidenhood" floated through my mind, but all I said was "That sounds positively medieval."

"What rumored engagement?" Isabelle asked.

"The Whitakers, or Jane at least, thought that Ian and Brittany were about to get engaged," I said.

"No idea where that came from," said Ian.

"You did say it might have been from Brittany herself," I said. "Jane had to have gotten it from somewhere."

"Right," he said, "and the fact that I kept trying to call her Thursday night to get it straightened out looks bad for me, according to the cops."

"Hmm, stalker behavior," Isabelle said.

Ian shot her a look.

"I'm just saying," she added.

"She's right," I said. "You didn't leave her any threatening voice mails, did you? Because the police have probably gotten into those, or will."

"Of course not," he said. "I only left a couple of messages. I did call several times—at first I didn't know where she was, but later I saw her coming and going from the cottage."

"So what exactly did you say?" I asked.

"Nothing threatening! The first one just said that we needed to get something straightened out and to call me. In the other one, I said I knew she was there and she needed to call me. Actually, there might have been two like that."

Isabelle and I exchanged a look.

"Ah," I said. "Well, it's possible the police are grasping at straws, but how about I call my lawyer friend anyway?"

"And I'll make you a sandwich," Isabelle said, "you must be hungry." She popped up and disappeared into the house without waiting for a reply.

Ian watched her go and looked at me. I raised an eyebrow.

"Okay," he said, taking a seat again. "You might as well. All my lawyers are on the West Coast."

I got out my phone and scrolled through my contacts. David was part of a busy practice, but I had his cell number and figured he'd get back to me in short order even if he didn't pick up. As I expected, it went to voice mail. I left a brief message and hung up.

"So you think this looks bad?" he said.

"I don't know," I answered. "The calls don't look good, but the motive is thin." I remembered what Jennie had said about motive versus opportunity and asked, "Were you at the boathouse alone for any of the night? Jeremy was at home, wasn't he?"

"He was out when I got home. He didn't come in until a couple of hours later. Then he was up after I went to bed. I was awake for a while, but he was in the main room sketching until I turned off the light. I woke up around three, and the lights were off. I went back to sleep."

"So either of you could have gone out at some point," I said. "You, before he got home, and either one of you while the other was sleeping. For that matter, Jeremy could have stopped at the cottage before he came back."

"He was back before I saw her drive away. At least I think so," he said. "At this point I'm not sure of anything."

My phone buzzed. My lawyer friend.

"So you want to go to a hockey game?" David said without preamble.

"I'd love to go to a hockey game, next time I'm in town, but right now I need a favor," I said.

Ian raised his eyebrows. I smiled at him and explained the situation to David. He did, indeed, have someone to recommend.

"He used to work for us but a couple years ago decided he'd had enough. He and his wife are both attorneys. They bought a place in the Adirondacks, set up a practice, and started spending the weekends hiking and fishing with the kids. They like all that outdoorsy stuff," he said, in the "go figure" tone of a born and bred city boy. "Anyway, he still likes to play hardball once in a while. I'm sure he'll take the case." He gave me the name and said he'd text the contact info. I promised to call the next time I'd be in town, and hung up.

"Got a recommendation, sounds promising," I said. "And here's the contact," I added as my phone pinged. I forwarded it to Ian, who hadn't said a word for some time.

"Friend of yours?" he finally asked.

"From grad school," I said.

He waited. I said nothing. As Isabelle came back out, he said, "Oh. That's nice," and took the plate she handed him.

"Yes," I said. If he thought I was going to give him any more information, he was mistaken. Other than Brittany, I knew nothing about the women he'd dated, not even their names. I didn't care. I'd never even asked about his ex-wives. That's what the internet was for. Not that I spent that much time on it. I was no more of a cyberstalker than the next ex.

There was a brief, awkward silence, interrupted by a tone from Isabelle's phone. She looked at it and excused herself.

"Jeremy's back and wants to get to work while the light is good," she said. "He needs to give his dad the SUV keys. Desmond has an appointment this afternoon. I'll get my things and go over to the boathouse. I gave you the spare keys to this house, didn't I, Greer?"

"I've got them," I said, patting my pocket. "We'll see you at dinner."

Isabelle went into the house and returned a few minutes later, heading across the yard to the boathouse. I waited until she was out of earshot and turned to Ian. "Here's our chance," I said.

"For what?"

"To search Desmond's office," I said. "You wanted a look at Brittany's computer. If it's there, we should be able to find it, and you can see if you can get in."

"How are we going to get in?" he said. "I'm sure that outside door is locked."

"I'm sure it is, too," I said. "That's why we're going to go through the house. The mudroom door is open all day. Jack and Sarah are out, and the rest of the family will be in their offices or rooms. If someone sees us, I'll make something up. It'll be fine."

"Okay," Ian said, "but I think we should have our story straight first."

"Where's your sense of adventure?" I asked. "Okay, fine. We need to wait a few minutes to make sure he's gone anyway. Let's sit over there. If you lean on the porch railing, you'll be able to see up the driveway. He'll probably come out that way."

"It sounds like you've done a lot of this sort of thing," he said.

"I keep forgetting you're an only child," I said. "Trust me, if you had an older sister or brother you'd have done a lot of this sort of thing, too. Now, can you see the house from there?"

"Yep," Ian said. He took a few bites of his sandwich. "There he goes. Headed around to the front of the house. Jeremy must have left the car there."

"We need to give it a few minutes. Hang on," I said.

I zipped upstairs and rummaged in my jewelry case. I found a dainty French hoop I'd purchased recently. Leaving its mate in the case, I wrapped it in tissue and put it in my pocket.

"Is he gone?" I said, once back on the porch.

"I saw the SUV pull away. Better still, all the ladies have set off for a walk. I think Jeremy said Barbara and Margaret take a long walk after lunch every day. Looks like Jane and Caro went along today. So who does that leave in the house?"

"Just the housekeeper, I think. I'm sure they have someone else in to help with the cleaning, and for parties, but I haven't had a chance to check that with Sarah. With any luck, it's just Mrs. Henderson, and she'll be in the kitchen."

"So what do we do? Sneak along the shrubbery until we get to the door?" he asked.

"Absolutely not. We stroll up the driveway and go in like we have every right to be there. I'm checking with Sarah, who I don't know is out, about an earring I found. You want to have a chat with Desmond to kill time while Jeremy is working in the boat-house. All very aboveboard."

Ian gave me an admiring glance. "How do you come up with this stuff?"

"It's not hard, Ian," I said, as we set off up the driveway. "We're telling the truth. We've just timed it to suit our purpose." *Also to allow me to stick to my rule—never lie about anything important.* "Don't you ever read detective stories? Watch *Sherlock*? Anything?"

"I read my dad's old copies of *The Three Investigators* as a kid. Does that count?"

"Good enough," I said. We'd arrived at the side door. As expected, it was unlocked. "Now, keep as quiet as you can unless we run into someone. If we do, act natural."

"Right," Ian said.

I opened the door and we slipped inside. I closed it gently behind us. Unlike the Granville house, everything here was well maintained and not inclined to squeak. I stopped near the door between the mudroom and the hall and listened. I could hear someone moving in the kitchen—Mrs. Henderson, most likely—and then the whistle of the tea kettle. She might be taking a break, which meant she was unlikely to stray from the kitchen.

I slipped around the corner and went toward the lake side of the house. Ian followed. There was no one in any of the main rooms, and no noise from above. We stopped on the second-floor landing and listened again. There was no sound from any of the rooms. Onward to the third floor. Once again we paused, and once again there was no sign or sound of anyone about. We were in the clear for a little while at least.

We went to the end of the hall. There were only three rooms and a bathroom up here, and the office door was the only one that was closed. I gave a brief knock, which is what I'd do if I didn't know Desmond was gone and, when I got no response, turned the knob and poked my head in. Empty, as expected.

Once the door was closed behind us, I looked around and said to Ian, "Where do you want to start?"

"Here," he said, going to the desk. It was an old-fashioned desk, not too large, with a kneehole and drawers on either side. That's where Ian started, pulling out a briefcase and a laptop case and going through both of them.

"Anything I can do to help?" I said.

"Keep a lookout. I'm not quite as comfortable with this breaking and entering thing as you are."

"We're not breaking. The door was unlocked," I said. I stuck my head back out into the hallway and was met with silence. Then I went to the window. Desmond didn't have a view of the garden, but looking straight down, I could see the patio and steps outside Jane's office. I could see down the driveway and onto the dock, as well as the edge of the Granville dock and part of the yard. Decent view of the lake. Also of the guesthouse, less so of the boathouse. The door to the outside stairs was next to the window, near the corner. I turned the handle. It opened, and I heard the mechanism relock. No need for a key once you were outside on the stairs.

"Gotcha," said Ian.

I turned and saw him pulling a laptop out of the bottom drawer. He'd removed some empty hanging files and put them on the desk.

"Brittany's?" I asked.

"Yes," he said. "She always had a dragonfly on her computer somewhere—a skin, a sticker, a picture taped on. I can see the wing wrapping the edge here."

He put the files back and opened the laptop. He pulled a piece of paper out of his pocket and put it next to the computer.

"How long until you know whether or not you can get in?" I said.

"Five minutes, maybe more. Then I'll need some time to look around," he replied, already focused on the task at hand.

"There's something I want to check," I said. "I won't be long. I'll come back and help you look for the tablet. If I hear someone coming, I'll call you and hang up. Then I'll slow them down. Go out the door to the outside stairs. It will lock behind you."

"Right," he said, still focused on the screen in front of him. I sighed, hoping he'd registered what I said. I went out into the hall. The house was still quiet. There were a few things I'd been wondering about, and this might be my only chance to investigate without being caught. I'd need to be both thorough and fast.

First, I wanted to know what could be seen of the garden, the guesthouse, and the dock from each of the rooms that faced the lake. It would be different in the daylight, but I couldn't go sneaking around the house in the middle of the night and hope no one would notice. On the theory that anyone could have been anywhere while Brittany was being murdered and hauled off to the lake, I started with the first room I came to—the bathroom. There was a window high up near the peaked roof, and a smaller, frosted one in the shower. Unlikely anyone had been in the shower, but I stepped out of my shoes and into the stall anyway. The window slid open easily, but I had to reach up to open it and stand on my toes to look out. This one was more for light and ventilation than the view.

I stepped out and looked around while I slipped my shoes back on. Not much to see, other than some nice hair care products, toothbrush and paste, and a hairband. No cosmetics. I looked in the medicine cabinet—nothing but Band-Aids and some calamine lotion.

Next, I stuck my head into the room on my right, which faced the street. It had occurred to me that maybe the garage was in sight, but when I went to the window, I found it was not. This room was tidy and looked almost uninhabited. An overnight bag was on the chair, and a handbag on the floor next to it. Margaret had said she didn't work nights, but she obviously came prepared for anything. I knew Barbara lived about an hour away, and Margaret had to live near her. A sudden storm or a downed tree would mean she was spending the night.

I went back across the hall. By process of elimination this must be Barbara's room. It was where Dan and I had once stayed. It was bright and sunny, with a comfortable chair by the window. I looked around, fighting a wave of sadness, and walked to the window. It had a nice view of the lake and mountains. I sat in the chair and looked down. From here I could see most of the garden. The area from the reflecting pool to the lawn would be visible to anyone sitting here.

I stood and turned in a circle. This room, too, was neat, but obviously in use. There were a few cosmetics and a travel-size jewelry case on the dresser. A pair of driving mocs, muddy around the edges, had been placed under a chair. There was a book on the nightstand—poems by Mary Elizabeth Coleridge. I noticed a black hoodie hanging on the back of the door as I left. No sign of meds, either here or in the bathroom, but I had a feeling the nursing staff took care of that.

I heard no sound from the second floor as I went down the stairs. Once I reached the hall, I went to the top of the next set of stairs and listened for noise from the first floor. All was quiet. I turned and studied the layout of the second floor. I knew from what Sarah had told me on previous visits that this floor had also been renovated. What had originally been four bedrooms, a bathroom, and a sleeping porch had been reconfigured into three bedrooms, two with bathroom en suite, one hall bath, and one small den. Sarah's room was at one end, the master bedroom at the other. Each had its own bathroom. Jeremy's room was in the middle, facing the lake. The den and shared bathroom were across from that and faced the road. I'd leave those for last. They might tell me something useful, but likely not, and I wasn't sure how much time I had.

I went to the end of the hall and walked into the master bedroom. There were windows on two walls, one facing the lake. I walked over, eased around a chair, and looked out. Not much view of the garden. I was beneath Desmond's office, but his windows were placed differently. Jane's office was somewhere around here on the first floor. All of them overlooked a sliver of garden, but more of the driveway and the area around the dock. Before leaving, I nipped into the bathroom and opened the medicine cabinet. While I usually found snooping through people's book-shelves more illuminating as to character, their medicine cabi-nets often yielded useful information. I wondered what prescription drugs Jane might be on, and if they had anything to do with her moods over the past few days. A quick check showed only one drug not available over the counter—a well-known brand of sleeping pill. A recent prescription, half full. Jane must use them regularly. I remembered Jeremy saying he thought he'd found his mother sleepwalking and wondered. One of these drugs was known to do that, but I wasn't sure which. Beyond that were vitamins, a bottle of ibuprofen, and something for swimmer's ear.

Back in the hallway, I decided to save Sarah's room for last, since that was the one place I had a logical reason to be. That put Jeremy's room, currently occupied by Caro, next on the list. This room had by far the best views. Jeremy had once told me that it was compensation for being smaller and colder, since part of it had been a sleeping porch back in the day. That part jutted out over the terrace, and I was sure no amount of modern construction or insu-lation could keep out the cold of an Adirondack winter. Today, though, the room was bright and inviting, the sunshine making it warm enough that the windows were open to catch a cooling breeze.

Once again, I went straight to the window to see what I could see. This room had a view similar to Barbara's, but you could see more of the garden. The lower floor made the angle less acute. I leaned to one side and could see the path to the driveway that ran by Jane's office. The hedge obscured the actual driveway, though the turnaround at the end and part of the Whitaker dock were visible. The Granville one was hidden by shrubs. That area looked murky even in broad daylight. This room looked a little more lived-in—a couple of popular thrillers on the nightstand, a jumble of tissues and cosmetics on the dresser, a soft black beret on the chair with Caro's spare cane nearby.

Sarah's room was next. It looked as it had on the day of the tea party, full of exploding suitcases. I didn't notice Jack's clothes. His were undoubtedly neatly folded away. I felt sorry for the newly-weds. They should be having a quiet few days visiting with family before leaving for a couple of weeks of honeymooning. Although, given Sarah's plans to leave the company and Jeremy's statement that a bomb was about to drop, those days might not have been that quiet.

I'd been in Sarah's room several times but hadn't ever studied the view. The windows that faced the lake and the garden gave a decent view of both. There were more trees on this side of the property, so some parts of the garden were obscured. With the hedge on the other side, I couldn't see much of the driveway and guesthouse. The boathouse and lawn were in view though, and the far end of the Whitaker dock. The windows in the bathroom were high on the wall, so no view from there.

I went back to the hall and was about to step into the den when I heard voices. Caro and Desmond, in the downstairs hall and near the stairs, based on how clearly I could hear them. I froze. Were they coming up? I strained to hear their words over my heart, which had started to pound. Desmond's low rumble was hard to discern, but Caro's voice was clearer. I caught ". . . can't keep up. My hip, you know . . ." followed by Desmond's response. The only word I heard clearly was "sunroom." Yes, please. If they both went into the sunroom, I could sneak up to the third floor, and Ian and I could make our escape via Desmond's private stairs. I slid my phone out of my pocket as I listened.

There was a little more conversation, then I heard "office" and, from Caro, "I really should lie down." This sounded much closer. They were on their way up, and I was smack in the middle of the hall. I bolted back into Sarah's room, dialed Ian, and let it ring a few times. I hung up, and just to be safe, texted "DESMOND." Then I shoved the phone back in my pocket, made sure I still had the stray earring, took a few deep breaths, and stepped into the hall just as they reached the landing.

"Oh, hi," I said. "I'm looking for Sarah. Do either of you happen to know where she is?"

Desmond answered. "Out with Jack," he said. "Lunch and errands, something to do with renovation next door."

"Oh, that's right. I think she mentioned it. I found an earring and thought it might be hers. I can check with her later," I said.

"An earring?" Caro asked. "Where did you find it?"

"Near the dock, the night of the party. I tucked it away and forgot. Would you recognize it?"

I walked over and pulled out the tissue with the earring in it, unwrapping it to show them. Caro let out a breath.

"No, afraid not. I've lost one, but that's not it."

"I'll check with Sarah when I see her. If it's not hers, one of the guests might have lost it," I said.

"Well, if you'll excuse me," Desmond said, "I've got some things to take care of in my office."

I said goodbye, and he went upstairs. I turned to Caro.

"I should be going, too. I thought I'd take a walk. I feel like I need the exercise. I'm used to moving around a lot at my job," I said.

"Lovely day for it," Caro said. "I wish my hip were in better shape. It hasn't been the same since I fell off that elephant. Barbara and Margaret walk a few miles every day after lunch. I couldn't do the whole distance. Jane's managing though."

"Does she still swim?" I asked. "I remember being in awe of the time she spent in the water on my last visit."

"I think it's been a while since she's done that," said Caro. "I'm going to lie down and finish my book. Enjoy your walk, Greer."

Caro went into her room, and I went in search of Ian. I'd reached the mudroom when my phone vibrated in my pocket. It was a text from Ian. "On the Granville porch," it said. "Slight problem."

I hoped that wasn't an understatement and that he'd made it out of Desmond's office unseen. I got to the porch in record time. Ian was there, pacing.

"What happened?" I said. "Did Desmond find you?"

"Almost," he said. "I got nowhere with the laptop. I gave up and started looking for the tablet. Then I got your call. I put everything back in the desk and was on my way out the door when I saw the tablet on the chair by the window, sticking up from the seat cushion, like it had slid down. Dragonfly skin, so I knew it was hers."

"So what did you do?"

He reached into his shirt and pulled out the tablet. "I couldn't think of anything else," he said. "I could hear Desmond coming up the stairs."

"Nice work," I said. "We'll see what we can do with it, and then find a way to sneak it back."

He looked at me. "Seriously? We're going to go through all that again?"

I waved a hand. "Don't worry. If there's anything on it related to the business, we're going to have to tell Sarah anyway. She can put it back pretty easily. The more important question is, can we get into it?"

"Haven't tried," he said.

"We've got some time before dinner. Let's go inside," I said. "I don't want anyone wandering by and seeing us."

We settled in the library. Ian hit the power button. Nothing happened. He tried again. Still nothing. He swore.

"No battery," he said. "Got a cable that might fit?"

I looked closer. "My phone charger should. Hang on." I ran upstairs and got it. It fit. We attached it and moved closer to an outlet. We got the charging icon on the screen.

"We're going to have to leave it here to charge while we're at dinner," Ian said.

I agreed. We started making a list of possible passwords, presuming there was a screen lock. Everything Ian had tried on the laptop was related to work. Apparently Brittany once told him she always used some version of something really important to her. I mentally rolled my eyes. He had a one-track mind.

"What do you know about her mother?" I said. "Or about her childhood?" Brittany didn't seem the type to have a favorite sports team or a pet.

"She was an only child. Single mother who died young. She rarely talked about it," Ian said.

"Do you know her mother's name? Where they lived? Anything?"

"Ally, I think. Allison Miles. That was it. They lived somewhere out in the western part of New York. I remember once she said "pop" instead of "soda." There were a couple of things like that. But only when she was tired. I think she tried to lose the accent, or anything that made her sound different."

"I don't suppose you know her birthday? Her mom's, I mean." Ian shook his head.

"Okay," I said. "Isabelle should be back any minute. We're all supposed to go to dinner in an hour. I'll see what I can find out about Allison Miles."

It was a stretch, but I thought Brittany's password might be something related to her mother. I used my grandmother's birthday, sometimes in combination with my father's, or lately, Danny's. It was a matter of finding the dates. Birth, death, either would be something she'd remember. Fortunately, I knew someone who was good at finding out that sort of thing with very little information. I checked the time. Millicent Ames, Raven Hill Library's archivist, had unsurpassed research skills. Every genealogist in the Albany area knew Millicent and consulted her often. She should still be at her desk. I called her direct line. I was in luck. She would be happy to help. It had been a slow day, and she liked a challenge. She'd stay late if need be, she said, and email me whatever she found out.

Isabelle walked in as I hung up. Ian left, saying he'd be back in an hour. I gave Isabelle an abbreviated version of our afternoon adventure. If we were going to be putting all our cards on the table at dinner, it would come out anyway.

"I'm not sure how Sarah's going to take it," I said. "But I think we need to know if Brittany was up to anything in relation to the business."

"That makes sense," she said. "And the sooner this is wrapped up, the better for everyone."

We debated hiding the tablet somewhere and finally left it where it was, but concealed under some books and papers. Then we both went upstairs to get changed.

It was going to be an interesting evening.

Chapter Seventeen

Sarah had arranged dinner at a local restaurant a little off the beaten path. She and Jack were running late and texted to say that they would meet us there. The rest of us piled into Ian's SUV. When we arrived, we were shown to a small patio with a firepit, well away from other diners. Sarah and Jack were already seated. Once we were settled and had ordered wine and appetizers, Sarah pulled out a notebook and pen.

"I'll take notes," she said to me. "Where do we start?"

"We should start with the facts," I said, mindful of Jennie Webber's comment about motive. "What do we actually know for sure? Then maybe a time line. Who was where and when, that sort of thing. We have to figure out who had the opportunity and who could have physically done it. I'm sorry, but we have to consider everyone."

"In other words, we're all suspects until we can prove we're not," Jeremy said.

Sarah bit her lip. She still wanted to believe that this had nothing to do with the Whitakers. But she nodded, took a sip of her wine, and opened the notebook.

"So, what are the facts?" she said. "Other than that somebody killed Brittany Miles."

"Well, we don't know that for sure," Isabelle said. Everyone turned to look at her. "I mean, we know she drowned, and we know that someone moved her body, but we don't know that anyone killed her. Though it's a logical assumption, we can't prove it."

There was silence as we processed this. Isabelle looked around, blushed, and reached for her wine.

"Isabelle is right," I said. "While it's likely that someone moved her body to try to cover up the fact that they killed her, we don't know that. We think so, and it looks like the police think so, but we can't state it absolutely."

"Okay," Sarah said. "Then let's start with this: Brittany Miles is dead."

"She received a blow to the head, didn't she?" Jack asked.

"Yes," Jeremy said. "But that's not what killed her. She drowned in the reflecting pool."

"Do we know that? Weren't the police taking samples elsewhere?" Ian asked.

"The police completed their analysis. It was the reflecting pool. My father's lawyer called him this afternoon," Jeremy said.

We went back and forth like this for a while. We finally ended up with:

Brittany had a head wound, origin unknown.
Brittany drowned in the reflecting pool in the garden.
Brittany's body was found in the lake, under the Granville dock.
Brittany's car, phone, handbag, and possibly some of her jewelry were missing.

That last bit was also courtesy of Desmond's lawyer. I was glad I didn't have to admit to searching the cottage or checking out the

Whitaker garage, but there was something about the jewelry that bothered me. I couldn't put my finger on what.

"This doesn't make a lot of sense," Ian said. "Unless someone robbed her? Even that doesn't make sense."

"To my knowledge, no one's ever been mugged in our garden, but I suppose there's a first time for everything," Jeremy said.

"It's interesting, though, that it looks that way," Isabelle said. "Why would she be in the garden in the middle of the night? She had to have been meeting someone."

"But who?" Sarah asked.

"I'm a likely suspect," Ian said. "I'd been trying to reach her, and she wouldn't hesitate to meet me somewhere."

"She'd be willing to meet me as well, and the rest of the family," Jeremy said. "Though we could leave Aunt Barbara out, and probably Isabelle and Jack."

"You can't honestly think—" Sarah said.

"We have to," Jeremy said.

"I find it unlikely—" Jack began.

The conversation devolved into people speaking over one another, sustained by a steady stream of sibling bickering between Sarah and Jeremy. The Dublin Murder Squad we were not. This was why my favorite girl detectives worked alone. Not an option at the moment. We needed to pool our information. I drank some more wine. The debate, if you could call it that, came to a halt when the waiter appeared to take our order. Thank God. I pushed my wineglass away. I'd only get a headache if I kept at it.

I ordered my dinner, complete with a martini made to my specifications, and took control of the conversation once the waiter had left.

"Okay, we're getting hung up on why," I said. "We need to figure out how, remember? Who could have done it?" I still thought motive was important, but no one could think of a good one, so back to the time line. That might shake something loose.

Sarah flipped the page in her notebook. "When do we start? Thursday?"

"We start when she got to town, which could have been as early as Monday or late Sunday," I said.

"I still find that hard to believe," Sarah said. "I'm sure my father would have known if she were here."

"The bartender at the inn recognized her. He saw her Monday night. He remembers because it wasn't too busy," I said. "She was joined by a man. I saw her Wednesday night, also with a man, and I'm pretty sure it was the same one. When I asked her about it on Thursday, she denied it. But there's something else you should know."

I told them about seeing Desmond with Brittany in the lobby. Ian added his story about the sudden halt in the business deal he'd been analyzing and the inclusion of some guests that surprised him. Back to me, witnessing Desmond's removal of the computers from the guest cottage. Now to finesse the office search.

"So Ian thought he should talk to your father about one of the projects he was working on being called off so suddenly. Given everything that's happened, something unusual could be important. I was on my way over to see if an earring I found belonged to you, so he came along. I met Caro in the hall, and we chatted for a few minutes. Anyway, your dad wasn't in, but Ian spotted Brittany's tablet."

"I figured if she was up to something, she wouldn't keep it on her work computer, but she'd want the information handy. I'd just picked it up when Greer called to say you weren't home. I'm embarrassed to admit I walked out with it. I must have just missed your dad," Ian said.

All true enough. I patted Ian's knee beneath the table. He really was catching on.

"I don't care how you got it," Sarah said. "I want to see what's on it. This may all come down to something shady that woman was involved in."

Everyone would certainly like to think that. I wasn't so sure.

"It needed to be charged, and it's an older model, so that won't be fast. We left it charging. We should be able to look after dinner," Ian told her.

We went back to the time line of events, with the result that we verified what we already knew. The last time anyone had seen Brittany was late Thursday night. Ian had seen her drive away, and an hour later Jeremy had seen her walking into the garden. He didn't think her car was in front of the guest cottage at that time but couldn't be sure. The turnaround wasn't lit. Ian had gone to bed. Jeremy had tried to sleep as well but was restless and had gotten up again to sketch. He'd seen someone moving around in the cottage, and then the lights had gone out. Isabelle had seen Desmond near the cottage late on Thursday and, in the early hours of the morning, had heard a splash and then gravel crunching as someone walked up the driveway. No one had seen anyone hitting Brittany on the head, holding her under in the reflecting pool, or hauling her body across the lawn and onto the dock.

"But let's face it—in the dark, anytime after we'd all gotten back from dinner, anyone could have done it. It was late when I saw her walking to the garden, and it must have been around three when I saw the lights go out in the cottage," Jeremy said.

"It was around then that I heard the splash and someone walking up the driveway toward the road," said Isabelle. "But that wasn't necessarily Brittany."

"No, but if we go on the assumption that someone killed her, and I think we have to, it could have been the killer," I said. I turned to Jeremy. "You told me that the lights in the garden weren't working, didn't you? How hard would it be for someone who was unfamiliar with the new design to find their way around?"

"The lights work," Jeremy said. "But they're solar, so the later it gets, the dimmer they are. But it wouldn't be easy, even with a lot of moonlight. Things look different than they do by daylight. And there was some cloud cover that night."

"Oh, I must have misunderstood," I said. "And that's true about the moonlight. So Brittany would have a hard time finding her way around, and so would anyone else."

"Unless it was someone familiar with the garden and the grounds. But I have a hard time seeing how our landscaping crew could be involved," Jeremy said. "What about your people?" he said to Jack.

"Small crew, all local, with some subcontractors in the mix," Jack replied. "I'm sure a few of them know some of the landscaping crew, but I've never seen them near the garden. I have a hard time seeing any of them being involved at all, unless one of them has some connection to Brittany we don't know about."

"It's possible, I guess," Sarah said. "But it sounds like it has to be one of us, one of the family."

"Or someone close by," I said. "Other than Mrs. Henderson, do you have any household staff in regularly?"

"Someone helps with the cleaning a couple times a week. And of course the caterers have been in and out. My mother nearly always uses the same firm, but it's not always the same staff."

"That's what I figured," I said. "Of all of these people, who has keys?"

"I checked on that," Jack said. "My mother thought she heard someone in the house," he added, with a glance at Isabelle. "The foreman on the renovation has a key to the back door of the Granville house. If someone needs to get in and he's not here, Mrs. Henderson lets them in."

"And there are no spare keys to any of the buildings on the property floating around?" I asked. "I know once when Dan and I visited, there was a key to the guesthouse hidden somewhere. And some of Brittany's things are missing."

Sarah and Jeremy exchanged a look.

"I'd forgotten about that," Sarah said. "You've been here more, Jeremy. Any idea?"

Jeremy shook his head. "I really don't know. I don't think so, though I'm not sure about the guesthouse key. Mrs. Henderson has keys to everything, but she keeps those in the kitchen."

"I'll ask her if she knows," Sarah said. "I think both my parents use that master set of keys to get into the guesthouse and boat-house, but I don't know for sure. I'll find out."

"And find out if anyone else has borrowed them. It's easy enough to get copies made," I said. Though given how simple it was to get in and out of the house undetected, someone could have borrowed a key long enough to have it copied. I didn't think the keys would get us anywhere, but it didn't hurt to check. .

"What I've been wondering is where Brittany was after the tea party," Isabelle said. "Could she have met someone then? Or could someone have come to the guesthouse and no one noticed?"

"I was wondering about that, too," I said. "There are a few hours unaccounted for. What she was doing might be significant. I didn't see her again after you introduced us, Sarah."

"I did. She was there until nearly the end of the party, I think. I saw her talking to a couple of people, and then she asked me about one of the sideboards, of all things. Said she loved antiques. I told her to feel free to wander around and look, the place is loaded with them," Sarah said. "After that, I went upstairs to freshen up and say hello to Aunt Barbara. I didn't see her after I came back down."

"She was looking at the furniture," Isabelle said. "I saw her. I was talking to Caro. She walked right by us and then turned around and asked if either one of us knew anything about the desk we were standing near. Caro said it had belonged to Desmond's mother. Then Brittany said her grandmother had had one. She'd seen a picture. Her phone buzzed, and then she excused herself to take the call."

"I thought she didn't have any family to speak of?" I said.

Ian answered. "Just her mother, but that doesn't mean her mother didn't have old family pictures."

"True," I said. "So do we know when she actually left?"

"Caro said she saw her walking down the driveway toward the guest cottage, remember? That's what she told the police. She'd gone out for some air as the party was wrapping up."

"I must have just missed seeing her," I said. "I saw Caro in the garden when I was looking for my sunglasses. That's when I saw you, too," I said to Isabelle.

"That's right. She must have left right before I did, because I didn't see her either, and I sat on the Granville porch for a few minutes after I left. I didn't see anyone but one of the landscapers."

"There were no landscapers there that afternoon," Jeremy said. "No work crews at all. They had to finish up and leave by noon."

"Yes, they did," Jack said. "Are you sure it wasn't one of the guests, Isabelle?"

"I'm sure. I only saw them from the back, but whoever it was had on jeans and a sweatshirt and one of those caps they all wear."

"Man or woman?" I asked.

She thought for a moment. "I thought it was a woman, but it could have been a man with a slender build. I only saw them from the back."

"Maybe someone left something and came back for it," Jack suggested. "That's the most likely explanation. But we can check."

Jeremy nodded.

Jack was right. It was the most likely explanation. But still.

Having determined what time Brittany left the party, we ran through where we all were. Sarah had said goodbye to her guests and gone upstairs to relax and change for dinner. She and Jack were meeting some out-of-town guests. Jack had been working at a coffee shop and come home after the party was over. Jeremy was picking someone up at the airport, then he and Isabelle had gone out. Ian had done some work in the boathouse but had set up his computer facing the lake. Then he'd met me for dinner. According to Sarah, her parents had taken Barbara and Caro out. Margaret had gone with them but driven separately. She'd gone home from there, since Melissa, the night nurse, would be at the Whitakers' when they got home.

"I'm sorry, Sarah, but I have to ask. Do we know for sure where Dad was all afternoon?" Jeremy asked.

"He took his car in for service. Anything to get out of the house during the party, he said. Then he was in his office on a conference call. But I'll check all of that," Sarah said.

I had to give her credit. Sarah wanted her family, especially her father, in the clear, but she was going to check up on him anyway.

"So it was just Mrs. Henderson at home while everyone was at dinner?" I asked. "And Brittany, in the cottage. Unless she went out and came back. Or unless someone came to her."

"Mrs. Henderson might have noticed, but that's not a sure thing. I'll ask her though," Sarah said.

"So where does this leave us?" Jack asked.

"We know when Brittany left the party. We know that she went out and came back, and we know she went into the garden that night and when. We know that she, or someone with a key, was in the guesthouse later and turned off the lights. What we don't know is if she met anyone between the party and the time she died, and if that person was on the property. And we don't know where her car is, though it seems likely the killer left in it."

"Find the car, find the killer?" Ian said.

"Maybe," I answered. "But we all have some things we need to check out."

Sarah rattled off a list of our assignments. Our food arrived, and we continued to debate various aspects of the case, as I thought of it. Isabelle's earlier statement aside, it was clear that everyone thought that Brittany had been murdered, and her killer had dumped the body in the lake.

"There's something I still don't get," Ian said. "If the killer dumped her body late Thursday or early Friday morning, why was it still there late Friday night? Why didn't it float away?"

"I think I can explain that," Jeremy said. "I was there when the police pulled her out. She was caught in my mother's swim tether. Tethers actually. There were at least two attached to the Granville dock."

"What's a swim tether? One of those things that lets you swim in place?" Ian asked.

Jeremy nodded. "When she was younger, my mother used to swim out to a float that was anchored in the lake. As she got older, she didn't feel comfortable with the distance, so she'd use the tethers, and she used the Granville dock so they didn't interfere with the canoe or the kayaks. There's a harness that goes around your waist, and a long rope attaches to the back of that at one end and the dock at the other. She'd usually remove them at the end of the summer, but some were either knotted or caught in the wood of the dock. It was quite a tangle. We've been planning on replacing that dock, so not a big deal. When Brittany went into the water, she got caught in the old tethers. They had to cut her loose."

"So she was there the whole time," Sarah said. She shuddered. "Don't tell Mom."

"Pretty sure she already knows," Jeremy said. "When the police came back yesterday, they had a piece of an old tether that had wrapped around Brittany's leg. They wanted us to tell them what it was."

They could have figured that out. What they wanted was a reaction.

We moved on to the car. If the police hadn't found it, it was either long gone from the area or well hidden. I shared Mike's theory about the used-car lot but admitted there were flaws in it. For one, how to get from wherever the lot was back to wherever our killer was staying.

"Aren't there a lot of empty houses around the lake this time of year?" Isabelle asked. "They're mostly vacation homes, right?"

"There are a few. Some people don't come up between Labor Day and the first good snow. Why?" Jeremy said.

"Because you could park a car in one of the driveways or find an open garage. It's not as anonymous as a car lot, but it would buy time. And not every house has a security camera. It's worth checking," Isabelle said.

"You're right," Jeremy said. "I know of a few places that are unoccupied right now."

"And so would the landscapers, if they had a service contract," I added.

"We'll add that to the list," Sarah said. "But right now, I want to go home and take a look at Brittany's tablet."

"If we can get into it," Ian reminded her.

"Right," she said. "Thoughts?"

I told her about my theory and that I was waiting for an email with what I hoped would be helpful information. I checked my email on my phone as we settled the check. Nothing yet. Millicent must be having some trouble finding Allison Miles. I had faith in her though. We'd get it eventually.

Chapter Eighteen

We all arrived back at the Granville house at the same time and piled into the library. I got the tablet out of its hiding place and hit the power button. Success! The screen popped to life.

"Is it password protected?" Ian asked.

I swiped the screen. A bunch of icons appeared, including a few reading apps.

"No," I said.

"Let me see," Sarah said.

I handed her the device. She swiped and tapped, then swore.

"There are some files that are password protected. So is her email. Nothing else is," she said.

"Let me try," Ian said. "I'll run through the password ideas I came up with."

Sarah gave him the tablet. He worked for a few minutes while we all watched. Then he shook his head.

"Nothing," he said. "It was a long shot anyway. We'll have to hope Greer's source comes up with something we can try."

Sarah was frustrated. "When do you think you'll hear? It's getting late," she said.

"She'll work on it until she finds something or has exhausted all her options," I said. "I may yet hear from her tonight. Would you mind leaving that with me? There's some things I want to look at, and if Millicent sends anything, I'll try it and let you know right away."

Sarah was reluctant to leave the tablet but nodded. Ian handed it to me.

"Call if those dates you asked for get you in," she said. "No matter how late. Promise?"

"Of course," I said. I meant it. If there was anything related to the family business in those files, Sarah would recognize it faster than I would. I wanted to do some general nosing around. You never knew what you might turn up.

It was getting late, so Sarah and Jack said good night. Ian and Jeremy stayed, and we ran through all our theories one more time. I decided to ask Jeremy a question that had been on my mind for some time.

"When you said the family was in for a big surprise, what did you mean?" I said.

Jeremy sighed, and then said, "I guess you might as well know. My father was exploring options for a merger. It wouldn't be an outright sale—he'd continue to manage part of the business but slowly wind down and then retire. Sarah would keep her job, if she wanted it. Eventually, the new entity would go public."

"So what happened?" Ian said. "I'm pretty sure some of the analysis I was doing on systems and so on was related, but as I said, the plug got pulled pretty suddenly."

"I suspect a better offer came along," Jeremy said. "And I think there was some connection to Brittany."

"Do you think she and your father were having an affair?" Isabelle asked. I'd been trying to think of a tactful way to pose the question myself.

"I don't know," Jeremy said. "I don't think so."

"What does your mother think? Do you know?" I asked.

"I'm not sure. She hasn't been herself for a few months. It's not like I can ask. I can't even talk to Sarah, really. I only found out about all this because I overheard my father on the phone discussing it. I confronted him, and he had to come clean. He asked me to keep it to myself. He wanted to talk to Sarah and my mother when he had all the details."

"Why now?" I said. "Even if he wants to retire, wasn't he planning on handing things off to Sarah?"

"I think he's just tired of it all. Things are very different than it was when he took it over. It's a different world. And truthfully, I'm not sure he ever wanted it. It was simply a given that he'd take over the family business. But I don't want to work there—I tried and hated it. Sarah seems to be getting restless, not that she'd admit it. It's really hard to tell. What can I say? Our usual family dynamic is off."

Because you're all keeping secrets from one another, I thought, but I couldn't say it without betraying a confidence.

"I think you should talk to Sarah," I said instead.

"I agree," Isabelle said.

Ian had been silent through Jeremy's story, his brows knit, one finger tapping his leg. Now he stirred and said to Jeremy, "Do you have any idea who this better offer might have been from?"

Jeremy shook his head. "No, only that it wasn't someone we've done business with in the past. When I heard my dad on the phone, he said he'd prefer to deal with a known quantity but would entertain any proposals. I thought it was a bargaining chip, but it looks like he meant it."

"Do you have a history with any of these people?" Ian asked, and then rattled off some of the names from the wedding guest list and a couple of company names.

"Yes," Jeremy said. "But not recently. Whitaker grew so fast, they weren't playing in the same league."

"They are now," Ian said. "Couple of acquisitions. I looked into it when I saw the names on the guest list. "

"I thought they were invited for old times' sake," Jeremy said. "One's an old college friend of my father's, and another gave me an internship." He shook his head. "I need to have a talk with Sarah. And then we need to sit down with my father. Whether or not we find anything useful on that tablet. But I need to call it a night. There's a lot to think about."

Isabelle walked him out.

"Can you find out if any of those people have some connection to Brittany?" I asked Ian.

"I can try," he said. "I'm beginning to think that's our best bet."

"Maybe," I said, as I turned the possibilities over in my mind.

"Sweet dreams," he said, giving me a kiss on the cheek. "Good luck with the passwords. I'll see you tomorrow."

"'Night," I said, lost in thought.

I heard Ian walk out, then say good night to Isabelle. A minute later she came back into the library.

"I'm tired," she said. "Want to help me check all the locks before I go to bed?"

"Sure," I said. "I'm going to go up, too." I wanted to go through whatever I could get into on Brittany's tablet, but I didn't intend to hang around downstairs by myself. I had no desire to encounter whatever was roaming the Granville house in the middle of the night.

We checked all the doors and left a few lights on both inside and outside, then went upstairs. I was hoping for a quiet night. I had some research to do.

Once I'd said good night to Isabelle and washed up and changed, I propped up some pillows and settled on my bed. I'd pulled a small notepad and pen out of my handbag. Still no email from Millicent, so I turned on the tablet. While a reading app was not as visually appealing as a bookshelf, it could yield the same information, so I started there. Brittany had saved shortcuts to two on her home screen—one a popular commercial app, and the other from her library. It was in character. She had a habit of thrift. I tapped the library icon and was happy to find that she'd stayed signed in.

I don't know what I'd expected Brittany's reading habits to be, but I was surprised by what I found. There were only a couple of titles on her loans shelf, both stories of happy families and communities. More of the same on her holds shelf, with a few soon-to-be-released Christmas romances thrown in. I was familiar with these books. They were all about close-knit groups in quaint small towns whose problems were solved with the care and help of their neighbors. There was not a murderer in sight. These authors had obviously never visited Raven Hill. No, these stories were all relaxing getaways to places you might want to live or at least vacation. There was an element of wish fulfillment to them. Maybe for the only child of a single parent, that's what it was. I'd escaped into books often enough myself, so I could relate.

I checked the other app and found more of the same. There were also a few business and personal finance books, one on capsule wardrobes and another on staging your house for sale. Back to the home screen. She had shortcuts to her personal email, a couple of news sites, a word game, and three different real estate sites. I was finding Brittany more simpatico. I loved real estate sites. While roaming around peeking in other people's windows would get you arrested, with one of these apps you could look around any number of houses with no one the wiser. You couldn't count on interior shots of any particular home, but you could get the sales and tax history. They could tell quite a story. And sometimes you got lucky and found old photos still attached to a house that wasn't for sale.

So was Brittany a lookie-loo, or was she in the market for property? Given that title on readying for a sale, she might have been planning a move.

I opened the first app and checked the menu. I wanted to see if Brittany had claimed her own home, if she owned one. She did, a condo within commuting distance of the Whitaker headquarters in Westchester. No photos. Her saved homes list was more interesting. It contained both the Whitaker and Granville homes, though there was little information on either, and no photos. They'd been in the same family so long only public records info was included, and that was sparse. There were a few small, charming, ridiculously expensive homes in towns along the Hudson. Then there was a small tract home in a suburb of Rochester. I couldn't see the appeal. It wasn't for sale, and there were no pictures. The only other saved home was a beautiful older house in Ithaca. This one had sold a few years ago, and the pictures hadn't been removed. I scrolled through them. Gorgeous, if a bit dated. That was it. I checked the other apps and found roughly the same thing. The homes for sale varied, but the Whitaker, Granville, and western New York homes were all there. Slightly different information on each, but I didn't see the point of saving them all three times.

I was about to start on her browser history when my phone pinged. I grabbed it. An email from Millicent. She apologized for the delay—it had taken a while to track down the information I needed. She provided birth and death dates for Allison Miles. "And thanks to a colleague in Rochester," she wrote, "I was able to get a copy of the obituary. Obviously written by the daughter, who was just out of college at the time. Her mother died young, and so has she. A sad story. Let me know if I can do anything else. It's been very quiet this week."

The obituary was attached. I read it quickly. Allison Miles, a native New Yorker, had been born in the Finger Lakes region. She gave birth to her only child, Brittany, at the age of nineteen. In spite of having no family support, she had managed to graduate from the State University of New York at Oswego in five years. She and her child had then moved to the Rochester area, where she worked for a local real estate developer. She had been active in the PTA and coached field hockey. She later volunteered at the local historical society. She had died of cancer two days before her forty-second birthday.

There was more to it, but those were the essentials. It was a tribute to a woman whose daughter thought her an exceptional parent. Well, raising a kid on your own wasn't easy, and Allison Miles did sound like a nice woman, the kind you'd want for a neighbor. I found it interesting that Brittany had made the point that Allison "had no family support." Not "no family to support her." There was a difference, and I thought the phrasing was deliberate. I read through it again. Yes, Brittany was making a point. She was giving a verbal middle finger to someone. Subtle though— she hadn't named names.

I picked up the tablet again, then hesitated. This would eventually end up in the hands of the police. I didn't know how sophisticated their tech department would be, but they might call on the state police for help. Maybe I should wait and use Ian's computer tomorrow. No. There was a story here. With a little digging, I should be able to find it.

I could wipe my browser history, or use an incognito window. I didn't know if it would help, but I also didn't know how much checking the police would do. Before I did anything else, though, I wanted to see where on the internet Brittany had been before she died.

Nowhere that interesting. Shopping, news, Lake Placid hotels, and a couple of auction sites. I used my phone to take pictures of the last two weeks, then went back to the real estate apps and wrote down the addresses of the houses near Rochester and Ithaca, and the name of the developer Allison Miles had worked for. I opened a private window for my own research.

I pulled up a map of New York. I wasn't that familiar with the central and western parts of the state. The home in Rochester and the developer's offices were not far apart, an easy commute. The home's property sales history showed a transaction a few months after Allison Miles had died. So this was likely her house, the place where Brittany had grown up. I looked up the developer. It was a local business, but successful. I read through the company website, noting down names and reading brief bios. It may have grown considerably since Allison had worked there. No guarantee that any of these people had known her, or Brittany. I then checked the house in Ithaca. The only sale date was several years ago. There hadn't been any other movement on it, at least none since the records had been digitized. Like the Whitaker and Granville homes, it had probably been owned by one family for a long time. I'd like to know who, and who owned it now. I scrolled through the pictures again, glad the realtor had forgotten to remove them. It was an elegant place, well designed and beautifully furnished. Update the color scheme, swap out some appliances, and it would do nicely. Something caught my eye, and I stopped mid-swipe. I enlarged the picture, and there it was—a twin of the desk in the Whitaker house.

I studied the picture. I couldn't remember all the details of the small writing desk Sarah said had belonged to Desmond's mother, but I could picture it pretty clearly. If this wasn't an exact match, it was close. According to Isabelle, Brittany had said that her grandmother owned a desk like it. So the age of the items matched. Which begged the question: Was this Brittany's grandmother's desk and, therefore, her home?

If that was the case, Allison Miles came from an affluent background. Maybe not the kind of money the Whitakers had, but her family was certainly comfortable. Yet they hadn't helped their daughter raise a child by herself. That could explain the tone of the obituary. Worth checking.

It didn't take long to find what I needed. According to the local property appraiser, the last sale of the Ithaca house had been a transaction between the Estate of Victoria Miles and Ruth and Christopher Edgemont, husband and wife. Bingo.

Victoria Miles must have been Brittany's grandmother. It was likely her grandfather had died earlier, but that could be verified by finding the obituaries. If they weren't online, Millicent would be able to track them down through her network.

Now the files and the email. Files first. I started with the dates related to Allison Miles's birth and death. Nope. The house in Rochester next. I tried the numeric address, the street name, and various combinations. Still nothing. Now Ithaca, same sequence. *Third time's the charm*, I thought, as the files opened. I scanned the contents. Standard financials from the looks of them, but Sarah would know for sure. I tried the same password on the email, but no luck. I stopped after two tries. No reason to get locked out. I'd gotten into the files. That was enough for tonight. I checked the time—well after midnight. Too late to call Sarah, no matter what she said. First thing in the morning would have to do.

I powered off the tablet and put it and my notes on the night-stand, then turned off the light and crawled under the covers. The sleep of the righteous eluded me, however. I kept spinning through the information I'd found. The background on Brittany's family was interesting, but I couldn't figure out how to connect it to her death. The financial statements might yield a clue, but that could lead right back to Desmond somehow. What was I missing?

The phone. I'd checked with Sarah—no one had called to say they'd lost one. I got out of bed, took the phone out of my hand-bag, and powered it on. Once the screen lock came up I put in the four-digit street number of the house in Ithaca. It worked. This screen was blank—no icons for apps. But the voice-mail indicator was active. I tapped it, hoping it wouldn't require a password. It didn't. Brittany had two new messages, and one saved message. I started with that.

Saved message, received Thursday at 4:17 PM.

"Call me. Something's come up."

It was a man's voice. It sounded like the voice on the call I'd picked up, but I wasn't sure.

First new message, received Thursday at 6:42 PM.

"You need to tell me how it went. We don't have time to screw around. You'll see that I'm right about this."

That phrase was familiar. The man I'd seen with Brittany at the inn had said that to her.

Second new message, received Friday at 12:02 AM.

"Don't play with me, Brittany. You'll be sorry."

End of messages.

Well, well, well.

Chapter Nineteen

I played the messages again. There was no mistaking the tone. What had started as irritation had become anger, and a threat. Whoever this was, I was ready to nominate him for prime suspect. I checked the call history. No name, and only this number appeared regularly, incoming and outgoing. That was strange. The phone belonged to Brittany—the caller had addressed her by name—but why wouldn't she have any other calls? Because she had another phone, I thought. This one was for one purpose only. Finding out the who and why of it was beyond me. That was a job for the police. I'd turn this over tomorrow. I put the phone away and crawled into bed. I was pleased with my progress and fell into a deep, dreamless sleep.

It didn't last.

"Greer, wake up!" A frantic whisper pulled me back to consciousness. I opened my eyes to see Isabelle's face a few inches from my own.

"There's someone downstairs," she whispered. "I got up to go to the bathroom, and I heard a door close."

I sat up. Isabelle stood back. She was in her pajamas and a hoodie and had a flashlight in one hand and her cell phone in the other.

"Do you want to call the police?" I asked, keeping my voice low.

She hesitated, then shook her head.

"What if they come and there's no one there again? No, I think we should check."

"Okay, but keep your phone handy," I said. "We'll sneak down, and if we see anyone we don't know, we sprint for the other house and call the cops."

"Good plan," she said.

I slipped out of bed, pulled on my sweatshirt, and grabbed my own phone and flashlight. We crept down the hall, keeping to the outer edge to avoid squeaks. When we got to the top of the stairs I stifled a gasp. An eerie red glow spilled out of the library. I looked at Isabelle.

"Lava lamp?" I whispered. "What's it doing down there?"

Isabelle shook her head.

We went down the stairs, again sticking to the outer part of the tread. We stopped at the bottom, listening. A minute passed with no sound other than our own breathing. And then a creak, and a shadow crossed in front of the light. We waited. There was a faint rustling, and then silence. Isabelle and I looked at each other. I nodded, and we walked carefully across the hall to the library door. Isabelle peeked around and motioned me forward. We stopped on the threshold.

A small figure, hooded and all in black, was on the far side of the room. One pale hand moved slowly across the carved wooden panel next to the window, tracing the shapes. When it reached the bottom, the hand dropped, the head drooped, and the figure slowly turned.

"Hello, Barbara," I said.

She started, and then reached up and pushed back her hood.

"Oh, dear," she said. "I've woken you. I'm so sorry."

"It's all right," Isabelle said. "I was awake. I was going to make hot chocolate. Would you like some?"

"That would be nice, Isabelle. If it's not inconvenient. It's gotten chilly, hasn't it?" Barbara pulled her hood up around her neck, like a scarf, and wrapped her arms around herself.

"It has gotten chilly," I said. My feet were freezing. "Let's go into the kitchen."

Barbara came across the room and followed Isabelle into the kitchen. I turned on the desk light, then turned off and unplugged the lava lamp. I wrapped the cord around the base and put it on a shelf. When I got to the kitchen, Barbara was seated at the table. Isabelle had the kettle on and was getting out mugs.

"It's instant, but it has extra marshmallows," she said.

Barbara smiled at her. "I love the marshmallows."

"Me, too," I said. I sat next to Barbara and tucked my feet up. We waited quietly until Isabelle had brought us our mugs and seated herself.

"Well, you girls must be wondering what I'm up to," Barbara said. She wrapped her hands around her mug and looked from me to Isabelle.

"Looking for something?" I asked.

"Yes, that's right," she said. "I thought they would be upstairs with my other things, but they're not. I've looked all over. I know Jane wouldn't throw them away. But I can't ask her. She gets upset when she thinks about—Jane gets upset."

"Your journals?" Isabelle said.

"Yes. You two are awfully clever. That's exactly right."

"You're a poet, aren't you? Caro mentioned it," I said.

Barbara gave a little laugh. "Not in a long time," she said. "But you know, I want to write again. My doctor said it would be all right, that it would be good for me. With the new medication, I think I could do it. But I want to see my old work."

"Haven't you written at all, in all the years since—you left?" I asked.

Barbara shook her head. "There's so much I don't remember. I know I did at first, when I was in the hospital. I had paper, and a pencil. The nurse would watch. But it was hard, hard to get the words to come. I don't know what happened to those papers. They took them, I think. They took my words, my thoughts. They're gone."

"We'll find them for you, the journals," Isabelle said. "Right, Greer?"

"Yes, we will," I said. "Do you think they're in the library?"

Barbara shook her head. "Jane would have hidden them, her room or mine. My mother—Jane would have put them in a safe place. But I can't find them. So I thought, maybe the library. She used to sit on the window seat and draw while I practiced the piano. I can't figure out where."

"We'll find them," Isabelle said. I nodded.

"Thank you," Barbara said. "Now, I should get back"

"Yes, Melissa will worry if she notices you gone," I said.

"Oh, she won't wake up," Barbara said. "She's sound asleep. She works so hard. Every night since we've been here, I've helped her study. She has these little cards, and I quiz her. But she gets tired, so it's good for her to rest. I'm very quiet."

"Then we'll walk you back," Isabelle said.

"It's too cold," Barbara said. "You're both barefoot. Watch me from the side door. That's what I did when Desmond and Jane were small. All right?"

I looked at Isabelle.

"I think that will be okay," she said.

We got up and went into the hall toward the side door.

"Barbara," I said, "why did you bring the lava lamp down?"

She looked puzzled. "The lamp?" she said. "I didn't. That was in the library when I got here. I just turned it on."

Isabelle and I exchanged another look. In unspoken agreement, we decided not to pursue it.

We stood in the doorway and watched Barbara cross the driveway. As she got close to the other house, Isabelle stirred.

"I think it was her. The day of the party. I think it was Barbara in that hoodie and a cap," she said.

"Are you sure?" I asked, as Barbara disappeared inside.

"Pretty sure," she said

We locked up and went back to the kitchen.

"I'll talk to Margaret tomorrow," Isabelle said. "And Jeremy."

"You should mention that Jane has sleeping pills."

"Do you think she—Melissa?" Isabelle said. "I'm not sure how she could."

"Neither am I, but it doesn't hurt to mention."

Isabelle nodded. "I'll tell her. I'll tell her about the journals, too. That we're looking, and that we already found one. She might want to check with Barbara's doctor."

"Okay," I said. "Let me know what she says."

The rest of the night was quiet, but too short. I was up with the birds the next morning. Bird, actually. The hooded crow was perched on a branch outside my window, cawing at high volume.

"All right, all right, breakfast in a few," I said through the window. After I showered and dressed, I sent Sarah a text letting her know I had gotten into the files. I was making coffee when she responded with "Be right over." I messaged Ian next. Isabelle stuck her head into the kitchen, still in her pajamas, to say she'd spoken to Margaret and Jeremy and given them the whole story. She gave me Margaret's number in case anything else came up, then went up to shower. I figured the whole gang would be here shortly. I was not mistaken. I had just poured my second cup of coffee and tossed some toast crumbs to the birds when Sarah bounded onto the porch, followed by a yawning Jack.

"Where is it?" Sarah asked.

I handed her the tablet and gave her the code. Jack went straight to the coffee maker. By the time Ian and Jeremy arrived, Isabelle was downstairs and making a second pot. Sarah was still scrolling through the files on the tablet.

"Anything?" Jeremy said, once we were all settled around the kitchen table.

"It's all financial, some of it not public," Sarah said. "Also, some projections I've never seen before. New accounts. It doesn't make sense."

"Would it make sense if the company was merging?" Jeremy asked.

"Maybe? Some of these potential partnerships are only in the discussion stages," she said. She didn't seem surprised by the question. "Jeremy called me last night and told me about the conversation he had with Dad," she explained. "It looks like we were all making assumptions and working at cross-purposes. But I still can't believe he'd do something like this without telling us."

She was angry, and sad. I could see it in her face.

"Maybe he was only exploring it," I said.

"Maybe, but still," she said.

"I think he only said something to me because I confronted him, and I was already out of the business," Jeremy said. "The question is, what do we do with this information now?"

"Before you decide that, I have some things you need to hear," I said.

I told them what I had learned about Brittany's background, and how I'd come up with the code. I finished up with the voice mails, playing them for everyone to hear.

"Wow," Ian said. "And to think you were worried about my messages. That last one was definitely a threat."

"I'd say so," Sarah said. "Do we know who this guy is? Because he sounds like our murderer." Everyone agreed.

"I don't know his name, but I'm sure it's the man I saw with Brittany Wednesday night. I told the police about him, but I don't know what they did with the information." I knew Bill Kent had taken me seriously, but I hadn't given him much to work with. I had a feeling they were still looking closer to home for the killer.

"We need to turn this over to the police, too," Jeremy said. "Along with the tablet."

Sarah held up her hand.

"Not just yet," she said. "I want to talk to Dad first. And I'd like to know how this all ties together. Then we'll hand it to the lawyer and let him deal with the police."

There was some debate about this between Sarah, Jack, and Jeremy. Sarah wouldn't budge.

"Look," she said, "we're going to have to finesse this time line anyway. We give the attorneys the bare minimum of information, and then they take it from there. They're not lying because they don't know. This is what we pay them for. We just have to get our story straight and stick to it."

"We don't even have to lie—much," I said. "We found the tablet late yesterday, it wasn't working, we charged it up, and made sure it was Brittany's this morning. It *was* after midnight when I got into the locked files. As for the phone, I tried calling the number I had for her from my own phone the night I found it. It didn't ring, so I thought it belonged to Shelby or another guest. We've been trying to find the owner ever since. Dumb luck I thought to try that code."

"Exactly!" Sarah said. "Now, are you coming with me to talk to Dad?" she said to Jeremy. He nodded. "Good. We'll all meet back here at lunchtime and see where we stand."

With that, she picked up the tablet and left, Jeremy and Jack right behind her.

"Well," Isabelle said, "I'm going for a walk. If Brittany's car is stashed around here, I'm going to find it."

"Are you really going to go looking in other people's garages?" Ian said.

"Sure. If anyone asks, I'll tell them I'm looking for my cat," she said. "They don't need to know she's at home in New Hampshire with my parents." She took a last swallow of coffee, set her mug in the sink, and then she, too, was out the door.

"I guess that leaves us," Ian said.

"Yep, and I need your laptop," I said. "Why don't we work at the boathouse? I'd like to get out of here for a while."

Ian helped me clean up from breakfast. We walked to the boat-house and in short order were set up in the living room, with more coffee and Ian's laptop.

"What exactly are you looking for?" he asked.

"Exactly? I'm not sure. I'm going to cast a wide net and see if I can find something to tie all these loose ends together," I said. I pulled out my notebook and said, "Let me show you what I found last night and see if you come up with something I haven't thought of."

I ran through everything, showed him the pictures of the houses, and gave him my theory on Brittany's family, admitting that I had no idea if any of it related to what was going on with Whitaker Inc. or Brittany's death.

"I'm going to see if I can find some connections," I said. "It's a long shot but worth a try."

I started searching for an obituary for Victoria Miles. The only thing I could find online was short. It gave no real sense of the woman but did state that she was predeceased by her husband, Kenneth Miles. I tried him next. He'd been dead for fifteen years, according to his obit, leaving his wife, one daughter, Elizabeth Miles Endicott of Syracuse, and two grandchildren, Jennifer Endicott of Boston and Miles Endicott of Westchester County, New York. No mention of Allison or Brittany anywhere.

"Must have been some family feud," Ian said, when I pointed that out to him.

"Seriously," I said. "See if you can find out anything about the daughter or grandchildren. I'll see what else there is about Kenneth."

Ian took out his phone and went to work. I didn't find much on Kenneth. He was a typical successful small-business owner, decent golf handicap, member of the Chamber of Commerce, blah blah blah. Nothing philanthropic.

"Hey, take a look at this," Ian said. "Do you think this woman looks like Brittany?" He handed me his phone.

He'd found a photo from a charity event. The woman in it did look like Brittany, or like Brittany aged twenty years. What interested me more was the man standing next to her. I wanted a better look.

"I think that's him, the man from the inn," I said. "Where's the picture from?"

Ian read off the information, and I typed it into a new browser window. Up popped a series of photos. I found the one I wanted and clicked on it. The man in it was the man I'd seen with Brittany. The picture was from a newspaper article and was captioned "Elizabeth Endicott, longtime symphony supporter, and her son, Miles."

"So that's Brittany's aunt, and that's her cousin," I said.

"And the cousin is here, or was," Ian added. He leaned closer. "Make it a little bigger."

I zoomed in.

"I've seen that guy," Ian said.

"Here? In Lake Placid?"

"No, but I'm sure he was at one of the events I went to with Brittany. I think she even spoke to him briefly, but she didn't introduce us. I only remember him because he seemed to be watching her until he left."

"Creepy. We'll definitely be showing this to the police," I said. "I'd better let Sarah know."

I emailed her the link and what we'd discovered, and then sent a text telling her to check her email before talking to the lawyer.

"But I'm guessing she's still having it out with her father," I said. "What a mess."

"Do you really think Desmond and Brittany were having an affair?" Ian asked.

"I don't know. From what you've said about her behavior, that she may have been using you, it sounds like she was involved with someone, and he's the obvious choice. Maybe not a full-blown affair, but there was something going on. Or maybe it was just all part of whatever game she's playing."

"He and Jane have been married a very long time," Ian said. "I couldn't do it. Obviously. I've concluded marriage is just not for me."

"I'd never do it again either," I said.

"Really? Why not?"

"Not to knock what I had with Danny, but in retrospect, I started to feel—confined, I guess you could say. I can't really explain it. I'm happy I married Dan. We were happy together. But I realized at Sarah's wedding that I would never do it again. Long-term partner? Maybe. Marriage, no."

Ian was silent for a minute. Then he said, "I can see that." Another pause, followed by, "Have you ever thought about—"

My phone pinged. I grabbed it. Message from April.

"Got into the records. Frank's last call was to William Warren. CTO New Leaf. Will let you know if I find anything else."

Well, now, this was interesting. But how did it tie in? The mysterious hospital visitor was a woman. But then again, so was the CEO of New Leaf.

"Was that Sarah?" Ian asked.

"April Benson," I said. "What do you know about the New Leaf CEO? Something Philips. Claire?"

"Clarice Philips," he said. "Well, we've met a few times. She's not really—I mean—I don't . . ." he trailed off.

"What?" I asked. "You don't what?"

"I don't keep in touch with her. Haven't since shortly after she started New Leaf."

"Oh. Well, I'm going to have to learn a lot more about cannabis. From the corporate angle, I mean," I added when Ian raised his eyebrows.

My phone pinged again. Sarah.

"Thanks! Lawyer wants phone and tablet. Strategize at lunch."

I showed Ian.

"I still think Sarah's plan is sketchy," he said.

This from the guy who searched someone's office and walked off with one of the devices under discussion. I shrugged.

"We'll have to keep our stories straight. I'm sure your light-fingered ways don't need to come into it," I said, and smiled.

"Oh. Right," Ian said.

I looked at the picture on the screen, then got Brittany's phone out.

"So you never saw her with this? You're sure she had another phone?" I asked Ian.

"I'm sure," he said. "No dragonfly. It was her signature, for the devices anyway."

"Kind of like the seasonal pashmina," I said. I scrolled through the call history. Other than a couple of things marked "Spam," it was all the same number. No name attached.

"It looks like she had this phone for only this contact," I said. Since I was going to be handing over the evidence, I wanted to listen to the messages again and write down the exact words. I went through them, noting exact phrasing, date and time.

"It really sounds like we found our killer," Ian said.

"Maybe," I said. I was studying the call history. Something seemed strange. I took out my own phone and snapped some pictures.

"You don't think it was him?"

"Hmm? Oh, well," I said, as I shut down the phone, "he didn't strike me as the type to want to get his hands dirty. He's more the 'cut off your allowance' type. Not that she was getting anything from him that we know of. But in the right circumstances, anyone can be a killer."

"That leaves us with the family, or someone who was here at the time."

"Like us," I said. "Though no one seems that interested in me for it. Are the cops still sniffing around you?"

"Not really, though I talked to that lawyer you recommended, and he said no one is in the clear until they find out who did it. He also said the clock is ticking, and if they don't come up with something soon, they may not. Then we're all looking at years of this. The story will never go away, he said."

"We can't let that happen," I said. "We're going to figure it out."

"So if it's not this Miles Endicott, who was it?"

"Well, if Desmond was having an affair with Brittany, it could be Jane, or Desmond himself if things went south," I said.

"Or if he found out she was trying to pull a fast one in terms of the business," Ian said.

"True. I think the two biggest motives for murder are love or money, or both."

"Where does that leave everyone else?"

"If Brittany was up to something with either Desmond or the business, or both, it could be Jeremy or Sarah. Jeremy less so, I would think," I said.

"Because he had moved on," Ian said. "But he could have been protecting his parents, Jane particularly. So could Sarah, I guess."

"Yes, and she didn't like Brittany. She found her threatening but couldn't put her finger on why. But I don't see her as the killer either. She's planning on moving on as well." I told Ian about Jack's job in Europe and that it was still a secret as far as I knew. "And at this point, it wouldn't surprise me if she wanted out completely."

"That leaves us with Barbara and Caro, unless we consider the staff," Ian said.

"Barbara may have been protecting Jane. Or Caro protecting Desmond. But I'm not sure either one of them is strong enough. The initial blow, yes. But what if Brittany wasn't out cold? Holding her under and then moving the body would require some real strength."

"That's true," Ian said. "That's why I keep coming back to Endicott. It had to be either a man or a very strong woman."

"If we're going to consider the staff, both Margaret and Melissa are strong. Mrs. Henderson less so. But Margaret leaves at dinnertime. Mrs. Henderson and Melissa have no known connection to Brittany. I'm sure that's something the police have checked. Which brings us back to Endicott."

"So what's the problem?"

"Loose ends? That it seems out of character, from the little I've seen of him?" I sighed. "I don't know. Maybe I'm overthinking. It's nearly noon. Let's go back to the Granville house and see if anyone else has come up with anything."

Someone had. We met Isabelle in the driveway. She was bouncing with excitement.

"I found the car! Well, actually, the police found the car, but I found the police searching it," she said.

"That's great," I said. "I don't suppose you could tell if any of her stuff was in it?"

"I got a good look," she said.

"How did you manage that?" Ian said.

"I walked right up, stopped where I could see into the car, and started asking about my missing cat," she said. "I made sure I sounded upset and described her in detail. Hypatia has very unusual markings, so that took a while. Then I asked if they'd mind if I looked in the bushes, since she's shy and might be hiding. They were very nice. I hunted around for as long as I could and listened to them. They said the car was clean, no personal items, not even any trash."

"So no keys, phone, or handbag," I said.

"Nothing," Isabelle said. "And the car was unlocked, I heard that, too. Looks like whoever left it there left in a hurry. I'd have locked it. You would if you were leaving your car for a while at your vacation home."

She was right. I'd have locked it, too. I'd have to make Isabelle an honorary member of the Raven Hill Irregulars. She had great instincts.

At that point Sarah, Jack, and Jeremy arrived. Isabelle repeated her story. Jeremy asked her to describe the house where the car was found.

"That sounds like the Griffin house," he said. "They're never here this time of year."

"Then whoever left the car would have to know that," Ian said.

"Not necessarily," Jack said. "I've noticed that house—it has some interesting features. There's never any lights on, and the landscaping isn't well tended. It looks like no one lives there."

"That's true," Sarah said. "My mother complains about it every time she goes by. I think the Griffins only come up for the month of July and ski weekends."

"So that widens the field again," I said. "And it leaves Miles Endicott in the picture."

"It must be him," Sarah said. "Nothing else makes sense."

I could think of several things that did, but she didn't want to hear that, so I moved on.

"What did your father say about the files we found?" I asked.

"He admitted that he wants to merge and then retire in a few years," Sarah said. "But he wanted to examine his options before he said anything. He wanted to make sure there would be a place for me in the new structure, if that's what I wanted. He said he didn't want me to feel stuck though, so he'd also be open to an outright sale. He said he thought I might be getting restless. I was surprised." She fiddled with her rings. "Surprised he noticed, I guess. I should have said something."

"We were still figuring it out," Jack said, taking her hand.

"Yes, yes, we were," Sarah said. "But there's something else. We downloaded those files onto a drive and printed them out. Dad says some numbers are off. When I said I thought Brittany was up to something with the potential sale, he agreed, but he said he couldn't figure out her endgame. A lot of her projections were reasonable, and the ones that were inflated might be bets that would pay off, but you wouldn't know that for a while. If you based a sale price on them, the buyer might end up overpaying by quite a bit, or they might do very well. He needed to study the numbers some more."

"Is there any connection, even way back, between your family and the Endicotts? Or Brittany's grandparents?" I asked.

Sarah shook her head. "I asked my father. None that he knows of. The Miles family was in manufacturing but sold their business a long time ago. I did some digging while my father was looking at the files. Endicott is an officer in a holding company. They have interests in social analytics, streaming, and various media. It's relatively new, and there's no sign of any connection to Whitaker in the past at all. But I can see why he's interested in adding our company to the mix—they don't have anything like it, and we're small and independent. Compared to their other options, we're inexpensive. I don't think this is a deal my father would have entertained without Brittany pushing it though. He's still pretty traditional and thinks putting people with no experience in the business in charge is a bad idea."

"Would Brittany get a big payday regardless?" I asked.

"She could do well financially in a lot of ways, depending on the deal structure and how long she stays with the company after. Especially if Endicott is also paying her for inside information."

"And she could already be gone by the time those projections don't pay out and leave Endicott holding the bag," I said.

"She could. Cold, but clever," Sarah said.

"And will your lawyer be sharing all this with the police?" Ian asked.

"Shortly," Sarah said. "He didn't sound happy on the phone, but he's going to get in touch and meet them here. He said they'd have questions, so he's coming early to make sure we're all clear on everything. Mrs. Henderson is doing another buffet lunch. Should be ready now."

"And then we make ourselves scarce unless the police want us?" Ian said.

"Something like that," Sarah said. "Let's go. I want to get this wrapped up so we can get on with our lives."

I admired her optimism, but I still felt like we were missing something. As we walked to the Whitaker house, I asked her for the notes she'd made at dinner the other night.

"Sure," she said. "Why?"

I shrugged. "I don't know. From everything you said, Endicott makes sense, but I want to be sure we didn't miss anything."

She nodded. "I'll run up and get them. You'll let me know, won't you? If you find something? Though I hope you don't."

"Me, too," I said. "I think we're all ready to move on."

"Yes," she said. "I should've talked to my dad sooner. Maybe we could have avoided all this."

"Maybe," I said. "Though it might have more to do with Brittany's family issues than yours."

"It's awful to say, but I hope so. I didn't like her, and now I feel sorry for her, but I still wish we'd never hired her."

We went in through the side door. I headed for the dining room, while Sarah went to get her notes. Ian caught up with me.

"What do you think?" he said.

"I don't know. I hope Endicott's our guy, but I'm not sure. I'm going to go over everything after lunch. If I can stay awake," I added, unable to suppress a yawn.

He nodded. "I have some work to do, and the police may have questions. Want to meet for dinner? Depending on what's going on."

"That would be nice," I said.

Sarah came back with her notes, and I tucked them into my pocket. We got ourselves some lunch. A short time later, Desmond's local attorney arrived. Tom Jocelyne was a "just the facts" guy. I'm sure there were things he didn't want to know. I handed over the phone and told him the story of finding it and trying to find the owner. I ended with the lucky guess on the code to unlock it. His eyebrows went up once or twice but he didn't say anything. Then he turned to Ian.

"And you found Ms. Miles' tablet?" he asked.

"Yes," Ian said.

"She had forgotten it in Mr. Whitaker's office after a meeting, I understand," Jocelyne said, making some notes.

"Apparently. I was looking for Desmond and noticed it on the chair. I thought I recognized the cover. I had just picked it up when Greer called. I got distracted and walked out with it."

"Absentminded, are you, Mr. Cameron?"

"Sometimes, yes," Ian said.

"Hmmm," Jocelyne said, and closed his notebook. "Thank you. The police may have some questions, but I don't think I'll need to be present. We're all trying to help, after all. However, if you'd prefer to have me there, here's my card. And I'd like to know if they do speak to you."

He handed each of us a card and disappeared into the hall. I excused myself, telling Sarah I wanted a nap and promising to call her later. I snagged a couple of cookies and wrapped them in a napkin on my way out. A nap would be nice, but I had some things to figure out, so a little walk and some fresh air, followed by cookies and caffeine, would have to do. I wanted another look at the reflecting pool.

I went out the side door and down the path from the driveway, past Jane's office, and down the steps. I saw no one along the way and, when I got to the clearing with the pool, found only the hooded crow.

"Having a bath?" I asked, as I seated myself on the bench. The bird hopped from rock to rock at the rim of the pool, head tilted as she looked into the water.

"You're right, it's too chilly," I said. It was getting cooler. I was glad I'd put on my jacket. I looked toward the lake. There were clouds moving in. The day was breezy, bringing autumn leaves to earth. Several were floating in the pool. Maybe that's what was putting the crow off her bath. I reached into my pocket and pulled out the napkin full of cookies. I unwrapped them and tossed her a bit.

"Here you go—it's peanut butter," I said. I broke some off for myself. The crow hopped over, gobbled down the cookie, and went right back to her perch by the pool, where she stared into the bright surface, sparkling in the midday sun.

"More interested in shiny objects today?" I said. And then I remembered. Shiny object. Something sparkling as Brittany pushed her hair back at the tea party, and again as she twisted out of sight beneath the surface of the lake. And here, in the pool. When was that? I stuffed the cookies back in my pocket and walked over to the pool. The crow took off as I approached but didn't go far. There was something she wanted in there.

I knelt and leaned over the water, pulling out some of the leaves. There it was, glittering deep in the water. Brittany's missing earring. It was half hidden in some debris, the motion of the water pushing dirt and dead leaves around it. Without the crow and the angle of the sun, I wouldn't have seen it. I took off my jacket, leaned on one of the beach stones that edged the pool, and started to reach in. The stone moved under my hand, and I pulled back to regain my balance. I'd put one of these back, hadn't I? The day after the tea party? And that must have been when I'd glimpsed the earring, a small spark of light, different from the glimmering surface of the pool.

That didn't seem right, though. A memory swam up—the glimmer beneath the surface, I was walking, and talking to Caro. But that was Thursday. Brittany had died here Thursday night. Could she have lost it and not noticed until that night, and been followed into the garden as she came looking for it? I shook my head. No matter how it got here, the police would want it. It must have been buried when the forensics team was here, though if they were here taking samples they might not have looked. Maybe I should leave it. *Take it.* A whisper from my subconscious. I ignored those at my peril. If I had seen this, someone else might. *Take it.* I reached again, bracing myself on the ground this time. The water was cold, but I got the earring. I gave the rest of the peanut butter cookie to the indignant crow and examined my find. It was an old-fashioned clip-on earring. The clip moved easily. She could have taken it off when she was on the phone and dropped it, or it could have come loose and fallen. Odd that she hadn't noticed.

I put it in my pocket, pulled my jacket back on, and went through the garden back to the Granville house. Time for more coffee and the remaining cookie. Fuel for what Poirot called the little gray cells. I had some thinking to do.

Chapter Twenty

Isabelle was on the porch with her laptop and a notepad when I got back. She had arranged a meeting on Friday with a mathematics professor in the Albany area and wanted to review some of her work.

"My father is right. I need to finish my doctorate, and Dr. Arsenault is one of the best people working in my field. She's brilliant. I don't want to sound like an idiot when I meet her," Isabelle said.

"I'm sure you won't," I said. "I'm going to be working in the library. I'm making coffee, if you want any."

"Maybe in a bit," she said, her attention back on her screen.

I went into the kitchen and put on some coffee. I noticed that where I had left the Whitakers with only two cookies, Isabelle had come back with an entire plateful. Not bad. While the coffee brewed I went into the library and spread out Sarah's notes, then got my own notebook and phone. Finally, I pulled out the earring I'd fished from the reflecting pool. Brittany's, I was sure, but there was something else I wanted to check.

I went to the photos app on my phone and pulled up the pictures I'd taken of Brittany's browsing history. There had been a couple of auction sites. I loved auctions, though I preferred live to online. I looked through the sites she'd saved, finding one that handled a lot of estate jewelry. Then I went to past auctions. There was a decent search function. I typed in "sapphire diamond" and then scrolled through the results. There were a lot. I'd gone through several pages before I found them. A match to the earring I had in hand and, below that, a bracelet and necklace. All part of the same set, all old, classic, and expensive. And, I was willing to bet, all once owned by the Miles family.

I looked around the rest of the site and the others. Plenty of furniture and jewelry were the right period and style to have come from the Miles house. Maybe that's why she had saved all the pictures. To get back what she thought should have been hers, or her mother's. To reclaim parts of a family she hadn't had, a more luxurious life. Her salary was high, according to Sarah, but was it enough? Desmond had said he couldn't figure out her endgame. Maybe she was looking for a big payoff. Or payback, if the plan involved screwing over Miles Endicott. It couldn't happen to a nicer guy, from my brief experience of him.

I heard the door open as the coffee pot beeped. I shoved all the notes under an atlas and tucked both earring and phone into my pocket. I walked into the kitchen and found Bill Kent eying the plate of cookies.

"Hello," I said.

"Hello, Ms. Hogan. Ms. Peterson said I'd find you in the library. Said to go ahead in. She seems engrossed in whatever she's doing."

"I'm sure she is. Coffee?" I said. "I was about to have some."

"Thank you. That would be nice."

"Have a seat," I said, waving him toward the kitchen table. He sat, and I placed some napkins and the cookies in front of him. He'd worked his way through a couple by the time I returned with two mugs and the cream and sugar.

"Lieutenant O'Donnell said some nice things about you," Kent said, as we fixed our coffee.

"How flattering," I said. "He found me helpful with a local case last spring. Now, I'm sure you want to know about the phone."

I'd already decided what I was and was not going to tell him, so I wanted to take charge of the conversation. I also wanted information, which I wasn't sure I'd get. Being helpful and forthcoming increased my odds.

"Among other things," he said. "But why don't you start there. How'd you find it?"

I was sure the lawyers had told him, but I was willing to go into detail. I hadn't done anything wrong. I started with Shelby screaming and ended with unlocking the phone. He asked a few questions but for the most part let me talk.

"One other thing about the phone," I said. "Someone called the night I found it. I was sound asleep, so I fumbled when I picked it up. By the time I could hear anything, a man was already talking. I was surprised—I'd expected it to be Shelby. He was saying, 'Are you there? Say something! Don't play games.' Something like that."

"Same voice as the messages?" Kent asked.

"I think so," I answered. "Same number, anyway. I checked the call history once I'd unlocked the phone. I had thought the phone belonged to someone who'd come to the party, so I tried to match the number to the guest list. I was helping Sarah with some last-minute things, so I have a copy. No match."

"And you've been looking for the owner among the wedding guests since you found it?"

"Yes," I said. "We didn't have a number for everyone. We didn't have Shelby's, for that matter. Her contact number was the same as Frank's. We asked around, then figured we'd hear from someone. And to be honest, with everything that happened, I kept forgetting."

"Understandable," Kent said. "Anything else?"

"It struck me as odd that she had a phone to communicate with only one person. Like something out of a spy novel. Did you find her personal phone?"

"We have not," Kent said. "Nor her work phone, though we were able to access those records through her employer."

"And did she have contact with that number, who I'm presuming is Miles Endicott, on her work phone? Because I'm guessing no."

He raised his eyebrows. "Not that we have found—yet," he said.

"But there were other personal calls on it? Friends, salon, doctor—stuff like that?" I asked. I had the beginning of a theory.

"Where are you going with this, Ms. Hogan?"

"I don't think she had a personal phone. I think she used her work phone for everything to save money. That second phone—I'll bet Endicott gave it to her to stay under the radar. No chance anyone at Whitaker would stumble onto the connection between the two."

"Why would she want to save money? She made a very nice living," Kent said.

"Same reason she took the mints and the hand lotion— the habit of thrift. And I think she had her eye on a big purchase."

"Go on."

"Did Mr. Jocelyne tell you what we discovered about Brittany's background?"

"He did. From what I understand, you found most of it. We'll check it out."

Not surprising. The lawyer would have been happy to share anything that pointed away from his clients but was unlikely to linger on anything that highlighted how long we'd had evidence in a murder inquiry before turning it over.

"Yes, well, I also had information from Sarah and Ian," I said. "And a lot of this is guesswork, you understand."

Kent nodded.

I told him about the unlocked apps on Brittany's tablet, and my curiosity about her reading habits. About our mutual love of real estate and auction sites, and how I'd started to see a pattern. Her mother's obituary. The fascination with the Mileses' house.

"And then I found this," I said. I laid the sapphire and diamond earring on the table. "Brittany's. I'm sure of it. She was only wearing one when she was found, right?"

Kent leaned forward in his chair. He didn't look happy.

"Where and when did you find this Ms. Hogan, and why did you take it?"

"About an hour ago, in the reflecting pool. One of the crows found it. I had to trade an entire peanut butter cookie to get it. I took it so it wouldn't disappear again. Crows collect shiny things, you know. Besides, I figured I'd see you this afternoon."

Kent looked up at the ceiling and tapped his fingers on the table. I got the feeling he was counting to ten. I had that effect on law enforcement. I took another cookie and waited.

"You shouldn't have moved it. You should have called us."

"Couldn't risk it. That was one very determined crow. But as long as I did take it, do you want to know what I found out about it?"

More finger tapping. A long sigh.

"Tell me," he said.

I wiped my hands and picked up my phone. I'd saved the page from the auction site. I showed him.

"I'd put money on these having belonged to Victoria Miles. I'd bet a lot of her estate was sold at auction, and Brittany found some of it. Maybe her mother had mentioned some things, or Brittany spotted them in the pictures from the house sale or by researching the family. I think she was looking for a big payoff because she wanted the house, too."

Kent looked surprised. "That is a leap, Ms. Hogan." He thought for a minute, then nodded. "But I can see how you got there."

"Call the agent who handled the last sale and see if there have been any inquiries," I said. I'd thought of doing it myself, but I'd have to make up a story. Kent could get it done faster. I was sure I was right though.

"So you think Ms. Miles was trying to broker a deal between Whitaker and her cousin, even if it wasn't in Whitaker's best interest, in return for a lot of money?"

"Maybe. Or maybe she wanted the money and a chance to screw over Miles Endicott and the family who disowned her mother. Endicott figured it out and killed her. Do you know where he was the night she died? Or where he is now?"

"We're working on that. I have to give you credit—up until now, everything we've found pointed in all kinds of different directions. Now everything's pointing in one—Miles Endicott. Though it isn't lost on me that everything you've said moves suspicion away from your friends. Still, you've unearthed an impressive amount of information in a short time.

I gave him a look over my coffee cup.

"I'm a reference librarian—I have a particular set of skills."

Kent smiled. "I guess you do," he said. He picked up the earring and stood. "Is there anything else?"

"No," I said. "Not that I can think of."

He took out a pen and wrote something on the back of his business card.

"Here," he said. "My home and cell are on the back. If anything else comes to you, or even if you see something, or someone, that makes you nervous, call me right away."

"Thank you," I said, and pocketed the card. I followed Kent to the door. Isabelle was still on the porch. She didn't even look up when Kent walked down the stairs. I went inside and poured her a cup of coffee, then put some cookies on a plate and brought them to her.

"So you don't forget to eat," I said, setting them down next to her. "Also, can you spare some blank paper? My notebook is too small for what I want to do."

"Hmm? Oh, thanks," she said. "Here you go."

I went back to the library and pulled the notes out from under the atlas. I smoothed them out and spread them on the desk, anchoring them with a couple of books. I yawned—my lack of sleep was catching up to me—and pulled my jacket closed. The denim was lined, but I'd have been better off with the fleece style that seemed to be standard issue in the Adirondacks. Caro's had kept me nice and toasty the other night.

I read through everything Sarah had written twice. Some of the questions we had answers for, but some of those answers led to more questions. And there was that gap in the time line, when no one had seen Brittany and anyone could have come and gone from the guest cottage. That bothered me. So did the sense that I was missing something obvious. I yawned again. All right, then. Back to the beginning.

I found the list we'd made of the things we knew for sure. This could be updated. "Brittany had a head wound, origin unknown." I added, "But probably one of the stones that lined the reflecting pool, either because she fell/was pushed, or someone hit her." Most of those stones were seated pretty firmly, but not all.

Next up, "Brittany drowned in the reflecting pool." Either because someone held her under or because she was unconscious when she went in. I thought there would be marks on the body if someone had held her down, different from what would happen from being in the water for twenty-four hours. Neither Kent nor the lawyer had mentioned that, so I was going to presume that she was out cold when she hit the water.

Up to this point, it could have been an accident. Brittany trips, falls, hits her head, drowns. She was wandering around the garden in the dark. It could have happened that way, except for points three and four. "Brittany's body was found in the lake, under the Granville dock," and "Brittany's car, phone, handbag, and possibly some of her jewelry were missing."

Why move the body? If I were Miles Endicott, I'd leave her where she fell and make myself scarce. When she was found, either the accident theory would hold or suspicion would fall on the Whitakers. Of course, he might have thought dumping her in the lake would get rid of physical evidence on her body. Or he wanted to buy time to get away and thought she wouldn't be found right away if her body was in the lake. By moving her car and taking her handbag and phone, it would look as if she had left voluntarily.

This is where the Endicott theory broke down for me. It was possible, but unlikely. It was possible that he'd been in the garden before and could find his way around, but unlikely. It was possible that he could find his way to the Granville dock while carrying a body, but unlikely. It was dark. It would be hard for someone who was familiar with the place, and next to impossible for someone who wasn't. Even Jeremy, who had designed the garden, said everything looked different at night. Moonlight cast different shadows, and there had been some cloud cover that night. Then he'd have to ditch the car and her stuff in places where no one would find them right away, and get back to wherever he was staying, all without being seen. No, as much as I wanted it to be Endicott, I couldn't make it work. Maybe the police could, but I was going back to the drawing board.

Jennie had said to forget motive and figure out who could physically have done it, who had the opportunity. Back to the time line. I pulled those pages closer. I'd start with the day of the tea. Brittany had died that night, so what she'd done that day was important.

The party had started at two. Sarah and I were downstairs on the hour, per Jane's instructions. I'd mingled for an hour, spent some time with Caro, then Sarah had joined us. Shortly after, she'd introduced us to Brittany. Brief chat, then Brittany had excused herself, and I'd gone outside. Say, a little after four? I wandered through the garden, visited with Jeremy, and then came back in. I hadn't seen Caro or Isabelle, but I had spoken to Sarah and then to Jane. From what Sarah and Isabelle said, Brittany was still at the party somewhere. First she talked to Sarah, then Isabelle and Caro, and then stepped out to take a call. That must be when I had heard her on the path. The last time any of us had seen her was as the party was ending, when Caro saw her walking down the driveway to the guest cottage. Based on when I'd seen Isabelle and spoken to Caro, that had to have been a little after five.

After that, no one had seen Brittany until after dinner, fairly late in the evening. I looked at Sarah's notes. Ian had seen her moving around in the cottage and kept trying to call her. He had then seen her leave in her car, around midnight. He gave up and went to bed. Jeremy saw her walk into the garden about an hour later but couldn't say whether or not the car was there. Later still, he saw someone, presumably Brittany, turn off the lights in the cottage. Isabelle had seen Desmond near the guest cottage late on Thursday, around midnight but after Brittany had driven off, and in the early hours of Friday had heard a splash and the sound of someone walking up the gravel driveway. My feeling was that by then Brittany was already dead. Jeremy was the last to see her, and that was hours before.

The time that was unaccounted for must hold the key. Everyone had been out, or getting ready to go out. She could have gone somewhere, but it was more likely that someone had come to her. Late in the afternoon, she had gotten a call important enough that she had stepped away from the party. Endicott? I checked the pictures I had taken of the call history on her second phone. She'd gotten a message during the tea but hadn't called back. Kent said she hadn't used her work phone to call Endicott. Maybe it was a legitimate work call. She hadn't called Endicott at all that afternoon or evening. Could he have come looking for her?

Isabelle had seen someone she thought was one of the landscapers walking around. Then last night she said it could have been Barbara, that she didn't see the logo on the hat. Either way, if it was someone built like Barbara, it wasn't Miles Endicott. It couldn't have been Brittany in a different outfit. Even without the heels she was several inches taller than Barbara, who was petite, like Jane.

Brittany in a different outfit. I mentally walked through the cottage bedroom again. There had been jeans and a cute top on the bed. More casual clothes and shoes in the closet. I hadn't looked in the little jewelry case on the bureau, but odds were she had more low-key pieces as well. At the party, she had been wearing a sheath dress, sleeveless, the sapphire and diamond jewelry, and very high heels. We all noticed those and thought maybe she had caught one in the dock, fallen, and hit her head. Also her signature wrap, in a bright coral. She wore that with everything. I could see that—you could dress it up or down. Versatile, a thrifty approach. But the shoes. Easily ruined on gravel and in a garden. Why hadn't she changed?

Maybe she had. And if she hadn't, did it make a difference? I thought of everything I'd learned about Brittany, the things Sarah and Ian had said, and I thought maybe it did make a difference.

I got Bill Kent's card and dialed his office number. He answered after a couple of rings.

"It's Greer Hogan," I said. "I'm hoping you can answer a question."

"I will if I can, Ms. Hogan," he said.

"What was Brittany wearing when she—when they pulled her out of the water? Do you know?"

"You were there, weren't you, Ms. Hogan?"

"Yes, but I saw her from the dock. I only saw her arm and a little bit of her face. It was dark. Please, are you allowed to tell me?"

I heard papers shuffling, then the clicking of a keyboard.

"I can do that. A dress, dark blue."

"And the jewelry? Sapphire and diamond, like the earring I gave you?"

"One earring, yes, and a bracelet. No matching necklace, but there was a long silver chain with a dragonfly pendant."

"Shoes?"

"One. As you all said, a four-inch heel."

"The other could have come off in the water," I said, thinking out loud. "But nothing else?"

"You're correct about the shoe, and no, nothing else. How is this important, Ms. Hogan?"

"I'm not sure," I said. Kent made a sound of annoyance. "I'm really not," I said. "I just think it might be." If it was important in the way that I thought, I didn't want Kent getting ahead of me. Distraction was in order. "What about Endicott?" I asked.

"He's in the area. Won't come in to talk to us without his lawyer, but he did say he had people who could vouch for him from seven onward."

"Okay, thanks," I said.

"Ms. Hogan," Kent said. "Listen to me. We don't have anyone in custody, not Endicott, not anybody. You need to be careful. If there's something you haven't told me, now would be a good time."

"I don't have anything but questions. If any answers come to me, I'll call."

I heard a harrumphing noise. He wasn't happy.

"Call my cell," he said. "And be careful."

He hung up.

I went back to my time line. I started with my arrival at the party and ran through to the end. I added some notes about Friday. I double-checked everything Sarah had written and circled some questions. Then I looked at the pictures of the call history from Brittany's phone. I mentally reviewed her wardrobe once more. Jennie Webber was right—the how was more important than the why.

If Brittany was killed after Jeremy saw her walk into the garden, anyone could have done it.

If Brittany was killed when I thought she was, no one could have.

That left only one possibility—someone was lying.

Chapter
Twenty-One

❧

I tapped my pen on the table. Was I reaching? Maybe, but there was only one way to find out. I walked out to the porch. Isabelle was shutting down her laptop.

"How's it going?" I asked, as she stood and stretched.

"So far, so good," she said. "I need a break though, so I thought I'd start searching for Barbara's journals. We promised her we would. Want to help?"

"In a little bit. I'm trying to figure something out first. Can you give me Jeremy's cell number? Do you know where he is?"

"Working on something for his art class. He should be around." She gave me the number and went upstairs to get a flashlight.

I called Jeremy. I wanted to start with the last Brittany sighting and work my way backward.

"I have a question," I said when he picked up. "When you saw Brittany walking into the garden, what was she wearing?"

"What was she wearing?" he repeated. "Well, she had on that pink shawl thing, I forget what it's called. That's how I knew it was her."

"What else, though? Dress, pants, heels?"

"I'm not sure—it was dark. And I only saw her briefly, and from the back. But heels, maybe. She seemed a little unsteady. Why?"

"I'm trying to figure something out. So you didn't see her face, you saw her walking away from you, into the garden?"

"That's right."

"Is Ian there?" I asked.

"Yeah, he's working in his room."

"Could you put him on the phone?"

"Hang on," Jeremy said.

I heard some muffled conversation, and then Ian took the phone.

"What's up, Greer?"

"You saw Brittany driving away from the cottage, right?"

"Yes, I did."

"Tell me exactly what you saw," I said.

"I heard a door slam, so I looked out the window. I saw Brittany sitting in her car. She seemed to be fiddling with the radio. She backed up and turned, and then stopped. Then she pushed her hair back, you know that nervous habit she has? And after a second, she started up again and went up the driveway."

"Did you see her face?"

"Yes. Well, not really. Just a glimpse, from the side, when she pushed her hair back. She was turned away, like she was looking at the dash."

"So you can't be sure it was her?"

There was silence. Ian said, "She was driving Brittany's car, and wearing Brittany's—pashmina, I think you called it. But I never got a good look at her face."

"Are you sure it was a woman? In the car, walking around the cottage, in the garden? Ask Jeremy. Are both of you sure?"

I heard Ian repeat my question to Jeremy. There was some back and forth, and then Ian said, "We're sure it was a woman, but neither one of us saw her face. Are you saying that wasn't Brittany?"

"I think Brittany was already dead. I'm not sure who you saw. Listen, I've got to make some more calls. I'll call you back."

"No need. We'll be right over."

I hung up. There was a noise behind me. I turned and saw Isabelle with a flashlight in her hand.

"Did you hear all that?" I said.

"Most of it." Isabelle perched on the arm of a chair. "You think Brittany was killed earlier Thursday? We were all out for a while—it could have happened then."

"I think it might have been even earlier." I told her about finding the earring and being sure I saw it in the pool as I was leaving the party. "It's possible she lost it and didn't notice right away, but all afternoon and evening? Those clip earrings get uncomfortable. I'd have taken them off right after the party, even if I planned to wear them later. And Brittany wasn't the type to appear less than perfectly put together, so she wouldn't roam around with only one earring."

"That makes sense," Isabelle said.

"Another thing—when they found her, she was wearing the same outfit she'd had on at the tea. Unless she was planning on going somewhere or meeting someone she wanted to be dressed up for, why didn't she get changed? I would've."

"Me, too," Isabelle said.

Jeremy and Ian arrived, wanting all the background on the questions I'd asked. I ran through the story and explained my logic. I also updated them on my conversation with Bill Kent.

"So if Endicott has an alibi for any time after seven, and you're right that Brittany was killed earlier, that puts him back in the picture," Jeremy said.

"Yes, but it's a short window of opportunity," I said. "I'm not sure he could pull all of it off in that time frame without being seen. And the two of you swear you saw a woman."

Silence.

"Isn't there a sister?" Jeremy said.

"There is," I said, "but that would mean coordination and planning. Premeditation, even. And bashing someone over the head in the middle of the garden in broad daylight seems more spur of the moment."

"It could be both," Isabelle said. "Miles kills her, then panics, and gets his sister to help him cover it up. Of course," she added, her head tilted as she thought, "there are a lot of variables. You'd need a high risk tolerance."

"Not to mention luck," Ian said.

"Right," I said. "There are a couple calls I need to make. Maybe the guys could help with your search?" I said to Isabelle. "You could probably get all of the third floor done before you lose the daylight if they help."

"What search?" Ian asked.

"I'll explain. Come with me and we'll get more flashlights," she said. She turned as they reached the doorway.

"Thank you," I whispered.

She smiled and went out. I could hear her talking as they went upstairs. I picked up my phone and found Caro in my call history. Maybe she could be more precise on the time she saw Brittany.

"Greer, darling, how are you? Did I see that red-headed policeman coming to call earlier? Fond of the gingers, aren't you?"

"Fine, thanks." I stifled a yawn. "A little tired. Yes, he did come by. That's why I'm calling." I gave her a condensed version of my current theory and the Miles Endicott angle and asked, "I was wondering if you knew what time, exactly, you saw Brittany at the party, and then leaving."

"Exactly? Let me see. She asked about a desk that had belonged to Desmond's mother. Isabelle and I were both there. Then she said she had to take a call. Isabelle saw someone she knew—a cousin, I think, and went over to say hello. That was all around four thirty. And then, what did I do? Oh, yes, I went upstairs for a few minutes. I was getting a headache and wanted to take something for it. Then I went out for some air. I saw her walking down the driveway to the guesthouse. That was shortly before I saw you. I was enjoying the last bit of sunshine—dusk comes so quickly in the mountains, doesn't it? So five thirty or quarter to six? Is that helpful?"

"Yes," I said, writing it down. "Did you see anyone else?"

"Mmm, no, I don't think so, though I confess I might have dozed. Too many cocktails. Why do you ask?"

"I thought I heard people talking as I was leaving, but it was faint. I wasn't sure. Then Isabelle said she saw one of the landscapers, but—"

"Oh, that's right! I did see someone walking down the driveway in one of those caps they wear. Just a glimpse. But I didn't see him leave. As I said, I might have nodded off."

That was strange. Isabelle thought it was Barbara she'd seen. But Caro might have caught a glimpse and made the same assumption Isabelle had. I'd leave it for now.

"Just one more thing, Caro, and I'll let you go. What time did you all leave for dinner?"

"Around six thirty. Maybe a little later. Jane was worn out, and Barbara had been napping. Everyone wanted to get changed, and none of us were moving too quickly. We were the last to get out of the house. All the kids were gone."

"Thanks, Caro."

I hung up and stared at my notes. Something wasn't making sense. I had seen Isabelle and Caro, but not Brittany, and I'd heard some movement and conversation in the garden as I left. Isabelle had seen me and someone we now thought was Barbara, but she hadn't seen Brittany. Caro had seen Brittany and me, and might have glimpsed Barbara, but hadn't heard or seen anyone else. Did that timing work? Could Caro have seen Brittany shortly before seeing me and later caught a glimpse of Barbara, while neither Isabelle nor I saw Brittany?

The problem was there was no exact time for anything. And was that actually Barbara? And if it was, had Barbara seen Brittany, or anyone else? Per Isabelle, Margaret had said she was going to talk to Melissa about Barbara slipping out at night, tell the Whitakers and ask them to secure any meds that caused drowsiness. Barbara had a history of getting into mischief, Margaret said, but everything had been quiet for over a year. New doctor, different treatment plan. Barbara was a night owl but a heavy sleeper when she did sleep, whether in bed for the night or napping. Sarah had said she went up to say hello to her aunt during the tea party, knocked on Barbara's door, and gotten no response. She'd presumed her aunt was asleep. But she hadn't opened the door.

Was Barbara there? Would Margaret have checked? One way to find out. Isabelle had given me Margaret's number that morning. I called and gave her the current status of the investigation.

"So we're trying to figure out the last time anyone saw Brittany, or if anyone was on the property after the party ended. Isabelle saw someone she thought was one of the landscapers but last night decided it could have been Barbara. In fact, she's sure it was. If it wasn't, we have a stranger roaming around. If it was Barbara, she might have seen Brittany. Did Barbara go out for any reason between the time you arrived and the time you left for dinner? Maybe to get some air, or to greet someone?"

"I would have said no, if it weren't for last night. I'm not sure how she could have. We arrived around three and went right upstairs. Barbara unpacked, and we talked about the wedding. She was excited to be here—she had barely slept the night before. Mrs. Whitaker came up to say hello about an hour later. She said that

Mr. Whitaker was out but would be back by six to take us all to dinner. Then Mrs. Whitaker went back to the party. Barbara said she was going to read, and she settled in the chair by the window. So I went to my room and started proofreading an essay for my son. I finished that at about twenty-five after four. We usually have tea at around four thirty every afternoon. I let her know I was going down to get it, but she said she didn't want any. She was closing the curtains and said she was feeling tired and wanted to take a nap before dinner. So I closed the door and went down for my tea. I brought it back up and spent some time reading."

"And you were there the whole time?"

"No, I took my mug down to the kitchen at around five fifteen. I ran into Ms. Quinn in the kitchen. She had broken a glass. I was back upstairs in five minutes. I used the bathroom, put away the papers I was working on, and then got the evening meds organized. I wrote up the daily diary for Melissa. It was just before six, so I went to wake Barbara. I walked out and she was in the hall. I said something to her, like 'I didn't know you were awake.' She said she had just woken—she got very warm and wanted to wash her face. She made a point of saying she'd been in her room, but it had gotten stuffy. It was odd though—I hadn't heard the door. I hadn't heard anything. But she's light on her feet, so I shrugged it off. Now I wonder."

"Is it worth asking?" I said.

"Doubtful. She knows if she wanted to go anywhere I would have gone with her, but there are days she doesn't want a minder. She's stayed with the family a few times recently, so she knows her way around. But her sister told her the party might be too much for her. Mrs. Whitaker is overprotective, but Barbara doesn't like to upset her. It would have to have been something Barbara thought was important for her to sneak out."

Margaret went on to say that she would be staying a little later that day to talk to Melissa, and that Barbara's doctor was aware of what had happened. "Please let me know if anything else comes up," she said. "I don't want the police getting the wrong idea."

I said I would and hung up. I added everything she had told me to the time line. It didn't help much. Barbara could have been outside anytime between four thirty and six but wasn't going to tell us if she had been. I was going to presume she had been and she was the person Isabelle had seen and go from there. I had seen Isabelle between five fifteen and five-thirty, and she had seen Barbara a few minutes after that. I saw Caro around five thirty. Caro claimed to have seen Brittany leaving. She had seen Barbara, though she didn't recognize her. But I didn't believe she could have seen Brittany. If not Caro, then who had seen her last, and when?

Back to the blasted time line. Isabelle and Caro had talked to Brittany at four fifteen, then she had stepped out to take a call. I had overheard her on the phone while walking back through the garden after my visit with Jeremy. Neither Sarah nor Isabelle had seen her after that, and Caro said she didn't see her at the party, only outside. So if Caro was lying, the last Brittany sighting was mine, hearing her voice in the garden at, say, four twenty. She had been walking toward me, on the stone path between the driveway and the reflecting pool. If I was right, she had walked into the garden and never left it. Not alive.

Which begged the question—who had managed to commit murder and dump the body in the lake in the middle of a party? In broad daylight, no less. Caro? I thought she was lying about seeing Brittany leave. She was also lying about the time of the phone call. Isabelle had said that the conversation about the desk happened shortly after four. I'd heard Brittany on the phone around twenty past. When I'd gone inside to look for Jane, I'd found Sarah, but not Caro. Sarah was on her way upstairs to say hello to Barbara, so that was about four thirty. I'd found Jane and gone upstairs. I hadn't seen anyone, but it was a quick trip to the second floor, and

I'd gone to Sarah's room and right back down. I was in Jane's office until ten past five. Margaret had seen Caro in the kitchen at five fifteen.

That left forty-five minutes. Caro follows Brittany outside, hits her, and then gets rid of the body. But not in the lake. She couldn't have pulled that off with so many people coming and going. Jeremy was in and out on the airport runs, Ian arrived, guests were leaving. So the body had to be hidden, and close to the reflecting pool. There was a lot of shrubbery. I pictured the scene. Shrubbery, some left deliberately overgrown to hide the pump. The tarps left by the landscapers, folded away beneath the bushes. Except they hadn't stayed that way. They were neat at first. But they were bunched and lumpy when I was talking to Caro. I had found her looking into the pool. I thought she was searching for something. I'd been right, but she distracted me with talk of koi and then walked me to the edge of the clearing.

It was a risk, leaving the body. But with the party ending, the sun going down, and everyone going somewhere for dinner, the odds were that it would pay off. No one was likely to go into the garden after dark. Mrs. Henderson was home alone—everyone had left between six and six thirty and had come back around ten. Melissa, the night nurse, had arrived at nine, settled into her room, and started to study for her test. Barbara had quizzed her for a couple of hours and then gone to bed. Caro could have slipped out once the household was settled for the night, gone into the cottage, gotten Brittany's keys, handbag, and pashmina, and moved the car. She'd know what houses were likely to be empty.

Keys. Wait a minute. I remembered the fob in the pocket of her fleece jacket. Jeremy had said Caro's Range Rover was more than twenty years old. That meant actual keys, not an electronic fob. But she'd also need a key to the cottage. Brittany would have had one for the weekend, and she might have put it on that fob. Or

Caro could have gotten the key ring from the kitchen, the one both Sarah and Jeremy said was kept in a drawer until the keys were needed. Margaret had seen Caro in the kitchen, saying she'd broken a glass. So either way, she'd have been able to get into the cottage.

But why not ditch everything when she moved the car?

Because it needed to go into the lake with the body. Ian had seen the car leave at eleven thirty, and Isabelle had seen Desmond near the cottage at midnight. Perhaps Caro had nearly been discovered? With Desmond roaming around and lights on in the boathouse, any moving of the body would have to wait. Jeremy had seen a woman in Brittany's wrap walking into the garden after midnight. Later he'd noticed the lights in the cottage were out. Then nothing, until Isabelle was woken by something at three. She heard a splash, and then someone walking on the gravel driveway. That's when the body was dumped, I was sure of it.

Could Caro have done it herself? Again, maybe. She was in decent shape, for someone who was seventy and had a bad hip. I'd seen her dance—I wasn't convinced the cane was always necessary. She had the risk tolerance. And there were all those wheelbarrows lying around. But still. Could she move Brittany's dead weight all by herself? That was quite an effort, and why? No matter what Jennie Webber said about motive, Caro would need a good reason to do something like that. What was so important to her that she'd murder a woman she barely knew on the spur of the moment?

Desmond? He was like a younger brother to her. She'd always let him know how she could be reached, and she'd promised to always look after him, as Barbara always looked after Jane. What about Barbara? Caro felt terrible that she hadn't been able to help Barbara after the accident. Fifty years later, she still struggled with guilt. Barbara had been roaming around, wearing a hat left by a landscaper, and headed toward the wheelbarrows and other gardening equipment. Barbara was in her room, alone, from four thirty until six, but no one could say for certain she hadn't left. What had prompted her to go downstairs? Something important enough to risk upsetting Jane. She had been at the window, so something she had seen or heard?

I'd gone through all those rooms, checking the views. From the third floor it was unlikely she could have heard anything, even with the window open. She could see the garden though, and most of the clearing near the reflecting pool. Maybe she saw Caro bash Brittany and went to her. Always cool in a crisis, Caro had said of Barbara. But that brought me back to Caro's motive, and I couldn't find a good one. Unless she had overheard some of that phone call and something Brittany said had enraged her. She might have gone outside earlier than she said. Someone in that first small clearing could be heard from the patio. She might then have followed Brittany to the reflecting pool and chosen her moment.

Except that wouldn't work because I had come through the garden while Brittany was on the phone, and Brittany was on the path from the driveway. I guess it could have happened, but the timing was tight. And the motive was conjecture. I tossed my pen onto the desk and stood. This was getting me nowhere.

I stretched and walked around the library. I was tired, irritated, and feeling stupid. I went to a window and looked out. The sky was gray, and the wind was picking up. Nightfall would come quickly. The day was drawing to a close, and I was no closer to an answer. There were three people who could have killed Brittany: Caro, Barbara, and Miles Endicott. He was a stretch, but with everyone coming and going he could have met Brittany in the garden. Maybe the phone calls later were a ruse, and they'd had a prearranged meeting. Doubtful. Or he could have called her work phone from a different number. I wondered if Kent would tell me who that call had been from.

I left the window and wandered over to the shelves of old mysteries, hoping to draw some inspiration. I knelt and ran my finger along the blue spines of the original Nancy Drew series. The shelf ended at the little hiding place I had found. I put my pinkie through the knothole that served as an eye for an owl carved into the wood and pulled open the door. Barbara's journals were probably hidden in a cupboard like this, perhaps smaller and more cleverly disguised. Barbara. I sighed and closed the door and returned to the window.

Barbara had no reason to kill Brittany Miles. Neither did Caro. Not one that I could find. But there was no denying that the two of them had the best opportunity. Barbara could have seen something. Caro could have heard something. I traced the carvings on the shelf nearest the window. Ravens, Isabelle's mother had said. Not only an unkindness, but a conspiracy of ravens. A conspiracy. What had Bill Kent said? Clues pointing in all different directions. Poirot had said that in *The Hollow*, when an entire household had conspired to misdirect. Yes. Barbara and Caro working together. It was the only way to get rid of both the body and the car. Barbara didn't drive, hadn't since the accident. But she was strong. I'd felt that in her grip when we met, and she walked every day. Working together, they could hide the body and then move it. Caro could get rid of the car. If she hadn't been able to toss Brittany's stuff into the water right after, she could hide it and do it later. Or Barbara could, since she was adept at sneaking out.

I kept circling back to why. Caro to protect Desmond or Barbara. Barbara to protect Caro. Or Jane. I went back to the desk and looked at my time line. I had ruled out Jane early on. She didn't like Brittany, perhaps suspected an affair. She had scratched out Brittany's name on the seating chart hard enough to tear the paper. And then there was the bloody knife sketch I found in the margin. Jane had some anger issues. But she'd been in view of someone all afternoon and evening. Hadn't she? All evening, certainly, but what about the crucial time in the afternoon, from the last time anyone saw Brittany until I walked back to the reflecting pool to talk to Caro and glimpsed the earring and the lumpy tarp.

According to Margaret, Jane had gone up to greet her sister around four. She had stayed for a few minutes and returned to the party. I had gone into the house looking for her right after hearing Brittany on the phone. I couldn't find her, but Sarah had said her mother was going to her study. She had, because she'd knocked over the vase. When I found her, she said she needed a few minutes. That was about ten minutes, maybe fifteen, after I'd heard Brittany in the garden. I'd gone upstairs, come back down, and snooped through Jane's desk. The door from the office to the patio had been ajar. I'd been alone in the office for less than ten minutes. Jane had arrived carrying a towel, with her dress wet. Not very, but a little. And she seemed distracted. In one of those short intervals, she could have killed Brittany.

On to the cover-up. Was she part of that? I thought not. She had been with me in her office during the initial hiding of the body. She wouldn't have dragged Barbara into it, and she was unlikely to confide in Caro. I was sure that her shock wasn't feigned when she heard that Brittany had drowned not in the lake but in the reflecting pool. She was convinced it was a closed head injury and that Brittany had gotten up, walked down to the lake, and drowned. No wonder she'd been doing a slow unravel—she hit someone over the head with a rock and left her for dead, only to have the body disappear, and then reappear somewhere else a day later.

No, Jane didn't know what happened, at least not right away. But she had to suspect. I remembered the look of surprise on her face when her sister walked over to sit with her, saying, "We all understand it was an accident." *We understand.* Caro had said something similar, about Barbara. "I want everyone to understand." Not know, understand. Understand why they did what they did. That choice of words mattered. The cover-up had begun with Barbara, who had drawn in Caro. Barbara, who had seen something from her window that triggered her lifelong need to look after Jane. They would stick to the accident story. Maybe the police could prove otherwise, based on the location of the head wound. Brittany had been banging around under the dock for a while though, so maybe not.

I stared over at the Whitaker house, different parts coming in and out of view as the wind moved the trees outside the window. Lights were on against the early darkness, creating warm pools at the edge of the shadowy garden. Sarah must have finished breaking the news by now. I wondered how it had gone over. Desmond might well be relieved, happy to sell the company and move on with his life. Jane? The future she'd worked to create for herself and her family was not going as planned. Learning about that possibility through an overheard phone call may well have caused her to snap and attack Brittany. Now her sister was involved, adding another layer of fear and uncertainty. In Jane's shoes, I'd be having a breakdown, too.

I had to tell the others what I'd come up with. Sarah and Jeremy had to decide how to proceed. I couldn't prove anything. I wasn't sure the police could either, but Bill Kent wasn't stupid and he had resources that I didn't

Deciding that it would be easier to explain my deductions to everyone at once, I went to the desk and got my phone. I'd call Sarah and see if she and Jack could come over. I walked back to the window. The light in her room was on. There was a light in Desmond's office as well. The moonlight reflected off the French doors of Jane's office, which remained dark. I dreaded having to tell my friend what I'd concluded about her family.

I'd unlocked my phone when a movement caught my attention. The door at the base of the outside staircase had opened. Desmond was briefly illuminated in the light from within. He stepped out and the door shut. The trees swayed, momentarily blocking my view. When they were still, I could see him again. He hesitated, and then turned to the path that led past Jane's office to the reflecting pool. He disappeared into the garden. The wind keened. The trees and shrubs began an agitated twitching. I shivered, from fatigue and cold and growing anxiety. I stood, watching the scene change as a cloud covered the moon, knowing I was stalling.

The cloud drifted on, and the moon returned. But something was different. Jane's office, still dark, but the reflections somehow different. A shadow in the glass, where a minute before there had been moonlight. The shadow moved. Jane Whitaker stepped into view. She stood on the patio, head tilted, arms at her sides. Then she went down the steps and onto the path. She turned right, to the garden, and as she did the moonlight flashed on what she was carrying. A knife, and a big one.

"Holy shit," I breathed. I froze. *Sarah*, I thought. *No, Kent.* I pulled out his card and dialed. I started talking the minute he answered.

"You need to come. It's about the murder. The Whitaker garden. Bring help," I said, not sure I was even making sense.

"Ms. Hogan, what's happening?"

"Jane and Desmond Whitaker. A fight—a knife—I've got to go!"

"On my way. Stay where you are." He hung up. Like hell I'd stay where I was. My brain unstuck. I wasn't going to tackle Jane on my own, but with enough of us we could distract her until help came. I hoped.

I ran to the hall and yelled up the stairs.

"Help, everyone, come on!"

I heard footsteps. Jeremy appeared first.

"Call Sarah and Jack. Your parents are in the garden. Jane has a knife. I think she's really lost it, Jeremy."

I turned and sprinted for the door. The fastest route to the reflecting pool from here was the one Jane and Desmond had taken. I went all out until I reached the path, and then slowed, moving carefully. I didn't want to startle her. I paused at the edge of the clearing, out of sight. I could hear voices, alternately clear and then lost in the sound of trees in the wind. Desmond's voice, a low rumble, indistinct. Then Jane. I edged forward, still screened by a shrub, but able to see. The two faced each other across the pool. Desmond stood by the bench. Jane opposite him, knife in hand.

"I should have killed you," she said. The calm, measured tone was chilling. "I made us a beautiful life. Beautiful and comfortable, for you, for our children. And you were ready to throw it all away. For what?"

I heard footsteps behind me, and then a clatter as the doors to the sunroom opened. Jeremy, his voice by my ear, asking, "What's happening?"

"Your mother has a kitchen knife, a big one. I saw her follow him out with it. I called Kent. I'm sorry, Jeremy. I think she killed Brittany."

Silence. Then a sigh. "Let me," he said, gesturing. I moved aside, and he slipped into the clearing, still in the shadows. I followed, Ian and Isabelle easing in behind us. I could see Sarah and Jack on the path from the house. Barbara slipped into sight. Jane didn't notice. She was focused on Desmond, who had started to speak.

"Jane, no. There was nothing going on, no affair. And—"

"I know that." Jane nearly spat out the words. "She was after bigger game. And she twisted you right around her little finger. I saw it over and over again with my father. And my mother, playing stupid, keeping up appearances. But I'm not stupid. And you—selling the company? Not even asking me?"

"I wasn't going to—"

"I heard her!" Jane's voice rose. She lifted the knife. "She walked past my office, talking on the phone, all about the great deal she'd put together. A sure thing, she said, but the owner had to get it past the wife. The wife!" She started to walk forward. At the edge of the pool, she stopped.

I heard a siren. Isabelle disappeared toward the driveway. She'd have the sense to tell them to approach quietly. Jane started speaking again, her voice back to the calm and cold tone she'd used before.

"The wife. Who funded every major initiative. Whose money kept the company private. The wife. Who provided every good idea *you* ever had. I followed her. I followed her out here, and I told her that, and I told her it wasn't happening. And do you know what she said? She said it wasn't what I thought, that if I went along with it I'd see that her plan was right, and that she understood. That she understood!"

Brittany had been telling the truth, I thought. She must have realized she was in danger.

Out of the corner of my eye, I saw Bill Kent at the edge of the path. Ian moved in front of me, leaving enough space for me to see. Two uniformed officers appeared near Sarah. But Jane didn't react. She seemed to be in a trance, staring at Desmond. She began to circle the pool, getting closer.

"I could kill you. I should have—"

"Janie, no." Barbara moved out of the shadows, walking toward her sister. "You don't want to kill anyone. You didn't kill anyone. It was an accident. I saw it from my window. Put the knife down, Janie."

Barbara turned to Bill Kent.

"It's my fault. I take full responsibility. Jane did nothing wrong."

"NO!" Jane screamed this time. "You did NOT! It was never your fault! I won't let them take you. No one is going to lock you up."

"It's all right, Janie. I'll go with them and tell them. I was only trying to help," Barbara said. "It'll be all right, you'll see."

She was moving closer to her sister, small steps, keeping eye contact. Her tone was soothing, but it didn't work.

"NO! NO! It won't be all right. I saw, Barbara, I saw what happened. You didn't do anything wrong. But they came, and they took you. They dragged you out screaming! I watched them. I won't let it happen again!"

My stomach turned. No one knew where Jane was that morning, Caro had said. I knew—in her little hiding place, her reading nook, listening to her beloved older sister practicing the piano. Barbara's parents had her committed, against her will, a week before her eighteenth birthday, and Jane, twelve, had watched it happen.

"Oh, Janie, no. I never knew," Barbara went to her sister and put her arms around her. Jane started to sob. Margaret appeared and took the knife from Jane, who offered no resistance.

"I'm so tired, Barbara. I tried so hard. I always did what I was supposed to. I thought I did everything right," Jane said.

"You did, Janie. You always have," Barbara said. She kissed the top of her sister's head and pulled her closer.

Margaret turned to Kent. "I'll be contacting Ms. Granville's physician," she said. "It is my professional opinion that neither she nor her sister should answer any questions or leave the premises without a proper medical evaluation."

Kent nodded. Margaret had no official standing, but her tone had all the authority of an experienced ICU nurse on a rough shift. There was no upside in hauling everyone off to the police station, and plenty of risk.

"I'll call the doctor," Jeremy said. "Would you take them inside, please, Margaret?" He looked up at Sarah. She was already on the phone, no doubt to the lawyer.

Margaret handed the knife to Kent. She said something to Barbara, and all three women moved toward the path to the house. Isabelle and Jeremy followed. Kent gestured to his officers. One headed for the driveway, and the other toward the house. Desmond had collapsed on the bench, his face in his hands. Caro stood next to him, one hand on his shoulder.

Kent sighed and shook his head. He turned to me. "Care to tell me what happened?" he said.

"I will," Caro said. She stepped forward and leaned on her cane, the brass lion's eyes winking in the moonlight. "I was involved in all of it."

Kent glanced at me. I nodded. She had been, and I wanted to hear her version.

"Jane Whitaker overheard a phone call that distressed her considerably. She's been under a great deal of strain of late. She followed Brittany Miles into the garden, here, to ask for an explanation. She felt the young woman wasn't taking her seriously and lost her temper. Jane shoved her and stalked off. She had no idea that the woman was badly injured. Her sister, Barbara, saw it all from her window and came down to help. By the time she arrived, Brittany Miles was dead. But of course you heard all of that."

We had heard something like that, but Caro's spin was impressive. Kent raised his eyebrows, but said nothing. Caro went on to point out that Barbara had a history of mental health issues and believed that she was protecting her sister by hiding the body. She, Caro, had seen Barbara slip into the garden and followed. By the time she reached the reflecting pool, Barbara was wrapping Brittany's body in a tarp. Barbara had convinced Caro that Jane would be accused of murder and gotten her to help. Together they'd come up with a plan. The rest was pretty much what I'd thought, except that Barbara had been the one to toss Brittany's wrap, handbag, and phone into the lake at three in the morning. She hadn't realized she'd dropped the phone.

"We shouldn't have done it," Caro said. "I can see that. We panicked and then didn't know how to undo it. Jane had nothing to do with that part, and I'm sure that's what put her over the edge. I'm terribly sorry. Once Mr. Jocelyne or his associate arrives, I'll be happy to make a statement. I'm sure you'll find that Barbara will say the same."

"I'm sure I will," Kent said. He looked at me. "Anything to add, Ms. Hogan?"

I shook my head. "That's pretty much what I'd figured out, right before I called. Then I saw Jane with the knife, and . . ." I started to sniffle. "I'm sorry. It's just that I didn't know that part, what Jane saw." I started to cry in earnest. Ian put his arms around me.

"None of us did, darling. None of us did," Caro said.

Chapter
Twenty-Two

The rest of the night passed in a blur. Doctors, lawyers, police. After a discussion with Tom Jocelyne, I gave the police a brief statement as to what I had seen from the window and in the garden. Ian and Isabelle did the same, and we were allowed to go. After a brief consultation with Jeremy, it was decided that Ian would spend the night in the spare room at the Granville house, and Isabelle would stay at the boathouse. Changes of clothes were packed. Shortly after midnight, I was tucked into bed and Ian was lounging in the chair next to me.

"Do you believe her? Caro?" he asked.

"Only to a point," I said. "But I can't prove she's lying." I explained the time line and what I'd seen and heard.

"That's a lot for Kent to sort out," he said.

"Yes, and so much of what Caro said is true, I don't think he'll be able to prove the parts that aren't. I guess we'll find out. Jane's story about Barbara, though. The more you learn, the worse it gets."

"Yeah," Ian said. "Are you okay?"

"Just tired. And sad," I said. "I feel awful for all of them. And for Brittany."

"I know," he said. "Me, too." He stood. "Breakfast out tomorrow?"

"Not before eight. Or nine," I said.

"Deal," he said, and stood. "I'll be right down the hall if you need me. Sweet dreams, gorgeous."

He turned off the light and left. I was asleep in seconds.

* * *

At a reasonable hour the next morning, we were sipping coffee and eating pancakes. We rehashed the events of the past few days. There had been a flurry of texts and calls that morning. Isabelle would be staying on until her trip to Albany and then planned on wrapping things up in Boston and coming back. She and Jeremy would spend the winter in the Granville house. Jack and Sarah had canceled their honeymoon and would stay in the area until things were sorted out with the police investigation. Both would telecommute and, eventually, go to Europe for Jack's project.

"Jeremy has said he'll handle things," Sarah told me. "He wants to be here. He's always been better at dealing with my mother than I have. Both he and my father want me to move on. My dad said it's time all of us stopped living for other people. And I'm only a plane trip away." I told her I thought it was a good plan. She invited me to stay another day or two but said she'd understand if I left that day. I thanked her and told her I wanted to go home. I was longing for my little carriage house apartment, but there were a couple of things I needed to do before I left. Talking to Ian was one of them.

"So," he said, once the pancakes were gone and our coffee cups were full, "what now?"

"I don't know exactly. I have some things to figure out," I said. "Dan."

"Yes. I can't move on until I know for sure what happened. I feel like I failed him. I feel like I failed myself."

"I'll give you whatever help I can," he said. "But I think you need to move carefully."

"I know," I said. "And I appreciate the help. What about you? Back to work?"

"I've decided to quit my job," he said. "Been thinking about it for a while. I'll take some consulting gigs here and there, but I only want to do what I want to do, you know? And I want to spend time with my parents. They're not getting any younger. So I'll be coming back east."

"Ah," I said. "They're in Delaware, aren't they?"

He nodded. "I'll stay near them until I figure some things out. So, if you need me . . ."

"I'll call," I said. "Thank you. You make a great detective's sidekick."

"Thanks," he said. "And once we both get things figured out . . ."

"We'll see what happens," I said.

And that's where we'd left it. An uncertain place, but one we were both comfortable in.

That left one task. Barbara's journals. I had a couple of hours before I had to leave. I had a dinner date with Henri that I wasn't going to miss. But Isabelle and I had made a promise to Barbara, and I wanted to keep it. Isabelle had covered most of the upstairs, but there was one place I wanted to check. I took a flashlight and went to the third floor.

Barbara's room was no different than the last time I'd seen it, but it seemed sadder and emptier now that I knew her story. I faced the mirror. It was as compelling as ever—the carved figures so life-like, the fey creatures of the woods appearing and disappearing in the corner of my eye. Shadows moved beneath the surface of the rippling glass. This time, the only face I saw was my own.

I pulled at the frame, working it slowly forward. Then I slipped behind it with my flashlight, and knelt down on the floor. This was

Jane's hiding place, so it was worth exploring. There was some carving in the wood back here—I hadn't noticed it before. I'd been too shocked by the writing on the back of the mirror. I moved the flashlight over it. There were inlays on one wall, hard to see from anywhere in the room because of the angle. I ran my hands over each, pushing and prodding. At the very bottom, something gave. The inlaid portion popped down, like a small drop-front desk. I leaned down and shone the light in. There they were. A pile of notebooks of different sizes and shapes. I slid them out and carried them over to the bed.

They were Barbara's. I recognized the handwriting. There were drawings, too, at first quite simple and then more detailed. I gathered them up and brought them to Isabelle's room, and left them on her dresser with a note about the hiding place. I sent a text letting her know they were there. She could give them to Barbara, along with the one hidden in the library.

I got my luggage and went downstairs. After loading up my car I came back in for some water for the road and to take a last look around. I checked the desk—I'd given all my notes to Isabelle to give to Jeremy before she left last night. I hadn't missed anything. I walked around the library and into the music room. I thought I understood now why Jane kept the piano tuned. For Barbara. I picked out the notes of the song, "The Unanswered Question," and then put the sheet music in the piano bench.

I looked around. There were still things I couldn't explain. The figure at the window, and the red light that first night. That could have been Jane and a trick of the light. How the lava lamp got downstairs. Jane again? Or Barbara, misdirecting. Both were good at slipping away unnoticed, and both had been roaming the Granville house more than they let on. I'd put money on it. The pull of memory, the need for closure—both sisters felt them strongly. There were ghosts to lay here, but it could be done. Isabelle's parents were right—this could be a happy house. Cut back the trees, let in some light, freshen up the furniture. A whole lot of sage smudging couldn't hurt either.

Bill Kent was standing on the Granville dock when I went outside. I walked over to him. He was staring at the lake. It was a sunny day. The surface gleamed. I could see nothing beneath it, and I was fine with that.

Kent and I stood silently for a minute.

"What will happen to them?" I asked.

He shrugged and blew out a breath. "I'm handing it over to the DA. I've got three people confessing to different things, none of which is the murder of Brittany Miles. They're all sticking to the tragic accident story, when they're talking at all."

"The head wound?" I asked.

"A glancing blow on one side and another that looks like she hit her head when she fell. Either could have knocked her out, and then she drowned. We could get to manslaughter and make it stick, but not murder. There's so many doctors and lawyers involved—I just don't know. Mrs. Whitaker and her sister are both in the hospital for observation."

"Jane had some kind of breakdown. I've never seen her like that. She may be in some kind of facility for a long time. And Barbara hasn't been truly free for most of her life," I said. "She told me that the night of the accident, the boy tried to strangle her, and that's why she drove off the road. Nobody believed her."

"Somebody did. I talked to a retired cop who was a rookie at the time. He was at the accident site. Another motorist saw something, and then they had the other girl's statement. If the boy's parents hadn't made so many threats, he said the whole thing might have been written off."

And maybe Brittany would still be alive, I thought. But there was no telling. I sighed.

"Anything else you think I should know?" Kent asked.

I shook my head.

He waited a minute, and then said, "Well, if you think of anything, you know where to reach me."

He walked up the driveway. I watched him go.

I got into my car. I'd told him everything I knew for sure. There was one thing though, that I couldn't be certain of. Had I heard it right? Jane's voice, rising above the wind. "I should've killed you." Had she said "should've" or "should?" It made a difference, because the emphasis was clearly on "you." "I should kill *you*" or "I should've killed *you*." Desmond, not Brittany. Had murder been her intention the minute she stepped into the garden that day? Did she regret the victim, but not the act?

Maybe it didn't matter, if the intent was there. It wasn't clear to me. An unanswered question.

And what would I do when I found the person who had upended my life? What if I felt justice was beyond reach? Would I do what Jane had done? Would I strike out at the killer? Or let justice take its course?

I suspected I knew the answer. But I'd only just begun. There was work to do. More unanswered questions. I started the car and turned it toward the road. With one last look in the rearview mirror, I headed home.

Enjoyed the read?

We'd love to hear your thoughts!

crookedlanebooks.com/feedback

Acknowledgments

Writing is a solitary pursuit. Completing a book and getting it out into the world requires the help of many people. Special thanks to my husband, Mark, for keeping our lives running while I was immersed in writing. I'm grateful to my family for always being my biggest fans, and equally grateful for the support and encouragement I received from the staff of the Lee County Library System, especially Angela Ortiz. For her generosity in sharing her time and incredible knowledge of the advertising industry, I thank Liz Rosenthal. Any errors in the portrayal of the Whitaker family firm are mine and not hers. Many thanks to my agent Julie Gwinn. I couldn't have done it without any of you.

Read an excerpt from

THREE CAN KEEP A SECRET

the next

GREER HOGAN MYSTERY

by M. E. HILLIARD

available soon in hardcover from
Crooked Lane Books

CROOKED
LANE

NEW YORK

Chapter One

～

Raven Hill Manor was silhouetted against a blazing scarlet sky. I stood in the shadow cast by the gothic pile of stone and wood, admiring the irregular outline and odd angles—the peaks and valleys of the slate roof; the false fronts and dormered windows; and the unexpected, octagonal tower jutting from one corner. Clouds moved across the setting sun, and red reflections flickered across the upper windows.

"'Last night I dreamt I went to Manderley again.'" I quoted the opening line of *Rebecca* as I pocketed my car keys. I'd always been a sucker for a creepy old house, with or without a creepy old housekeeper. Raven Hill Manor fit the bill, though after a year of working at the library it housed, I found it more quirky than creepy. The manor was far from sharing all its secrets with me, but I had reached the point where its creaks and groans and sighs, its odd artifacts, and its overlooked nooks were a familiar part of my day. The Raven Hill Library was a busy, cheerful place in spite of its brooding exterior. If it kept itself to itself after business hours— well, that was fine with me.

I was reaching for the back door of the building when it opened.

"Oops, sorry, Greer!" It was Felicity James, president of the Friends of the Library. The annual book and bake sale, the group's biggest fundraiser, was only five days away, and several of the volunteers had gathered to work out some final details. In spite of her recent widowhood, or perhaps because of it, Felicity had stepped up to finish out someone else's term as president and had thrown herself into the book sale organization. A few other members of the group were right behind her. We stepped to one side.

"So, any last-minute issues?" I asked Felicity.

"A couple of minor things—some confusion about schedules and who's doing what for the preview sale, but other than that, we're in good shape. As long as the weather's nice, I think it will be a success." Felicity looked toward the parking lot. Even in the fading light, large puddles and fallen leaves and branches were visible. We'd had a heavy rain that afternoon, but the clouds had given way to a brisk autumn breeze. Random gusts still set the trees thrashing in the fading light, but the forecast was for crisp, sunny weather through the weekend. I told her as much.

"Well, let's hope that holds," she said. "What brings you back?"

"I forgot something," I said. "I'm off tomorrow since I'm working this weekend, so I decided to come back and get it. I needed a couple things from the Market on Main anyway."

We chatted for a few more minutes, and then Felicity went on her way and I headed for my office. I moved a few files on my desk and found what I was after—a portable battery I could use to power or charge my phone or tablet. The battery was a gift from Ian Cameron, my one-time love, current friend, and future who knew? Since he was currently in Kuala Lumpur on a work project of several months' duration, I could think about that later. He'd sent a present to mark my one-year anniversary of working for the Raven Hill Library. The perfect gift considering how often we lost power. He'd included a headlamp as well. It was lightweight and on thick elastic. I had laughed, but I kept it in my desk drawer next to a flashlight. You never knew when you'd need to go hands-free.

I had big flashlights at home and in my car, but the battery was something I'd never thought of, and now that winter was approaching, I liked to keep it handy. An icy November storm could knock out the electricity all over town. Besides, it made me smile. Ian was a techie, a gadget guy, and this was his idea of a perfect gift. Some men never thought past flowers.

I decided to see if we had a copy of Hitchcock's *Rebecca* checked in. I had the DVD of Christie's *Hallowe'en Party* at home but decided to save that until the following weekend. The sky over the manor as I arrived had put me in a gothic state of mind. As I walked down the hall toward the reading room, I noticed a light on in the director's office. Helene Montague, our director, had been off today after working the weekend, so I decided to take a look. Very little in the manor was kept locked, and with a small staff in the evenings it was easy for people to end up in places they shouldn't be. I was surprised it didn't happen more often. I poked my head into the office and immediately regretted it.

Anita Hunzeker, who chaired the library board of trustees, was looking for something in a portable file box that she'd placed on a chair. Thankfully, she had her back to me. My relief was short-lived. As I began to ease back out the door, she spotted my reflection in the window and turned.

"Oh, Greer, it's you. You're not closing tonight, are you?" she asked, eyeing my jeans and sweater with disapproval. Anita was wearing her usual uniform of dressy slacks, blazer, silk blouse, and colorful scarf. If she owned anything denim, I had yet to see it.

"No, I was here earlier. I came back for something I forgot," I said. "I saw the light and thought I'd check and see who was in here. I know Helene is off."

"Yes," she said. "I've been using her office. Board business, and then the Friends meeting. I wanted to make sure they had things in hand. Felicity had to step in rather late in the process. And now

I've misplaced my new glasses. I'm supposed to use them for driving at night. Of course I can manage without them, but I'd rather not."

"Would you like some help?" I asked. It was the last thing I wanted to do. Anita Hunzeker was regularly referred to as "Attila the Hunzeker" by the library staff, the volunteers, and most of the rest of the residents of Raven Hill. She was ruthlessly efficient, had boundless energy, and was completely lacking in sensitivity. Though she had been involved in hiring me, I had fallen out of favor while investigating a murder on the manor grounds the previous spring. My stock had gone up when I solved it, leaving the library with no legal liability, but Anita still felt I had a tendency to stick my nose into things. This was true, so in general I tried to avoid her.

"Well, if you wouldn't mind checking to see if they're on the floor somewhere. Richard dropped off some files for me and knocked over my bag—men are so careless. I was sure he picked everything up, but he might have missed them. They're not in here—let me check my handbag again."

I heaved a mental sigh and knelt down. Helene had a little table and some chairs on one side of her office for smaller meetings. This was where Anita had been working. I looked around, feeling along the shadowed area by the baseboards. I heard Anita yawn. Odd, she was usually the Energizer bunny.

"Long day?" I said, as I backed up and then moved toward the radiator. It was too dark to see underneath it.

"An early appointment and several meetings. The historical society cannot wrap their minds around the need for a better facility. The proposed library would be ideal, but they're very territorial. Combining our archives and their collection makes perfect sense. Why let everything molder away in the dark when you can house it all in a bright, new research center?"

"Better climate control would certainly help. Some of those documents are fragile," I said, giving myself points for diplomacy. I liked working in the manor and would be happy to see the library stay there. Anita was determined that her legacy to the town she grew up in would be a new, state-of-the-art library and archive. She'd already picked out the location. She had a point about accessibility, air quality, and light—but she ignored tradition and history. The village was pretty evenly split on new versus old, and the preliminary discussions had been going on for nearly a year. I didn't see it getting any better. Add to that the terms of the Ravenscroft Trust and the deeding of the manor to the village for use as a library, and the whole thing got even messier. But Anita was determined.

"Exactly, Greer," Anita went on as I completed my search beneath the radiator. She was unusually chatty this evening, possibly happy to have an audience who seemed to agree with her. I moved to do one last check under the table as her phone rang.

"Richard!" she said. Her husband. She turned and walked to the office doorway, stepping into the small vestibule outside. I heard her ask about her glasses. I'd found nothing under the table but the portable file box Anita had placed there. I glanced up. She still had her back to me. I took a quick look at the files. Typical Anita—everything was neatly labeled except a couple of folders that had penciled names on the tabs. The labels were what I would expect—"New Building," "Historical Society," "Grants," "Book Sale." The penciled ones were harder to read—I'd need a closer look. Anita was still talking. I caught "wine—that new white I like" and "gift." I pulled the box toward me. I could make out "Millicent/Ames Family," "Margaret Emerson," "JP Walters," "Sean Harris," "J Bean," and something that looked like "Ravenscroft Deeds." It sounded like Anita was winding up her call. I could clearly hear "in my car? I'll look, I'm leaving shortly," so I backed out from under the table. I was standing, dusting myself off, when she turned around.

"Sorry, Anita, I've come up empty," I said.

"Well, thank you for helping," she said. "I guess I'll have to make do."

"Could they be in your car? Maybe they fell between the seats or something?"

"I guess it's possible, but I could swear I had them when I walked in. I picked up the new prescription this morning. Well, I'd better be going. It appears I still have things to do. Good night, Greer."

"Good night," I said.

I left Anita gathering her bags and boxes and headed to the reading room for my DVD. I saw Millicent Ames, our archivist, going out the front door as I went into the hall. She often parked in the old lot near the front of the building. Staff usually only used it when we were expecting a big crowd for programs or meetings, but Millicent had been parking there for decades and said she often did it by habit. The reading room was quiet. There were a few patrons browsing, a page shelving in the new book section, and two other staff members. David, an older gentleman who had retired from his regular job, gotten bored, and come to work for the library part-time, was at the circulation desk. Jillian Bean, our Youth Services librarian, was at Reference, her attention on some papers in front of her. It was a peaceful scene.

"Hi, Jilly," I said.

She jumped. "Oh, hi, Greer. What brings you back?"

"Forgot something and then decided to pick up a DVD as long as I was here. I ran into Anita. She was remarkably chatty."

Jilly frowned. "I thought she'd left," she said, her tone flat.

"Packing up. Couldn't find her glasses. She should be gone by the time you close up." I looked at the clock. "I'd better get moving."

I waved to David and went to the videos. I was pretty sure *Rebecca* would be checked in—the book wasn't usually assigned until later in the school year, so those who wanted to either skip it entirely or see how the film stacked up wouldn't be asking for it yet. I hadn't liked the novel when I'd read it in high school. The nameless heroine had been, in my opinion, also spineless and therefore irritating. It wasn't until I was older and heard a lecture on Du Maurier that I started to come around. According to the speaker, the author had been disappointed when her critics and readers saw the book as a gothic romance rather than a story about a man who had power and a woman who had none, which is what she'd intended. That, and the fact that I was older and wiser, had made me revise my opinion. Revisiting many of the things I'd read and judged in my teens and early twenties would undoubtedly be edifying. The view from forty is different. There are some things that never change, though. Tonight, I wanted junk food and Hitchcock. I plucked the movie from the shelf, checked it out, and went home.

Chapter Two

⁓

I woke for the first time at four AM on Tuesday when my phone chirped. It was a text from Officer Jennie Webber, my friend and workout buddy.

Can't make our run. Working accident scene all night. Call you later.

Calling it a run was kind of her. The part she did with me was more of a brisk walk/slow jog combo. I knew that after we were done, or sometimes before, she did a couple miles at a faster pace. She never missed a workout, whereas I would use any excuse. I squinted at the screen, turned off my alarm, rolled over, and went back to sleep.

I was awakened for the second time at a little after eight. It was Helene's ringtone.

"Greer, I'm sorry to disturb you. I know it's your day off. I'm afraid I have some bad news."

I sat up. "No problem. What's going on?"

"It's Anita. She's been in a car accident. She apparently died at the scene."

"Last night," I said, thinking of Jennie's text.

"Yes, after she left here. She was on her way home. You know she lives down that winding road. I'm not sure exactly what happened, but it sounds like she skidded and went into the trees. I really don't know much. Sam O'Donnell called me. He said they'd have some questions. Routine, according to Sam. I'll have more information after I speak to him."

We'd have more information, but only what Lieutenant Sam O'Donnell wanted us to have. He was a small-town cop, but he was a good one.

"Wow, that's awful. Hard to believe, even. She always seemed indestructible," I said.

"True," Helene said. "Anyway, the library will be open as usual, and the book sale will go on. It's what she would have wanted."

That phrase so often sounded trite, or convenient, but in this case it was absolutely true. Anita would never have let the death of a board member, volunteer, or even employee get in the way of a fundraiser.

"Yes, it is," I said. "Listen, it's probably not important, but I did see Anita last night before she left the building."

I explained about my late errand back to the manor and seeing the light in Helene's office. She agreed that my conversation with Anita probably had no bearing on anything, but said she'd let Sam know, and then hesitated a moment before saying, "I hate to impose, but would you be able to take care of a couple things today? I'm not going to be able to leave the office. I was supposed to be picking up some brochures from the printer and dropping them off at a few places around the village. After the book sale, I'll be able to give you a few hours of comp time."

"Sure," I said. "I'm out running errands today anyway."

"Thank you," said Helene. "That's such a help. I'll email you everything you need in a few minutes. It shouldn't take too long. I really appreciate it."

We hung up. I got out of bed and made coffee, mentally reviewing my conversation with Anita the night before. Maybe she *had* needed those glasses more than she let on. For someone near-ing seventy, Anita had been in great shape and proud of it. Her entire family, she said, had always had "iron constitutions." It was an old-fashioned phrase, but it suited. She had recently mentioned a little arthritis in her knees but stated that it would not keep her from skiing this coming winter. She'd wanted some information on different kinds of pain relievers, both prescription and homeo-pathic, and I'd helped her find good sources. She must have taken the issue with her vision as a personal insult. The only glasses I'd ever seen her in were sunglasses. Could she really have gone off the road in the dark?

I'd had a little more trouble seeing things at night lately. Or far away. Did I need glasses? I covered one eye, then another, trying to make out things across the room. Meh. Then I tried to read washing instructions on the little labels on my clothes as I got dressed. Hmph. I scribbled "make appt. eye doctor" at the bottom of my day's to-do list. No harm in checking. Squinting created crow's feet, after all.

I had a busy week ahead and a lengthy list of errands now that I was handling some things for Helene. Since I'd missed my workout that morning, I decided to group anything in the vil-lage into the afternoon and walk. I'd visit only my more far-flung locations—grocery store, printer, historical society—by car. I was adding them to my list when I got a text from Jennie.

Questions about Anita. Java Joint later?

It looked like Helene had mentioned my conversation with Anita to Lieutenant Sam O'Donnell, Jennie's boss. I texted back, and we confirmed a time. After making a few calls and putting away my clean laundry, I set out. I stopped first at the printer, picking up a couple of boxes of brochures and handouts. Groceries next. I liked to use the Market on Main whenever possible, both because they were local and because they had a great selection of prepared foods. I wasn't much of a cook, and Raven Hill's takeout options were limited. For paper goods and pantry staples, I used the bigger chain supermarket in the next town. As I drove, I mentally reviewed all the stops I had to make that day, and wondered if there would be much talk of Anita's accident. I didn't have to wait long to find out. I was walking into the store when I ran into Dory Hutchinson on her way out. Dory was a circulation assistant at the library and a walking repository of village gossip. She was a lifelong resident of Raven Hill. That, and the fact that she had relatives scattered all over the Albany area, made her a great source of information as long as you took the time to sort out fact from salacious speculation.

"Greer! I'm so glad I ran into you. I suppose you've heard about Anita?" Dory steered her cart out of the lane to the door. She was ready to settle in for a gossip. I stepped over to her.

"Yes, Helene called me this morning," I said.

"Well, did she tell you that Anita was run off the road? Deliberately!" Dory said, looking not at all distressed. Dory had never liked Anita.

"She did mention the police weren't sure what happened, and they'd have some questions for us. Sam O'Donnell told her it was routine," I said.

Dory rolled her eyes. "Not likely. Bill went by Winding Ridge Road this morning. He had an early job out that way—burst pipe. He said the local police were there, but so were some state troopers. And you know what that means. They think something's fishy."

She was probably right. Raven Hill shared a police department with several other towns and villages in the area, but the force was small. Traffic accidents were one thing, but if anything required more sophisticated forensics, they'd need some help.

"So what's the theory? That road has some treacherous curves, doesn't it?" I asked. I'd only driven on it a few times, but the "winding" in the name was an understatement.

"It does, but she went off it along one of the straightaways," Dory said. "Bill had to go right by it. The police were directing traffic—it was down to just the one lane—and he had to wait for a few minutes while a car came the other way. He said she went down the bank *before* that hairpin turn, right where it's so steep and rocky. I think she was forced off the road right there."

"That *is* strange. It's still hard to believe."

Dory snorted. "The only thing hard to believe is that no one did it sooner. The police have their work cut out for them, that's for sure. Although . . ."

Dory paused. I knew my cue. I raised my eyebrows. Dory looked around. Satisfied that there was no one near enough to hear her, she leaned closer.

"Well, you know about Anita's feud with Cynthia Baker, right?"

I shook my head.

"Cynthia is president of the Raven Hill Historical Society. Has been for years. Her family has lived in the area forever. She and Anita went to high school together, and they've never gotten along. Started out fighting over who would edit the yearbook and moved on to the PTA and then every other committee in town."

"And you think that after all these years she snapped?"

"Sort of," Dory said. "Anita finally did something that pushed her over the edge."

"What?"

"I'm not exactly sure," Dory said. "But my cousin Angela was there at the last meeting—Monday afternoon it was—and she told me that afterward Anita and Cynthia had a closed-door meeting"—Dory put little air quotes around the last bit—"and that she heard them yelling at each other. Well, as much as you can hear anything through the doors of that place. Solid oak, every single one. Those Victorians knew how to build to last. Anyway, Angela said Anita sailed out, saying something like 'We'll see about that,' and that Cynthia was fuming." Dory gave a little nod. "And Cynthia lives up the same way that Anita does. Not the same road, but near it."

"So, she stewed all afternoon and then went after Anita that night?" I said. "How did she know when Anita would be on the road? I don't know, Dory."

"Well, listen to this. Angela was at the historical society building for a couple of hours after the meeting. She volunteers there doing office work, and they're closed to the public Mondays so that's her day. Anyway, she said that Cynthia stomped around for a while, and then went into her office. She made a few calls—Angela couldn't hear—but then she seemed to calm down. Right as Angela was getting ready to leave, she heard Cynthia shout 'hah!' or something like that. Angela looked into the office as she was walking out, and asked Cynthia if everything was okay. And Cynthia said, 'Everything's fine. Anita Hunzeker is in for a surprise. I'll teach her a lesson.' Something like that. And I'm sure she knew Anita would be at the library for the meeting—she was always going on about how busy she is." Dory rolled her eyes.

"It does sound suspicious," I said. "But I still think the timing would be tricky."

"True," Dory conceded. "But Cynthia has hated Anita for a long time. Of course, she's not the only one."

We paused while Dory greeted someone she knew. A natural salesperson, Dory threw in a pitch for the library book sale. "And we always have a wonderful bake sale at the same time," she said. Hard to go wrong with that.

Once the woman had left, we went back to our conversation.

"Who else is on your suspect list?" I asked Dory.

"I'm glad you asked," she said, "because I'm sure if you and I work together we can figure this out. Of course, since you and

Jennie Webber are friendly, you may get inside information." She gave me a pointed look.

I shrugged. "Not likely. She's very tight-lipped about work, you know." Which was mostly true, but if Jennie did tell me something, I wasn't going to share it with Dory. She was the closest thing Raven Hill had to a town crier.

"Hmm," Dory said. "Then it's even more important that the two of us put our heads together." She went on to rattle off a list of names, followed by her theories on how likely a suspect each one was. A few names were familiar, but many weren't. According to Dory, Anita had alienated most of the town.

"Of course," she said, "there's always Richard and Sloane. They say it's usually the husband, don't they? Although I know Sloane and her mother never really got along. Still, I don't see either one of them having the nerve to stand up to her, let alone kill her."

"A cornered animal will attack to defend itself," I said.

Dory considered this. "That's true, Greer. But Richard never seemed to have any issue letting Anita run the show, and Sloane has a family of her own now and lives in the next county. I don't think they see each other that much. Of course, Richard spends a lot of time with his grandson now that he's retired, but Anita is always too busy. Well, we'll just have to keep our ears open, won't we? See you tomorrow?"

I told her I would and said goodbye. I ran through all Dory's theories as I pushed my cart around. I wasn't familiar enough with the Winding Ridge Road to argue with her, but the fact that Jennie wanted to meet and ask me some questions about Anita suggested that her car accident was being treated as suspicious. Dory was right in her assessment of Anita—she had alienated a lot of people. I knew that after only a year of living in Raven Hill. When people found out I worked at the library, the discussion inevitably turned to Anita and her plans for a new building. Whether for or against the idea itself, the comments on Anita's approach were uniformly negative. But were any of these people upset enough to kill?

Richard Hunzeker and his daughter merited a closer look. Years of proximity to an abusive personality could breed the kind of rage it took to commit murder, even in the most mild mannered. And then there was Cynthia Baker. I'd met her once or twice, but I couldn't say I had a good read on her. I hadn't known about the longstanding feud, but I'd bet anyone who'd lived here for any length of time did. Jennie probably didn't, so I'd mention it when I saw her. And since I was stopping to drop off brochures at the historical society, I'd drop Anita's accident into the conversation. If someone wanted to talk, I was always willing to listen.